The Last Dreamwalker

Also by Rita Woods

Remembrance

The Last Dreamwalker

Rita Woods

A TOM DOHERTY ASSOCIATES BOOK
NEW YORK

This is a work of fiction. All of the characters, organizations, and events portrayed in this novel are either products of the author's imagination or are used fictitiously.

THE LAST DREAMWALKER

Copyright © 2022 by Rita Woods

Map by Rhys Davies

All rights reserved.

A Forge Book
Published by Tom Doherty Associates
120 Broadway
New York, NY 10271

www.tor-forge.com

Forge® is a registered trademark of Macmillan Publishing Group, LLC.

Library of Congress Cataloging-in-Publication Data

Names: Woods, Rita, author.
Title: The last dreamwalker / Rita Woods.
Description: First edition. | New York : Forge, a Tom Doherty Associates Book, 2022.
Identifiers: LCCN 2022008261 (print) | LCCN 2022008262 (ebook) | ISBN
    9781250805614 (hardcover) | ISBN 9781250805638 (ebook)
Classification: LCC PS3623.O6766 L37 2022 (print) | LCC PS3623.O6766 (ebook) |
    DDC 813'.6—dc23
LC record available at https://lccn.loc.gov/2022008261
LC ebook record available at https://lccn.loc.gov/2022008262

Our books may be purchased in bulk for promotional, educational, or business use. Please contact your local bookseller or the Macmillan Corporate and Premium Sales Department at 1-800-221-7945, extension 5442, or by email at MacmillanSpecialMarkets@macmillan.com.

First Edition: 2022

Printed in the United States of America

0 9 8 7 6 5 4 3 2 1

For Serenity,
My living, laughing dream made real.
And my parents,
who would have adored you.

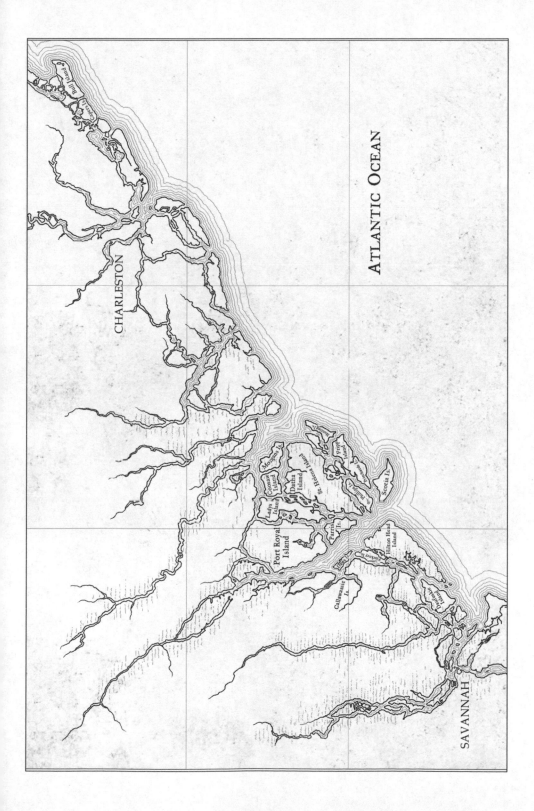

The Last
Dreamwalker

Gemma
1861

Gemma's master was dreaming of the war again. He did that more and more now, returning in sleep, night after night, to the same time, the same place.

It was as if as Rupert Everleigh's life grew shorter, his dream world grew emptier. He dreamed of his wife, long dead, and Nell, his daughter, most likely so. He dreamed of his son, disowned, dissolute, lying drunk in yet another cat house. And of the expensive cigars and aged whiskey he'd enjoyed with the other rich, white planters in his big house in Savannah, back when his body was strong and the money seemingly endless. And of course, on many nights, he dreamed of the rice harvest here on Scotia Island.

But it was the war, always the war, that began and ended most of his nights. And she was there too, watching, waiting, walking inside those dreams with him, skirting the edges of the shadows cast by his memories.

An explosion like thunder shook the ground under her feet and Gemma looked up to see dark smoke drifting above a too-green hill, toward a too-blue sky.

War.

The buckras—the whites—they were always making a war about one thing or another, blowing each other to bits over this piece of water, that smidge of mountain top. They were making one now, out there, in the waking world. She'd heard the rumors the wind carried, the rumors that seeped up through the dark, rich soil. Heard that this war was different, that this war concerned them: the slaves that worked Master Everleigh's rice. Heard that there was a buckra named Lincoln, up North ways—the master of all the buckras—who was saying that blacks might not be slaves no more.

Gemma pressed her lips into a tight line. That faraway war, that white master, Lincoln, had nothing to do with her. Tonight, she was searching for Rupert Everleigh in his dreams, walking the twisted wreckage of his memories. Tonight, she would try once again to grab hold of him there, bend him, shape him, take from him what she wanted.

There!

She'd found him.

He lay at the edge of a narrow mule track, alone, his belly pressed flat into the swampy earth, half-hidden between the gnarled roots of a black cypress tree. From a distance, she watched him cradle his rifle in the crook of his arm, take aim, then fire into a thick wall of mist and smoke. Flashes of red—uniforms, the vague shapes of men—appeared, then disappeared, as if no more than a trick of the eye. She watched her master rip the paper of an ammunition cartridge with his teeth and pour powder into the muzzle of his rifle before firing again.

She smelled the gunpowder, the blood. But the sharp bite of gunpowder was from the dark caverns of his memories, the blood, from the corpses of soldiers long dead and rotted into soil.

This war that haunted him night after night was from when he was young, from a half century past. From when his whole life spooled far out ahead of him, instead of far behind. This was his dream, and she was walking in it with him.

She waited. She could wait forever. In dreams, time was meaningless. The roar of cannon fire crashed over them, and Rupert Everleigh fired his rifle again and again at the ghosts of the long-dead British, near a place called New Orleans.

The instant he saw her, she knew.

His eyes went wide, and suddenly, he was no longer a young man, but bent and frail, his old man skin the color of rice water.

She approached him, taking her time. She was in no hurry. She had all the time in the world. Her master dropped his rifle and struggled to get to his feet, his arthritic hands clawing desperately at the gray trunk of the cypress for support. The cannons had gone silent and around them the world swirled, changed. The ground dried, grew sandy, the vegetation more sparse, the air taking on the salty smell of the sea. They were back on Scotia Island, back on the plantation where she'd spent every waking moment of her life.

He held up one twisted hand, as if to hold her back, and in the warm sunlight she saw that he was trembling.

"Stop," he cried. "You are an abomination, a damned creature. You stop right there, you hear?"

Gemma's lips pulled back from her teeth and she made a sound, half laugh, half snarl. This was his dream, but there was nothing he could do to make her leave it.

She was a Dreamwalker.

She could slip into the world of a sleeper and wander at her will, a spectator in the theater of the unconscious. Or, if she was of the mind to do so, she could twist those dreams, change their shape, change their meaning. And what she did as she meandered in and out of those dark nooks and crannies of the night world could even change the dreamer himself.

Tonight, and the night before, and the night before that, she was exactly of that mind. This dreamer—her master—had something she wanted, and she intended to use what she could do, what she had been born to, to make sure he gave it to her.

1

SPRING

The day before her mother's funeral it rained—alternating between a determined downpour and a vague, half-hearted mist that covered the city in a twilight haze long before actual nightfall. As Layla pulled her car into the driveway just after eleven, it was still raining.

She killed the engine and sat, staring through the windshield at her mother's house, the only light coming from a streetlamp near the end of the block. It'd been months since she'd been on this street, and yet, even in the hazy darkness, everything looked exactly as it always had. The newspaper soggily perched in the Pryors' bushes. The mound of damp leaves piled at the edge of the Calhouns' curb. The Browns' bright yellow Hummer parked in its usual spot next door, taking up an obscene amount of street real estate. The lawns all neat and well cared for.

She twisted a strand of hair round and round her finger. There was not a single thing in the world she would've rather done less than go into that house. Finalizing the arrangements at the funeral home with Will, she'd offered to pick up their brother Evan and his family from the airport, or to drop the programs off at the church, or to check in with the caterer about the repast.

Anything.

Anything else but this.

Instead the single task she'd been given for the funeral had been to go to the house and retrieve the pink crystal heart brooch their father had given their mother, the one piece of jewelry Elinor Hurley was never seen without, and make sure it got to the church in time for the service.

Layla'd argued with her brother, suggested someone else should get the brooch, said it was ridiculous to drive all the way to their mother's and hunt for the brooch with so much else to do. But Will had gotten that look: eyes narrowed, his full lips clenched so tightly she could see the muscles spasming in his jaw. The look that said that, once again, she was being ridiculous, that she was a disappointment.

And she'd flinched. Hated that she flinched. Hated that he could still make her feel like a badly behaved child. That he could make her feel stupid. So here she was, sitting in her mother's drive in the middle of the night, her stomach a clenched fist beneath her rib cage.

Muttering an obscenity, she pushed herself out of the car and dashed through the rain to the front door. On the narrow porch, she unconsciously touched the bottle nestled in the branches of the holly bush that framed the railing. For as long as she could remember, her mother had insisted there always be a bottle in the tree by the door: to catch the evil spirits that came in the night, she said.

Blue.

Because blue attracts the evil spirits and once caught inside, they couldn't get out.

One of Layla's earliest memories was of her and her mother on this porch, the scent of her mother's perfume, as they bent together just after sunrise to check the bottle. Listening for the telltale hum that would indicate the presence of an evil spirit trapped inside.

Hunching her shoulders against the rain, she struggled to open the door but the key wouldn't turn.

"Damn it, Mom!" she swore.

The lock had stuck for forever, since before her freshman year of high school. How many times had she reminded her mother that it needed to be fixed?

The realization struck her like a blow that she would never again have to complain to her mother about the lock—or about anything else—and for a long moment, she stood shivering on the porch, oblivious to the rain soaking her hair, running down her face. Swallowing hard, she tried the key again, with the same result.

"Shit," she screamed.

Kicking the door in frustration, she fought the urge to throw herself down onto the small porch and wail at the top of her lungs, neighbors be damned. Instead, teeth clenched, she stomped toward the back of the house, her tennis shoes soaking up water as she squished through the wet grass.

The back door opened easily, and Layla stepped into her mother's kitchen. Wet moonlight spilled through the window over the sink, turning the black granite countertops a shimmering silver. The faint scent of coffee and vanilla, and her mother's perfume—Chanel No. 19—hung in the air. She kicked off her wet shoes, scrunching her toes to keep from slipping on the smooth tile floor. Her heart fluttered fast in her chest, and she forced herself to take slow, deep breaths as she moved through the house. In the dining room, the table was covered with pies and cakes and homemade breads dropped off by neighbors and friends, mingling the aroma of yeast and butter with her mother's scent.

Her mother was everywhere in the house: watching, disapproving. Disapproving of what? It didn't matter. If her mother was watching, she was disapproving: of Layla's hair, of her job, of the fact that she never wore pantyhose.

Stopping just long enough to pour herself a glass of wine from the wine rack, Layla reluctantly made her way down the hall toward her mother's bedroom. The last time she'd been in this house had been nearly two months before. As usual, she and her mother had argued. She couldn't remember now how it started, most likely the way it always did, with her mother criticizing something she'd done, or hadn't done; with her offering to get Layla a "real" job teaching at one of the schools so that her education, her "talent" wasn't completely wasted.

Layla may not have remembered how it started but she remembered with painful clarity how it ended.

Her mother's voice—hard, the consonants sharp, clipped—seemed to still ricochet in the shadow-filled hall.

"It's time to grow up, Layla. Compromise is what grown-ups do. Dreams are for children. There are things you have to give up as an adult because there are things that need to be done to survive in this world."

"I am surviving, Mom. And I still have my art."

"Art?" Her mother's laugh had been like a physical blow, the sound like wind-whipped sand against her skin. "That's not art. If you're going to settle, Layla, at least settle for a job with dental insurance."

Even now, all this time later, Layla could feel the way her lungs had constricted in her chest, forcing out all the air.

"You would never say something like that to Will," she'd finally managed, barely recognizing her own voice. "Will dreamed of being a dancer and he's a dancer."

"Choreographer," snapped her mother. "And women don't have the luxury of indulging their fantasies the way men do. Women have to live in the real world."

Layla had stared, open-mouthed.

"Loving something, doing something that makes you feel whole inside yourself, isn't real?" she said slowly, trembling with rage. "I feel so sorry for you, Mom. To have spent your whole life living a halfway life. Living a life without a single dream!"

Layla'd stormed out of the house. Those were the last words she'd ever speak to her mother. Her mother had called the next day and the day after that. Had left voice messages inviting her to lunch at the Florida Avenue Grill, asking her to drop by the museum for coffee. Her version of a truce, of an apology. But Layla had ignored her, ignored her brothers' pleas to just move on. The wound inflicted by this latest argument was too raw, too deep. She hadn't expected her mother to die. Her mother *couldn't* die. Elinor Hurley was a force of nature, indestructible, like the wind, or lightning. Dying was simply an impossibility.

Now, back in her mother's house, Layla fumbled in her trench coat pocket, hands shaking, until she found what she was looking for: the little blue pills. The pills for her anxiety. She hesitated. She'd already taken one earlier in the day at lunch.

A small voice whispered in her mind that she was taking too many of them lately, but she shook that voice away and popped a pill in her mouth, washing it down with a large gulp of wine. She closed her eyes and pressed her back against the wall, inhaling deeply through her nose. She waited, motionless, until she began to feel that familiar unspooling in the pit of her stomach, until she felt the weight of the world rolling away from behind her eyeballs.

Sighing, she opened her eyes and pushed open the door to her mother's bedroom, flicking on the light. The champagne satin duvet was neatly folded on the end of the bed, as if her mother were simply spending the night somewhere else and would be returning in the morning. Through the half-open closet door, Layla could see shoes neatly stacked in their boxes, clothes meticulously arranged by color. Everything in its place. Everything perfect.

A wave of light-headedness washed over her.

Just get the brooch and go, she thought, setting the glass on the dresser. Just get it and get out of this house.

The jewelry box sat in the center of the dresser, a large silver box inlaid with mother-of-pearl. She lifted the heavy lid and managed a half smile. Her mother was nothing if not a creature of habit. The heart lay right on top, nestled on a square of white velvet, the facets throwing off shards of pink light. She ran one finger lightly over it, feeling the irregular shape under her fingertip.

She'd been six when her father had woken her late on Christmas Eve night, still wearing his heavy coat. She could smell the cold on him, mingling with the scent of cigar smoke and the Old Spice cologne he always wore, all of it merging into the smell that was uniquely her father's.

"Do you think your mother will like it?" He held out a small box. "It's Swarovski crystal."

Her breath had stopped. In the moonlight streaming through her window, the crystal heart shimmered, seeming to faintly pulse in its white velvet nest, as if it were an actual living thing. She hadn't known what Swarovski crystals were, but she was still young enough to believe in magic, and this heart had clearly come from the land of dragons and fairies and princesses. She nodded. Of course her mother would like it. How could she not?

And she'd been right. Other than her wedding ring and the ornate silver cross she wore on a chain under her blouse, the crystal heart was the only other piece of jewelry her mother always wore.

Layla picked up the heart, velvet square and all, and pushed it into her pocket before backing from the room and closing the door. In the hallway she stumbled and reached to brace herself against the wall. She felt watery, as if her spine, her legs, were turning to jelly. She frowned. The pills didn't usually hit her so hard, so fast.

"Shit!" She suddenly remembered.

That hadn't been the second pill of the day. It had been the fourth . . . or maybe the fifth. She couldn't remember anymore. There'd been the one at lunch. But also, the two she'd dry swallowed in the parking lot right after storming from the funeral home. Three pills in two hours. The little voice was nagging at her again.

"It's fine," she muttered to the empty house. "It's fine."

Without the pills she couldn't sleep. Without sleep, she could barely make it through a day. They just calmed her, made her feel more like herself. And her mother had just died, so of course she was taking them.

Maybe a few more than usual, but who wouldn't under the circumstances?

She squinted at her watch. Blinked in confusion. Along with everything else, she was losing track of time. It was twelve thirty; "half past middle night" her mother would have said. Standing in the darkened hallway, she debated whether or not to risk the forty-minute drive back to her apartment. She shook her head, trying to clear it, and the floor swooped sickeningly beneath her feet. She grabbed, once again, for the wall.

She did not want to spend the night in her mother's house, but she doubted she'd make it to the end of the driveway like this. She should lie down, just for a few minutes, let the medicine wear off a little. This house, her mother's house, might be filled with ghosts, but Layla didn't really believe in ghosts anyway, did she? Especially not with that little blue pill coursing through her veins.

She gave a harsh laugh and walked unsteadily down the hall to her old bedroom, the room she'd slept in as a girl. Stepping through the door into the room, she winced.

When she was fifteen, she'd insisted the room be painted a deep eggplant hue because the color felt powerful, royal. Now the walls were a soft, pastel pink, the curtains a delicate lace. But aside from the color, it was exactly as she'd left it the day she'd gone away to college: louvered French closet doors, the paisley patterned cushion on the rocking chair. Swimming trophies lined the top of the bookshelf; a small stuffed lamb, her favorite childhood toy, lay curled in the center of the rocking chair. Layla knew without looking that behind those louvered doors were old art books, neatly boxed, the dress her mother had forced her to wear to the prom she hadn't wanted to go to.

Acid rose in the back of her throat, and she swallowed hard.

Pulling a knitted afghan from the back of the rocker and wrapping it around her damp shoulders, she stared at the room. Since flaming out of art school four years before, she'd only spent a handful of nights here, preferring to couch surf with friends or spend a few nights here and there with Will, until she'd found her own place. One more thing she and her mother had exchanged heated words about.

On a whim, she pulled open the louvered closet door. Pushing aside the clothes, she let out a pained groan. It was still there, tucked deep into a back corner. Their Adventure box.

Layla sank to the closet floor and pulled it close. The pale wooden box was six inches high and eighteen inches wide. Lifting it into her lap, she was surprised by the unexpected heaviness of it. She lightly stroked the plain, unornamented top, sadness, grief, anger roiling together inside her. This box contained the best of her and her mother, their happiest memories.

Hands trembling, she lifted the lid and let out a shaky laugh. Like everything else her mother did, the contents had been painstakingly arranged. Photos, menus, store flyers, receipts, bundled together and organized by date, everything tied neatly with a thick purple ribbon.

Layla plucked one bundle from near the bottom. Their trip to San Francisco from when she was about nine. There were receipts from Eastern Bakery in Chinatown and the cable car, a grease-stained menu from Zuni Café. And there, a picture of her and her mother on the Golden Gate Bridge, her mother's green silk scarf swirling around her face in the gale force wind. Layla remembered that day. Remembered how terrified she'd been at the high, wide-open view from the bridge, how cold and miserable she'd felt, and it showed in the picture. She remembered her mother had only been able to coax her to walk the length of that bridge with the promise of cake and hot chocolate at Ghirardelli's.

She picked up another bundle and then another. New York, Mexico, Montana, London, Rome. Sometimes these adventures included her whole family, but as the years went by, usually just her and her mother. She stared at the picture, at her mother's face. Her mother had seemed so happy on these trips, the further from home, the happier, like a completely different person. But that different, happy person always faded away once they returned home, sometimes after a week or two, sometimes in just a few days.

Layla picked up another picture. Their last trip. Her mother was kneeling before a tombstone in the Necropolis in Glasgow. Her head was bowed as she leaned far forward, making a rubbing of one of the tombstones, her white sweater seeming to glow against the grays and greens of the cemetery, the crystal heart there near her shoulder.

It had been the last time Layla had seen the laughing, carefree woman that existed now only in her memory and on bits of paper inside the Adventure box. Six months later her father had been killed. There'd been no more adventures.

Sagging under the weight of the memories and her sadness, Layla pushed the box aside and closed her eyes. She just needed to rest a minute, until it felt safe to drive, then she would get up and go home.

The rich, greasy smell of bacon woke her.

Sunday. It must be Sunday. The only day her mother allowed them to eat bacon. Too many chemicals, she said. Too much fat.

Or maybe it was the birds that had awakened her.

Not the soft cooing of mourning doves in the trees that shaded her neighborhood but something different: a harsh, aggressive sound that filled the air, her head.

She opened her eyes, and the deep purple walls—eggplant—seemed to pulse around her like a heart. She stood, following the aroma of Sunday breakfast into the kitchen. Three strips of bacon lay side by side in a skillet on the stove, past crisp, burning, but the kitchen was empty. Through the open back door, she saw her mother on the lawn, wearing her pink bathrobe, staring up at the sky.

Layla frowned; something had happened to her mother, something bad. She twisted a strand of hair around her finger, trying to remember what. Stepping closer to the door, she looked up, following her mother's gaze. The sky was dark with birds, large black birds, their feathers iridescent in the sun. They seemed to sense Layla watching them and swooped lower, charging at the screen door before breaking away at the very last moment, their dark eyes locked on hers. Then suddenly, they were no longer wheeling away, no longer avoiding the collision. She cried out, shrinking back, as bird after bird slammed into the screen, the mesh pulling free of the frame a little more after each assault. Behind her, the burning bacon set off the smoke alarm.

"Layla."

Her mother stood beside her. The pink bathrobe was gone, replaced by a wedding dress. Not the sleek, designer gown that Layla knew from the photo on the mantel, but an old-fashioned, overdone thing, frothy with lace and crinoline, a dress like nothing her mother would ever wear.

They were standing in a house she didn't know. It was old: the floors warped and uneven. Doors hung crookedly in their frames, the peeling, windowless walls and the ceiling seeming to glow like a carnival fun house.

"Mom?" There was something off about her mother, something . . . wrong. Her usually flawless makeup was caked thickly atop her skin like a mask, and she seemed . . . frightened.

"I have to go," her mother said.

"Where?"

Without answering, her mother turned and began to walk away, down a corridor cluttered with bits and pieces of decrepit furniture, seemingly oblivious as the lace of her dress caught and shredded on the edges of the half-broken things in her path. It was hot, the still air as thick as pudding. And the smell: the air smelled like the ocean.

"Who ebben you be?"

The voice came from behind her, and Layla whirled to find a tall figure—a woman—forming in the oily light of the hallway. The words sounded both familiar yet heavily foreign, the accent bright as music.

"Who ebben you be?" the woman asked again. "How come you be here?"

The woman was narrow through the shoulders, with a wide, round face and skin the color of perfect morning toast. She frowned, stepping closer. At the end of the corridor Layla's mother stood watching in silence.

"Wait!" The woman's gaze swung between Layla and her mother, the whites of her eyes glittering in the impossible glow of the walls. "I knows you!"

Her expression twisted, changed, settling on a place somewhere between shock and rage. The hair on the back of Layla's neck stood up.

"Elinor?" The woman's lips pulled back from her teeth in a snarl as she addressed Layla's mother. "You made this here . . . thing."

Layla took a step back. The woman followed.

"You can't be here. You not b'long." The woman gave a harsh laugh. "That's what you try hidin' all this time, Elinor? This here devil Dreamwalker?"

Layla didn't see her move, but suddenly the woman's face was mere inches from her own, her breath damp and hot, the smell of her oddly sweet.

"You not one a us. You not the third a three."

Layla shook her head. "What?" she whispered. "What does that mean? I don't know what that means."

She tried to take another step back, but something blocked her way. A dresser? A table? She was afraid to look, afraid to turn her back on this strange woman.

"Knowed it would come to dis by and by," hissed the woman. "Knowed it jes a matter a time. But you ain't trick me, no. You am the devil walkin' dreams and she can't protect you no more."

"Who?" cried Layla. "Who can't . . ."

The blow stunned her, throwing her off balance. Tears of shock and pain momentarily blinded her.

"Charlotte!" Her mother was there, the front of the wedding dress bunched in her arms, her bare feet showing. Layla stared at those bare feet. "Stop it!"

"No!" screamed the woman named Charlotte. "No! You go 'way! This punkin-skin chil' come to me! She want take me dreams? She break covenant and take me dreams? Me last dream? She want to take Ainsli Green? Not never!"

The big woman drew back her hand as if to strike again and Layla cringed. Then came her mother's voice, whispering in her ear.

"Wake up, Layla! It's time to wake up!"

She jerked awake, heart thrumming hard in her chest, unsure of where she was. She looked around, wild-eyed, the afghan bunched around her knees. The Adventure box was on the floor, inches away.

Mom's, she thought, I'm at Mom's. Today we're burying my mother. Pale morning light from the window reached the closet where she slumped. She glanced at her watch. It was just after eight.

"Jesus hell," she murmured. She raked her fingers through her hair and groaned. She ached everywhere, and a spot just below her left eye throbbed inexplicably with pain in time with her heartbeat.

She touched the sore place on her cheek and scrambled to her feet. There was just enough time to grab a cup of coffee before heading to her apartment to get dressed for the funeral. Head pounding, she padded to the kitchen. When the coffee was ready, she poured herself a huge cup and shuffled into the dining room, bleary with fatigue. Her stomach churned acid up into her throat, as it always did whenever she was stressed, but if she was going to get through the next hour, let alone the rest of this day, she needed this infusion of caffeine. She glanced at her reflection in the mirror over the buffet and froze.

"What the hell?"

Her left cheek was swollen, a bruise already beginning to form, a hint of the black eye to come. With shaking hands, she gripped the cup and gulped down the coffee, ignoring the scalding sensation on her tongue. It had been months since she'd had one of *those* dreams. It was another reason she took the pills—to keep the dreams away.

She'd had them—dreams like this—her whole life. Dreams so real that for most of her early childhood, she hadn't understood that there was a difference from what she dreamed at night and the world she walked around in during the day.

Sometimes the dreams were nice: like when she followed Mr. Pryor to his grandmother's house, watching from the shadows as the old woman sat humming in her rocking chair, shelling peas. Or when her grandfather taught her daddy how to catch fireflies in a jelly jar in the field behind their house in Michigan, even though he'd died when her daddy was still in college. She liked those dreams. When she had those kinds of dreams, she woke up happy.

But then there were the other ones.

The ones where she woke up bloodied and bruised. When she found herself standing alone in the dark, in the middle of a stranger's yard. Those were the bad dreams.

And as she'd gotten older, there were fewer and fewer of the kinds of dreams where she watched the old lady across the alley dance in red sparkly slippers, and more and more where people she barely knew whispered things in her ears she didn't really understand but somehow knew were terrible.

Growing up, Evan had listened patiently as she confessed her growing fear, rubbing her back and telling her to just think of nice things before she went to bed. Will mostly just rolled his eyes then, after a while, stopped listening to her altogether, excusing himself from the breakfast table whenever Layla began recounting her latest dream.

It was Daddy who'd insisted she go see the doctors, worried about the scratches, the bruises, the torn clothes. Night terrors the doctors called it. She'll grow out of it, they said.

And her mother . . .

Her mother pretended it wasn't happening. Refused to even listen to Layla's dreams about lying in head-high grass as alligators slithered across her feet and gunfire split the air, or the scary man, his face swollen with rage, hitting the little girl with red hair who looked just like her teacher at school. Her mother always changed the subject. She would ask about Layla's next swim meet or history test, or if she really intended to go out with her hair like *that*. Her mother seemed not to see the scratches, the bruises. Her mother, who saw everything.

And Layla learned to pretend too. To pretend that when she went into her room at night and lay in the bed, she fell asleep like everybody else. She learned to cover up any evidence of a bad night.

By the end of high school, she'd discovered a glass of wine, or four, helped her fall asleep, helped keep the dreams away. And now the pills, especially the little blue pills, those helped too. Sometimes weeks passed without one of those dreams, weeks when she woke feeling refreshed, feeling normal.

But not this week. Not since the call that her mother had been found lying unconscious on her office floor. Ever since then, nothing seemed to keep the dreams away. But it had been a long time. A year? More? Since they'd leaked into her waking life, since they'd left their mark on her body, her face.

"I have to get out of here," she said aloud to the empty room. "I knew staying here was just stupid! I have to . . ."

She gulped the last of her coffee and searched the kitchen for her shoes. They weren't there. She frowned, trying to remember if she'd picked them up and taken them into the bedroom with her the night before.

Fighting panic, she walked quickly back down the hall. The door to her mother's bedroom stood slightly ajar. She frowned. She'd closed it the night before; she was sure of it. Gritting her teeth, she pushed it open with one finger.

"No!" Layla cried, stumbling back. "No!"

Her mother's bedroom was in shambles. Dresser drawers had been yanked out, the contents strewn across the floor, the bed. The bedside lamp lay half under the bed, the satin shade crumpled. The closet door yawned wide, and from the hallway she could see that her mother's clothes had been ripped down and dumped in a heap on the closet floor, the hangers dangling, empty on the rod. The silver jewelry box lay upside down on the floor.

Atop the dresser, looking obscenely out of place, even in the midst of the chaos, were Layla's black Converses, perched next to her empty wineglass. But it was the mirror that held her transfixed. Clinging to the center of the glass was a soggy picture, a page torn from some old magazine. The picture was tattered and creased, but she could still clearly see the image of the Eiffel Tower. And holding the page in place, smeared onto the otherwise spotless glass, was a muddy handprint, the mud dried to a pale gray, the handprint clearly not hers.

And the smell.

The room reeked, a strange, pungent odor, reminiscent of rotting eggs, hanging in the air. Layla made a gagging noise. She snatched her shoes from the dresser, upsetting the wineglass, then turned and ran barefoot from the house.

2

By the time of the funeral, the sun was still a no-show. The rain had finally stopped but a blanket of thick, soggy air lay heavy over D.C., smothering the city. But, in spite of the weather, the turnout was good.

The pews of her mother's large church had been filled. Layla recognized many of the people: her mother's coworkers from the Smithsonian; the Calhouns, the Pryors, and Mr. and Mrs. Brown from the neighborhood; ten or so women from her mother's book club; her sorority sisters. But there were scores more she'd never seen before.

She was surprised. She was always surprised at how many people knew and genuinely liked her mother.

Elinor Hurley was a woman with a great sense of humor. Never forgot a birthday or an anniversary. Was the go-to person when one needed a sympathetic ear, or uncritical advice.

Layla had heard about that Elinor Hurley her whole life, and to be fair, there had been moments when she'd caught a glimpse of that patient, uncritical, witty woman. But, for the most part, these anecdotes made her feel as if people had her mother confused with someone else, some other tall, striking, black woman who favored crisply tailored suits and ridiculously high heels. And it made her angry that she'd so rarely encountered that woman.

Her mother, the Elinor Hurley she knew best, was serious and intense, propelled by some quivering, unrelenting drive. And she drove everyone in her immediate orbit with the same unremitting energy: her husband, her sons. But it was Layla, her only daughter, who seemed to bear the brunt of her mother's most intense efforts.

The repast was being held at her mother's favorite restaurant, and now, well into the second hour, Layla felt drained, irritable. Across the room, a woman caught her eye and nodded then began to slowly make her way toward her. She was a petite, middle-aged woman, expensively dressed, with graying dreadlocks that reached midway down her back. Layla had noticed her at the church, standing near the back, apart from the rest of the mourners. As she approached, Layla tried to place her, but quickly gave up. There'd been so many people she hadn't recognized.

"You're Layla," said the woman, stopping in front of her. "I used to work with your mother."

Layla nodded, the polite smile she'd worn all morning fixed firmly on her face.

"Your mother was . . ." The woman's expression twisted into a sneer. Anger flashed in her eyes, lingering there a moment until the woman seemed to catch herself. With obvious effort she rearranged her attractive features into a mask of bland civility before saying, "I'm sorry for your loss."

"Thank you for . . . ," began Layla, but the woman had already turned and was walking away.

Frowning, Layla stared at the woman's retreating back, the air seeming to vibrate with the weight of ugly words left unspoken.

"What the . . . ," she muttered as the woman vanished through the restaurant door.

Unnerved, Layla retreated to a corner, wedging herself against a tall potted palm. She realized she was shaking and closed her eyes, trying to focus only on the coolness of the palm's leaves against her cheek.

"Can I see your hair, Auntie?"

Layla started. She opened her eyes to find her niece, Ashley, standing a few feet away. Nodding, Layla bent forward, holding herself still as the girl examined her hair. Small hands moved gently through the twisted strands.

"It's really red," said Ashley. "I like red."

Layla grinned and tickled the girl's nose. Evan's daughter was six and endlessly fascinated by the things Layla did with her hair: the colors, the asymmetric haircuts. Sometimes she did things with it just to amuse the girl: weaving tiny bells into her curls, braiding it with gold thread.

"Are you sad, Auntie?"

Layla blinked. "Yes," she said, realizing as she said it that it was the truth. "I'm very sad."

"Me too." Ashley nodded solemnly. She wound her small fingers through Layla's. "But it's okay to be sad, because one day it'll be alright again, right?"

Layla felt the tears well. "Yes," she managed to say. She squeezed her niece's fingers. "It's okay to be sad until everything's alright again."

They stood, holding hands in the quiet corner, watching the guests mill about the restaurant.

"Would Gram have liked your hair?"

Layla inhaled sharply, laughing. "No! Not one little bit."

Ashley grinned and deep dimples appeared in both cheeks, a trait she'd inherited from her father. Layla reached up and pulled at the cranberry-colored strand near her right temple. No, she thought. Her mother most definitely wouldn't have liked it, would have, in fact, most likely have given her version of a fit: eyes narrowed, her jaw muscles clenching and unclenching. Layla smiled grimly as another wave of sadness washed over her.

"Here comes Uncle Will."

Looking over her niece's head, Layla saw her brother striding across the restaurant toward them. Despite the obstacles of the closely placed tables and chairs, and the infant strapped to his chest, he moved gracefully, like the dancer he was.

"What are you two doing hiding back here?" he asked when he reached them.

"We're not hiding," laughed Ashley before Layla could think of a lie.

"Looks like hiding to me." He gave his niece a quick hug. "Your daddy's looking for you."

He pointed across the room to where Evan stood talking to a woman Layla recognized as her mother's hairdresser. Ashley stood on her tiptoes to kiss the baby Will was carrying, then, with a wave goodbye, trotted across the room to join her father.

Will stood silently next to his sister and peered out across the restaurant. The crowd was finally thinning. Aside from their immediate family, there were only a handful of people still moving about looking at the photos of their mother arranged in frames near the door, picking at the remnants on the dessert table.

"Well?" he said, finally.

"Well, what?" she said, bristling slightly at his tone.

"Well, what happened to your face, for one thing?" He was staring pointedly at the burgeoning bruise near her eye that she'd tried, unsuccessfully, to cover with makeup.

"My feet are killing me," she said, ignoring the question.

She stepped around him and limped back to her table. Seconds later, Will slid into the chair beside her. She poured herself another cup of coffee, her sixth of the day. The coffee was lukewarm and bitter. Wincing, she added three packets of sugar, then took a gulp.

"I'm proud of you."

She squinted in surprise. "For?"

"For . . ." He hesitated. Her brother looked tired, tired and troubled. "For holding it together at the service."

"What are you talking about?" Easing her feet from her shoes, she grunted with relief. She rarely wore heels, and she could feel her toes throbbing angrily in time with each beat of her heart.

"Well, when Father Mike started talking about the gentleness of her soul." He shrugged. "You know . . ."

She snorted and rolled her eyes. "What did you think I was going to do?"

Her brother grinned. "Shoot, girl, I don't know. Start slinging prayer books?"

"There weren't any in my row." She gave Will a crooked half smile. "And besides, St. Basil's prayer books have soft covers. It's impossible to have any kind of a decent fit throwing soft stuff. Not enough damage. Everybody knows that."

"She loved you, you know."

She groaned softly. "Will, not now, okay? Not today. Just let it alone."

Her brother was silent for a long moment.

"I loved her," he said, finally, sighing. "But Mom could be . . . difficult. Christ, she could be a straight-up hard-ass sometimes."

He gazed down at his sleeping son. "And you and her . . . ? Jesus." He shook his head. "She had her own way of moving through the universe. Things always had to be just so," he persisted despite his sister's silence. "And you and her . . ." He blew out a hard breath. "You two . . . Man!"

Layla twisted her hair around her finger and stared at the sleeping baby in her brother's arms.

"Me an Ev could never figure it out. Was it because you were a girl? Because you were so much younger?" He rocked the baby gently. "All I know is if we could've harnessed all that crazy between you and her, the government's search for alternative energy would've been solved."

Layla fought the urge to smile. She knew that was what he wanted, to make her laugh. It was what he'd always done when there was tension between her and her mother—which was most of the time—ignore it or try to get Layla to laugh, to apologize, to shake off the latest conflict.

"Lay," he said, when she didn't respond. "Mom had issues . . ."

"Issues?" Her head snapped up. She saw the few remaining guests look in their direction and forced herself to lower her voice. "You're kidding, right? Her biggest *issue* was that she was either criticizing everything I did, or said, or thought, or wore, or ate. Or she was treating me like I was a crazy person!"

"Lay!" Her brother's handsome face twisted.

"Unh-unh! Don't 'Lay' me." She held up a hand to stop him. "Do you know she even once corrected the way I breathe."

He snorted in disbelief.

"Layla," She lowered her voice, imitating their mother's husky contralto. "Breathe quietly. A lady does not make sounds like a barn animal when she exhales."

Will bit back a guffaw.

"You and Ev. Always trying to act like our family was some TV sitcom. Like at the end of a half hour, we'd all be sitting around the kitchen table sharing a big ol' laugh while the credits rolled. What did you think? That one day me and her would be sharing secrets and getting mani-pedi's together?"

Her brother shrugged, his expression both sad and amused. "Well . . ."

She raked a hand through her hair and took another sip of the cold, oversweet coffee. Suddenly, her anger evaporated as quickly as it had flared. She sighed. "Don't even worry about it. It's fine. I'm over it. I made my peace about Mom a long time ago."

"Unh-hunh. I can see that," he said, one eyebrow raised.

She pressed her lips together, holding back a retort. She felt a ripple of regret remembering all of his texts urging her to just return her mother's calls.

She took a quivery breath and forced a smile. "You and Ev, you did all the right things. Married well. Had babies. You matched your socks to your tie. And then there's me . . ."

She pointed one paint-stained finger at the slightly wrinkled dress, at her secondhand high heels lying discarded under the table. Her bare feet.

Will frowned at her for a long moment, then began to laugh. "Well, when you're fierce, you're fierce," he chuckled.

"Shut up," she said. Movement by the door caught her attention. "Who is that?"

Her brother twisted in his seat to follow her gaze. Two vaguely familiar older women were making their way across the room toward them.

"Shut up," he muttered, standing up. "I don't believe it."

"What?" She squinted. "Who is that?"

"It's the Aunts," he said.

"The Aunts?"

And then, before he could answer, they were standing right in front of them: two tall, solidly built, late sixty-something women, both wearing shiny purple dresses and black patent leather pumps.

"William!" they cried in unison, gathering him in a hug.

Layla stared, wide-eyed.

The Aunts.

She and her brothers had always referred to her mother's two older sisters as if they were a single, interchangeable unit.

They were simply: the Aunts. Layla studied them now as they oohed and aahed over her baby nephew. They did look very much alike, the same milk chocolate skin, the same shiny pin-curled hair, but there were differences. One was nearly a head shorter than the other, a bit less stocky. The taller one's hair was more salt than pepper and she held herself back just a bit, in a way that reminded Layla a little of her mother. Both had deep dimples in their cheeks like her mother, like both her brothers, like her.

The aunt closest to her, the shorter one, turned and pulled her close, gripping her more tightly than she would have imagined possible.

"Layla, give me some sugar, baby," she cried, and Layla was suddenly enveloped in a thick cloud of perfume, something sweet and lemony.

Jean Naté.

The name of the perfume surfaced from some deep cavern of her memory.

"My turn, Therese."

She tried to catch her breath in the brief instant before she was engulfed in the arms of the other aunt.

"Well," said the woman, finally releasing her. "You surely don't remember us, do you?"

Layla blinked. "I . . ."

The women laughed, their voices those of women decades younger. "Of course you don't. The last time we saw you, you were missing your two front teeth and had just learned to ride a bike. It's all you talked about. That bike."

Another memory surfaced: a big blue house, a winding road, moss dangling like tinsel from the branches of huge silver-colored trees. She glanced at her brother. Will stood smiling as he rocked the baby side to side.

"I'm your aunt Jayne and this is your aunt Therese."

"From South Carolina?"

"That's us, baby," cried Aunt Therese. "I told you she'd remember, Jayne."

"She doesn't remember nothin', Therese," said her sister. "I just told her who we were."

"Oh, hush, old woman." Aunt Therese waved a hand dismissing her sister before wrapping Layla in another hug.

Aunt Jayne and Aunt Therese.

Elinor Hurley rarely spoke to her sisters. Rarely spoke of them. She'd left Port Royal, South Carolina, for college, only going back occasionally to visit, and even those sporadic visits had stopped when Layla was born. The reason was as mysterious to Layla as everything else about her mother.

But every year, for as long as she could remember, up until she'd left for college, a huge box had arrived from Port Royal, exactly one week before Christmas, with gifts for her and her brothers. And every November until she'd turned eighteen, six years before, she'd received a birthday card containing a crisp five-dollar bill.

Layla smiled, remembering the outsized pleasure she got opening that card every year. Each birthday she looked forward to that crisp bill, inexplicably delighted even at eighteen at the arrival of that five-dollar bill, smelling faintly of lemons. In the years since, every so often, on a whim, she sent the Aunts a note, a postcard, a tiny sketch she'd done, and they would respond with a note of their own, gushing with enthusiasm, as if she'd gifted them a Renoir.

She only remembered visiting them once, when she was six or seven. Her mother had refused to go, had found a reason to keep Will and Evan from going. She remembered her parents arguing, bitterly, the long car ride to South Carolina, the longest ride she'd ever taken in her life, just her and her father. She'd sat in the front seat next to him, playing I Spy and singing along with the radio. She remembered a pecan tree growing in the Aunts' backyard, like something from a fairy tale.

Pecans.

On a tree.

And there had been pie. Pecan pie.

"Of course I know who you are. You came all the way from South Carolina?" she asked, and not for the first time that day felt tears threaten to spill over.

"Course, sugar," said Aunt Therese. "Rode the Greyhound right up from Port Royal. Can't stand no airplane. Not natural for a man to be up in the sky with God's flying creatures, but that dang bus got us in so late, we about missed the whole funeral."

"Did miss it," groused her sister. "But at least we made the repast, thank the Lord."

"Thank the Lord," agreed Aunt Therese. She loosened her grip and Layla took a deep breath.

"Your momma and us, we had our differences," said Aunt Jayne.

"We surely did," agreed Aunt Therese.

". . . but Elinor was our baby sister. Our family. You all our family. Long as we had breath in our body we were going to make it here for her goin' home. Isn't that right, Therese?"

"You right."

"Are you . . . ?" Layla stopped. The bad coffee, the overwhelming lemony perfume, the fatigue left over from the restless night of sleep. She felt a swoop of dizziness and gripped the back of the chair beside her. "Where are you staying? There's plenty of room at Mom's."

She thought of the chaos of her mother's room and pressed her lips together.

"Lord no, sugar. That ain't necessary. We got us a real nice room at the Motel 6," said Aunt Jayne.

"It's got a pool," added Aunt Therese. "Shoulda brought along our bathing suits."

"Girl, hush! What we look like paradin' these old, fat bodies around in a bathing suit? Like to make some poor child go blind from the sight," said her sister.

"You got that right," cried Aunt Therese, laughing. "Ruin them poor babies for life!"

Layla's mouth dropped open. She caught her brother's eye and grinned.

Evan walked up and placed his arms around his aunts. "Ladies, let's fix you a plate and then I'd like you to meet my daughter."

"That pretty child over there?" cried Aunt Therese.

"Must take after her momma," said Aunt Jayne. "Too cute to take after our people."

"I beg your pardon," said Evan with mock indignation. Layla and her brothers laughed.

"Come on, aunties, I'll take you so Evan can talk to Layla for a minute," said Will. He led them across the room to where Ashley stood snuggled against Will's husband, Chuck.

"Whoa," said Layla, looking up at Evan. "They are . . . something."

Evan laughed, shaking his head. "Don't much remind you of Mom, do they?"

"No." She laughed. "Not so much."

She smiled up at her brother. In his midthirties, he was the oldest of the three Hurley siblings. Only three years older than Will, he was nearly a decade older than she was. He lived on the other side of the country and was always teasing her that he was from the "other Washington. The cleaner, greener Washington." They all, her two brothers and their families, managed to get together two or three times a year, and Layla tried to video chat with Ashley every Sunday, but it never felt like enough. Even with Will living less than a half hour away, she often felt lonely for family—or at least the image of family she carried around in her head. She was glad Evan was here, even if it was for their mother's funeral.

He touched her shoulder. "You doing okay?"

She shrugged. "Awesome."

He gave her a quick squeeze. "Yeah."

Across the room, Aunt Therese was waving her purse over her head like a banner.

"What in the . . . ?"

"I think you're being summoned," laughed Layla.

"Wow, they *are* something," said her brother. "I better go before she starts whistling for me."

He gave her a quick kiss on the forehead.

"You coming to Mom's house for breakfast in the morning?"

"Of course." He smiled. "And with the Aunts in tow, apparently."

She watched him walk back toward the women, then turned to pick up the coffee cup. There were only a few drops of coffee left and she debated whether or not to ignore the flames smoldering in her stomach and finish it off.

"Baby?"

Layla jumped. Aunt Therese had materialized behind her. The woman leaned close, and once again Layla found herself inside a sweet citrus cloud. Her aunt pressed a hand, soft and warm as a biscuit, against Layla's cheek. She blinked hard. When was the last time her mother had touched her face like this? Had touched her at all?

"We have something for you," said the old woman.

Layla frowned. "You . . . do?"

For a moment an image of a five-dollar bill flashed in her mind and she almost smiled.

Aunt Therese nodded. "We have something. Something we've been holdin' on to for all these years."

Her aunt glanced over at her sister and seemed to hesitate. ". . . Because we knew that there were things that Elinor . . . didn't . . . that she wouldn't . . . tell you."

Layla shook her head, confused. She felt another surge of dizziness. It had been a long day and she was exhausted.

"And we weren't sure," her aunt went on. She straightened as her sister came to stand by her side.

Layla blinked. "Aunt Therese, Aunt Jayne, I am so sorry, but I don't . . . I'm not sure what you're talking about."

She tried to laugh, raking a hand through her hair, as a thick haze of fatigue settled over her, mixing unpleasantly with the caffeine jitteriness.

Aunt Jayne stared at her, her expression unreadable, and Layla felt the hair on the back of her neck stand on end.

Aunt Therese took a deep breath and smoothed her dress across her thighs. "I know you don't, sugar. We'll talk." She smiled. "We'll talk real soon."

3

"Sugar, you look like somethin' the cat drug in."

Layla glanced up from the pile of condolence cards she was sorting on the couch and exhaled a sharp laugh. From some deep recess of the pantry, Aunt Therese had unearthed a secret Santa gag gift her mother's coworkers had given her years before. Bright green and covered in red glitter Christmas trees, the apron flashed on, then off, barely covering her aunt's ample front. Twinkling in the late May sun streaming through the living room windows, it looked spectacularly ridiculous.

"Just tired," said Layla, still smiling.

"Well, just sit there and rest yourself," said Aunt Therese. "Me and Jayne got all this covered."

"All this" apparently meant everything. Since the morning after the funeral, the sisters had blown through the house like a Jean Naté–scented derecho: vacuuming carpets, cleaning out the refrigerator, watering plants, warming up one of the dozens of casseroles brought over by neighbors and coworkers.

"You remember I told you we had something for you?" asked Aunt Therese.

Layla glanced past her. Through the patio door windows she could see Evan pacing back and forth on the patio, a phone pressed to his ear.

"Yes?" she said slowly.

With a groan, her aunt plopped into the green velvet armchair next to the couch, bending to rub one plump foot. The apron blinked on, then off. "Could you get me my pocketbook, sugar."

A purse the size of carry-on luggage sat by the front door.

Layla grunted at the unexpected weight. "Jesus, what do you have in this thing? A dead body?"

As the words came out of her mouth, she cringed. Her mother's funeral had been barely seventy-two hours before. But Aunt Therese only chuckled.

"Oh, sweetheart, it would just be plain bad taste to be carryin' a corpse around our nation's capital. Not to mention a violation of some kinda law. I done took that out at the Motel 6."

Layla let out a surprised whoop, her aunt's dark humor catching her off guard. "Well, even without the dead body, I don't know how you carry that thing around all day," she said, setting the bag at the older woman's feet.

Her aunt flexed a fleshy arm. "Years of hard work, sugar. I'm strong as any fifty-year-old man."

"No doubt," Layla laughed.

Aunt Therese peered into the purse. "Let me see now," she muttered.

She thrust one arm in and began to rummage but, seeming not to find what she was looking for, began to haul the contents out. She barely glanced at each item before dropping it on the floor next to the chair.

Out came a foldable cane, a freezer bag full of pill bottles, a small phone-book, a tattered map, and a pair of pantyhose. Aunt Therese squinted at the stockings for a moment, then sucked her teeth before tossing them on the pile.

Layla watched, eyes widening, as her aunt pulled out wads of tissue, ink pens, two folded brochures from the Motel 6, and a small jar of Vicks VapoRub.

"Well dang it!" Aunt Therese grumbled irritably, tossing a pink se-quined change purse on the floor. "Course, it was just gonna have to be at the very bottom. I swear, I keep meanin' to clean this thing out."

She struggled to pull something from the monstrous bag, before finally managing to extricate a thick, ragged, legal-size folder.

"Here we go. Finally." She was breathing hard. "This belongs to you."

She held the folder out. Layla hesitated, momentarily distracted by the cornucopia of items from Aunt Therese's bag that were now strewn around the chair.

"Baby?" Aunt Therese shook the folder.

Held together by thick green rubber bands, it was covered in ink doo-dles and coffee stains, the edges shredded and crumbling. Layla took it and balanced it on her lap.

"No," said Aunt Therese, sharply, grabbing her wrist as her niece tugged at the rubber bands.

Layla jerked, nearly dumping the folder and its contents onto the floor.

"No, baby, not now," Aunt Therese said, more softly. "Don't look at it now. Be better for you to wait 'til we gone. This is somethin' you might want to go through in private. Somethin' you gon' need to chew on a bit. Then when you ready, when you got questions, you call us. Can't promise we'll have all the answers, but we'll most likely have a fair some."

She was smiling, but there was an edge to her voice, a stiffness in the way she held herself that made Layla uneasy. From the corner of her eye, she saw Aunt Jayne hovering in the kitchen door, silently twisting the dish towel around and around her hand, her expression unreadable.

Layla glanced again through the patio doors. Outside, Evan was still pacing, the phone still pressed to his ear, gesticulating with his free hand. She looked back at her aunts. They were watching her, Aunt Jayne from the doorway, Aunt Therese from the green armchair.

Her mother's sisters.

She was surprised by how much she liked them, how funny and warm they were. How safe they made her feel. And she felt a flash of resentment at her mother for denying her the opportunity to have had them in her life. She tried to smile, to speak, but her throat clamped tight, trapping so many emotions there: grief, confusion, anger.

"What is it?" she asked finally, pushing the folder to the other end of the couch with one finger.

"Your inheritance," replied Aunt Therese.

Aunt Jayne made a sound and her sister shot her a look.

Layla frowned. "My . . . what?"

Inheritance?

Evan was their mother's executor. What of any significance could the Aunts possibly have of her mother's? Old photos, mementos from her mother's childhood? What treasures from her mother's past would the Aunts have held on to all these years that they could think were so precious that their youngest sister's only daughter might cherish them?

The sisters exchanged another look.

"Not like that," said Aunt Therese quickly. "Not exactly. It's . . ." She hesitated and Layla felt another flicker of unease.

"It's complicated, baby," she went on, finally. "Your momma shoulda . . . She wanted . . ." She sighed. "Elinor was always funny about . . . some things. Tried to pretend that . . ."

"It's complicated," interjected Aunt Jayne quietly from the doorway.

"Complicated," echoed her sister, softly.

Layla looked from one round, brown face to the other, watching as an unspoken conversation passed between them.

"But she's gone now, so this belongs to you," said Aunt Therese, sighing. She pointed to the folder. "You the last, and you should know."

Layla frowned, confused. She opened her mouth to tell them she didn't understand, to ask, *"The last what?"* just as Evan burst through the back door.

"Ladies?"

The sisters turned to him, and the peculiar mood that had descended on the living room evaporated. The Aunts smiled broadly at him.

He strode to Layla and kissed her forehead. "Time to hit the road, little sister. Gotta get these two ladies to the bus terminal, then pick up Ashley and her mom and head on to the airport."

Layla felt tears well as Evan pulled her close.

"Come on, Lay. It's okay," he whispered in her ear. "I'd stay if I could. But I've got to be in London for the next several weeks. I'll get back as soon as I can to help you and Will settle things. I'll even bring Ashley with and you two can hang out on the National Mall. She loves that." He squeezed her hard.

She nodded, burying her face in his jacket. He smelled like soap and musky aftershave. Suddenly, there was a gentle pressure against her back. The Aunts had come and wrapped them in a hug, Aunt Therese behind Evan, Aunt Jayne behind Layla.

Aunt Jayne's body was thick and warm. Layla closed her eyes. Being huddled between her brother and the Aunts was like being encased in a Jean Naté–scented cocoon. For the first time since she'd received the call that their mother had died, she felt something like peace.

They stood there a long moment, the four of them, wordlessly embracing in her mother's living room. Then Evan cleared his throat and the cocoon dissolved. Aunt Therese pulled off the Christmas apron and began scooping her belongings back into her bag while Aunt Jayne disappeared into the kitchen to hunt for their shoes.

"I'll call you when we land at Sea-Tac," Evan said as he wrangled the Aunts out the front door.

On the porch, Aunt Therese stopped. "We'll be talkin' to you soon, sugar," she said, smiling at her niece. "Call us. For anything."

And then the two sisters were following her brother down the walkway to the car. Layla stood in the door waving until the car turned the corner at the end of the block, disappearing from view.

Back in the empty house, the ticking of the grandfather clock seemed louder, her heart catching hold of the sound, beating in time with it. She pressed the tips of her fingers against her breastbone until it hurt, feeling the slow, monotonous thrum of her heart inside her chest.

She needed to get out. Out of this house. Out of her skin. Just out.

Striding into the kitchen, she snatched plastic containers from the cabinet and began frantically filling them from the dozens of food trays and casseroles lining the counter before shoving them into plastic grocery bags. She had no idea what she was taking, but anything was better than the cold cereal and frozen pizza waiting at her apartment.

She grabbed her purse and the folder the Aunts had given her and headed for the door. She was tired. And sad. And her head throbbed. She didn't want to think about anything. Not her mother. Not the dream that had left her with the black eye that was now turning an ugly greenish purple. Not the peculiar exchange with the Aunts about some unexpected inheritance.

On the front porch, she balanced the bag of Tupperware against her knee and prepared to wrestle the key from the lock. She yanked hard and the key slid easily from the lock, catching her by surprise. Thrown off balance, she found herself flying backward off the narrow porch, the bag of casseroles and the Aunts' file sailing over her head.

"Son of a bitch!"

She landed hard on her back in the grass, narrowly missing the concrete walkway that led to the porch. Winded, she lay motionless on the lawn, dampness seeping through her cotton blouse and up the back of her thin skirt. One flip-flop teetered on the top step, as if mocking her.

"Outstanding," she muttered through clenched teeth once she'd caught her breath. She pushed herself slowly, painfully, to a sitting position, legs spread wide. "Freaking outstanding."

An old man, walking an even older dog, passed by. Layla raised a hand in greeting, but the man squinted at her suspiciously and hurried past.

She inhaled sharply in surprise, then began to laugh. She laughed until tears ran down her face and she toppled backward again into the grass. Her stomach began to cramp, and she rolled over, pressing her forehead into the cool grass, forcing herself to take slow, deep breaths.

The Aunts' folder had landed halfway beneath the azalea bush and she considered leaving it there, considered just picking up her scattered casseroles and going home. For a long moment, she lay there, face down, arguing with herself.

Her inheritance.

The Aunts' cryptic words about her mother rolled over and over in her mind.

Finally, reluctantly, she pushed herself to her hands and knees and crawled to the azalea. Stretching, she just managed to grab the folder by one soggy corner and pull it toward her. Cursing under her breath, she limped to the porch and slumped on the bottom step, staring at the damp mass of papers bursting from the top of the folder.

She gripped the edge of a wrinkled, yellowing envelope and tugged it free. Inside was a newspaper clipping dated from thirteen years before. Unfolding it, she read the smeary headline: THE MYSTERY OF AINSLI GREEN.

Layla frowned.

Ainsli Green?

Why did she know that name?

There was a photo underneath the headline, and she squinted at it. It was nearly as smudged as the typeface, and at first, in the bright sun, all she could make out were indecipherable shades of gray. For a long moment she squinted, letting her eyes adjust to the individual details.

And then she saw.

With a strangled cry, she leaped to her feet, flinging the clipping away from her. It lay crumpled in the damp grass like a dead bird. She closed her eyes and tried to swallow, but her mouth was dry as sand.

The photo.

There in the center of the old newspaper clipping was the woman from the dream. The woman who had slapped her in the cluttered hallway that smelled like the ocean as her mother watched in an old-fashioned wedding gown. A slap from which she had awoken with a very real bruise.

And she heard the voice, once again, echoing in her head: *She want to take Ainsli Green? Not never.*

4

GEMMA

The sun lit the sky on fire as it raced westward toward the mainland. A dozen yards away, out where the water became suddenly deeper, she could just make out the dark shape of a dolphin pod, heading north through the sound. Gemma glanced over her shoulder. Ainsli Green's manor house stood at the highest point of Scotia Island, lights flickering in every window.

The slave woman laughed softly to herself.

He was afraid.

That was good. That was very good.

But all the light in the world wouldn't protect him, any more than that pathetic pistol she knew he kept tucked beneath his pillow. The colonel would have to sleep sometime, and when he did, she would be there, walking beside him in his dreams.

Gemma inhaled deeply, smelling the salt from the ocean on the eastern side of the island. Marsh hens rustled, unseen, in the tall grass as the sun slowly dipped below the horizon and the sky cooled to hues of purple and blue. With a sigh, she stepped out of the marshy water and began to make her way back toward the slave quarters.

Out here, on the barrier islands, night fell fast. Within minutes the only visible light came from the sliver of yellow moon and the big house, perched there on its mound of sea grass and shifting sand, like a lighthouse on a dark ocean.

But even without that little bit of light, she could have easily found her way. She had been born on this island, had never been further away from it than the few feet she walked into the marsh each night to watch the sun set. She knew this place by the feel of the uneven sand beneath her feet, by the sight of the bright hibiscus that bloomed in the spring, and by the lumbering manatees that swam the shallows. This island beat in her heart. It was as much hers as it was Colonel Everleigh's—more.

And she intended to have it.

As she made her way through a stand of live oak, the dozen squat, wooden buildings of the quarter came into view. A fire burned low in front of her cabin down the lane, the aroma of cooking food greeting her as she cleared the trees.

"Mama!"

Lavender materialized from the shadows and Gemma frowned. Her youngest daughter had inherited her height but, unlike her, was a thin creature, all sharp, bony angles. And the girl had an unnerving way of moving through the world, silent, stealthy, like warm sea air whispering through the grass. Studying her, Gemma felt a shiver of dread. Lavender was her third daughter, as she herself had been the third, and there was so much yet that the girl needed to know, so much that Gemma wanted to teach her. But things were changing, not just with the buckra—the white folks—but inside her as well. Things she couldn't explain. The faintest current of fear rippled through her.

"Mama?"

Gemma blinked. Lavender had linked her arm with Gemma's and was watching her as they walked, eyes narrowed.

"You come to fetch your mama, then?" Gemma asked. She forced her lips upward, feigning a smile, and felt her daughter relax beside her.

"Hey there *ooman*! You catch you *d'et* quick soon you keep standin' in that water every night."

Gemma stopped in the center of the rutted path. Her friend Bekka was sitting on the ground in the shadows in front of her cabin, weaving a basket of sweetgrass by the light of a smoky lantern, her newest baby asleep in another, smaller basket nearby.

"Ain't died yet," laughed Gemma.

"Still time," called Bekka. "I speak the truth. Tell'um Mama stay out that water, Lavender."

"Stay out that water, Mama," said Lavender obediently, grinning.

"Don't bad mout' me, Bekka," said Gemma. She gave her daughter a playful pinch. "*D'et* come for me, we go together then."

Her friend laughed softly, waving as Gemma and her daughter continued on their way. When they reached their own cabin, Gemma dropped down in front of the fire and stretched her hands toward the glowing embers. The night air was thick and warm, but she felt a chill through to her bones.

"Mama."

She looked up. Jessamine, her middle daughter, held a bowl of soup out to her. She nodded her thanks as she took it, relishing the heat against her cold hands.

She spooned a bit of okra into her mouth, then rolled it on her tongue as she studied her oldest daughter from the corner of her eye. While her younger daughters teased each other, tending the fire and stacking the pots from supper, Marigold had yet to acknowledge her mother. She sat apart, silently mending a piece of linen from the big house. Gemma could feel anger surging off the girl like an incoming tide. She sighed. This was nothing new, Marigold's anger. Every day it grew. It felt sometimes as if she and her other two daughters were sharing their cabin with a feral cat: suspicious, unpredictable, stingy with affection.

Gemma took another spoonful of stew and closed her eyes, savoring the thick tomato broth, the small chunks of crab as it warmed her throat.

Sleep.

How long had it been since she'd been able to sleep? Really sleep? To dream her own dreams? This thing she was doing to Colonel Rupert. It was dangerous. One couldn't live in another's dream world night after night without paying a price. But there was no other way. War was coming to Scotia Island. There were nights when the sea was flat as a skillet bottom, the stars sparkling in the navy-blue sky, that they could hear the sound of cannon fire wash up on the edge of their island with the tide, all the way from the mainland. War was coming to Scotia, and she had to get that old white man to put his mark on those papers, to deed the island to her true.

Marks on paper.

It was the only thing the whites respected.

"D'em gon 'way," Marigold said, finally speaking. "Penny and her man."

Gemma jerked. She had been drifting, floating along in that gray place between awake and not. She opened her eyes and squinted blearily at her daughter.

"You hear me, Mama?" snapped Marigold.

Gemma rolled a curl of okra round and round on her tongue, tamping down an angry retort. Swallowing, she glanced at Jessamine and Lavender. They had gone still, watching their mother and their older sister warily.

"Dem take one a Colonel's bateaus this mornin'," Marigold went on. "Dem go to the mainland. Dem say dem free there."

Gemma studied her daughter. Marigold was old enough to be mated—Otis, Ainsli Green's head boatman, had long fancied her—and yet here she sat, still mending linens around her mother's fire. She suspected the blame lay with Marigold. The girl was hard as iron. Gemma loved her, but her oldest daughter was like one of those sharp-toothed creatures the fishermen sometimes hauled up from the sea: all dangerous, pointy teeth, ready to bite anything foolish enough to get too close.

"We'un should go way, Mama," said Marigold when Gemma didn't respond. "Go way from here. Go up to Chaa'stun. Dem say solduhs from up North, say we'un slaves no more. The colonel can't stop us. We—"

"No!" Gemma's voice was harsh. Jessamine and Lavender flinched and gripped each other's hands.

Gemma set her bowl down and ran her hands over her face. She was so tired. She was so cold.

"And where Penny and her man go to?" she asked, struggling to keep her voice even.

"Off island," cried Marigold. "To the mainland."

"And what dem do once dem get to the mainland?"

"Anything dem want, Mama," said Jessamine, speaking for the first time. "Dem be free over there."

Gemma looked at her daughters sadly, so young, so hopeful, so naïve. Did they really think their future lay on the other side of that water? Did they really think that life would be so much better off island?

"You b'lieve in this freedom then?"

"It be on the paper," Lavender said quietly. "And not just here on Scotia. Everywhere."

It was true. Gemma had seen it with her own eyes, the newspaper crumpled on the floor of the colonel's bedchamber, just days before. The edges scorched as if the master had tried to burn it up. She couldn't read the marks, but Aron, the crippled boy who helped the master dress most days now, could, a bit. He said it was about that white master Lincoln. Said that Lincoln man say wasn't going to be no more slaves, that some colored men been joinin' up with the buckra soldiers.

And there were rumors.

Of slaves building boats or stealing boats and deserting the sea island rice and cotton plantations up and down the coasts of the Carolinas, Georgia, Florida. Of Union soldier men taking over Port Royal and blocking the Confederate ships. Of planters fleeing, abandoning their plantations to their slaves.

"Those North soldiers say us free, then us free. Us be free here. More free maybe than off island," said Gemma, evenly. "Don't need to go no where's else then."

Marigold threw her mending into the dirt. "Here? You want to stay here?" She flung out an arm, taking in the quarter, the manor house, all of Scotia Island. "For what, Mama? For what you want to stay here? To work the rice sunup to sundown. 'Til oonah feet is rot? To root for yams in this dirt like a wild pig?"

Gemma leaped to her feet, spilling the rich soup. "And wuh you t'ink waits the other side of that water, daughter? You spec a pretty house wit' soft beds? Fancy buckra bittle and shiny new pots to boil 'taters? A fancy girl to bring 'em?"

The cold was gone now, replaced with a fire that blazed hot in her gut. Marigold stood, too, more slowly. "Don't know. Somethin' bettuh. Somethin' . . . not this."

"*This* what me give me whole life to. *This* where me lay down me sweat, me blood. *This* where me bury me man, me momma, two a me babies." Gemma hissed the words through clenched teeth. "This here *b'long* to me. It speak to me. It hold me roots. Me soul. Me am Ainsli Green and Ainsli Green mine."

Marigold gave a harsh laugh. "Oonah don' even b'long to you own self. You think you haunt that man long-long, he give you this place? You think you break he mind he forget you a slave when he wakes? Walk his dreams, Mama. Walk 'til you break both you minds! He as like to give Ainsli Green to that mule out yonder!"

Gemma swung. The back of her hand connected with Marigold's cheek, knocking her backward against the cabin wall.

"Mama, no!" cried Lavender. She grabbed her mother around the waist and pulled her away. Jessamine ran to Marigold's side. Sprawled on the ground, her sister laughed. In the flickering firelight tears sparkled on her cheeks.

"This thing you do not free, Mama. You gon' pay. It gon' swallow down you soul," she hissed. "You be alone on this islan'. You and that crazy old *buckra*."

Gemma shook free of Lavender's grasp. "Go on 'way from here then, if that be in your heart. Go on out in that world and be free. But you remember this warnin', girl. Oonah never be as free as you be right here on this island. As you be at Ainsli Green."

She whirled and stormed into the night, only vaguely aware of the other slaves hovering in their darkened doorways, watching, listening.

She crouched, hidden in a clump of giant cattails, the splintered moon, the color of churned butter in the sky, high overhead. Something rustled behind her, and she jerked, squinting into the darkness, every muscle tense.

Voices.

She thought she heard voices—like a faint echo inside her head. Sweat crept downward between her breasts. A boo hag was out running free on the island. She was certain of it.

"Be gone from this place," she whispered. She fingered the wooden cross that hung from a length of woven, blue-dyed hemp at her neck. "Leave me be."

Trembling in the thick air, she waited for the evil spirit to come for her, to leap from the rushes and tear at her flesh with jagged, blood-stained teeth. But there was only the murmuring of the wind across the grass, the screech of an owl deep in the trees.

A fox, she thought, swallowing hard, clutching at the cross. Or perhaps it was merely the rats that scrabbled through the fields every night searching for stray grains of rice to eat. But she didn't really believe that. *They* were out there, in the darkness, waiting for her: the haints and the boo hags that haunted the night.

She pinched the soft flesh near her armpit hard, the pain centering her, sweeping the fear off her skin. She took a deep breath, the sound loud in the darkness. From her hiding place, she had a perfect view of Rupert Everleigh's window. Gemma licked her lips. They felt dry and cracked. For the first time since she had begun to stalk the old man's dreams, she felt a shiver of doubt.

Marigold was right. There was a cost for what she was doing. One could not walk unbidden in the dreaming house of another, night after night, without payment coming due. Each time you walked, you took a little of the person with you, left a little of yourself behind, and the cost was highest when you were unwelcome.

She closed her eyes. She still felt the sting on the back of her hand where she'd struck her daughter, still felt the sensation of Marigold's cheekbone against her knuckles. She clenched her hands to stop them shaking. She'd almost never struck her children in anger, left that for the buckra to do, but what was done could not be undone. She groaned deep in her throat, feeling her heart break a little.

But Marigold . . .

Could she be so stupid? So anxious to get off island, so anxious to believe the pretty words about the Yankee soldier men. They were just another kind of buckra, weren't they? Marigold would leave and that big land over the water would eat her alive, digest her like an acorn in a pig's belly. This was where she belonged. This was where they all belonged— right here on Scotia Island, right here at Ainsli Green.

Gemma pushed the pain in her heart down, back into that dark place where all her sorrows lived. She would walk the master's dreams, force herself inside his nighttime mind because she had no other choice. The buckras' war was coming. Soon, there would be soldier men sailing their ships out into the sound, maybe even pouring out onto the pale sand of Scotia itself. And then what? What would happen to Ainsli Green if that old man was foolish enough to die without a will? It would most likely go to his worthless nephew who cowered in his big house in Savannah, hiding from the Yankee men. The same nephew who'd abandoned the old man here on Scotia with his slaves and a handful of foul-smelling drivers. Gemma spit into the sandy earth.

War was swirling out there: white men fighting over this and that and she didn't know what. But she could not—would not—have her fate, the fate of her girls decided by a white man who'd set foot on Scotia Island fewer times than the fingers on her one hand. The buckras had their war and she had hers, and she would fight it in the old man's dreams. She intended to belong to herself and herself alone. And no matter what the white men did out in their world, she would have Scotia Island for her children and her children's children and all the children that came after that carried her blood in their veins.

There was a loud crack and Gemma's eyes snapped open. She had nearly drifted off. On the lawn in front of the house, just beyond a magnolia tree, stood three white-tailed deer, trembling, alert, staring toward the clump of cattails. She shook herself and looked once more toward the window. The curtain was drawn but she could see his shadow at the window, unmoving, as if looking out over Ainsli Green, though she knew he could see nothing in the darkness.

"Go on now," murmured Gemma. "Go on to sleep now, Colonel."

She shivered. It was late fall, and though the days were still hot, a salt-laden fog blew over the island at night, encasing everything in a damp, brittle chill.

"Sleep, Colonel," she whispered again.

The sliver of moon disappeared behind the clouds as she waited, the night growing cooler, wetter. It wasn't until the earliest hours of the morning that Rupert Everleigh finally fell asleep. The slave woman felt it the instant he crossed the threshold into the realm of dreams. Deep in her cushion of the cattails, she closed her eyes and followed him in.

Rupert Everleigh's house of dreams was big, stretching long and straight as a plane, its main corridor disappearing into the far distance. Gemma hesitated on the doorsill, uneasy. From where she stood, she could see rooms hanging off the sides of the long hallway like berries on a stem. To her right, a window hung crookedly in its frame, the glass blacked out. The house seemed to breathe around her, expelling thick air that smelled of rot.

She shook herself. This was the colonel's dream. She was just a visitor, unwanted yes, but still a visitor. She had no control over the house his mind built, only what happened once she entered. And even that was not entirely predictable. Warily, she stepped inside.

The colonel was nowhere to be seen, but he was here . . . somewhere. He had to be. This was his dream, after all.

She moved down the long corridor. Shadows oozed along the cool, yellow pine floor and dripped down the walls, leaked from beneath the closed doors. Behind each door lay the colonel's hopes, fears, and memories, hidden away, waiting. Around her, the house breathed, a living thing, just as fears and memories live. In dreams, all things were possible.

Unconsciously, she stroked the white shell bracelet at her wrist, the talisman that ground her to the dream world. There was an unease growing in the pit of her stomach. But why should she be afraid? She was the third daughter of a third daughter. She was a Dreamwalker. It was the old colonel that should be afraid.

And he was. She felt his fear. Felt him fighting to wake up. She smiled grimly. Not yet, Colonel. Not just yet.

She stopped. A door had suddenly appeared at the end of the corridor, different from all the others. It was set high in the wall, its sill nearly a foot above the floor. She could hear the sound of a piano coming from behind the closed door. She grasped the handle. It turned easily in her hand, and she pulled herself up into a large sitting room, lit by dozens of candles.

A tiny man, no bigger than a lap baby, sat playing the piano in the corner, his gray skin as pale and puckered as milk curds. A woman stood in front of a tall window, and though it was full day on the other side of the glass, there, in the room, was the darkness of night, broken only by the glow of candlelight. The woman turned at the sound of Gemma's footsteps on the polished floor, and Gemma recognized her instantly: Nell, the colonel's daughter.

But it was a Nell from another time, a much younger Nell, not the Nell that peered out of the painting that hung in the parlor, a gift to her father two Christmases past. The woman in that portrait was a wasted creature with expensive-looking clothes and dead, sunken eyes. The Nell that stood watching her from near the window still had the plump face of her youth, the same dark, shiny hair she'd had on the day she'd wed her Englishman here at Ainsli Green. And Gemma knew that but for the dim light, she could have looked into Nell's face and seen the colonel's pale, blue eyes peering back at her.

The woman held a child in her arms, a dark-haired boy, whose head dangled awkwardly on his neck.

"Have you come to take us to heaven?" asked Nell.

Gemma shook her head. The woman sighed and shifted the lifeless child in her arms.

"What then?"

"Me come to find your daddy."

"My daddy?" Nell looked confused. She gazed sadly down at her son and stroked his cheek. "I don't think my daddy wants to see you."

Gemma shrugged. "Don't reckon so."

"My baby's dead," said Nell, looking up at her.

"Seems like."

Across the room, the tiny man pounded out waltzes on the piano, seemingly oblivious to their presence.

"And you're not to take us up to heaven?" Nell's voice sounded hopeful.

"No, miss," replied Gemma. "Me just needs to speak wit' your daddy."

Nell sighed again and cocked her head toward a corner of the room, then turned to stare back out of the sunlit window. Another door had appeared in the corner, just beyond the piano-playing man. It was the way of dreams.

Gemma pushed it open and stepped into a sun-drenched field. She didn't know the place, but she knew the man who stood cowering against a young oak tree.

"Colonel?"

He turned, trembling, to face her. He was wearing his uniform from the war, or at least most of it. His blue short coat hung open over his bare chest, and his gray pants gaped, unbuttoned, his manhood dangling limply at the opening. He pointed his musket at her face. She didn't flinch.

"I know what you want from me," he said, his voice hoarse.

She glanced up. The light in the sky seemed to be coming from everywhere. And nowhere.

"'Spects you do, Colonel Rupert," she said, meeting his eyes.

"You can't have Ainsli Green," he screamed.

"Ain't no one else to have it," she replied, reasonably.

"I got my daughter. Her children."

"You know that ain't true. Yo' boy dead. Miss Nell's chillun dead. She good as." She felt a twinge of pity as she said this—she'd always had a fondness for the young mistress—but she pushed it away.

Locking eyes with her, the master straightened his uniform coat, and suddenly she was aware that something had changed, some subtle shift in the dream. Instantly, she was on guard.

The air grew cooler, and they were standing on a sidewalk in front of a big house, the bricks smooth beneath her bare feet. And Rupert Everleigh was younger. Not young, but much younger than the failing master asleep in his bed at Ainsli Green. Her master was old and he was sick, but to her astonishment, he'd found some hidden well of strength, of will. And he was fighting back.

"You're some kinda witch! A black, Africa witch," he hissed, watching her through narrowed eyes. "I see you followin' me, slinkin' around in the shadows like a stray dog beggin' for scraps."

She watched him, saying nothing as he paced in front of her, growling curses. Suddenly he stopped and stared at her, the heat of his hate nearly blistering her skin.

"You want to sign them deed papers," she said finally, her voice low. "You want to sign them in my name."

"No," he snapped. "I don't."

He jerked the musket so that the barrel was only inches from her face, and Gemma felt a ribbon of fear unfurl down her spine. She had underestimated this man. He was strong, stronger than she could have ever imagined. She swallowed hard, locking the fear away from her face.

"May be some thing I can give you back."

The colonel threw back his head and laughed. "You ain't got nothin' to give me, gal! You ain't yo momma. I'm a sell you! Sell your girls. See that youngest one shipped off to the Louisiana cane fields. She's a skinny thing. Mayn't last a season, but can't never tell with nigras can ya? What you say to that?"

She flinched, then forced a smile. "Ain't nobody to buy us. Masters is runnin', not plantin'."

He spit at her feet, cursed again. They stared at each other in that strange, everywhere light, locked in silent battle.

"There is a thing I can do for you," she said finally, the words barely audible, even to her ears. "A thing only I can do."

She had walked his dreams, his memories and his fears. She knew his greatest desire: that his son would live again to inherit Ainsli Green. That his daughter would return to him, whole, happy. That he would not die a man alone, without heirs. And she could do that for him, at least within the borderlands of dreams.

She could hold him forever in that vague, drifting place that was not awake, yet not quite sleep, where he could float with Nell, and his wife, and all those he'd ever loved. In that place, he would never be old. He would never be alone. But to trap a dreamer in their own dream, whatever the reason, was a perversion of her gift. The dark side of dreamwalking. A sin before God and the ancestors. It meant flirting with her own madness. And there would be a punishment exacted.

She hesitated, a warning sounding deep in her soul. She turned the shell bracelet round and round her wrist. This was a path with no way back. She thought of Marigold, her rage-filled oldest daughter, wanting a world bigger and shinier than Scotia Island. Of sweet, easygoing Jessamine, happy wherever her family was. And of Lavender, her quiet, ever-watchful Dreamwalker daughter. Marigold was right, she could do this thing. Lead her master to the place of his greatest desire, leave him dreaming there forever. But to do this also meant risking being trapped there with him, losing her way in that gray never-waking place.

Gemma ground her teeth.

But wasn't the awake world as much a trap? Waiting for the buckras to beat *each other bloody? Waiting for them to divide the spoils among the victor? One buckra bad as the last?*

She had already spilled her blood and her tears. This *was her war, this battle in the dreams of a frightened old man. And Ainsli Green was the prize she sought. If this battle broke her, then . . .*

She clenched her fists and focused everything she had on him. She would promise him whatever she had to promise him, do whatever she had to do to get that deed paper signed, to gain freedom for her girls. Madness and damnation wasn't such a price to pay.

The deed papers appeared in her hand.

"You get to be with your girl. Her boy. Get to see him grow," she said, her voice soft, soothing. "You be strong again. Won't nothin' pain. Put your mark and I do that for you."

She held the thick papers out and took a step toward him, saw him flinch, took another step.

"You do this thing I ask. Small-small thing. I do this thing for you."

She saw a flicker of hope in his blue eyes, the longing. She smiled. A mistake. The yearning faded to be replaced by . . . rage.

"I'll give you the grave!" he snarled.

He jerked up the musket and the world exploded in fire and the sharp smell of gunpowder. When it cleared, they were standing in a dark, featureless room: no windows, no furniture.

There was a terrible pain in her face, and she felt a spasm of panic. The first thing—the most important thing—a Dreamwalker learns is how to not come to harm in the dream world. She could not remember the last time she had brought back the marks of her dreams into the waking world.

"Keep their dream theirs, lest you get pulled in and find yourself kilt."

Again and again her mother had whispered those words in her ear just before she dropped off to sleep: "Don't lose yo' grip on what theirs and what yours."

And yet now, her face burned under her left eye where her master had aimed his musket: a low-pitched, brutal pain. She clenched her fist at her sides to keep from touching her face, and forced herself to smile. He would not see her fear.

"Ainsli Green mine, Colonel. Oonah just doesn't knows it yet," she said. She turned and walked away, out of his dream.

5

Her tongue lay thick and heavy as a sock in her mouth, and there was a faint warning twinge at the base of her neck, but it had been a blissfully dreamless night. She felt almost rested. Groaning, she pried open her eyes, sending up a silent prayer of thanks for the inventor of her little magic pills. The last thing she remembered was curling up on the living room couch, but sometime during the night she had migrated to the floor and now lay sprawled atop the newspapers and sketch pads and partially finished drawings that covered most of the living room carpet.

The ringing phone jolted her fully awake. Pushing herself upright, she scrabbled through the chaos, papers crunching beneath her knees as she tried to locate it. She found it on the fifth ring, tucked between the couch and a long-dead asparagus fern.

"You're not up yet?"

She groaned.

"Will, it's . . ." Layla glanced at her watch. "Barely eight."

"I know. I let you sleep in," Will chuckled. "You're welcome."

"Will . . ." She gritted her teeth. Her brother's morning cheer was like a nail in her eye.

"I have coffee."

"Shit," she muttered.

Will laughed. "Nice! You are just so adorable in the morning. I so want to be you when I grow up."

She squinted against the sun streaming through the living room blinds. She had agreed to meet Will at their mother's to start the long process of clearing out the house.

"Lay?"

She heard the concern in his voice when she didn't answer. She imagined him, eyes narrowed, lips pressed together, his long frame draped over the railing of the balcony at his condo overlooking Rock Creek Park. In the background, the baby began to cry.

"There's no rush to do this, you know," he said into the silence. "It can wait a few days."

She shook her head no, though he couldn't see it. What was the point of waiting?

"Did you know that morning people are seventeen times more likely to die prematurely than people who aren't?" she asked. She slogged through the debris on the floor toward the kitchen.

"That right?" Will's voice was still serious. She pulled coffee grounds from the refrigerator and began to spoon them into the coffeemaker.

"I read it on the internet. So, you might want to try being just a little less perky in the mornings. You know . . . for your health."

She heard him chuff, amused. "Internet. Perky. Got it. If I do die prematurely, will you take care of Chase?"

The thought of her moon-faced nephew, his big, one-toothed grin, made her smile. "What about Chuck?"

"Chuck? Chuck is genetically incapable of sleeping past dawn. Or of having a bad day. So he should be dead in . . . let's see . . . damn . . . he should already be dead!" Her brother laughed.

Layla snorted. She leaned on the counter as the smell of freshly brewed coffee filled the small kitchen. "I always knew Chuck was not quite right."

Will laughed again. They both knew Layla adored her brother-in-law.

"You sure you're okay doing this today?" he asked, serious again.

She grimaced. The thought of going to her mother's house, of picking through her things, made her queasy.

"Yeah, I'm just super." She sighed, then winced, hoping he hadn't heard. "I'll meet you at Mom's in about an hour, okay? And Will?"

"Hmmm?"

"There damn well better be coffee."

Back in the living room she slid into the purple, plastic picnic chair she'd rescued from the curb on garbage day months before. She'd been meaning to sketch it, or paint it, or somehow rehabilitate it into a clever art piece, but, like so many other things, she had never gotten around to it. Now it just took up precious space in her already cramped apartment.

She sipped her coffee and stared at the wall in front of her. It was covered with her latest assignment.

Layla pushed herself out of the chair and went to stand in front of it. She'd taped white craft paper to the wall on which she'd drawn a human tongue, three feet wide and three feet high. Drawn in pinks and blues and angry reds, the taste buds clustered near the back and along the edges like islands in the sea. The frenum, the part that connected the tongue to the mouth, rose up like a wave, the thick tongue muscle surfing its leading edge.

She'd already completed the assignment in ZBrush, modeling the tongue in 3D. She still had a few days to render the colors and download the file before it was due to the clients. By the end of the year, reprints of her tongue would find their way into doctor's offices and medical schools everywhere. This one was a normal tongue. Her next assignment was to draw one riddled with cancer.

She twisted her fingers through her hair. She didn't need to do these sketches on canvas and paper, but she liked doing it. Liked the feeling of the pens and chalks and charcoals in her hand. It felt more real, more like the art she'd envisioned doing when she'd left home for school. She glanced around her living room. The floor was littered with drawings of kidneys and eyeballs and testicles.

"If you're going to settle, at least settle for a job with dental insurance."

She gripped her coffee cup, her mother's words echoing off the apartment walls. Layla had always envisioned herself spending cool autumns somewhere exotic, sketch pad in hand, paints nearby. She'd imagined her work in some beautiful, brightly lit boutique gallery in SoHo or Montmartre. Instead, an accident of fate combined with a crisis of confidence had landed her here, creating medical illustrations.

"It's not settling," she murmured to the empty room. "And it *is* art."

She had a vision of her mother telling people what her daughter did for a living, of Elinor Hurley having to use the word *testicle* in a sentence, and the thought made Layla laugh out loud.

She turned from the sketches, feeling a vague sense of agitation as she stared at the chaotic jumble that was her apartment. Dropping to her knees, she began raking pens and watercolor brushes from under the couch. She pushed papers and unopened mail together into piles, stacked textbooks and anatomy photos in one corner. A frenzied momentum took hold, and her face glowed with a faint sheen of sweat as she swept through the apartment gathering shoes, empty food containers, discarded sweaters and jeans as she went. It suddenly seemed important—imperative—that she get her apartment in order.

She raced around, feeling a growing exhilaration as she hung up clothes, emptied and reloaded the dishwasher, threw out old newspapers. She knew Will was waiting at their mother's, but the impulse to clean, to organize, was an itch she had to scratch.

Finally, she took a step back and looked around. Though far from spotless, the floor was visible, and for the first time in weeks, she could sit on the couch without risking an avalanche of paper. She felt calmer, as if even the air she was breathing was somehow cleaner.

She glanced at her watch. "Crap!"

If she didn't hurry, Will's hair would be on fire by the time she got to her mother's. She hurriedly wriggled into the faded flowered housedress she'd bought for three dollars at the flea market, then rummaged through the dirty clothes basket on her bedroom floor for something to throw over it. She pulled a sleeveless denim blouse from the middle of the pile and sniffed at it. It smelled fresh enough for cleaning out her mother's house. Tossing it on, she hurried out.

Yanking open the car door, she froze. The Aunts' envelope lay on the front seat where she'd left it days before. She stared at it and the strange woman's face—the one from her dream, the one from the newspaper clipping—floated up to her again. Standing there in the parking lot behind her building, the morning sun warm on her arms, she unconsciously touched her face. Though it was fading, turning to faint shades of yellow and green, the corner of her eye was still tender.

Her father used to say that the dreams she had, the dreams that were as real to her as her two brothers, were simply little pieces of her life, memories seasoned with her vivid imagination.

But they were more, so much more than that.

In her dreams, she'd learned to knit. Miss Effie, Mrs. Calhoun's long-dead grandmother, had shown her how. She liked Miss Effie, liked it when Mrs. Calhoun dreamed of the long, white porch looking out over a bright green sea of growing corn. Liked the softness of the yarn in her fingers, the hypnotic rhythm of knit one, purl one.

She remembered the look on her mother's face when she'd asked for knitting needles.

"You don't know how to knit."

But she did. She knit her father a tie of burgundy and blue yarn, not a very good tie, but still . . . Tried to explain to her mother about Miss Effie and the corn. But her mother had recoiled, her lips pressed tight, as if tasting something foul. Told her to go outside and play.

And then there was Butterscotch.

Her best friend growing up had been Evie Russell. Evie lived at the end of the block and across the street. Mostly they played at Layla's house because Layla was afraid of Mr. Russell. He said bad words and he smelled funny. But sometimes they did play at Evie's because Evie had a dog. Butterscotch had soft, golden hair that ringed his face like a beard. He liked to curl up on Layla's lap and have his tummy rubbed. One day he disappeared.

Mr. Russell told everyone that Butterscotch had run away. But Layla knew that was a lie. Every night for a week, she had the same dream. She stood shivering at the edge of the Russells' backyard, her bare feet numb on the frost-coated mud. And Mr. Russell was always there, an unlit cigarette dangling from his lip. His eyes were bloodshot, and he had that funny smell again. Every night for a week, she watched as he dug a hole beneath the catalpa tree. Watched him pick up something wrapped in a pale blue towel and toss it in the hole. Watched as a tiny corner of the towel fell back at the last minute, just a little, just enough for her to see golden hair curled around a tiny face. And every night she screamed.

Mrs. Russell caught her on a cold Sunday morning trying to dig Butterscotch up. Layla had been grounded for three days, and Evie was never allowed to play with her again.

And still the doctors said night terrors. And she began to pretend.

Layla stared at the folder on the front seat and tried to remember every detail of the dream from the night at her mother's: the house with the mismatched furniture, her mother in that odd wedding dress, everything the woman had said to her.

Her cell phone rang, startling her out of her reverie.

Will.

"Crap!"

Layla slid into the driver's seat and headed for her mother's house.

Her brother stood in front of the open garage door. As she stepped from the car, he made a great show of checking his watch.

"You said there'd be coffee," she said, ignoring the gesture.

He pointed to a thermos propped on top of a metal picnic cooler. "Nice outfit, Lay."

She eyed his baggy overalls, the pink bandana tied around his neck, then flicked her hand, dismissing him as she poured the coffee. "It's already got creamer?"

"And sweetener too," he said, grunting as he hauled a large box marked "Christmas Ornaments" from a shelf. "You know . . . because I'm wonderful like that."

"Will. A legend in his own mind," she muttered, taking a sip. It was exactly the way she liked it.

"Yep, that's me," he said, grinning at her.

She rolled her eyes and sipped her coffee. For the next few hours, they boxed up shoes, coats, dishes, and lamps for the Goodwill, threw away outdated books and moth-eaten sweaters. They sorted through old family photos and grade school art projects, laughing at the macaroni hearts, hand turkeys, and yarn Christmas trees. Layla was amazed at what her mother had saved from their childhood.

"Uncle," cried Will finally. He stood and arched his back with a groan. "I'm calling uncle." He snatched the pink bandana from around his neck and swiped at his face. "Break time."

Layla glanced at her watch. They'd been working nonstop in the hot garage for nearly three hours.

"I'm getting some ice tea," he said. "Want some?"

She nodded as she stuffed her old Brownie uniform into the metal garbage can. She dropped into a tattered lounge chair and slid down until her head rested against the back, her long legs stretched out in front of her. The denim shirt had long been tossed in a corner and the flowered dress was soaked with sweat. Every muscle ached, but they'd managed to organize and empty nearly half of the garage as well as a section of the basement storage area.

She stared at the wall in front of her where rusting woodworking tools hung from hooks near the ceiling, remnants of their father's foray into yet another of his short-lived hobbies. She smiled, remembering her mother's dismay at the trail of sawdust her father left everywhere he went during that time. In a far corner of the garage stood one of his projects, a bookcase that had never made it into the house. It leaned crookedly against the wall, balanced precariously on its uneven legs. It had ended up being used to store hammers and nails and the endless rolls of duct tape her father was forever buying.

"What happened to Mom's room?"

Layla jerked upright in her chair. Will stood staring at her from the step that led down from the kitchen into the garage.

"I . . . ," she began, then fell silent. She hadn't been back in her mother's room since the night before the funeral. In her mind's eye she saw the clothes strewn on the closet floor, the dresser drawers yanked open. She wondered what he'd seen. Had the Aunts cleaned up in there? She couldn't remember.

Her brother stood watching, waiting. When she didn't answer, he stepped down into the garage and squatted in front of her.

"Layla?" His voice was tight.

She pleaded silently with him to drop it, but he grabbed her hands and held them, staring into her eyes.

"I had one of those dreams, Will," she said finally. She locked eyes with him, her chin thrust out, defiant.

"Oh, for Christ sake!" He stood abruptly, dropping her hands.

She pursed her lips and said nothing. There was nothing to say.

"Again, with this? You're doing this again? Now? I thought this was all over." He sounded more tired than angry. "I thought you were seeing someone or taking some kind of medicine or something?"

"There's nothing wrong with me!" she snapped, bristling at the pity she saw in his eyes.

He reared back as if struck and stared at her, eyes narrowed. He pointed at the nearly healed bruise on her face. "Really? That's nothing? And that in there, that's nothing too?" he said sharply, jerking his arm in the direction of the house.

"No," she yelled. "No, the dreams aren't nothing. They're . . ."

"Layla, I don't care!" He held up a hand to stop her. "I don't give a good goddamn what they are, okay? I don't want to hear about your crazy dreams. Jesus Christ . . . !"

He slammed his fist down onto the garbage can, denting the top, and she gasped.

"I'm sick to death of it, okay? Sick of it! Aren't you sick of it?" He glared at her, then seemed to deflate. "Jesus, Lay! This is just so seriously messed up. We're not kids anymore."

He stared at her in silence, his expression a mix of sadness and anger. Most of the time he pretended that her . . . problem . . . didn't exist, but when he was forced to acknowledge it, when it smacked him full in the face . . .

"You need to see something," she said, blinking back tears. He shook his head as she walked to the car and snatched the Aunts' envelope from the front seat.

"Here," she said, holding the envelope out toward him. "I dreamed about this woman. In my dream she was talking about Ainsli Green."

"Who the hell is Ainsli Green?" He frowned at the envelope.

"I have no idea," she admitted. "But, Will, there's a picture in here of the woman who attacked me in my dream." She pointed to her face. "And when I woke up Mom's room was trashed."

She shook the envelope at him.

"What is that?" asked Will, staring at it.

"The Aunts gave me this before they left." She forced it into his hands.

Slumping back into the lounge chair, she crossed her arms and waited. Will held the envelope for a long moment, then, with an exasperated sigh, opened it. Layla watched as he pulled out the yellowing newspaper clipping and studied it.

"I don't . . . what is all this?" he asked, frowning. "The Aunts gave you this? Why?"

She shrugged, chewing on a strand of hair.

"You didn't read it?"

She shook her head. The shock of the photo still vibrated beneath her skin. She'd been too unnerved to examine the envelope's contents further.

"It's a place," said her brother after a moment. "Ainsli Green is a place. The name of an old rice plantation. On Scotia Island."

She squinted at him. "Where?"

"Scotia Island. It's a Sea island. One of those islands off the Carolina and Georgia coasts." He studied the piece of paper in his hand.

She'd heard of them, barely. "Like Hilton Head?"

"Like Hilton Head." He smiled slightly. "Only smaller, I think, if I'm reading this right. Way smaller."

She blinked. "O . . . kay. So?"

He pulled the rest of the papers from the envelope and spread them on the garage floor, kneeling as he arranged them in two rows. As he read,

Layla watched his expressions cycle rapidly between disbelief, confusion, then back again.

"What?" she asked, finally. "What is it?"

"Oh my god!" he murmured. He rocked back on his heels, blinking up at her. "It's yours!"

"What?" She frowned, confused. "What's mine?"

"The island! The plantation! Or whatever's left of it, belongs to you!" He held a wrinkled jumble of papers out toward her.

She want to take Ainsli Green? Not never!

She gave a sharp laugh. "I don't . . . what? What are you talking about?"

"This!" Will was on his feet. He shook the papers in her face. "This is a deed. To the plantation. To the island."

He dropped the documents in her lap. Dense lines of legalese blurred together, but there, near the bottom of one of the pages, was her name: Layla Elise Hurley, dated October 31, on the year she'd turned seven.

Aunt Jayne had said that the envelope contained her inheritance. "But why?" she asked. "Why would I have a deed to an island?"

"You remember Granny Bliss?" Will was quickly scanning the other documents on the floor.

"No." She shook her head.

There was a picture of her mother's mother in the living room: a handsome, older woman with a square face and open, friendly eyes. Her mother rarely spoke of her, but more than once Layla had caught her staring at the picture, hands clenched tight at her side.

"Oh, right," he said. "Well, Granny Bliss had a twin sister named . . ." He shuffled through the papers on the garage floor. "Mercy. She had a twin sister named Mercy. They both inherited Scotia Island, which apparently has been passed down through the family for generations. Granny Bliss deeded her half to Mom. Mom deeded it to you. And voila! You own an island."

"So, Granny Bliss had an island that she willed to Mom, who then willed it to me?" The words sounded ridiculous to her ears.

Will peered at another tattered document.

"Well, technically half a plantation and half an island. The other half is owned by Mercy's daughter. A Charlotte Fortenberry. So, our second? Third cousin?"

He squinted as he did the calculations in his head, but Layla had stopped listening. She was staring at the photo of the woman on the garage floor. She bent to pick it up. Her brother leaned to look over her shoulder.

"Damn." He gave a low whistle. "That sister looks like she eats glass for breakfast."

Layla said nothing as she studied the picture. The same chocolate-brown face. The same piercing eyes and wide, unsmiling mouth from the dream.

Charlotte Fortenberry. Their distant cousin.

"You're rich, Lay."

She forced her gaze from the photo and peered up at her brother. "What are you talking about?"

"This." He shook the newspaper clipping in front of her face and pointed. "This says that developers have been trying to buy or find some way to take control of the island for years to build some sort of fishing or camping resort or something. Some luxury something or other. They've been offering millions. And half that island is yours now."

Not never.

"And you are going to love this part." He sounded amused.

"I doubt it," she muttered.

"Part of the reason it hasn't sold is that supposedly the island is cursed."

She reared back. "It what?"

"Oh yeah, girl. That article? 'The Mystery of Ainsli Green'? Well, seems that all kinds of wild, creepy stuff has been going on out there since . . . well, since forever. Folks disappearing, losing their minds. Every single time a developer even comes near to closing a deal on that island, some absolute craziness happens. Going back at least to the 1960s." He grinned. "Man, this is awesome."

She made a noise in the back of her throat and gripped the plastic arms of the lounge chair.

"Layla?"

She forced a smile through clenched teeth. "Yeah," she managed to say. "Awesome."

She stared at the smeary picture of the woman from her dreams. The woman that was her cousin.

6

Moonlight streamed through the living room window, bathing everything in a soft, milky light. The apartment smelled peculiar—yeasty and unpleasantly sweet—like something forgotten in the garbage pail. Layla screwed up her face. Whatever it was would be worse in the morning, but she was too exhausted to investigate, much less remedy the problem.

Without bothering to turn on any lights, she slogged toward the bedroom, grateful that during the morning's cleaning frenzy she'd removed at least most of the obstacles on the floor. Sidestepping the basket of dirty laundry in the doorway, she flung herself facedown on the bed.

An island.

Her mother had bequeathed her an island.

Layla felt a pressure forming just above the bridge of her nose, signaling the onset of a headache. According to Will's interpretation of the paperwork they'd read, she now shared ownership of this island with a distant cousin. The cousin she'd met in a dream a week ago and who had, for some unknown reason, attacked her.

"Jesus Christ, Mom," she muttered, burying her face deep into her pillow. "Why couldn't you just leave me your fur coat, or jewelry . . . like a normal person?"

An island.

Like so much else about her mother, it made absolutely no sense. Other than the fact that she'd grown up in South Carolina and was the youngest of three sisters, Layla knew next to nothing about her mother's life before she'd left for college.

She often wondered what horrific thing could possibly have driven her mother to try so hard to erase that whole part of her life: her family, her past.

But an island.

Even in the face of her mother's determination to obliterate her beginnings, it seemed incomprehensible that she would have never mentioned owning a whole island. And why, if she was so bent on severing ties with her past, had she even held on to it all this time? Why not sell it? Or give it to the Aunts?

Layla frowned. The Aunts. The deed had specified that the island had belonged to her mother, to be passed to her. There'd been no mention of the Aunts. Why would her grandmother pass the island to only Elinor, the one daughter that had turned her back on her home, her family? Why not give it to her older daughters, the ones who'd stayed and lived their whole lives in Port Royal?

And for that matter, there'd been no mention of Will or Evan in the deed. Nothing about this made any sense.

Layla rolled onto her back with a groan. The air in the apartment was warm and thick. Her skin felt sticky and damp. She could smell herself. The pressure in her head grew as the questions continued to swirl, bumping up against each other.

Why had the Aunts been so mysterious about all of this? Surely the island and who owned it was no secret. At least . . . she could think of no good reason why it should have been.

And what was all that talk about being the last? The last what? Remembering the look that had passed between the sisters as Aunt Therese pushed the packet into her hands, she felt a shiver of unease.

"Jesus Christ," she whispered.

She jerked upright on the bed and clutched her hair in her fists. It felt damp and gritty.

She and Will had spent the better part of an hour combing through the articles in the folder about the strange happenings surrounding the island. One told of a developer driving his car into the Port Royal Sound in the middle of the night and drowning. Two other developers had gone bankrupt, one after burning down half his company's million-dollar properties on another high-end resort island. Most recently, five years before, the banker financing the buying of properties out on the Sea Islands had simply vanished, leaving a wife and four children.

"Jesus Christ!" she said again.

She shivered and blew out a frustrated breath. Aunt Therese had said there'd be questions. Well, she'd been right about that. Her head was near to exploding with questions. With effort, Layla forced herself to her feet and headed toward the shower.

She peered into the refrigerator. Nothing inside had changed since the last time she'd looked.

And the time before that.

And the half dozen times before that.

There was half of a salmon casserole, two bags of whole coffee beans, a pint of creamer, a partially eaten protein bar, and a container of expired cottage cheese. She closed the door again and drifted into the living room.

She paced the small apartment, picking up pen and sketch pad then putting them down again. She'd been on edge since leaving her mother's the day before yesterday, restlessness chafing at her skin like a rash. Her brothers had been calling, but she let the calls drop into voicemail. She knew she would have to call them back eventually, unless she wanted Will or Chuck to show up and start pounding on her door.

But not today.

Probably not tomorrow.

But eventually.

She caught her ankle on the purple picnic chair and swore. What had she been thinking? She was never going to sketch it. It would never become anything beautiful or interesting. It was always going to be exactly what it was now, an ugly thing, useless and out of place. She kicked it, hard, watching as it bounced off the bookcase, then fell—in slow motion—onto its side.

A strangled cry escaped Layla's throat and she grabbed her car keys and purse; the only thought in her mind was to go . . . somewhere, anywhere. Halfway out the door, she pivoted and, reaching into the apartment, grabbed the purple chair. Hoisting it high on her waist, she headed for the car.

She drove aimlessly, weaving in and out of traffic on I-95, the chair bumping against the back of her seat whenever she braked. When she saw the sign for the Beltway leading into Washington, she was only slightly surprised. Rush hour traffic was just starting to congeal on the freeway as she took the exit for her mother's house. By the time she pulled up, the sun was low in the sky, golds and oranges reflecting off the trees and rooftops.

In the two weeks since her mother's funeral, she'd spent more time on this street than she had in the whole year before. She was tired. The pills seemed to be losing some of their magic. There'd been no sharp-edged, confusing dreams, but these past few nights, in the hours before dawn, she found herself wide awake, sweat soaked, heart racing, feeling as if there was something she needed to do, but not knowing what.

And now, here she was, sitting in her mother's driveway. From the driver's seat, she watched the house, feeling oddly safe there in the waning daylight, less lonely—in a way that she hadn't in all the time she'd lived in this house.

A girl rode by on her bike, her long, blond hair streaming behind her from beneath her bicycle helmet. She gave a quick wave as she passed. Layla didn't recognize her but waved back anyway.

Across the street, a teenager was driving a riding mower around the Pryors' yard, carving concentric circles in the lush lawn. Layla laughed softly. Her brothers had mowed the lawn for their neighbor for years. Mr. Pryor was very particular about his grass. He wasn't going to like those circles one bit.

Up and down the street, American flags fluttered from porches. Layla'd forgotten all about the upcoming holiday. The Hurleys had always put out a flag too. It was probably still in the basement in one of the boxes she and Will had yet to sort through. She wondered if it would be odd to hang it this year, now that no one lived here. She turned back to her mother's house. It had always been her mother's house, not her parents' house, not her house, her mother's house.

She pushed open the car door and strode up the drive, moving fast, before she could change her mind. This time, she went directly to the back door.

The last of the day's sun poured into the kitchen through the window over the sink. Her mother's scent still lingered in the air, and she wondered how long that would last. Maybe it would smell like her mother until the house was completely emptied out. Maybe even after that. Maybe forever.

"Mom?" she called softly. She held her breath, listening. "Mom?"

Tears pricked at her eyes, and she brushed them roughly away. Her mother would be so pissed off that she was dead. The thought made her laugh, though the sound came out as a choked sob. Jaw clenched, she walked slowly through the house, opening cabinets and drawers, peering into closets looking for . . .

She didn't know what she was looking for. The muffled sound of the riding mower came to her from outside, mingling with the rhythmic ticking of the grandfather clock in the foyer and the low hum of the refrigerator.

In front of her mother's room, she came to a stop. The door was closed, and she pressed her face against it, the wood cool against her cheek. For a long moment she stood like that, then, steeling herself, opened it.

The jewelry box was once again on the dresser where it belonged, her mother's clothes arranged neatly in the closet. The only sign that the room had ever been other than how her mother left it was a small crease in the bedside lampshade. She felt a hot stab of embarrassment at the realization that Will must have come back at some point and put the room back together. She tugged at her hair, found a loose strand, and began to twist it. He wouldn't bring it up again, she was certain of that, but he would never forget either. It would become just one more thing for him to file away about her. To confirm for him that there really was something wrong with her.

Folded neatly in a basket at the foot of the bed was a red woolen shawl. She pulled it out and pressed it against her face. It was what her mother threw around her shoulders to run out to retrieve the newspaper from the end of the drive on damp days. What she wrapped herself in to watch television or sit at the kitchen table reading the paper on winter mornings. Layla wrapped it around her shoulders, then crawled into her mother's bed. It wasn't lost on her that the last time she'd curled up in this bed had been after her father died.

She was thirteen when the two policemen came to the front door to tell them there'd been an accident at the pharmacy her father owned: that her father wasn't coming home ever again. Her mother had grabbed hold of the front door handle and hung on. It had taken Mrs. Calhoun and one of the policemen to pry her hands loose. That was when the front door lock began to stick.

If her mother said anything after that, Layla didn't remember it. She'd turned away from the policeman and Mrs. Calhoun and grabbed Layla's hand, dragging them both into her bed. She remembered her mother gripping her hand so hard that she could feel the bones grinding against each other, but she hadn't pulled away. She lay there next to her mother, neither of them speaking, her mother hanging on to her hand the same way she'd hung on to that door handle.

When her brothers came home the next day, her mother hadn't made her get up. Without a word, she climbed from the bed and wrapped her in Daddy's cardigan—the ratty green one he wore all the time, the one her mother hated—then left her alone. For two days Layla lay there, seemingly forgotten by everyone. She lay, wrapped in her father's sweater, sleeping, dreaming dreams of Daddy covered in sawdust, of the way his toffee brown skin burned at the beach, his deep belly laugh.

Layla closed her eyes and rubbed the wool shawl against her cheek. This would probably be the last time she'd ever lie in this bed. She had run out of parents to die.

"A big girl doesn't chew her hair."

She tried to look up, to see her father's face, but she was bent over the bathtub. Soapy water dripped between her eyes and into her ears. As he washed her hair all she could manage was a glimpse of his wrist where a soap bubble perched on the leather band of his Timex.

She laughed. "I'm not a big girl, Daddy."

"But you are, sweetie."

She leaned her forehead onto her arms, felt the shell bracelet on her wrist bite into her skin. A dream. She didn't know why, but the bracelet was always there in her dreams, the tiny white shells shimmering bright against the golden brown of her skin. She was dreaming, but it didn't matter. She was with her father and she was happy.

As he massaged shampoo into her hair, she could feel his fingernails on her scalp, feel his fingers rake gently through her hair, smoothing out the curls, feel the strength of his hands as they cupped her head. When he leaned over her back to rinse her, she turned her head so that her nose was near his armpit. He smelled like the bleach her mother used on his undershirts, and Old Spice. He squeezed water from her hair, and suddenly she had a clear view around him. The bathtub was not in the bathroom but in the middle of the playground near her house. A crowd of children waited their turn on the slide. A little boy was standing on the swings, knees bent, his feet planted wide on the wooden seat, pumping hard to make himself go higher. She began to laugh.

"Hold still so I can get all the soap out."

Her father's voice sounded muffled, far away. She took the towel he handed her and wrapped it around her dripping hair, but when she turned to ask if he'd braid it too—he was good at it, better than her mother, who was impatient and too rough—he was gone. Instead, there were the Aunts and her mother. They were sitting on red velvet theater chairs, next to the dragon teeter-totter. Aunt Therese waved, but her mother just looked at her, her mouth pressed into a hard line. Layla felt a knot form in the pit of her stomach. She knew that look, that look of sour disapproval. Despite the towel, water ran down the back of her neck, soaking her blouse.

Her mother leaped from the velvet seat.

"Do you see this?" she cried, waving a crumpled paper at her sisters. "Do you?"

The Aunts stared at her in silence.

"This comes from the real world," cried her mother. "A world you can see. A world you can touch. That other people can see and touch."

The Aunts were shaking their heads, but their younger sister ignored them. Suddenly, she was in front of Layla, leaning close, her eyes locked on her daughter's. Layla clutched at the towel, forcing herself not to look away. They were no longer in the sunny playground but in a dark room, a room Layla didn't recognize.

"You are not the third of three. You are my daughter. My only one." Her mother's voice was thick, as if the words were catching in her throat. "And you are going to be normal. Normal!"

Wild-eyed, she threw the paper on the floor, and for the first time Layla could see that it was a page from a sketch pad. She caught a glimpse of blue and green pastel swirls just as something moved at the corner of her vision.

Charlotte!

The woman from her dreams, the woman from the newspaper article, her cousin, stood on the other side of the room, half-hidden behind a panel of black lace that hung across a darkened window. She saw Layla and her mother at the same time they saw her, and her face twisted into a mask of unadulterated fury. She thrashed at the lace curtain, trying to get free of it.

Layla stood frozen as Charlotte tore free of the curtain and charged, teeth bared. She was screaming something.

Abomination?

Layla felt herself pushed aside, felt her feet slip on the pastel painting, as her mother stepped forward to face the enraged woman.

"Wake up!" she screamed over her shoulder. "Layla, wake up now!"

Layla cried out. Her heart tripped crazily in her chest. She lay, jaw clenched, staring up at the ceiling, her body shaking. She grabbed at her hair, half expecting it to be wet. She had dreamed of her father. And her mother. She could still feel her mother pushing her aside to confront Charlotte, still hear her screaming for her to wake up. Trembling, she pulled her mother's shawl more tightly around her shoulders. Through all the years of her inexplicable dreaming, she had never dreamed of her mother.

She dreamed about her brothers and her father. About her friends from school. About neighbors and even strangers. But never about her mother.

Ever.

And now she'd dreamed of her twice in two weeks.

Layla had asked her about it once. Her mother had been stuffing the turkey for Thanksgiving dinner. She'd looked up at Layla's question, had stared at her for a long time. Layla remembered how cold it suddenly seemed in the warm kitchen, the way the hair stood up on her arms.

"The women in our family aren't allowed to dream about their mothers," her mother finally answered.

"Why not?"

She regretted the question as soon as it was asked. Her mother had laughed, a laugh like the ones in the movies, the ones where the woman goes crazy and someone has to slap her. But she hadn't slapped her mother. She'd stood frozen by the dishwasher, watching as bits of dressing dropped from the spoon to the floor unnoticed, until finally, the laughter stopped.

Her mother stood silent, looking past her, through her, then, without another word, turned back to stuffing the turkey. Layla was almost out of the room when she heard her mother say, "Because it costs too much. Because if we dream of our mothers then we run the risk of losing . . . everything."

That was the last time she ever mentioned her dreams to her mother.

"Jesus Christ," she whispered. She licked her dry lips.

She glanced at the clock on the bedside table. It was that weird time of morning—too late to drive home and go to bed, too early to get up and start the day. She sat up, shivering. Her blouse was soaked with sweat, the dream clinging to her skin like a film. What was she doing here? She was an idiot to have come.

She folded her mother's shawl and placed it back in the basket. She could hear the ticking of the grandfather clock, the creaking of the house as it settled around itself. It was still hours before sunrise, and the only illumination came from the small light above the stove. Shoes in hand, she snatched her car keys from the counter. Go home and stay home, she thought again. Showing up here in the middle of the night, sleeping here, was making her crazy. Well . . . crazier.

Reaching for the door, she slipped on something on the floor. Flailing, she managed, just barely, to grab hold of the stove and catch herself. She cursed under her breath and flicked on the overhead light.

Her throat constricted.

On the floor, halfway under the stove, was a large sheet of sketch paper. She could see swirls of blue and green pastels. She remembered this drawing. It had lain tucked in a leather portfolio in the back of her bedroom closet since forever. It was an abstract of a dragonfly, its free-form body a dash of silver. It was part of her other life: from when she'd dreamed of living in Paris or New York, when she'd dreamed of painting pictures that would hang in galleries or on living room walls, instead of in textbooks or in doctors' offices.

She stared at it a long time under the glare of the kitchen light, afraid to touch it, the night still heavy outside the window. And suddenly she knew what it was—the something that had been gnawing at her since her mother's funeral—the thing she had to do.

7

"This is so not a good idea," said Will.

"Why not?" asked Layla.

"Because we hardly know these people."

"*These people* are family."

"The Mansons were a family."

"Wow, Will. Really? Really?"

"Maybe Will can go with you?" Evan chimed in, his voice clear despite the more than three thousand miles between them. A half hour before, she'd announced to Will that she was leaving for South Carolina, and he'd immediately called Evan in London. Now they were on a conference call, and she'd barely managed to get a word in.

"I can't go," said Will.

"Why not?" asked Evan.

"Because I have a commercial that starts shooting tomorrow."

"It can't wait?"

"No, Evan, it can't wait," snapped Will. "I know this may be hard for you to wrap your big-shot corporate head around, but what I do is actually a real job."

"I never said . . ."

Layla put the phone on speaker and lay back on the floor. Since she'd gotten rid of the purple chair, the living room felt almost spacious.

Before leaving her mother's the night before, she'd snuck over to the Browns' and left the chair in their driveway, in the exact spot where they always parked their ridiculously huge Hummer—her small environmental protest. She chuckled.

"Lay? You still there?"

The clatter of dishes sounded in the background. She did a quick calculation in her head. It was just after dinner in London.

"Yes," she answered.

"Well, say something," demanded Will.

"Oh, I'm part of this conversation now?"

"Don't do that, Lay," said Evan. "We're just concerned about you."

"Why?"

Her brother's silence set off an alarm deep in her brain. Grabbing the phone, she jerked upright.

"You told him, didn't you, Will?" she snapped.

"I . . ."

She hung up.

She waited until the sixth ring before picking up.

"He told you, didn't he? He told you about the dream. About that Charlotte woman," Layla barked before either of them could speak. "He told you about Mom's room!"

"Layla . . . ," said Evan.

"Just shut up! I am sick of you both treating me like a crazy person!"

"And I'm sick of you acting like a crazy person," Will snapped back.

"Will . . . ," said Evan.

She hung up. This time she picked it up on the first ring.

"Stop hanging up," yelled Will.

"Stop being a dick!"

"Enough!" The international connection collapsed the word in the middle. "Jesus Christ, Will, leave her alone! And Lay, why can't you just wait until I get back? I have a friend in D.C. who does probate, estates, that kind of thing. Let me have him check into this island situation just to make sure it's legit before you go charging down there and end up in the middle of some mess."

"I'm going," said Layla.

"Layla . . . ," said Evan.

The brothers began to protest, talking over each other.

Layla placed two fingers in her mouth and let loose an earsplitting whistle into the phone.

"I was not asking for permission and I don't need your approval," she said into the sudden silence. "I was simply letting you know where I'll be for the next few days."

She could feel her brothers' displeasure through the phone.

"Well," said Evan finally. "At least be careful."

Miles away, in her small apartment, Layla smiled grimly.

———

Aunt Jayne arrived at the airport to collect her in a battered pickup that was more rust than red. As soon as Layla climbed up into the cab, Aunt Jayne thrust a brown paper bag into her hands.

"Probably only got stale pretzels and bad coffee on that plane. Don't even know why they bother." The old woman shook her head. "Cost of tickets, it's just disgraceful."

The truck gave a violent shudder as they pulled from the parking space, the cab suddenly filling with dark smoke. Layla shot her aunt a worried look, but Aunt Jayne merely shrugged.

"It's old but it still runs. Not like it used to, but it'll get us where we need to get." She grinned. "Kinda like me."

After a mile or so, the old truck seemed to find its rhythm and Aunt Jayne turned on the radio. Gospel music surged through the truck cab, merging with the sound of the warm air blowing through the open windows.

The late afternoon Carolina sky was overcast, coloring everything in shades of gray. Only the irregular line of gray-green trees showed where the sky broke free of the earth. Layla clutched her paper sack, stealing glances at her mother's sister, who swerved around the endless potholes, humming loudly, barely seeming to watch the road.

And the water.

Water was everywhere: thick tidal marshes pushing hard against the road, wide, slow-moving creeks meandering through the trees, and, every so often, flashes of something bigger—a river, or a lake—off in the distance. By the sixth or seventh bridge, Layla had completely lost her bearings. They sped along, twisting and turning, looping through one thick patch of forest then out again, only to flow into another.

"You not hungry?" Aunt Jayne pointed at the bag in Layla's lap.

Layla opened the bag and peered inside.

"Egg salad," said the old woman.

She was hungry, but the sandwich inside was the size of a toaster and there was no way for her to eat it without it exploding all over the inside of the truck. Shaking her head, she closed the bag just as they lurched around a corner and crossed yet another bridge. Aunt Jayne hummed, occasionally interrupting herself to honk the horn and call a greeting from the open window at a passing vehicle.

They finally turned onto a narrow, sandy road, lined by broad trees, moss hanging from the branches like window dressing. As they crossed one, final bridge, a house appeared.

Though the two-story frame house had clearly faded, it was still a bright spot of blue against the darkening gray sky. Two porches stretched across the front, one on the first floor, a matching one on the second. Above the upper porch, tucked beneath the eaves, was a large, eight-sided window.

Layla squinted, trying to recall the house she remembered from her childhood—the magical house with the pecan trees—but nothing seemed familiar except this bit of blue color.

"Home sweet home." Aunt Jayne jerked the truck to a stop beneath a sugarberry tree and stepped out.

Layla climbed from the truck and stopped. Dozens of blue bottles hung suspended from branches above them like ripe fruit, swaying gently in the breeze. She stood, mesmerized by the faint music the bottles made as they twisted and turned in the fading daylight. She reached a hand to touch the nearest one, remembering her mother's perfume as she leaned close, listening for the hum of a trapped spirit.

"Woo-hoo! Hey there, baby!"

A voice pulled her back and she turned to find Aunt Therese on the upper porch, waving a white cloth back and forth like a flag.

"Hey, sugar!"

"Therese, have you lost your mind? Get back in that house before you kill yourself, you hear me?" yelled Aunt Jayne.

"That old porch ain't barely fit to hold a toothpick and she ain't hardly no toothpick," she groused as her sister vanished back inside the house. Still grumbling, she led Layla onto the front porch and into the house.

A narrow staircase rose steeply on their left. A long hallway ran to the back of the house toward the kitchen.

"I got some sweet tea made." Aunt Therese appeared on the stairs.

"This girl don't need no sweet tea, Therese," said her sister. "She needs to get some real food inside her. Didn't even touch her sandwich."

"You don't like egg salad, baby?" asked Aunt Therese.

Layla looked down. She'd forgotten all about the bag she still clutched in her hand.

"That used to be your momma's favorite. I swear, that girl would just eat 'em 'til she was fit to explode. Yolk all over her face. Momma would about have a hissy . . . Elinor eatin' up all her eggs like that. Girl, she was . . ."

"Therese!" hissed Aunt Jayne.

Aunt Therese stopped midsentence.

"This child don't want to hear about all that old-timey stuff," Aunt Jayne said quietly.

Layla touched her face, startled to find tears there.

"You don't have to eat that old thing." Looking stricken, Aunt Therese yanked the bag from her hand and steered her toward the kitchen. "We got hush puppies and gumbo. And I can make some biscuits. That alright?"

Layla swiped at her face, nodding.

Her mother had loved egg salad as a girl. She hadn't known that. Not until this very second. Such a trivial thing. And yet realizing that she hadn't known that, hurt in a way she could barely describe.

The two sisters bustled around the kitchen, pretending not to notice her distress as they loaded the table with food. Aunt Therese placed a jelly jar of tea in front of her, patting her shoulder as she brushed past. When the women finally sat down at the table, Layla picked up a hush puppy forcing a smile.

The first bite filled her mouth with hot oil and sweet cornmeal, unlocking the tension in her jaw. Taking a deep breath, she began to eat in earnest. The food was delicious.

As she ate she looked around her. The Aunts' kitchen was large, dominated by an old metal sink nearly big enough to bathe in. Crisp white curtains hung at the wide window over it. Speckled green linoleum, worn in places to the wooden subfloor, covered the floor. Through the open back door, sheets fluttered on a clothesline, and the garden just beyond seemed to stretch nearly to the distant trees.

"You remember bein' here with your daddy when you were a little girl?" asked Aunt Therese.

"Let the girl eat in peace, Therese."

"Shush!"

"Who you shushin'? All I said was let the girl eat."

Aunt Therese sucked her teeth.

Layla smiled at the sisters' bickering. "I remember the pecan tree." She bit into another hush puppy.

"Pecan tree?" asked Aunt Therese, frowning.

"The pecan tree in the yard. I remember I couldn't believe that nuts came from a tree." She gazed out the back door, smiling at the memory. "I remember thinking it must have been some kind of magical tree."

The two sisters frowned.

"You made pie," she went on.

Aunt Therese shook her head. "We ain't never had no pecan tree, sugar."

"Well . . . we did," her sister said, slowly. "But not since we was itty-bitty. Elinor was barely in school when Daddy chopped that thing down. It got all full a stink bugs, remember?"

"Oh, goodness! I forgot all about that. That was something awful, wasn't it?"

Layla frowned. She tugged at her hair, grabbing hold of a strand and twisting it around her finger. She remembered it clearly. The tree towering so high that the whole sky was blotted out by dark green leaves. She remembered trying to walk beneath it, the earth shifting and rolling under her feet as she navigated the nuts on the ground in her brand-new white tennis shoes.

And she remembered the pie, the color of sunshine, sweet and sticky.

"But . . ."

Her frown deepened. Her father had been there. He'd pulled a tiny knife with a red handle from his pocket and carved their initials: AH + LH. Andrew Hurley + Layla Hurley. A tiny heart between.

The pie. She remembered the explosion of the thick custard, the feel of the sugary nuts on the roof of her mouth.

"You and your daddy were here in the spring, baby," said Aunt Jayne quietly. "Pecans don't come in 'til fall."

"Maybe I . . . ," she began. She stopped, frowning. She didn't know a single thing about harvesting pecans, but she clearly remembered the tree, the pie.

"Maybe . . ." Aunt Therese was watching her closely, her expression guarded. She shot a glance at her sister. "Maybe you and your daddy stopped somewhere. On your way here. Maybe that's what you rememberin'. Pecan trees down here like ticks on a dog. They everywhere. And you were so little then."

Aunt Jayne opened her mouth to say something, and her sister shot her a warning look. Layla looked from one aunt to the other. She felt the familiar swoop in her head, that feeling when her memories—the things that happened to her during the daylight hours—got tangled up in the things that happened in her dreams. The dreams she'd learned to pretend she no longer had. Sitting here with the Aunts, she could still clearly recall her mother's narrow-eyed, tight expression, the lips pressed into a hard line before she'd learned to pretend. And, for the first time, she was struck with a realization. Her mother hadn't just looked angry, she'd looked frightened. The Aunts were still watching her. And she saw a faint echo of that fear, there just below the surface. She locked eyes with them for a long moment, there in the warm kitchen, the things unsaid swirling around them.

"Yes," Layla said, finally, looking away. Her eyes fixed on the sheets swaying in the darkening yard. "Yes, that's probably it."

8

A burst of thunder shook Layla upright in the bed. Confused, she squinted into the darkness around her, struggling to get her bearings. Pale, green-tinged light flickered through the large octagonal window, creating strange patterns on the floor in the near darkness and faintly illuminating the small room, the sharply sloping ceiling.

Her eye fell on her backpack near the door.

"Port Royal," she whispered.

She raked a hand through her hair, flinching as another clap of thunder rattled the house. She loved thunderstorms—normally—but here, in this tiny room, at the very top of this old house, she felt exposed, vulnerable. Pulling open the the bedroom door, she inhaled. The house smelled of aged wood and damp carpeting, of the fried hush puppies they'd had for dinner and the Jean Naté the Aunts wore.

As the storm gained momentum outside, the house seemed to sigh and shift itself around her. She had no idea what time it was, but there was an echo of wooziness deep in her head—faint, but insistent—a reminder of the pill she'd taken earlier in hopes of ensuring a dreamless sleep.

Holding her breath, she inched her way down the narrow flight of stairs outside her door, guided only by touch and the intermittent flashes of lightning.

Warm milk.

She had a sudden craving for a glass of warm milk.

When she was little and woke terrified and confused in the middle of the night, her father always brought her warm milk with honey, fortified with a drop of whiskey. The milk had tasted peculiar, both oversweet and fiery. But it, and her father's presence, never failed to ease her back into a quiet sleep. She remembered the way he pulled her tight against his side. The tickle of his mustache on her forehead; his pajama buttons pressing into her cheek. He nearly always fell asleep before she did. And he snored. It was always the last sound she heard as she fell into her own sleep.

She felt an ache, a faint spasm of sorrow in that deep-down place where she never stopped missing him.

Milk and honey, and a drop of whiskey. Surely the Aunts had all those ingredients in the house. And surely, they wouldn't mind if she helped herself.

At the bottom of the first set of stairs was a narrow landing leading to a short hallway. At the end was a small bathroom, flanked by two closed doors, which she assumed were the Aunts' bedrooms. She paused, listening, but there was only silence. Cautiously, she continued down the stairs. In the doorway to the kitchen, she fumbled along the wall for the light switch.

"Couldn't sleep, sugar?"

Layla jumped back, letting out a sharp yelp.

In the suddenly bright kitchen, Aunt Therese sat blinking at the table, her head bristling with blue plastic rollers, a bottle of Canadian Club whiskey open on the table in front of her.

"Jesus Christ, Aunt Therese! What are you doing down here in the dark?"

The old woman took a slow sip from her glass and studied her niece over the rim of her glass.

"Are you alright?" asked Layla finally.

"Me?" Aunt Therese raised an eyebrow. "I'm fine, baby. You the one screamin' and flailin' around like you done seen somethin' raised up out the grave."

She gestured toward an empty chair with her glass, and Layla sat. Her aunt pulled another glass from the low cabinet behind her and poured three fingers' worth of whiskey into it before pushing it across the table.

Layla hesitated. "Do . . . do you have any milk?"

Her aunt frowned before pointing toward the refrigerator. She watched, one eyebrow raised, as Layla filled a coffee mug with milk, then added a teaspoon of honey, and finally a tiny bit of the whiskey from the glass between them. Layla took a sip and gagged.

Aunt Therese laughed out loud, the sound thick and throaty. "Sugar, you got to warm up the milk first."

"It's fine," said Layla, flushing.

The old woman shrugged, suppressing a grin. "Okay, then."

Layla took another sip before wordlessly standing and placing the mug in the microwave.

Aunt Therese sipped her whiskey and gave a loud, closed-eyed sigh of pleasure. "You wanna know how I come to live so long, lookin' this good?"

Layla sat back at the table, the steam from her now warmed milk warming her face. She eyed the whiskey bottle in front of her aunt. "Good genes?"

"Well, yeah. Course, that too." The old woman chuckled, tugging at one of the blue rollers. "But you wanna know the other reason?"

Layla nodded and took a tentative sip from her cup, letting the sweet, whiskey-laced milk trace a shivery path to her stomach, where it bloomed into a small fire. Almost exactly like what her father used to bring her.

"It's 'cause I learned a long time ago how to chill out. That's how the kids say it, right? Chill out?"

Layla grinned. "Yep, that's how they say it."

"Well, that's how you live long. How you live happy anyway." Aunt Therese made a face and sipped her drink. "Life always be tryin' to trip you up, doesn't it? Always messin' with your head. Can't afford to be gettin' all scatty over every little thing. That'll kill you faster than a gun."

"That's Aunt Jayne's philosophy too?"

A shadow flitted across Aunt Therese's face.

"Jayne?" The usual good-natured expression was back. "Oh, Jayne, she chills out in her own way." She held up her glass and grinned. "But she frowns on spirits. Says it makes smart men simple and simple men worthless. Can't say that ain't the truth."

The two women sat drinking in silence, listening to the sounds of the storm outside. The more Layla drank, the more pleasant her milk whiskey became. Despite the raging storm outside, she felt an unaccustomed stillness, sitting there with her mother's sister in the warm kitchen.

There was a flash of lightning and the lights flickered out.

"Dang it," muttered Aunt Therese in the darkness.

Layla could just barely make out the older woman rummaging in the cabinet. There was a sharp hiss and suddenly her aunt was framed in pale candlelight.

"Happens about every other time we get a storm," said Aunt Therese.

The wind rattled the windows hard, and Layla peered uneasily into the darkness. "You don't think we need to worry about a hurricane, do you?"

Aunt Therese squinted toward the back door. In the dim light, the window was only a black rectangle. She shrugged. "Probably not. A bit early in the season for 'em."

"Oh. That's good then," said Layla, not reassured. "I guess."

She leaned back and tried to relax into the warmth of her drink.

"She had them you know."

Layla opened her eyes. The drink and the storm had begun to lull her, and she squinted, struggling to focus on her aunt.

"What?"

"Your momma," said Aunt Therese. "She had them."

Layla shook her head and the room blurred slightly. "Had . . . what?"

"The dreams."

Layla tensed, suddenly on alert. Aunt Therese's face seemed to stutter in the flickering candlelight.

"I don't . . . know what you're talking about."

"No?" Aunt Therese gave a high, girlish laugh. She drained her glass in a single swallow, then slammed it onto the table, where it skidded, stopping just before going off the edge. "Now see, sugar, I know that just ain't so. I believe you know exactly what I'm talkin' about."

Layla gripped the edge of the table. She felt strangely weightless, as if it were only the table keeping her from falling upward, into blackness.

"Your momma had the dreams, but over time she stopped appreciatin' what a gift it was. A gift from the ancestors. From God," her aunt went on. "Somethin' happened to her. Somethin' terrible. Don't know what. But she started hatin' the thing she'd been given. Started hatin' *us*. Like we, and whatever happened, was one in the same."

Her aunt fixed her with a look filled with sorrow.

"Elinor couldn't never seem to understand that it wasn't *where* she was. It was *what* she was."

She leaned across the table and stared into Layla's eyes. There was sorrow but something else. Something like rage.

"She refused to acknowledge what she was," she said, her voice low, hard. "She refused to acknowledge what you are."

"What?" whispered Layla, not even sure she'd said the word out loud. The fire in her belly had been replaced with ice. "What am I?"

"The third of three, baby. That's what."

Their eyes locked for a moment, then Aunt Therese seemed to deflate. She shrank back in her seat, her expression camouflaged by the weak candlelight. Layla lunged forward and grabbed her wrist.

"What does that mean?" She could feel the woman's bones under the skin. "Aunt Therese, what does that mean?"

Aunt Therese gazed down at the hand on her wrist.

"Jayne, then me, then Elinor. The third of three daughters," she said, not looking up her voice low. "For as far back as anyone can remember. Always the third daughter of a third daughter."

Layla closed her eyes, then opened them again, her head pounding, fighting the urge to scream into the old woman's face, to shake her until answers started falling out of her mouth like confetti.

"The third daughter of a third daughter . . . what . . . ?" she said, her voice strangled.

Aunt Therese sighed then slowly stood. As Layla loosened her grip, her aunt took a step back, staggering a bit before bumping into the low cupboard behind her. Layla heard the soft clink of glass. Outside, the wind hurled rain against the kitchen window.

"Dreams," Aunt Therese said, the words barely audible. "Your momma was a Dreamwalker."

Layla blinked.

"You momma . . ." Aunt Therese stopped. She sighed, staring off into the distance. "Your momma . . . and Charlotte out there on the island. Both third daughters of third daughters. They . . ."

She made a walking motion with her fingers.

Layla felt the familiar swoop in her head. She shot a glance at her wrist. A dream. This must be a dream. But there was no white shell bracelet glowing on her wrist. Only shadows flickering across the bare skin.

She looked up, startled to find Aunt Therese inches from her face, the faintest whiff of lemons mixing with the whiskey on her breath.

"Your momma could walk inside the dreams of other people. Fiddle with their minds. Their memories. And you," she said, her words vaguely slurred. "You can too, can't you? You shouldn't ought to. Elinor's first daughter. Her *only* daughter, but you can. Knew it from that first time you came down here with your daddy. Could feel the special comin' off you. Somehow you can too."

"What are you talking about?" Layla moved her head slowly from side to side. "What does that even mean? Walk in someone's dream? That's not a thing. It's not . . . it isn't even possible."

But even as she said the words, a knowing was forming deep inside her.

Aunt Therese straightened, that faraway look on her face once again. "You know what scared Elinor the most?" she asked, not answering the question.

Layla held herself still.

"It was that sometimes, the dreams followed her back. Sometimes, she said she couldn't tell if she was awake or if she was still sleeping."

She shook her head, and for a moment she looked every one of her nearly seventy years.

"And," she went on. "And I think she was afraid that you would turn out just like them. Like her and Charlotte."

The old woman walked from the kitchen, and Layla sat, long after the candle had burned to nothing and she was in total darkness.

9

Layla lay watching as the sunlight moved across the scarred wood of the floor, spinning and twisting, the panes of the octagonal window fracturing the light into red- and yellow-tinged rectangles and diamonds.

When she finally rose, she made her way, as quietly as possible, down the stairs and out onto the wide front porch. The previous night's storm had scrubbed the air, rendering everything around her—the trees, the tabby drive, the Aunts' truck—in Technicolor hues. A thick mist rose from the grass, while overhead the blue bottles dangled from their place among the sugarberry leaves, silent, no sign of trapped evil spirits.

Layla took a deep breath, savoring the fragrance of South Carolina, feeling a calmness in the morning light, the weirdness of last night's conversation with Aunt Therese receding for a moment.

"Drunk," she murmured. "She was just drunk."

But she felt a tremor deep in her gut. And she knew that even though she'd not understood their meaning, the words Aunt Therese had spoken there in the candlelit kitchen were maybe the truest anyone had ever spoken to her.

Sighing, she stepped back into the house and immediately heard sharp, angry voices coming from the kitchen. Layla hesitated, then tucked herself against the newel post to listen.

"Are you out your mind, Therese?" Aunt Jayne was trying to whisper, but the words were edged with steel and easily penetrated the shallow hallway.

"Shhhh."

"Do *not* shush me!"

"You gonna wake the child," hissed Aunt Therese.

"Wake the child? Sweet Jesus," snapped Aunt Jayne. "Oh, now you worried about the girl? Wasn't so worried when you was down here last night gettin' your liquor on and runnin' off at the mouth."

"I thank you to not be worryin' what I do with my own mouth in my own house, Miss Jayne," snapped Aunt Therese.

Layla crept down the hall, closer to the kitchen. Aunt Therese passed by the door, a large red mixing bowl tucked against her side, her expression stony. Layla pressed herself against the wall, out of sight.

"I cannot believe you got all stink faced and blabbed everything out to her like that," came Aunt Jayne's voice from just inside the door.

"I was not all stink faced," cried her sister, no longer even trying to whisper. "Somebody need to be tellin' her something. That's clear as day. Obvious Elinor never said a word to that little girl."

A cabinet door slammed.

"Child must have been scared to death. All those years rattlin' around in other folks' dreams. Thinkin' she was losin' her damn mind."

Layla slid a step closer, the plaster walls cool beneath her trembling hands.

"The island called to her, Jayne," Aunt Therese went on, her voice pleading now. "It belongs to her and it called to her and we got to try and teach her the little bit we can. Help her understand what she is."

Layla inhaled sharply as Aunt Jayne moved into view, her back to the door. "Don't be an idiot, Therese! This not one a your romance books. Wasn't no doggone island callin' to her and you know it! It's that damn fool Charlotte sittin' out there on Scotia gettin' meaner and crazier by the minute."

She slumped at the table.

"Charlotte." Aunt Therese sighed, coming to sit across from her sister. "Ain't been right in the head since the day Elinor left."

"Charlotte wasn't right, long before that."

The two sisters were quiet for a long moment, each lost in her own thoughts.

"It's every night now," murmured Aunt Jayne. "Every night I see her in my dreams."

"Me too." Aunt Therese nodded, her face grim. "Can't figure what she wants."

"What she always wanted," answered her sister. "Elinor back out there on that island with her. Back there or destroyed. Probably both."

"Well, it's too late for either," said Aunt Therese, her voice breaking.

"May be. But that child up there is the next best thing. If Charlotte can't have Elinor, then she'll have her girl. And Elinor can't protect her anymore."

There was another long silence. Layla barely dared to breathe.

"You think it was a mistake? Us goin' up there?" asked Aunt Therese. "Us tellin' that child about the island? You think we shoulda just let it be?"

"Charlotte wasn't never gon' let it be. She would a found her somehow, started tormenting her . . . if she hasn't done already. Don't see we had a choice. The only way to protect her, to protect ourselves, was to tell her. Tell her what she is." Aunt Jayne made a strangled noise in her throat. "Though I'm dangum sure gettin' drunk and just blurtin' everything out all at once like that wasn't the best way to go."

Her sister glared at her. "Maybe not, but . . ." She shrugged. "I just wish . . ."

"I do too," interrupted her sister. "Wish a whole lot a things."

Aunt Therese sighed. "Poor Elinor. It must have been so hard . . ."

"Elinor was selfish and stupid and a coward." Layla jerked as Aunt Jayne slammed her cup onto the table. "That girl layin' up there don't know nothin' about nothin'. All those nights dreamin' and no one to show her the way. Even if she didn't want it for herself, Elinor shoulda taught her own child. It's her right, her heritage. Surprised she ain't crazy as Charlotte."

"She shouldn't even have it. Shouldn't even be in her. Elinor couldn't—"

"What should be and what is don't very often have a close acquaintance, Therese," snapped Aunt Jayne. "The way Momma and Auntie Mercy got brung into this world twisted things all around. This mess shouldn't a been no big surprise." She flung her hands out. "And please sister, explain to me, why after all these years, you still stickin' up for that girl?"

"She just wanted something different for herself, Jayne. Somethin' different for her girl," said Aunt Therese, quietly. "You can't fault her for that."

Aunt Jayne lurched up from the table and stared at her sister. From her hiding place Layla could feel her anger. "I *can* fault her for leaving her own daughter defenseless. I *can* fault her for turnin' her back on her people, on her home. I *can* fault her for turnin' her back on Momma!"

"Hush, now. Past is past," said Aunt Therese, her voice breaking.

Aunt Jayne laughed, the sound low and ugly. "Please! You know good as anyone that the past ain't never really in the past. Not in this family. Not around here. She threw us away, Therese. While she was out lookin' for somethin', or hidin' from somethin', or whatever it was she was out there doin', she just threw us away."

Layla stepped into the kitchen. The sisters turned, and the silence that suddenly descended over the room was nearly a solid thing. The two old women stared at her, the only sound the ticking of the stove clock.

"Well, good morning, sugar," said Aunt Therese, springing to her feet, her voice unnaturally high and bright. "You finally get some sleep? Power came back on early this mornin'. I made coffee and we got some cold ham, and peaches picked fresh just yesterday."

She moved around the kitchen, talking fast. Aunt Jayne stared into her coffee cup, saying nothing.

Layla took the cup her aunt offered. Wordlessly, she drank her coffee, savoring the heat of the cup between her hands. She was halfway through the cup before she broke the silence.

"Tell me," she said, her voice low.

Aunt Therese stood frozen, a small bowl of peaches in one hand, a paring knife in the other, juice dripping, unheeded, onto the linoleum floor.

"My mother was a Dreamwalker. I'm a Dreamwalker. What does that mean?"

When neither woman responded, Layla set her cup carefully on the table. The air felt hot, gelatinous. "Okay then, how do I get out there?"

"Where?" asked Aunt Therese.

"To that island," said Layla. "Scotia. How do I get to it?"

Aunt Jayne's head snapped up. "No."

"You came to me, remember?" interrupted her niece, her voice hard. "I didn't know anything about any island. I don't understand what's happening, but if I own an island. Half an island," she corrected herself. "Then I want to see it."

She locked eyes with Aunt Jayne. "And I want to know what's going on."

Her aunt held the gaze for a moment, then stood and walked from the room.

The sound of laughter coming from the kitchen surprised Layla as she came down the front stairs. Two days had passed since Layla'd asked about going out to the island and there'd been no conversation about it since. Instead, the Aunts had driven her around town, pointing out museums, parks, the helicopters overhead from the nearby Marine base. The day before, they'd spent the morning at the Port Royal Farmers Market, where they seemed to know everyone. The mother and daughter vendors weaving sweetgrass roses, the tall, elegantly dressed white man selling fresh shrimp from a massive steel cooler, the tall, black woman with the blond dreadlocks standing beside her display of sea glass jewelry. They stopped at every booth, every stall, to introduce her.

"This Elinor's baby girl. She's an artist down from Washington. Don't she look like Elinor just spit her out. Come to visit awhile."

There were the quick hugs. The murmured condolences. A quick story about when Elinor was in school. How smart. How she used to love her some pecan pie. All morning, everywhere they stopped, and they seemed to stop at every single stall, there was the insistence that she try this peach jam, sample just a tiny taste of that blueberry cobbler, a bit of muscadine wine.

But there was something else, too, something darker flickering around the edges of the bright, sweet-smelling stalls. For every proud of hometown girl made good, there were the quick exchanges of looks, the flashes of distaste quickly covered by polite smiles that never quite reached the eyes. As they moved among the fresh bread and the colorful quilts, Layla couldn't shake the unsettling sense that her mother was lurking there, just out of sight, in the shadows.

By the time they'd headed for home, Layla was wilting, her head spinning from the food, the people, the stories both spoken, and not. What could possibly have made her mother turn her back on this place? These people?

She stepped through the kitchen door.

"Well, here she is," said Aunt Therese, turning as she entered.

"Layla, I want you to meet Gerta Williams, my oldest friend in the world."

A tiny white woman rushed forward to clasp Layla's hand.

"It is good to meet you," she said. Barely reaching Layla's chin, with snow-white hair and a nearly perfectly round face, she spoke with the faintest German accent.

"Our husbands were best friends in the Corps," explained Aunt Therese.

"Stationed together in Boeblingen. In Germany. My Joe and her Simon. Two peas in a pod."

"I come here and now we are best friends forever, yes?" exclaimed Gerta, beaming at Aunt Therese.

"BFFs," said Aunt Therese, laughing.

Layla smiled. Aunt Therese had had a husband named Joe. She filed that away with the growing list of information she hadn't known about her mother and her mother's family.

"You just missed Gerta's grandbaby. His first day out in cobia season he shows up soon as the sun rises. You can set your watch by that boy."

"My grandson already catch his limit," said Gerta, releasing Layla's hand to hold up two fingers. "And always the first one comes to his *tantes*."

Layla frowned. "Cobia?"

"Cobia," said Gerta, slapping a tiny hand lightly on the kitchen table.

"Jesus Christ!" Layla took a jerky step backward.

The kitchen table had been covered in newspaper, and sprawled across nearly the entire space was a big fish, brown and silver, and vaguely pre-historic looking.

"What . . . ? What is that?"

The two friends laughed.

"That's some good eatin', baby girl," said Aunt Therese. "That's what that is."

"You like to fish?" asked Gerta. "Viktor, my grandson, he take you. You catch your own, yes? Take it home to Washington, D.C."

Layla eyed the fish, hoping her dismay at this idea wasn't obvious on her face.

"Thought we'd run out to the island today, Gert," Aunt Therese said quietly.

Layla heard Gerta's sharp intake of breath. She looked as shocked as Layla felt. They both stared at Aunt Therese, who swiped her dish towel over the same section of counter again and again.

"Yes?" the small German woman said finally.

Aunt Therese nodded.

"And you think this is good idea?"

Aunt Therese made a sound halfway between a sigh and a laugh. "I think it's a terrible idea but . . ." She pointed at Layla. "But half of the place belongs to her now. She should at least see it."

"Why?" asked Gerta.

"Why?" The question seemed to catch Aunt Therese off guard.

She stopped pretending to clean the counter and turned to face her friend.

"*Ja!*" The white woman nodded. "Why? She can see it on the computer. She can visit it on . . . on the Google maps."

"Gert . . ."

Gerta waved her hand, cutting her friend off. "That is a bad place, Therese. Too much anger. Too much sorrow."

"Ain't the place that's bad," murmured Aunt Therese.

Gerta reached for her friend, who was silently wrapping the fish in the newspaper. "Therese . . . ?"

"Gotta get this thing on ice," said Aunt Therese, her mouth tight. With a grunt, she clutched the fish in her arms and pushed through the back door.

Gerta blew air through her lips in exasperation. She turned to Layla. "Your *tante*, your aunt. She has the brains of that cobia. She must show you this place? This terrible place?"

Layla blinked as a jolt of warning coiled up her spine. Gerta seemed genuinely afraid. For that matter so had the Aunts. What was on that island? They couldn't possibly believe all those rumors about a curse. She opened her mouth to ask just as her aunt stepped back through the door.

Gerta ignored her. "You go. Go see this island," she said to Layla. "Then you come back and sell it for lots of money. Take your *tantes* on a cruise so they can meet young husbands, yes?"

Layla laughed. Aunt Therese did not.

"Won't never sell Scotia," she said, the ice crackling in her voice. "Don't matter what's out there. Who's out there. Scotia belongs to this family. Won't nobody ever take that from us."

Layla felt a chill, the words echoing in her mind, eerily familiar.

"Therese . . . ," Gerta began.

"No. We beenyah. Always," snapped Aunt Therese, passion suddenly seasoning her words with the Gullah of her childhood. "Never sell to no comeyah. Not never!"

Layla stared, shocked, but Gerta merely held up her hands in surrender.

"I know this, *Schatzi*, I only . . ." She sighed. She picked up the straw bag that was draped over a chair, then reached up to pat her friend's cheek.

"You have the brains of that fish," she said.

For a long moment, Aunt Therese glared at her friend, eyes hard, lips pressed into a thin line, and then her face softened. She chuckled. "Girl, get out my house now."

Gerta laughed. At the door, she turned.

"Be careful, *mein lieber Freund*. Be very careful."

10

In the front seat, wedged between the Aunts, Layla felt oddly soothed, their fleshy arms like two chilled rolls of bologna, smooth and cool against her bare skin.

They rode in comfortable silence, the rich fragrance of the South Carolina backcountry wafting through the open windows. A quarter of an hour later, Aunt Jayne steered the truck from the main road onto a narrow, unmarked dirt road. As the vehicle reared and bucked its way through the trees, Layla held her breath, her nails digging into the faded dashboard.

Aunt Jayne chuckled. "You remember that time Elinor got drunk and brought Daddy's truck out here to race? Dang near tore the whole undercarriage out from under that ol' pickup."

Aunt Therese let loose a whoop of laughter. "Oh, Lord! I thought Daddy was gonna bust into flames. Wouldn't let Elinor outta his sight for nearly a month of Sundays."

Layla looked from one to the other.

"What do you mean?" she asked.

Aunt Jayne, concentrating on the obstacles in the road in front of them, shot her a puzzled look. "What we mean about what? About Daddy's truck?"

"No, I mean . . ." Layla blinked. "Mom doesn't . . . didn't drink."

Aunt Jayne did a double take. "She didn't what, now?"

She leaned forward and caught her sister's eye, and suddenly the truck's tiny cab was filled with raucous laughter.

"The hell she didn't," hooted Aunt Jayne. "'Scuse my French. Your momma was a lot of things, baby, but teetotaler wasn't one of 'em. Least not while she was still livin' down here. When she was in high school, her, Lane, Buddha, Puddin' Head, Charlotte, and who knows who all else, would be over to the island nearly every other weekend, drinkin' moonshine and darin' each other to do somethin' stupid. That girl could spend half the day drinkin' and still show up to dinner lookin' sober as a preacher. Momma didn't have no idea what that girl was up to out there half the time."

Layla stared at the Aunts, trying to imagine her mother—a woman who drank a small glass of sherry on New Year's Eve and maybe a flute or two of champagne on her wedding anniversary—sitting under a tree, drinking moonshine with someone named Puddin' Head.

"I . . ." She shook her head, then slid down the tattered seat, resting her neck against the fraying leather. She closed her eyes.

Who the hell was Elinor Hurley?

Her father was standing on a hill, waving for her to follow. He was far away but she knew him by his green sweater.

That ugly green sweater.

"Daddy!" She called to him, and he waved again for her to come. But she couldn't move. She was stuck, rooted where she was. From the corner of her eye, she caught sight of her mother in the shadow of a catalpa tree, arms crossed, face expressionless, silently watching.

She jerked awake. She didn't remember falling asleep, but Aunt Therese's hand was on her shoulder, gently shaking her.

"We're here."

They were parked on a narrow ribbon of asphalt between two large trees. A sandy path led down to a wooden pier.

"You feelin' alright?" asked Aunt Therese.

"Awesome," said Layla, and she laughed, realizing it was true. There was a lightness inside her, an excitement she hadn't felt in as long as she could remember. She was on an adventure. Heading out to a mysterious island, *her* island, a haunted island that seemed to spook all who even said its name. Where her mother had drunk moonshine and loved egg salad.

Scotia Island.

She grinned.

"Good." Aunt Therese took her arm, and they walked down the path toward the pier.

At the bottom of the path, Layla stopped, frowning, sniffing at the air. The hair stood up on the back of her neck as the acrid smell of sulfur and decay washed up her nose and crashed against the back of her throat. The image of her mother's bedroom flashed in her mind. The room trashed. The muddy handprint on the mirror. And the smell. *This* smell. Instinctively, she touched the place near her eye, the bruise now healed.

"What is that smell?" She'd noticed it off and on since arriving in Port Royal, quick whiffs, faint and in the background, but here on this little channel off the river, the odor was insistent, impossible to ignore.

Aunt Jayne, waiting on the pier, smiled.

"Pluff mud." She took a deep inhale. "The smell of home."

"It smells like . . . rotten eggs," said Layla, taking shallow breaths.

Aunt Therese pointed to a shallow area where the trees met the water. "You should be here at low tide."

Layla saw a strip of gray-brown mud, exactly like the mud that had formed the handprint at her mother's. The handprint on the mirror. Bile rose in her throat, and for a moment she considered turning back, following Evan's advice and waiting; considered that this might be a mistake. She turned to her aunts, but Aunt Jayne had already tossed the rucksack she was carrying into the small, drab-colored jon boat tied to the pier and was climbing down a metal ladder with surprising grace.

She slid onto the seat next to the outboard motor, her sister following and taking up a position near the bow. The Aunts looked up at her expectantly.

"Climb on in. Just mind you don't get yourself all tangled up," said Aunt Jayne, eyeing Layla's long sundress.

Layla glanced past the sisters. They were docked in a small marshy inlet that opened up onto a shimmering, seemingly endless body of water.

"Whose boat is this?"

"No idea." Aunt Jayne squinted at her. "We're stealin' it."

"What?"

"Jayne, stop that," laughed Aunt Therese. "It's our boat, sugar. Get in."

"You have a boat?" It struck Layla as somehow incongruous that these two matronly women owned a boat.

The sisters stared at her.

"Lord Almighty, this is South Carolina Lowcountry, girl. Course we got a boat," said Aunt Jayne. "Everybody got a boat."

Layla eyed the jon boat nervously. Small, maybe fifteen feet from bow to stern, it sat low in the dark water, a thin sheen of the thick pluff mud glazing the bottom. Feet still planted firmly on the pier, she nervously twirled a strand of hair. The Aunts' plan seemed to be for them to head for all that water out there on the horizon.

She'd been a swimmer in high school. A thing she did mostly because her father had been a champion swimmer. And she'd been good at it, the trophies lining the wall at her mother's a testament to that. But the truth was, she didn't love the water. Not like people thought she should. She didn't mind pools, defined enclosed spaces. But wide open, limitless water . . . ?

"Shit," she muttered.

It was an island. Of course there'd be boats. And water. Lots of water. She felt nauseous.

Seeing her reluctance, Aunt Jayne grinned.

"It's okay, sweetie," she said, not unkindly. "We been on the water since before we could walk. Your grandaddy was a oysterman, and his daddy before him. Men on both sides of this family been fishin' and sailin' these waters for more'n two hundred years. Women too."

"Ain't no more to drivin' a boat than is to drivin' a car," added her sister.

"How would you know, sister? You can't drive worth a tinker's dam," said Aunt Jayne.

Aunt Therese chuckled. "Well, that's true enough."

A jet from the nearby Marine base roared overhead.

"Okay," murmured Layla. "Okay."

She had been the one to insist on going out to the island, and this was obviously the only way she was going to get there. Teeth clenched, she grabbed hold of the ladder and clumsily climbed into the gently bobbing boat.

She plopped onto the slim metal bench just as Aunt Jayne fired up the outboard and accelerated from the pier.

"Nola. Our first ancestor was called Nola."

The wind caught the words as the small boat raced through the grass-choked water, ripping them away so that Layla wasn't sure she'd heard them correctly. She twisted in her seat and opened one eye to peer at Aunt Jayne. The nausea wasn't so bad with her eyes closed.

"Nola," Aunt Jayne said again. "Each generation tells the story. So we never forget where we come from. Never forget who we are. Nola was our beginning. The third daughter of a third daughter from way back in Africa. A seer. Like all her people."

"A seer?"

"They say her people, our people, had a . . . a connection to things, to the world around them. Could sense things." Aunt Jayne shifted in her seat, scanning the dark water around them.

"But the third daughters of Nola's tribe had something else too. They could see things in dreams: intent, truth. They could lay their hands on a person and know the soul of them, the way animals seem to sense the good or bad in a person. People came for miles to have the third daughters of that village dream a dream for them, to read their futures."

"It's how she knew," said Aunt Therese.

Layla leaned forward, unconsciously twisting her hair around her finger, absorbed in the story, her discomfort on the water nearly forgotten. "Knew what?"

"Nola was pledged to the son of a wealthy trader from another village. The day before their marriage, she traveled with her youngest brother to her betrothed's village. That night she dreamed a dream. She dreamed that when the rest of her family arrived for the wedding, the trader meant to sell them as slaves to the white men in the big boats. All of them, including Nola," said Aunt Jayne.

"Jesus," whispered Layla, her throat tightening in revulsion.

"Her brother managed to sneak out. To get word to their village," said Aunt Therese, her voice barely audible over the outboard's roar. "By the time the slavers came, everyone had vanished. Every man, woman, and child, gone."

"And Nola?"

Aunt Jayne shook her head.

A cold blade of sadness pierced Layla for this long-dead ancestor, a young girl, probably younger than she was now, betrayed by a man's greed, separated forever from her family, her home, and sold into slavery.

"She saved her village, but they took her," said Aunt Therese, staring out over the water. "And when Nola got here to America, something had changed. No one knows why or how. Maybe it was like takin' a plant and rootin' it in foreign soil where there's no natural predators. But whatever it was, from the day she stepped her foot on that island out yonder, she was more powerful than she had ever been in Africa."

Layla could just make out a gray shadow rising from the water on the horizon. "Powerful how?"

Aunt Jayne glanced down at her. "America. That island. Her . . . rage. Her hate. It turned Nola into a Dreamwalker."

"A Dreamwalker," repeated Layla, her mouth dry. The thing the Aunts said her mother was. The thing *she* was.

"A Dreamwalker," Aunt Therese repeated. "One who can step into folks' dreams, who can peek into all those strange, little cubbyholes where folks tuck things away from the light of day."

She touched Layla's arm.

"Before, back in Africa, she could just listen, watch. Say what she saw. But after they stole her from her home, her family. After they took her name. Something happened. She could become part of the dreams. Could change things in the dream that changed things in the awake world."

Layla looked out across the water, watching the shadow on the horizon grow larger. Saltwater spray misted her skin.

"Why the third daughter of a third daughter?" she asked finally.

The Aunts shrugged.

"Just how it's always been," answered Aunt Therese.

"And you can't do it?"

Aunt Therese was silent for a long time, staring out over the silver-gray water. "Momma always used to say that dreams are like a pond. You drop a pebble in that pond and a circle forms. The more pebbles, the more circles. We, me and Jayne, we like sticks at the side of that pond. Sometimes, we can feel those circles ripplin' over us, sense things happening out there in the water. Sometimes we even get a picture, clear for the tiniest time, a voice, a smell. Then it's gone."

She held a hand up as if feeling the vibrations in the air. "What we got is special too, but it's different. Passive. Like a kinda echo of what Nola's people had back in Africa. More like instinct."

Aunt Therese grinned. "Just two old sticks stuck in the mud at the side of that ol' dream pond."

Working the outboard, her sister snorted. "You the stick in the mud."

"Shush up, old woman," said Aunt Therese. "But you, your momma. Dreamwalkers," she went on. "You all can move around, pickin' and choosin' those ripples. Diving inside." Aunt Therese sighed. "Used to think I'd a liked to a been able to do that. To live different lives inside other folks' dreams. Seems like that could be some kinda wonderful."

Layla said nothing. She wasn't sure how much of what the Aunts said was true, but she did know that the way of her dreams wasn't always so wonderful.

The shape on the horizon had formed itself into an island that seemed to float atop the water, a gradual rise of greens and grays, jutting like a buoy out of the sparkling sound.

"Scotia Island," Aunt Jayne said, pointing.

"But . . . you said it . . . this thing . . . it passes third daughter to third daughter," Layla said.

"Yes," said Aunt Therese quietly.

As they approached the island, the boat seemed to skid sideways, lurching hard in the water. Layla inhaled sharply, gripping the edge of the boat.

"Blasted rip currents," muttered Aunt Jayne. Her mouth set in a hard line as she fought the boat toward a wooden dock. She managed, finally, to bring the boat parallel to the dock and cut the engine. In the sudden quiet, the sea birds wheeling overhead seemed especially loud.

"Then how can I be a . . . Dreamwalker? I'm an only daughter."

Aunt Jayne fixed her with a look she couldn't read, and Layla suddenly felt a watery lightness in her head.

"Yes," said Aunt Jayne, finally. "You are an only daughter and you are a Dreamwalker."

11

GEMMA

Pressed against the doorframe, Gemma watched from the lengthening shadows as Jessamine and Lavender cleaned out the rice pot, raked the ash from the night's cook fire. Huddled side by side, her two youngest daughters whispered to each other, giggling at some shared secret.

"Lavender, time to finish up and lay yourself down."

The girl's shoulders stiffened at the words.

"Don't think I can't hear you rollin' your eyes at me," said Gemma, suppressing a smile.

Lavender turned to face her. "Mama, don't need you watchin' over me. I knows how to walk. Knows how to find my way back. How to not gets hurt."

"Can't never have enough watchin' over," Gemma sniffed.

This time Gemma saw the eye roll. Out of the corner of her eye, she caught Jessamine's grin.

Gemma pointed a finger and scowled.

Jessamine's eyes widened. "I'm a just go fetch kindlin' 'fore it gets too dark," she said, grabbing a basket and a lantern from beside the door. She shot her sister a sympathetic look before melting into the woods behind the cabin.

"Mama, why . . . ?"

"Pick someone to walk with," said Gemma. "Someone you likes."

Lavender crossed her arms. "Fine," she said, sighing loudly. "I picks Aron then. I likes Aron."

Gemma chuckled. Nine years old, Aron was a smart, easygoing little boy whose dreams were almost always about fishing and chasing squirrels and wild pigs up and down the hills of Scotia Island.

And horses.

Gemma knew that the only horses he'd ever seen were in the paintings on the wall of the colonel's study, but the boy was plum horse crazy.

She liked Aron, too, but they both knew it was a mistake to assume that a child's dreams were always the safest. Children were unpredictable. The line between real and made-up was a fuzzy one for them, and that could make them dangerous. It was easier to get lost in a child's dream, to end up drifting in that gray place between awake and asleep, bumping against reality like a moth against a window. Lavender needed to remember that.

Gemma stepped aside and Lavender followed her into the cabin. Marigold was already there, unrolling their cotton mattresses.

"What you fixin' to do?" she asked, looking up when her mother and sister walked in.

"Mama thinks I need another lesson," Lavender answered. The two sisters exchanged a look that Gemma pretended not to see. "Want to come?"

Sometimes, if she focused, and the dreams were vivid enough, Lavender could bring her sisters along.

"Who you walkin'?" asked Marigold, settling down onto her mattress. She glanced out the door. Darkness was falling fast over the island.

"Aron."

"No, you go on by yourself then." She snorted, shaking her head. "That boy's dreams always the same: mud, fish, and horses."

She turned her back to them, curling into a ball. Within minutes, she was snoring softly.

Gemma pulled the dented lamp closer. The burning oil reeked of rotten fish, filling the cabin with greasy smoke and bathing her and Lavender in a murky yellow light.

"Go on now. Aron be about sleep now. Go on now and look for him."

As she watched over her daughter, she thought of the hundreds, the thousands, of dreams she'd walked, as she'd grown to womanhood in this very spot.

She remembered walking with her sisters, the other children in the quarter. She remembered walking the dreams of the buckras up at the big house: the colonel and Young Master, also named Rupert after his father. Young Master's dreams were mean and dark, like the boy himself, leaving her to wake feeling fevery, a sour taste in her mouth come morning.

His mother was another matter. Mistress Lucy's dreams were pretty, filled with sparkly music and bright colors.

At first Gemma had only followed the mistress, trailing far behind, quiet, unseen, watching in secret as she'd been taught. But each time she found herself walking the mistress's dream, she grew bolder, venturing closer to the woman, staring out of the tall windows of her mistress's dreaming place, where towering buildings made of stone seemed to reach for the heavens, and the sky was not the translucent blue that covered Scotia Island but the deep coppery color of old nails and smelled of smoke and metal.

And then on one of these dreaming nights, she turned to find Mistress Lucy watching her, her turquoise-colored eyes narrowed in her round face. Even now, all these years later, Gemma could recall the feeling of panic, how it had seemed to scratch and crawl its way up the back of her throat, how she'd held herself still, not even daring to breathe. Then Mistress Lucy had smiled and held out a raspberry tart on a tiny china plate, the crust golden brown and thin as an oak leaf.

And she remembered the sting of her mother's hand against her cheek the next morning, as she'd relayed that dream.

"Don't you never," hissed her mother. "Don't you never be walkin' up in no buckra's dreams for a sweet. Them got no souls! Them be infectin' you with darkness sure as the sun rise.

"I teach you," said her mother. "I teach you how to turn they dreams 'round so you be safe. And you children be safe. And they children. I teach you. You hear me?"

And her mother, Tuesday, had taught her. She taught her what her own mother, Nola, had taught her.

She taught Gemma the way of traveling free even as their bodies stayed held in bondage. She taught her how to use the dreams of others to protect herself, just as Tuesday used them to protect herself and her children . . . if only just a little bit.

Tuesday walked the dreams of the colonel, bound herself to him there. Night after night, she walked his dreams, showing herself to him. She touched him, whispered to him, her lips warm against his dreaming face, until he craved her beyond all reason, in his dreams and in the daylight too.

She bound the master to her so tightly in the night, that in the day she and her children were free to come and go about Ainsli Green unmolested. But, she told her daughter, there were rules.

Only the third daughter of a third daughter would ever possess the ability to walk a dream. Tuesday was Nola's third daughter, as Gemma was hers.

A walker could use what she found in the heart of a dreamer to her advantage, but to actively interfere, to force a dreamer to act against his true nature, could have unintended consequences, for both the walker and the dreamer. The dreams might crawl inside the walker, cleaving a walker and dreamer so close that all control was lost, vanquishing both into that place that was no place: not awake, not asleep, simply mad.

So many nights, Gemma lay dreaming, learning, Tuesday at her side. But even as she learned, growing in knowledge, growing in power, she snuck away, the dreams of the mistress proving irresistible. She followed Mistress Lucy into her dreams because there were always sweets: tarts and queen cakes and white pot pudding. And because Mistress Lucy dreamed of a place filled with music and horses, a place where boats were bigger than even the big house on Scotia, and people of every shape and color walked impossibly crowded streets paved with bricks, and ice fell soft as cotton lint from the sky.

A soft laugh escaped Lavender's lips, pulling Gemma back to the present, and she reached to stroke her daughter's cheek. On the other side of the cabin, her other two daughters were tightly curled against each other like newborn kittens.

Gemma gazed through the cabin's one window. Two large sphinx moths flitted at the edge of the splintered sill.

Dreamwalking.

A gift from the ancestors.

A weapon.

But like any weapon, it needed respecting, care taken, so as not to blow one's own self to bits with it in the using. When walking in the dreams of others, the space between dreaming and madness was narrow.

Gemma felt a chill. She looked down to find Lavender watching her, dark eyes glittering in the faint light.

"Mama?"

"Thought I told you to close your eyes, child. Now go on and find that boy."

Lavender watched her mother a moment longer, worry flickering across her narrow brown face. Then, with a nod, she closed her eyes again.

A few feet away, Marigold cried out from her own dream. In the viscous lamplight, Gemma could just make out the faint swelling on her daughter's cheek from where she'd struck her before. She swallowed hard, her heart twisting in her chest. She reached to lay a hand lightly on Marigold's face, and her eldest daughter sighed, seeming to settle.

Gemma turned back to her youngest. "Walk with Aron," she whispered. "Let him take you along."

Lavender murmured something incoherent, and Gemma felt a slithering sensation in the pit of her stomach and she knew her daughter had slipped away from the tiny cabin at Ainsli Green. Gemma hoped she'd found Aron. She held her daughter's warm hand in her own and waited.

"Mama?"

Gemma was cold, weighted down as if pressed beneath one of the mistress's velvet ballgowns. Someone was calling to her. She struggled to open her eyes, but she was so tired, tired to her very bones. She just wanted to rest, to linger in that dark, timeless place for a little while longer.

"Wake up. Mama? Please wake up."

Nell?

No . . . That wasn't right. Nell was the colonel's daughter. This voice was different. In the darkness behind her closed eyes, Gemma felt clammy with panic. Where was she?

"Are you sick? Oonah want I got Bekka?"

Bekka.

Her friend.

Gemma blinked, the inky nothingness slowly giving way. Lavender's face, golden in the light from the fish oil lamp, swam into focus. Jessamine and Marigold stared wide-eyed from the corner. Gemma had thought to watch over her daughter but had somehow lost herself.

"Mama?" said Lavender again, her voice high with concern.

"I fine," she snapped. In the dim light, Gemma saw Lavender stiffen, saw her mouth press itself into a hard line. Little by little, Gemma was losing control.

"I fine, child," she said, more gently. "You find Aron?"

Lavender smiled, even as she studied her mother through narrowed eyes. "Did. Left him climbin' trees up island."

Gemma patted her daughter's hand, waited for her to go lie by her sisters.

She stared up at the low, cracked ceiling. She'd gotten lost. Without even dreaming, she'd gotten lost.

From a deep corner of her memory, she heard Tuesday's voice: *"Ain't no wide space 'tween dreams and madness."*

"I's fine," she whispered.

Above her in the shadows, faces, memories, formed then melted away, her eyes playing tricks. Unconsciously, she stroked the space on her left wrist as she recited the lineage. "Lavender, third daughter of Gemma. Gemma, third daughter of Tuesday. Tuesday, third daughter of Nola, a seer from over to Africaland. Dreamwalkers."

Tears flowed unheeded down her face as she whispered into the darkness, "I's a Dreamwalker."

12

Scotia Island rose gradually from the sea, its grassy hills pocked with shoulder-high clumps of sea oats, their honey-colored frills bobbing in the light breeze. A narrow trail led upward from the dock, disappearing from sight in a clump of stubby trees at the crest of the dune. Sand stretched several yards on either side of the dock, forming a beach of sorts, before petering out into muddy flats. Layla grabbed hold of the wooden ladder attached to the dock and pulled herself out of the boat.

"How many people live out here?" she asked.

"Three, four dozen or so, full time. Maybe twice that still got places and come out time to time," said Aunt Jayne. "The full timers're mostly old folks."

She pulled her bag from the boat. "Back in the day, school only went to eighth grade. Kids got ferried off island if they wanted more schoolin'."

"Less and less young folks came home," added Aunt Therese. "Even those that wanted to stay. Well . . . ," she sighed. "It just got harder and harder to make it out here. Oysterin', fishin' guide for rich folks maybe. Workin' off island and commuting back and forth stretched folks thin. So . . ." Aunt Therese shrugged.

"Most folks stayed close though. Got small places in the Royal like Daddy, or maybe Charleston, Beaufort. Never far from their home place, their people," said Aunt Jayne. "But some, well they traveled further."

"Like Mom."

The Aunts nodded.

"Like your momma," agreed Aunt Therese.

Layla gazed at the island around her. A faint wind rustled the tall grass. Tiny brown birds on spindly legs ran jerkily along the water's edge. She tried to imagine her mother here, standing knee deep in the cold, salty water, lying on the beach shoulder to shoulder with her sisters, the sun shining on their faces as gulls wheeled in the crystal-blue sky overhead.

"Charlotte never left?"

In the silence, she turned to find the Aunts gazing up the trail.

"No," answered Aunt Therese.

"Why not?"

Aunt Jayne turned to look at her, her expression unreadable. "Charlotte just . . ." She sighed. "There wasn't nothin' off island for Charlotte."

Once more, the two sisters exchanged a look, a silent conversation passing between them.

"Well," Aunt Jayne said, finally. "Best start headin' up 'fore it gets too hot."

The trail leading to the top of the dune was steeper than it looked. Layla slipped again and again as she labored upward, the pluff mud on the soles of her sandals attracting the sand like a magnet. Almost immediately, her dress was damp with sweat. It clung to her thighs, her back, her buttocks. Something bit her near the shoulder, and she hissed. When she finally reached the top, she dropped to her knees and crawled gratefully into the shade of a stand of pine trees.

"Can you believe we used to run up and down these hills twenty times a day?"

Layla turned, watching in silent admiration as the Aunts slowly but steadily made their way up the hill behind her. More than four decades older, they seemed to be having less trouble navigating the trail than she had. They joined her in the shade of the trees, the ocean breeze washing up the sides of Scotia, leaving a fine salty glaze on their skin as it dried their sweat. From where they sat, the island rolled out in a palette of greens and blues, browns and golds.

Layla felt the familiar itching in her fingertips, that craving for her paints she felt whenever overtaken by the urge to capture an image on canvas. Below them, the sea rolled away from the island's edge, first a brown-tinged gray, then silver, then blue. She inhaled the complicated fragrance of earth and sea into her lungs. "It's beautiful here."

"Yeah." Aunt Jayne dabbed at her face with a handkerchief. "Sure can be."

"How often do you come out here?"

"Not so often. Not anymore," said Aunt Therese. "Way back when, we'd spend days and days out here. Would take the boat outta Port Royal for the oyster harvest in the fall and this place would be so full you couldn't barely find a place to put in. Everybody was here: folks who grew up here, their kids, their kids' kids. Good music. Good eatin'."

She was silent for a long time. "It was somethin'," she added finally.

Her sister, staring off across the wide expanse of water, said nothing. Layla studied the Aunts for a long moment.

"Aunt Terese, this Dreamwalker thing," she said at last, breaking the silence. "Let's say I believe it's a real thing."

She held up a hand as both Aunts leaned forward to protest.

"Wait, wait, wait! Okay, you gotta admit it's . . . Let's just say I believe it. I do. I mean, I think I do." She shook her head. "But it doesn't make any sense."

"What doesn't?" asked Aunt Therese.

Layla swallowed an incredulous laugh. None of it, she wanted to say. None of this made any sense. She tugged at her hair, wrestling with the questions that had been nagging at her since the Aunts had first told her the story in the jon boat. "Well, for starters, the whole third daughter thing. How does that work? I mean, Mom was Granny Bliss's third daughter and I assume Granny Bliss was . . ."

"Gracious . . . ," supplied Aunt Jayne.

"Excuse me?"

"Gracious," said Aunt Jayne, nodding. "Gracious Johnson. Momma's momma."

"O . . . kay," said Layla slowly. "But how could Charlotte and Momma both be the third daughter of a third daughter. Granny Bliss was the third daughter, right? Not Charlotte's mother. Mercy? And what about me? I'm an *only* daughter."

Aunt Therese reached into her bag, pulling out a slender bottle of ginger ale, condensation coating the glass. Layla took the offered soda, shivering as her hand wrapped around the near-frozen glass.

"That's the mystery, isn't it?" said Aunt Therese. "How things start. How things change. All those ripples that seem so small at that time but . . ." She stopped, sighed.

"Siamese twins," said Aunt Jayne. "That's when we think things changed. When the Siamese twins came."

"Conjoined," murmured her sister.

"What?"

"Conjoined," said Aunt Therese. "Not supposed to say Siamese anymore. Supposed to say conjoined twins now."

Aunt Jayne stared at her sister, her lips pursed in annoyance.

Layla sat staring, the soda frozen partway to her lips.

"Anyway," said Aunt Jayne, rolling her eyes. "Momma and Aunt Bliss were born Sia . . . conjoined twins."

"I don't . . ." Layla closed her eyes, opened them. She pressed the icy bottle to her cheek. "I don't understand."

"Conjoined," said Aunt Therese. "You know. When babies born connected to each other."

"I know what . . ." Layla dropped the soda into the sand and leaped to her feet.

She stood for a long moment, looking from one aunt to the other as confusion and shock slid slowly into anger. She felt the heat of it crawling up her neck and into her face.

Layla turned away and bent, hands on her knees, breathing hard. This woman, her mother, was more of a stranger than she could have ever imagined. She felt something crumple then collapse inside her.

"What the fuck," she muttered.

And then she laughed, the sound harsh and ugly. She felt herself empty out, could almost see her pain, a thick and oily mass, spewing into the damp, hot air. Aunt Therese reached to stroke her back, and Layla recoiled.

"No," she snarled, the laughter abruptly cut off. "No."

She straightened and stared off at the silver water, the only sound that of birdcall from the trees behind them. She stood there for a long time before finally turning to face them.

"Why?" she said. "Why keep all this a secret? The island. Her family. I don't understand."

There were tears glistening in Aunt Therese's eyes. "We don't know, baby."

Layla blinked, then slowly moved back into the shade of the pines, slumping onto the sand. "What happened to the twins? Why did that change things?" she asked, her voice flat.

"When Momma and Aunt Mercy were born, Grandaddy Finn, your great-grandaddy, bundled them into the bottom of his oyster boat and carried them off quick quick to Beaufort. White doctors told him nothin' to be done," said Aunt Jayne. "Told him take 'em home and let 'em die peaceful."

"But they didn't die," said her sister. "And they kept not dyin' and not dyin', until folks started hopin' for some kinda miracle."

Layla wrapped her arms around her knees and pictured her great-grandparents hoping, praying for a miracle, day after day, for the miracle that might save their babies.

"What happened?" she murmured.

"Island folk prayed over those baby girls night and day. Anointin' them with sweet oil to keep their little bodies soft," said Aunt Therese, her voice barely above a whisper.

"And then peculiar things started happenin'." Aunt Jayne was staring into the distance, a faint smile on her lips. "Folks all over Scotia started complainin' of headaches. Strange dreams, the same one over and over."

"What dream?"

"Every night, at dusk. Just as the sun was dropping below the horizon, a woman would come walking out the forest. A big woman. Naked as a jaybird. Folks said she looked familiar. Like somebody they oughta know. But no one could quite place her," Aunt Therese answered quietly. "They said that in the dream, the naked woman would walk right to the edge of the sea and just stand there until a huge black bird appeared in the sky. A raven. First one. Then another. And another. Until the whole sky was filled with black birds, blockin' out the setting sun. Screechin' so loud they drowned out the sea."

Layla's mouth went dry. "Black birds?"

Aunt Therese nodded. "Hundreds of them. Thousands. They dove at that naked woman, and she stared up at them like she was darin' them to come for her, darin' them to attack. And they got close. Comin' at her face over and over, before veerin' off at the very last minute."

"What happened?" Layla asked again, her voice hoarse.

"They say that just before the sun sank below the horizon and everything went dark, that woman, that woman nobody could quite place, threw her head back and screamed like some kinda demon. The sound just horrible. Like maybe she was talkin' back to all those birds. And then they say those birds surrounded her like a big, black tornado, whirlin' and screeching, 'til couldn't no one see her. They whirled and whirled. And when they finally flew off, that woman was gone."

"Layla? Baby?"

Layla blinked. The Aunts were standing, bending over her, their round faces pinched with concern, and she realized it wasn't the first time they'd called her name.

"You feelin' alright?" asked Aunt Jayne.

For a long moment she didn't answer as an image played in her mind: black birds slamming into the back door of her mother's house, the screen pulling loose, the deafening cawing, furious, dangerous.

"Here, baby, drink your ginger ale," said Aunt Therese. "This heat sneaks up on you if you not careful."

Layla reached for the bottle, her hands shaking, and took two large gulps.

"What happened to the babies?" she asked.

"Well, they lived didn't they or we wouldn't be sittin' here." Aunt Jayne chuckled. "Momma and Aunt Mercy kept right on livin' and growin'."

Aunt Therese placed her hands on her broad hips and stretched with a grunt. "Turns out what connected their two bodies was just a thick piece of skin. As they got bigger, the place that held them together started drying up—like some kinda strange umbilical cord. One night, the dreams, the one with the naked lady and the ravens, just stopped. Next morning, when Grandaddy Finn went to pick them babies up, there they were layin' face-to-face, and separate as you and me."

Layla gaped.

"Only thing showin' they ever been connected at all was this dark line on the middle of their chest that they both had 'til the day they died," added Aunt Jayne. She stood slowly and stepped from the meager shade back onto the crest of the hill. "We best be gettin' a move on if we want to see any fair amount of this island today."

"But . . . the change. What changed?" asked Layla, not moving. "How can there be two third daughters?"

Aunt Jayne turned to face her. "You don't see?"

Layla shook her head.

"Conceived together in the womb. Formed from one egg. Born joined together. Living as one, all those months. They were both, Momma and Aunt Mercy, the third of three. Both third daughters. Both with the power to dreamwalk, even after they separated."

Layla held herself motionless, afraid to breathe.

"But bound to each other, connected all that time. Something happened," said her aunt. "The power changed. The way it changed in Nola when she came to this island. Different, stronger. Charlotte's aunt Mercy's third daughter." She shook her head, her mouth set in a hard line. "And now there's you."

The hair stood up on Layla's arms and she shivered. Yes, she thought, scanning the trees uneasily, *and now there's me.*

The trail flattened out as it wove its way through the trees. In some places it was barely a foot wide, gray moss brushing their faces as it dangled from the tree branches, in other places, opening wide so that Layla saw flashes of lagoons and estuaries sparkling through the foliage. The air was thick with heat, insects forming a translucent cloud around their heads as they walked.

Layla plodded behind the Aunts in silence, replaying over and over the Aunts' story, struggling to make it fit everything she knew about . . . everything. Granny Bliss, whom she knew only from the few photos on her parents' mantel.

Conjoined twins.

Dreamwalkers.

The dream of ravens.

She gave an involuntary shudder.

She was so focused on her thoughts that it wasn't until she walked into the back of Aunt Therese that she realized they'd come to a stop.

They were standing beneath a stand of loblolly pines that opened onto a small meadow. To her left, another trail led to a thickly wooded area before disappearing into the shadows within. To her right, she could just make out the deep sound that fed into the Atlantic. Directly in front of them, perched atop a low hill, stood what appeared to be the ruins of a large house. Nearly completely overgrown, rotted timbers jutted toward the sky like javelins, the red brick remains of the two chimneys scattered in piles at either end, honeysuckle vines snaking their way through the remaining mortar.

"What's this place?"

"This is . . . was Ainsli Green," said Aunt Therese.

Layla inhaled sharply, shivering despite the bright, hot sun overhead. "This is Ainsli Green?"

She break covenant and take me dreams? She want to take Ainsli Green?

Aunt Therese nodded. "Ruins of the old rice plantation that used to be here long long back."

"The papers in the folder said it's supposed to be haunted."

"White folks think so," replied Aunt Jayne, laughing. "More's the better for us."

"Really?" Layla frowned. "Why's that?"

"White folks come from all over. Try'n to take what they got no rights to take. Buildin' fancy hotels. Raisin' taxes," said Aunt Jayne. Her voice was hard. "Not just on Scotia. All over the Gullah. Disappear us so they can have themselves another Hilton Head. They think us haunted. Good. They stay away then."

"But is it true? That stuff about what happened to the developers who came out here?" asked Layla. "The stuff they said in the papers?"

Aunt Jayne shrugged. "Ain't nobody studyin' them white folks and their nonsense," she said with a snort. "For all we know, they ran off somewhere with their mistress. Or maybe they hidin' out 'cause they were cheating their partners. Easier to blame it on ghosts and crazy Black folks than admit they doin' what rich, white folks always doin'."

Layla gave a sputtering laugh. Shaking her head, she walked slowly toward the ruin.

"Careful now," Aunt Therese called after her.

The house appeared to have been built on the highest part of the island. From where Layla stood, she could see the land sloping in stair-step fashion all the way to the sea, the indigo water fusing with the sapphire sky.

Besides the chimney and shattered timbers, little was left of the house, though the ruins hinted at the solidity of the structure that had once stood on the site. Crumbling stone steps led up to nowhere. A dwarf orange tree grew in a corner of what may have once been the front parlor. Though no one had inhabited this place for many decades, Layla couldn't shake the sense that she was trespassing. She could feel the Aunts watching her from the shadow of the loblolly pines as she picked her way along the remnants of the drive that ringed the perimeter of the ruins.

Halfway around, she stopped. The ground at her feet was littered with nutshells. And there, standing several yards away, was a lone pecan tree. It was old, reaching nearly a hundred feet into the air, its crooked branches heavy with dark green leaves. Still too early for pecans, the furry, yellow-green tassels of the pecan flowers swayed in the sea breeze.

Layla held her breath as she ran a hand over the rough, gray-brown bark, moving it lower and lower on the trunk, frowning at a memory that no one else seemed to share: a magical tree that grew nuts, her father's

Swiss army knife, the way he'd wrapped his hand around hers as he carved their initials.

She'd asked him if it hurt the tree, the carving into the bark with the knife, and he'd kissed her forehead. She could almost feel it now, his full, warm lips pressed against the skin between her eyebrows. No, he'd said. Trees are strong, just like you.

She blinked back tears.

She had come to South Carolina in the car with her daddy. They'd found a pecan tree. They'd carved their initials: AH. They'd had pie.

Or . . .

Maybe they hadn't.

Maybe the whole thing had been a dream that had followed her into the daylight all those years before. Like so many other dreams.

But if that was true, whose dream had she been in that would have brought her here? Her mother's? Charlotte's? Did Charlotte even know she existed back then? She laughed bitterly. She didn't know if it was better or worse that she finally had an idea about what had been happening to her all these years.

She stood for a long time staring at the tree, the sun hot on her bare shoulders. It was just a pecan tree, like the thousands of other pecan trees all over the South.

She ran her hands over the rough bark. She knew, just as she knew that the stories the Aunts had told her were true, that this was the place, this was the tree. And so, when her hand brushed the *A*, carved in the bark there, six feet up, she was not surprised.

13

GEMMA

The world felt blurry and distant, as if Gemma were seeing everything through silvery water. The slaves, the animals, everything, seemed to drift through the fields and orchards in bleary slow motion.

Every morning, there were fewer and fewer slaves working the rice, repairing the traps and fishing lines out near the marsh. They seemed to simply evaporate into the air like dew off morning grass.

The day before, the dark, hulking shape of a ship had appeared like a ghost on the far horizon from the direction of St. Helena's. Timon, Ainsli Green's cooper, said it was a Yankee ship. The colonel often loaned Timon to other planters off island to make their barrels. He heard things the other slaves weren't privy to, so perhaps he was right. In any case, by daybreak, the Yankee ship—if that's what it truly was—had vanished, as if it had never existed at all.

There was a terrible throbbing in Gemma's head. Things were happening out in the world that she didn't understand. It felt like she was waiting for a terrible storm to blow up on them.

"You seen him?"

She started and turned to see Bekka emerging onto the sand from the tree line, her baby secured to her back with a bright cloth. Her friend swayed as she walked, gently rocking the infant with each step.

"Who you mean?" asked Gemma.

"The hoo-doo man." Bekka rolled her eyes. "Who you *think* I talkin' about, ooman?" She jerked her head in the direction of the manor house. "You seen him?"

Gemma shook her head.

"'E dead?"

Gemma huffed a laugh. "Sweet Lawd, Bekka," she cried, her mood lightening. "Smattuh wit' you? Course he not dead."

"How you know?"

Gemma shook her head again and linked her arm in her friend's. They walked together back into the trees and up the narrow trail that led to Ainsli Green's slave quarters.

"'Cause I know that's all."

No one, including her, had seen the colonel in nearly a week, but every morning she placed his food tray in front of his door and every afternoon there were dirty dishes to collect.

"Plus," she said. "Chamber pot outside his door always full. Dead men don't piss." She didn't add that she'd visited the old man in his dreams just three nights before.

"Humph," groused Bekka. "Could be anybody pissin' in that pot."

Gemma sucked her teeth. "Lawd have mercy! You's a nasty thing, Bekka."

Her friend laughed and the two women walked in companionable silence until they reached the summer kitchen. They blinked as their eyes adjusted to the relative darkness inside.

"Folks leavin' day by day," said Bekka quietly.

Gemma turned from dragging a sack of cornmeal from a low shelf and studied her friend, a measuring gourd dangling loose in her hand.

"More, more every day," Bekka added.

"Somethin' botherin' you mind, Bekka?" Gemma asked carefully.

Bekka loosed her baby from the bindings on her back and began to nurse it. She was quiet for a long time. Gemma waited, her fingers absently working the coarse cornmeal. Bekka finally looked up and met her eyes.

"David says them Union men's offerin' freedom, land . . . if we fight." David was her husband.

"Ain't our fight, Bekka."

"Everything the buckra do, comes back at us by and by."

"That ain't no lie, but what if us listen to the Yankee men's sweet talk and they lose they fight?" Gemma pointed the gourd at her friend. "Least-wise here, us already got land."

Bekka shifted her baby and shook her head. "Ain't our land, Gemma."

"Old man can't live forever. Like you say. No tellin' what happenin' other side a that door." She smiled grimly.

Bekka sighed. "Got to go heat water for the wash."

"Bekka . . ."

You will not have this island!

The colonel's voice roared in her ear and Gemma cried out, clapping her hands over her ears.

"Gemma!" Bekka stepped toward her, her voice high with alarm.

You are a witch. A black-faced witch. And the only thing I will give to you will be the grave.

The white man's voice came from behind her, in front of her, inside her. Gemma staggered, blindly lashing out. The cornmeal toppled from the worktable, spewing a thick cloud of meal into the air as the sack exploded on the hard-packed earth floor.

"Gemma! What ailin' you? Oonah sick? What is it?"

As if from a great distance, Gemma heard her friend's voice, but her eyes felt weighted by penny nails as she struggled to open them. She was on the floor, wedged against the butter churn in the furthest corner of the kitchen, her arms, her legs, her clothes, everything, coated in pale meal, lending the summer kitchen an eerie glow. Bekka was leaning over her, her baby clutched to her chest.

"Oonah sick? Oonah want mi ax'um Granny Lee come?"

Gemma shook her head. She had no need of Granny Lee. The old slave healer was half-blind and stone deaf—as likely to kill her as to heal anything that ailed her. In any case, it was not her body that required healing. She stumbled to her feet, tasting blood and the grit of the meal on her tongue.

"Ain't nothin'," said Gemma, swallowing hard. The words sounded false, even to her own ears.

"You got the evil eye workin' on you plain as day," whispered Bekka. "You got to go see Granny Lee 'fore you soul turn black. Get you some anointin' oil."

"Bekka . . ." Gemma clasped at the cross around her neck, felt the rough wood scrape the flesh between her fingers.

She wanted to tell her friend it wasn't the evil eye, that there wasn't anyone working roots on her, wanted to tell her that it was because she'd broken a sacred covenant. She gripped the cross more tightly, a talisman against the evil she sensed crawling in the shadows. She had forced herself into his dreams. She had twisted his fears and used them against him. And now, she was bound too tightly. The night world and the waking world had begun to mix themselves up. She had broken the vow, and the cost was likely to be her soul—and her mind. She wanted to tell Bekka all of this. Instead, she forced herself to smile.

"I's alright. Sleepin' poorly, that's all. Got a little swim in the head."

"I go get one of the girls," said Bekka. "Jessamine winnowin' rice today but 'spects they could spare her a bit."

Gemma shook her head. "Go on now. I gots this mess to clean up."

Bekka hesitated, but Gemma pushed her firmly toward the door. "Git now."

"You gon' see her? Granny Lee?"

Gemma rolled her eyes and Bekka smiled uneasily, worry swimming in her eyes, but she let herself be shooed from the kitchen. Gemma watched her friend make her way toward the wash house. Once alone, she sagged against the doorframe and stared at the manor house a dozen yards away. The shutters to the old man's bedroom were closed but she felt him in there, restless, confused, angry.

She willed him to open those shutters, to see her. Beyond the house, she could hear the call and response of the slaves in the rice fields as they threshed the harvested rice plants. Eyes fixed on the house, she waited, her nails digging into the wood of the doorframe, but the shutters stayed tightly closed.

Despite the thick heat, she began to shiver. It took hold of her, building until her legs could no longer hold her upright. She slid slowly to the floor. It had broken, that line between the colonel and her, the barrier between their souls, between sleep and awake. He didn't know it yet, but soon he would be able to see into her head the way she saw into his. And then what would happen? She didn't know. Not for sure.

She touched her face. There was still a soreness there, an echo of the gunshot from the dream several nights before. She clenched her fists and grunted. She would walk his dreams again and she would push him hard, harder than she ever had before. Not just because the Yankee soldiers were coming, but because *he* was.

A man, sitting in the saddle straight as a pine sapling, was riding up the steep incline to the house. Gemma frowned, biting her lip, concentrating.

There were no horses on Scotia Island—a small herd of cattle that they used for milk and butter, a handful of ragtag mules, but no horses. There was no need for them.

Scotia Island was thickly forested and studded with boggy places. It was an island of steep hills and uneven ground, too treacherous for a horse to find its footing. And Scotia Island was small. A child could walk its entire perimeter in a matter of hours. There was no need for a horse on Scotia Island, and yet here one came, making its way slowly up the narrow, sandy trail from the south beach.

"Gemma."

Someone whispered her name, but she was alone on the porch of the manor house. Shading her eyes, she stepped out onto the tabby drive, feeling the sharp edges of the unground oyster shells through the thin soles of her shoes.

The sun was at the rider's back, but still, she could tell that it was a white man—a white man on a black horse.

"Gemma."

The air whispered her name again and she cried out, startling a flock of black birds. They swooped and spun, dark punctuation marks against the flat blue of the sky.

The rider was closer now—close enough for Gemma to see his face—if he'd had one. She backed away, her mouth open in a scream, but there was no sound. Overhead, the birds whirled, strangely silent too. All sound had vanished from the world.

A dream, she thought, this a dream.

But for the first time in her life, she had no idea if the dream was her own, or someone else's. Panic was a pure, sharp crystal in her gut.

Wake up! she thought. Wake up, woman!

"Wake up, Gemma!"

A voice came from behind her, echoing her exact thoughts and she spun toward it and gave another soundless cry. Her mother, long dead and buried, stood on the porch in the shadow of the doorway. She wore her white burying shift, and her face was as gaunt as the day she'd been laid in the ground in the slave cemetery.

"Mama," cried Gemma. "Help me."

Her mother stared past her—seeming not to hear. The faceless rider was closer now. Gemma could smell the horsey sweat, hear the crunch of hooves on the oyster shell drive.

"Mama," Gemma said again. But the ghost of her mother remained silent, oblivious.

Is this my dream . . . or his? Ain't no way out?

She felt it then, the hot breath on the back of her neck, the power of the animal's body towering over her.

Ain't gon' look in the face of no evil plateye. Ain't goin' where it wants to lead me.

"Gemma!"
She pinched the soft flesh on the inside of her arm.
"Got's to get woke. Got's to get free."
Above her, the black birds soared in silence.

"Gemma! Lawd have mercy! Look to me now, ooman. Open you eyes. You hear me? Open up you eyes now!"

Gemma blinked and Bekka's face floated into focus.

"What . . . ?" said Gemma. It was still dark, the sky just starting to purple toward dawn. Why was Bekka here? And why was she digging her bony fingers into Gemma's wrists?

"What . . . ?" she tried again, but the words wheeled away from her like black birds.

Black birds.

Gemma bit her lip and glanced toward the sky, but there were no birds, only the faint shadow of fruit bats spinning at the edge of the trees.

"Gemma, what in the name of heaven? What goes on wit you ooman?"

Bekka's grip tightened on her wrist, and Gemma sucked her teeth in pain. How could such a skinny woman be so strong? She tried to pull away, but Bekka was having none of it.

"You ruckuhnize me? You knows my face?"

Gemma peered at her friend and nodded. Her head felt as if it had been mounted on a rusted pike. "What you mean? Co'se I knows you face," she snapped. "Let me loose."

"Oh now you sayin' co'se. Like it every day you be standin' b'fo day out in the drive in you britches," said Bekka irritably, but she released her.

Gemma peered down at herself. She was wearing only a thin shift and a pair of woolen bloomers. What was left of the moon lit up the edge of the tabby drive a few feet away, making it glow.

She made a noise in her throat, and Bekka was back at her side in an instant, her thin arms wrapped around her friend's waist.

"Unh-unh," she said. "Don't never mind all that now, old 'oman. Bad dream. Skay'd you. That's all. Comin' down with a little sick most like and no wonder. Wasn't it me that told you to stop messin' around out there in that water every night? And now you wanderin' Ainsli Green half to nekkid."

She led Gemma back through the trees as she talked, back toward the slave cabins.

"There was a horse," Gemma said. "A big, black horse."

Bekka laughed uneasily. "Well, there it be. Ain't never been no horse on this island and you knows it."

"Buckra ridin' it didn't have no face."

Bekka jerked. She yanked Gemma to a halt and forced her around so that they stood facing each other. "You quit it now, Gemma! Don't you go givin' mout' to no juju. You just quit it right now!"

"Ain't got to give it no mout', Bekka. Plateye done took shape already. Saw . . ."

Bekka clamped a hard, bony hand over Gemma's mouth, cutting her off. She shook her head. "Nuh-unh, no. I loves you, Gemma, but you got somethin' bad bad inside youself. Somethin' undeesunt. Terrible juju. Too big for Granny Lee. Only thing to help you now be Jesus."

She poked hard at the cross resting between Gemma's breasts and in the lightening day, Gemma saw anger in her friend's eyes.

"The world unsettled enough as it is," said Bekka, her voice shaking. "Can't hardly ruckunize it from one day to next, but I got my babies on this place and I b'lieve in my heart, things gon' get bettuh. I do. And soon. So's if you seein' plateye on this island, you best keep it hush. Pray on it. Pray hard. Ask why it chasin' up behind you."

The two women stared at each other as the rising sun slowly pushed back the night shadows. From somewhere through the trees, a rooster crowed.

"You right, Bekka. I'm a pray on it. Set my soul right."

Bekka nodded, relief washing across her face. "Bit a willow bark and life everlastin' tea wouldn't do no harm either."

Gemma gave her a bleak smile.

By the time the women made it back to the slave quarters, the few remaining slaves had already left for the rice fields, leaving the place all but deserted.

"I got to get on," said Bekka quietly, not looking at her friend as they entered the quarter.

"Go on then," said Gemma.

Without another word, Bekka turned and walked back the way they'd just come. Shoulders hunched, Gemma walked alone through the quiet quarter. A slave, too old to be of any use in the rice fields, sat dozing on a low stool, a whittling knife in his lap. A half dozen bedraggled chickens ran, protesting, ahead of her.

She stopped in front of her cabin. Her daughters were already gone, but the coals of the cook fire were still smoldering under a dented kettle. She leaned over the pot, sighing as steam washed over her face.

Something crashed back in the trees, and she straightened.

"Hello?"

There was no answer except for the sound of something big moving through the murky thicket beyond the slave cabins.

"Hello?" she called again.

Gemma stepped into the gloom of the loblollies behind her cabin. The sun was still low in the sky, and the woods were filled with deep shadow. She squinted into the dimness. There was someone . . . or something out there . . . something terrible that had followed her out of her dream.

Her breath came fast and she felt a coldness to her marrow, as if the spirits were tracing their fingers along her collarbone, but she forced herself to keep walking, to keep moving deeper into the forest. There was an underground spring nearby and the ground beneath her feet grew soft and spongy. The squawk of birds overhead startled her, but they were only ordinary gulls, along with the occasional ricebird.

Something rustled in the trees behind her. She spun, losing her footing on the slick ground. From her knees, Gemma saw butter-colored sunlight shining through an opening in the trees ahead. With a grunt, she got to her feet and moved toward it, her heart pulsing hard in her throat.

"Lawd, let you righteous word be done," she whispered over and over as she shuffled into the light. She found herself in a space so small she could reach her arms wide and touch the trees on either side. At her feet lay a log, nearly eaten through by rot. Bright yellow jessamine grew from its center, winding upward into the nearby trees.

She laughed aloud, the sound tinged with hysteria.

"Foolishness," she muttered. "Bekka's right. Got to get right with Jesus 'stead a scarin' my own self to death."

She glanced up at the sky. The morning was getting on and here she stood in the middle of the woods, nightclothes covered in muck. She needed to get herself cleaned up and dressed so she could tend to the colonel's breakfast. Whether he ever left his room again was not her concern.

She had a job to do here in the daylight, at least for now. And she didn't need to lay eyes on him to get at him. She turned to go—she had to hurry if she was going to manage any kind of decent meal in time for breakfast—and froze.

The fingers of the spirits were back, and this time they clasped themselves firmly around her neck, stealing her breath.

In the soft, decaying earth, just beyond the log, was the clear imprint of a horseshoe. And there, in its center was a single gold button, exactly like the buttons she'd seen on the old colonel's blue coat. The one he'd been wearing in his dream when he'd shot her with that old musket.

Gemma gasped, frantic for breath, but the air had disappeared from the small clearing.

The covenant, I done broke the covenant, she thought frantically. And now the Lord done abandoned me to the devil.

Far back in the shadows, she thought she saw a figure. And though it had no face, she knew it was laughing at her.

I done broke the covenant and now I'm gon' die.

It came to her with the force of a blow, with a certainty as sure as the life of her children: it had been neither her dream nor his, but a joining of both. The colonel had started to figure it out. And he wanted her dead. He wanted her dead as much as she wanted his mark on that deed paper.

It wasn't the war, or the incomprehensible machinations of the buckras out in the world, she had to fear anymore. It was Rupert Everleigh. He was going to use the last of his strength to fight her—even if he didn't understand exactly what he was doing, or how he was doing it.

She folded to the ground. That old man wants me dead, she thought.

And then she began to laugh, the sound a broken wheeze.

She could live with that.

"Well good for you, Colonel," cackled Gemma. "Good for you. You can kill me dead but you gon' still give me Ainsli Green."

She gave a sharp bark of laughter.

"And then we both just see each other in hell."

14

Charlotte Fortenberry's house was only a short walk from the ruins of Ainsli Green, but from where they stood the remains of the old manor house were invisible.

Charlotte's house was a squat, one-story structure, the clapboard siding split and faded. A sleeping porch formed the front, jelly jars filled with wildflowers sitting in nearly every one of the many windows. In the side yard, a lone, pink nightgown fluttered on the clothesline. There was no answer to Aunt Jayne's knock.

"Maybe she's not here."

"It's an island," said Aunt Therese dryly. "Even when she ain't here, she's here."

"Might as well go on in and wait. She'll be around sooner or later." Aunt Jayne stepped to the door.

"You're not just going to walk into her house?"

The Aunts looked at her.

"Well, of course," said Aunt Jayne. "Why wouldn't we?"

Layla blinked. "Well, because . . ." The Aunts were still staring at her, their expressions puzzled. She shrugged, letting it go. "Is it okay if I look around for a minute?"

"Alright by us," said Aunt Jayne. She pulled open the screen door, the hinges screaming in protest. "Just don't stay out here too long. It's hotter than the devil's armpit out here."

Layla skirted a pile of firewood and rounded the side of the house.

"Oh," she exhaled in surprise.

The woods behind Charlotte's little house shimmered with light, flashes of color flickering from the branches of the trees. It took her a moment to realize that nearly every tree held a bottle: clear, brown, blue—every shade of blue—sunlight reflecting off the glass, filling the air with hundreds of flickering rainbows.

"Oh," she said again. She suddenly thought of the lone blue bottle her mother always insisted be kept in the holly bush by their front door and felt her throat tighten.

"Shit," she murmured, feeling tears threaten.

"Who you be?"

Layla jerked around. A woman stood several feet away, the sun at her back, obscuring her features.

"Jesus Christ! You scared me!" She laughed uneasily.

"What you want here?" asked the woman.

"I'm here visiting with my aunts."

The woman stepped free of the shadows and Layla's breath caught in her throat. The woman was short, well-defined muscles stretching tight over her small frame. She wore a faded man's work shirt and worn work boots. In one hand she gripped an intricately carved walking stick.

It was the woman from her dream, the woman from the newspaper: her cousin Charlotte.

Charlotte was staring at her. Her eyes, dark in her wide face, glittered, hard and bright as glass. Layla felt a frisson of unease as the memory of this woman's fury in her dream resurfaced.

But this was not a dream.

"I'm Layla," she said, pasting a smile on her face. She thrust out her hand, blinking in surprise when Charlotte seemed to recoil.

"Elinor's girl."

"Yes." Layla dropped her hand.

"What you want here?" Charlotte asked again, her voice hard.

"I want . . ." Layla hesitated. It was not a simple question.

The woman studied her, her expression indecipherable, then without another word turned and walked away. A few seconds later, Layla heard the screech of the screen door.

Layla sat behind the kitchen table, a massive thing that took up nearly all the space in Charlotte's tiny kitchen, watching as the woman bustled back and forth in the narrow gap on the other side, loading the table with food: deviled eggs, cold fried chicken, slices of watermelon, a pitcher of lemonade.

Charlotte had not spoken a single word to any of them since coming in the house.

Aunt Jayne caught Layla's eye and smiled, correctly reading her expression.

"Folks may be plann' to kill you and bury you in the backyard," she said under her breath. "But in the South, they gon' still feed you first. It's good manners."

Layla bit back a nervous laugh just as Charlotte slammed a jar of pickled okra onto the table and glared at the three of them.

"Me wish Jayne hab crack 'e teet 'bout oonah comin'. But come, come, oonah hab brekwus now."

Layla blinked. Her cousin was speaking Gullah, the native language of the Sea Islands. The sound was fast, fluid. Familiar words drifted up, then sank back beneath the surface.

"It was last minute," answered Aunt Jayne.

"You really ought to get a phone, Charlotte," said Aunt Therese.

"What I get a phone for?" Charlotte dropped into a chair. She shot a look at Layla before switching to deliberate English. "Then people be callin'."

Aunt Therese rolled her eyes. "Yes, sweetie, I believe that's the point."

Layla studied her cousin across the table. Charlotte was about her mother's age, her skin smooth, unlined, her hair, tied up in a scarf, barely gray at the temples.

"You heard from your sisters?" asked Aunt Jayne, after a moment of uncomfortable silence.

"Time to time. They still try to get me off island. Try to get me to Savannah." Charlotte narrowed her eyes at Layla. "You not hungry?"

Layla pressed her lips together and took a wedge of watermelon. She placed it on the plate in front of her as fragments of the dream came to her: Charlotte screaming in her face, lace shredding, Charlotte's hot breath against her neck. In the dream Charlotte had been tall, like Layla and her mother, like the Aunts, much younger than this woman who sat scraping egg yolk off her plate with her fingernail.

"Your house is very nice," she said, pushing the images aside. Charlotte stopped picking at the egg yolk and squinted at her.

Layla pushed on. "There's wonderful light in here."

Charlotte grunted and slammed a drumstick onto Layla's plate.

"This Momma's house," she said.

Momma's house.

"Your mother was Aunt . . . Mercy."

Charlotte nodded and pointed at the Aunts. "Our mommas is sisters. You know that story?"

Layla nodded.

"Connected in they flesh." Charlotte touched a fingertip to her chest. "Connected in they mind." She touched her forehead. "Connected for always."

Aunt Jayne made a noise. Charlotte ignored her, all of her attention focused now on Layla. She was smiling, but her eyes shot fire.

Those eyes.

The hair rose on the back of Layla's neck. There was no mistaking those eyes. The yellow walls in the tiny kitchen thrummed with heat, and the air felt suddenly too thick to breathe.

"Why you come here?"

"Charlotte," said Aunt Therese softly, a warning.

"Ain't talkin' to you." Charlotte pointed, her eyes never leaving Layla's face. "Talkin' to her."

Layla clenched her jaw and returned the stare. In spite of everything, she *was* Elinor's daughter. She had every right to be here and she was not about to let this woman intimidate her.

"Elinor's gone," said Aunt Jayne.

Charlotte flinched and Layla saw a flicker of something like pain in her eyes before she looked away.

"I knows that," snapped Charlotte, finally looking away from Layla. She stared down at the table. "Don't need no phone to know that."

"We were tryin' to reach you before we left," said Aunt Therese gently. "We thought you might a wanted to go with us to her homegoin'. Say your goodbyes."

Charlotte made a choking sound. "Why I want to do that for?"

Aunt Therese gasped.

"Because once upon a time she was like a sister to you," said Aunt Jayne, her voice hard. "More."

"Long, long time gone!"

A viscous, angry tension filled every corner of the tiny kitchen.

"Mom . . . ," Layla said into the sudden, lethal quiet. Three pairs of eyes turned to look at her.

"Mom left me her share of the island and I wanted to see it. Wanted to . . ." She stopped, struggling to articulate her churning emotions.

"I wanted to meet you," she finished weakly.

"Meet me?" Charlotte reared back, eyes widening in surprise. She laughed and the sound set Layla's teeth on edge. "'Cause all the good things you heard 'bout me then?"

Layla's face grew hot, but she did not look away.

Across the table Charlotte watched her warily. "Well," she said finally. "I s'pose you be wantin' to see the rest of 'your' island then."

"Charlotte . . . ," began Aunt Jayne.

"Yes," interrupted Layla. "Yes, in fact I do."

"You want to see where your momma was a young girl? Hear all 'bout what she was like?" Charlotte's lips were pulled back in a semblance of a smile. "Don't every girl want that?"

Layla heard the sarcasm, noted the malice in her cousin's eyes, but the truth was, she did. She did want to see where her mother had grown up. Did want to hear about her life as a girl. She nodded, not trusting herself to speak.

"Well, come on, then. Mornin' wastin'. Don't want be out middle day. Fry you head up."

In a few minutes they were all following Charlotte out the back door.

The sandy path led away from the back of the house, passing beneath the trees where the bottles sparkled like jewels. Charlotte, in the lead, walked in silence, gripping her walking stick. A short way into the trees, the trail bent out of sight.

"Just yonder is the Old Place," said Charlotte, stopping at a low hedge.

"The Old Place?" Layla ran a hand over the hedge, releasing a bright, sweet-smelling fragrance into the air.

Her cousin nodded. "Where most a the old folks built they homes."

"When the freedom came, the slaves moved away from Ainsli Green. Away from the slave quarters," said Aunt Jayne from behind her. "They built their own places all over the island, but down here mostly. Relatively dry, fair protection from the storms that blow up every fall. Generations that came after followed their example."

Charlotte grunted and pushed through an opening in the hedge. Layla followed. Just beyond the hedge the ground gradually dipped away, forming a shallow bowl, surrounded by dense vegetation. A dozen houses, all broad and low to the ground like Charlotte's, lined the sides of the bowl. But where Charlotte's house had seemed merely weatherworn and time frayed, most of these homes appeared in various states of collapse.

"Up and down these hills like wild goats. Me and Elinor. To the big house, down to the water, then back again," Charlotte murmured, almost to herself.

Without another word, she continued down the short hill, her stick throwing up small spits of sand.

"Here," she said, stopping in front of one of the houses.

Layla stopped beside her; her arm accidentally brushed the older woman's. Her cousin's skin was hot and dry, smelling of something sweet.

"Where is everybody?"

"Everybody?" Charlotte laughed. "Not many 'everybodys' left on Scotia."

"Well, where are the everybodys that are left?" Layla asked, a sharp edge to her voice. Charlotte's hostility was wearing her down.

"Weather changin' year by year. Storms gettin' worse. Most folks moved further inland. Beau Hampton and his family, they farm cotton over other side of Scotia. Sell it to some crazy white folks what use it to make funny lookin' pants for the rich folks over to Kiawah Island. Missy Leigh and her two daughters, they off island visitin' they people over to Atlanta 'til end of summer. The Everleigh brothers they be takin' folks out on the water for cobia season."

"Let's see," said Charlotte, squinting up at the sky. "Manda and her husband got good jobs at a hotel over at Myrtle Beach. They don't never come home. 'Cept every now and again. And Big Sam oysters with them folks in Port Royal. They's some others that be comin' and goin' but . . ." Charlotte gave a tiny shrug. "Ain't so much left of *your* island no more. This Auntie Bliss's house."

She'd changed subjects so quickly that it took Layla a moment to register that Charlotte was talking about the house in front of them.

"What?"

"This the house your momma got borned in."

"Mom was born on this island?"

"What you think?" Charlotte crossed her arms and peered at her.

Layla rubbed her forehead. What *did* she think?

She thought it was terrible to possess such tiny fragments of her own history, ragged pieces that added up to nothing whole.

She thought it was horrible and sad that it took her mother dying for her to finally start finding out anything real about her.

She thought it was incredibly strange that her mother had kept so many secrets.

And she thought she clearly didn't know anything about anything.

"Port Royal," she answered finally. "I always thought she grew up in Port Royal."

"We moved off island for good when your momma was 'bout six," said Aunt Therese, coming to stand beside them. She stared up at the house, a small smile playing around her lips. "Daddy fought it tooth and nail, but Momma insisted we all needed to go somewhere with good schools. And hospitals and libraries."

"Your momma was born right here," said Charlotte. "Aunt Bliss and Uncle Hannibel moved off island but it wasn't like they was true gone. They was back so much a the time."

She stepped up and placed a hand on the collapsing porch.

"Cousin Buddha lived here 'til he died, and Elinor, Jayne, and Therese was here plenty . . . for a while." She glanced at the sisters, then turned to Layla, her eyes blazing. "But Elinor moved on to better."

She spit the last word.

"You know about snakes, girl?" she asked.

Layla blinked, caught off balance once again by the sudden detour in the conversation.

"Charlotte!" hissed Aunt Jayne.

"They shed they skin over and over. Movin' along through life."

Layla narrowed her eyes, a spear of warning lighting up her spine.

"They don't never stay where they leave their skin. Just keep movin', but the thing is, they still snakes. Even in they new skin. Some people be like snakes."

Layla leaned in, shaking off the protective arm Aunt Therese had placed around her shoulders, lips drawn back from her teeth.

"That's true," she snapped. She had reached her limit with this mean-spirited, angry woman. This cousin she now shared an island with. "But one of the reasons snakes shed their skin is to get rid of parasites."

She was not sure why she said it, not sure why she chose that particular word, but she knew the instant it hit its mark. Charlotte growled deep in her throat, rearing back.

The two women locked eyes, staring each other down, until, without a word, the older woman whirled and stalked away. At the tree line she turned and pointed at Layla with her stick before disappearing into the shadows.

15

They walked in silence back to the jon boat, Layla and the Aunts each lost in their own thoughts. Confusion, shock, anger roiled in Layla's head, rendering her mute. At the head of the dock, she stopped, raking one hand through her hair.

"What the actual hell was that?"

Aunt Jayne, several feet ahead, went rigid, not turning, not speaking. A second passed, a single breath of time, then, without a word, she climbed down into the boat, taking her place at the tiller.

Layla turned, locking eyes with Aunt Therese. "They hated each other," she said, more statement than question.

"Wasn't always like that," murmured Aunt Therese. She glanced at her sister who sat in the stern of the boat, staring off into the distance. "Once, they was like two halves of the same person. Always together."

She climbed down the short ladder and settled herself into the boat. Layla hesitated, glancing over her shoulder back toward the island before following.

"Charlotte 'bout two years older than your momma. Always a little peculiar," Aunt Therese went on after a moment. "Sickly, screaming all the time. Didn't nobody know what to do with her. Wore Aunt Mercy clear out."

As her sister spoke, Aunt Jayne fired up the motor and pointed the boat toward open water. Overhead, a white heron took flight.

"Then Elinor came along." Aunt Therese raised her voice to carry over the sound of the motor. "Couldn't nobody explain it. Only body could get Charlotte to settle. Aunt Mercy started bringin' her by the house just so Charlotte'd go to sleep for a bit. Elinor the only one on this whole island could get that girl to eat, to mind."

Water sprayed Layla's face, cooling her. She tasted salt on her tongue.

"All the way up through high school. Charlotte was your momma's shadow. Never saw one without the other," Aunt Therese went on. "Summer before your momma left for college, somethin' . . . changed."

"What?" asked Layla, leaning toward her.

Aunt Therese shrugged.

"Asked them once," said Aunt Jayne, speaking for the first time since walking away from the Old Place. "Elinor said everything was fine. Charlotte didn't say nothin'. But somethin' was different. *They* were different. Elinor got quiet and Charlotte got . . . mean."

Aunt Therese opened her mouth as if she wanted to say more, then seemed to think better of it. She pulled her rucksack close and hunched low in her seat. The three women rode the rest of the way home in silence.

"Thank you," said Layla as they walked into the foyer. "For taking me out there."

"Welcome," said Aunt Jayne. She gave a tight smile. "I'm a go lie down for a bit. Feelin' a little worn."

"Want some tea?" asked Aunt Therese after her sister'd gone up.

Layla nodded and followed her into the kitchen.

"I hated her too," Layla murmured.

Aunt Therese froze, pitcher held in midpour, her expression stricken.

"I mean, she was my mother and I loved her, but . . ." Layla rubbed her face. "But it was so hard with her. Everything was just so hard."

"Oh, sugar." Aunt Therese slid into the chair across from her and reached for her hand. Layla pulled away.

"I don't . . . You have no idea what it's like. Growing up thinking something's wrong with you. And all the while . . ." Layla's voice trailed off.

She sat for a long moment in the warm kitchen, jaw clenched, poking at the ice in her glass with one finger.

Aunt Therese sighed. "She loved you, baby. No, no she did. All she wanted . . . She just wanted . . . I don't know. Something else. To be something else. Someone else. Normal. No dreamwalking. No island. Just . . . normal. After she had you, the one daughter, she thought she had everything she could ever want then. The fine man, the fancy job. And then you . . ."

She sighed again, sagging in her seat.

Layla laughed, a harsh, broken sound. "Do you think she thought I could be cured? That if she ignored what was happening it would just . . . stop? Like a bad habit? Like thumb sucking or cursing or something?"

She laughed again, but there was no humor in it. Part of her hoped that was true. Maybe she could forgive her mother—a little—if she could believe her mother was trying to help her, was doing her best.

"Oh, sugar, I don't know." Aunt Therese reached for Layla's hand again and this time Layla let her take it. "Hope is a powerful thing, but it can blind folks to some pretty big truths."

"Hope?" asked Layla. "Or denial?"

Aunt Therese flinched, sighed. "I think I'll go up for a bit too. You?"

Layla shook her head.

Her aunt stood for a minute, gazing through the back kitchen window. "We got a fair bit of your momma's stuff in the shed out yonder if you want to take a look."

Layla looked up, surprised.

"Couldn't never bring ourselves to throw it out. No idea what's out there. Mice might a got to everything by now." She turned to look at her niece. "Might want to wait for the sun to go down a bit though. Be cooler."

She studied Layla a moment longer, emotions playing across her face, then walked from the kitchen.

Near the tree line at the back of the property stood a small shed, just visible through the sheets fluttering on the line. It was the same shade of blue as the house, though it seemed to have had a more recent coat of paint. Pink, white, and violet sweet peas climbed a rusted trellis that leaned against one wall, scenting the air with their perfume. Late afternoon had brought clouds, but the air was still heavy and warm.

The lock hung loose, and as Layla pulled open the wooden door, the smell of oil and grass and dust assailed her. The only light came from the small, dirt-grimed windows, but it was enough to see that the shed was crammed top to bottom. There were garden tools, bits and pieces of several bicycles, two ancient-appearing push mowers, shelves overflowing with jars, some empty, others filled with nails and screws of various sizes, a wheelbarrow, a leaning pyramid of old paint cans, wooden fruit boxes, a stained mattress.

Layla played her flashlight over the space, the drifting dust sparkling like stars. There was nothing here that looked like it might belong to her mother. She was backing out when her light caught a low, tarp-covered mound in the corner nearest the door. She peeled back the tarp, coughing as gritty dust exploded into the air.

Two cardboard boxes were stacked neatly atop a battered suitcase, their corners crumbled and mouse chewed. On the side of the top box was written "Elinor."

Layla carefully dragged the boxes out onto the grass. She sat for a long time in the warm grass, the sky turning shades of gold and orange above her in the waning afternoon. The past weeks had been full of so many revelations about her mother, not all of them pleasant, and she felt a shiver of nervousness at what these boxes might uncover.

"Alright, girl," she muttered. She took a deep breath. "We got this."

Slowly, she pried open the first box and the smell of mothballs filled her nose. She ran a hand over threadbare sweaters and dry-rotted shirts, her heart thudding hard, surprised at the surge of emotion. Her mother had worn these things long before she was anyone's mother. She picked up an empty perfume bottle and held her nose close, hoping to catch a scent of the young Elinor. But there was nothing.

There were mildewed textbooks and old school assignments, her mother's faded handwriting loopier, more girlish, than it would become later. Layla took her time, savoring each object as if it might hold the key to her mother, to the things she was coming to know about the woman who would become her mother.

In the second box, beneath a Howard University sweatshirt, was a stack of old newspapers and *National Geographic* magazines. Sitting neatly atop the stack were two wooden cigar boxes, the word "CHURCHILL" burned into the wood.

She opened the closest one to find a wild jumble, postcards held together with twine or brittle rubber bands: the Statue of Liberty, the Waldorf Astoria Hotel, Niagara Falls. Most bore postmarks from four, five decades past, the signatures nearly worn away. But there were a few where she could see the addressee: Charlotte Fortenberry.

As Layla rummaged through the cigar box, sorting through the contents, she felt an echo of familiarity. There were matchbooks advertising the Roostertail supper club in Detroit, the Four Queens Hotel and Casino in Las Vegas, flyers from gas stations and universities and bowling alleys.

She inhaled sharply, realization striking her.

This was exactly like the Adventure box. Less organized and more haphazard perhaps, but otherwise, it was simply a shabbier version of the box that sat in the back of the closet in her mother's house. Were these trips her mother had made? And with who?

There were photos, dozens and dozens of photos. Mostly black and white and nearly all of the same two girls. Sometimes together. Usually alone. She plucked one from the center of the box. The photo showed two girls, maybe ten or eleven, their arms draped across each other's shoulders, standing in water to their knees.

The taller one was grinning, her free hand up, as if waving to whoever held the camera. The other girl was shorter, skin a shade lighter, lean. She was smiling, too, but she seemed more hesitant. She was turned slightly away from the camera, a half step behind the other girl, as if trying to disappear into her shadow.

Layla gasped, pulling the picture closer. The girl in the picture was Charlotte—Charlotte as a young girl—but unmistakably Charlotte. The young Charlotte had the same wide face, the same wiry build. And the girl next to her, the girl with the exuberant, gap-toothed grin, was Elinor Hurley. Her mother.

"Holy crap!" she whispered.

She opened the other cigar box. In picture after picture, there was Charlotte and her mother, her mother and Charlotte: dragging driftwood down a beach, sitting on a log beside a fire, on a porch swing. They were very young in some of the pictures, grade-school-aged with scuffed knees and wild, unkempt pigtails, in others they were teenagers, easily recognizable as the women they would become.

In every picture, her mother faced the camera, head thrown back in laughter, or mugging for the photographer, eyes crossed, tongue stuck out; and then there was Charlotte, always just a quarter step in Elinor's background.

Layla touched a finger to one of the photos. Her mother hung upside down by her knees from a tree branch, blouse falling free exposing her smooth, brown belly, mouth open in obvious joy. Layla traced her mother's face, barely able to reconcile this wide-eyed, laughing girl with the fierce, driven, everything-in-its-place woman she knew.

"I remember that."

Startled, Layla jerked, nearly spilling the contents of the cigar box into the grass. Aunt Jayne stood over her, gazing at a picture that lay in Layla's lap, a smile tugging at the corner of her mouth. Layla looked down. Her mother, eyes swollen, bandage covering one side of her forehead, was grinning, two fingers held up in a peace sign for the camera.

"I am too fat for this." Aunt Jayne groaned, dropping into the grass beside Layla. She picked up the picture. "Elinor ever tell you how she got that scar on her forehead?"

Layla shook her head. At one point, she and her brothers had all asked about the moon-shaped scar at their mother's hairline, but the only answer they ever got was that it came from "having more nerve than sense."

"Well, your momma read this story in school 'bout some boy that wanted to fly, so he made himself some wings. But they were made out of wax and when he flew too near the sun, the wings melted off and he ended up fallin' out the sky. Your momma said, 'What kinda jack-eyed idiot makes wings outta wax?'"

Aunt Jayne studied the picture, chuckling softly. "Next thing we know, Charlotte's screamin' bloody murder out in the yard and your momma's up on the roof of the house."

She shook her head. "Elinor had got Momma's best bedsheets and strapped them to a bunch of pine branches, then lashed that whole mess to her arms with Daddy's dress belt. Quicker'n you could say get your fanny down here, that fool jumps."

Layla gaped at her aunt. "That did not happen."

Aunt Jayne laughed out loud. "Oh yes, ma'am, it happened just like that. That idiot girl flappin' her arms all the way down. Thank the baby Jesus, she landed in a pile of brush Daddy had stacked by the house to burn. Still managed to gash her head wide open. Couldn't nobody believe she didn't kill herself. After her head healed up, Momma tried to beat the black off her . . . for all the good that did."

Layla was laughing. *Her* mother made wings out of branches and bedsheets and jumped off Granny Bliss's roof? Her brothers would never believe it.

"Momma made Charlotte swear to tell anytime Elinor started even thinkin' about some foolishness that was liable to end up with one a them dead. Charlotte swore, but there wasn't no stoppin' your momma. And truth be told, I believe the crazier the ideas your momma got, the better Charlotte liked it."

Layla lifted a handful of matchbooks. "What's this all about?"

"Oh goodness. I haven't thought about those in years," said Aunt Jayne softly, her expression darkening. "Didn't even realize all this was still out here."

She shook her head.

"Lord, those two would sit for hours clippin' pictures outta magazines, talkin' about the places they was gonna go when they grew up. All the amazin' sights in the world. The Eiffel Tower, the pyramids in Egypt."

She picked up the cigar box, staring at it for a long time. "They were gonna ride camels and climb mountains. Leave Scotia behind and have big adventures together. Anytime anybody left Scotia they'd bring those girls back a little somethin'. Matchbooks, playbills, napkins, or some such and they'd add it to their collection."

She was quiet as she gazed at the picture of her youngest sister, grinning at the camera despite her injuries.

"But then something happened," said Layla softly.

"Something happened," echoed Aunt Jayne, not looking up.

"It must have been really bad."

"Yes," agreed her aunt. "For the life of me, I can't even imagine what could possibly have turned those two against each other." Her aunt sighed. "But it must have been something hellacious. Getting late," she said, struggling to her feet. "Come on in for supper."

"In a minute," said Layla.

Aunt Jayne stood staring down at the pictures, the postcards a moment longer, then headed to the house.

Layla pushed the cardboard boxes back into the shed. As she swept the postcards, letters, and pictures into the cigar boxes to take into the house, one picture caught her eye. Charlotte and her mother were older, possibly late teens. They were sitting on a pile of bricks, the ruins of the Ainsli Green manor house recognizable in the background.

Her mother's hands were folded demurely in her lap, the broad, mischievous grin from earlier photos replaced by the tight, closed-mouth smile that Layla had known her whole life. Her hair, which in nearly every other photo had been an exuberant frizz, had been straightened and was pulled back from her face with a yellow headband.

Charlotte, crouching a few feet away and nearly out of frame, was staring at her cousin, her expression a mask of rage.

Layla felt the hair rise on the back of her neck. What was the thing that had happened between her mother and her cousin? Shivering, she closed the box.

16

High above, the sky stretched an endless robin's-egg blue, the sun bleaching sea and sand to shades of silver and white.

She was on Scotia Island. Far below, tiny sandpipers scurried along the beach.

Layla frowned. Was someone crying? Following the sound, she found herself back near the ruins of Ainsli Green, and there, standing several yards away, were her mother and Charlotte. Somehow, Layla realized, she had entered Charlotte's dream and instinctively clung to the shadows of the loblolly grove.

It was her mother who was crying. Head bowed, she was wearing a white blouse and white skirt, her hair wild around her head. Charlotte stood in front of her, holding a steaming cup.

"Drink this, Elinor. You need to drink this."

Layla's mother shook her head. "I can't."

"You can." Charlotte forced the cup into Elinor's hand. "He did this thing to you. This will make it alright. Like before. You and me. Everything be just like before."

Elinor, still sobbing, took the cup and drank. As Layla watched, a stain, dark maroon, appeared and began to slowly spread across the front of her mother's white skirt. Layla gasped. Blood. She could smell it in the air. Even as her mother's cries dissolved into hiccupping moans, the stain grew larger.

And then it was night. They were on the beach, the full moon reflecting bright off the water. Shaken, Layla held herself still. Her mother and Charlotte were only a few yards away, but they seemed oblivious to her presence. Her mother, still wearing the same blood-soaked skirt, was staring out over the water, her anger palpable even from a distance.

"Elinor?" Charlotte sounded uncertain, frightened.

"He did this thing. You said that. And you were right," said Elinor, her voice hard, barely recognizable. "Justice is not a sin."

She held out one hand. Charlotte hesitated for a long moment, then took it, and the two girls turned toward the trees lining the beach. Seconds later, a man *emerged onto the sand. He was young, well built. Barefoot and shirtless, he was carrying a gun, and Layla unconsciously took a step back.*

"Elinor?" Charlotte said again, her voice cracking.

But Layla's mother said nothing, merely clasped her cousin's hand and watched as the man made his way down to the water's edge.

Layla frowned. Something was off in the way the man moved, in the way he carried his rifle. Almost as if he was . . . sleepwalking.

Alarm spiraled through her.

This was wrong.

Something about this was very wrong.

Layla stepped forward. To call a warning. To intervene. To . . .

Whatever her intention had been, it was forever lost as the man walked to the water's edge, placed the gun in his mouth, and pulled the trigger.

Layla staggered backward, mouth stretched wide in a silent scream. And then Charlotte was there, eyes glittering in the moonlight.

"What . . . ?" said Layla. "What did . . ."

She was shaking badly, unwilling, unable to complete the question.

"Pretty clothes. Pretty life," whispered Charlotte, leaning close. Her skin smelled sweet. "Lies. You. The only daughter. Lies."

Layla backed away and Charlotte followed.

"No matter how many times a snake sheds its skin. It still a snake."

Layla shot upright, breathing fast, the T-shirt she'd slept in sweat sour, clinging to her skin.

Murder? Had she just dreamed of her mother and Charlotte committing a murder?

She leaped from the bed, hot fluid rising into her mouth. Barely making it to the trash can, she vomited again and again, then dry heaving when there was nothing left, spasms clenching her stomach.

Long after the retching subsided, she knelt, trembling, the image of the man at the water's edge, the gun, her mother standing there in her bloodied skirt holding hands with Charlotte.

"It's not real," she whispered. "Not. Real."

Her throat burned as she pulled herself upright and lurched over to the octagonal window, forcing it open. Leaning out as far as she could, she focused on the sensation of the wood frame pressing against her rib cage, the morning breeze rustling through the trees. Up this high, she could nearly touch the leaves of the tree shading the house. Far below, the Aunts' truck was parked beneath the sugarberry tree. She closed her eyes, taking deep breaths, letting the fresh air wash over her face.

She'd caught Charlotte's dream. She knew that with unwavering certainty.

She'd fallen into Charlotte's dream, and her mother and Charlotte had . . .

Justice is not a sin.

Jesus Christ. What had happened out on that island? What had her mother done?

She staggered into the shower, turning the water as hot as she could tolerate. She stood, letting the water wash away the stink of the sweat, the vomit, and the dream.

"It can't be true," she muttered, through chattering teeth.

But she knew that though she didn't always understand what she saw in dreams, and that there were times when dreams distorted facts, they didn't alter them. What she'd seen was real. The way she'd learned to knit was real. The way initials on a pecan tree were real. The way her friend's dog Butterscotch had been real.

A loud moan escaped from somewhere deep inside, and Layla clasped a hand over her mouth.

"I want to go home," she whispered. The thought made her laugh out loud. She'd come to South Carolina looking for . . . something. And though Baltimore wasn't exactly what she meant when she thought of home, it was close enough. At least it was a place she understood.

She dressed quickly, ignoring the puffy eyes and matted hair she saw reflected in the mirror. Grabbing the fouled trash can, she headed down the stairs, so distracted that she didn't notice the man at the foot of the stairs until she'd run into him.

"Shit!" She stumbled, nearly losing her grip on the trash can.

"Oh, sorry." A pair of hands grabbed her arm, steadying her. "Mornin'. You must be Layla."

The man at the bottom of the stairs, blocking her route to the kitchen, was of medium height and solidly built, and in the light streaming through the front door, he seemed to glow. Blond streaks ran through his amber-colored hair; his pale eyes flashed green, then brown, then smoky-gray in the early morning light that filtered into the entryway, his honey-colored skin a muted shade of gold. Her hands tightened around the stinking trash can.

She could almost see her color sticks laid out in front of her, the colors she would use to sketch him. The yellows: honey, gold, and flax. The browns: raw sienna, light ochre, titian. Endive green to bring out the highlights in his eyes, flamingo to show how the light sparkled on his skin.

She swallowed hard. "I . . . mm-hmm, yeah, no."

She nodded, trying to tuck the trash can behind her.

"Beg pardon?" said the man.

"I . . ." She took a deep breath, her face on fire. "Yes, Layla. But I wouldn't trust anything I say until I've had my first cup of coffee."

The man grinned. "My daddy was the same way. Momma used to say he wasn't fit for man nor beast 'til he had his first cup." His voice was deep and lightly accented with the South. He held a hand out toward her. "I was hopin' we'd get a chance to meet while you were here. Viktor."

She hesitated, fighting the urge to bolt for the kitchen. She took his hand. It was rough and warm, a working man's hand. He released her and made as if to step aside, but Aunt Therese appeared suddenly from the kitchen and wrapped her arms around his waist, holding him fast from behind.

"Here's my baby," she said. "Well, officially, he's Gerta's, but that's just a technicality, isn't it, sugar?"

Viktor laughed and squeezed Aunt Therese's plump arms. "Yes, Tante. Everybody knows I really belong to you."

"The fish guy," blurted Layla. She cringed inwardly.

Viktor frowned.

"She's talkin' 'bout that big ol' cobia, baby," explained her aunt over his shoulder.

Viktor threw back his head and laughed. "Only my absolute nearest and dearest friends call me the fish guy, but yes, that would be me."

Face hot, Layla forced a smile.

Aunt Therese patted Viktor's cheek. "Come on now, babies. Breakfast is on the table."

Clutching the trash can against her chest, Layla scooted past them and deposited it on the back porch.

"So, you have met my Viktor."

Layla turned. Gerta sat at the table sipping coffee from a flowered teacup. "I did."

"Is he not the most beautiful boy?" said Gerta, beaming.

"He is," said Layla, glancing self-consciously at the man who now stood in the kitchen door behind Aunt Therese.

"Well, my goodness, ladies. If my head ain't about fixin' to bust." Viktor leaned to kiss his grandmother. "I need to get to work, Oma."

"You can't stay for breakfast?" exclaimed Aunt Therese.

"No, ma'am. Ain't got the time. All these folks in town and most of 'em bound and determined to get into some kinda mischief."

"Well, let me wrap you up somethin' at least," said Aunt Therese.

"It's fine, Tante." He kissed her. "I'll be by later. Tell Tante Jayne I said hey."

He bowed toward Layla. "Pleasure. Hope to see you again."

"Such a good boy," sighed Gerta after he'd gone.

"You should get to know him while you're here," said Aunt Therese. "Don't need to be spendin' all your time hangin' around us old folks your whole visit."

"What does he do? I mean other than catch big fish?" asked Layla, changing the subject. She poured herself a giant mug of coffee and sat across from Gerta.

"He is policeman with Fish and Wildlife," said his grandmother. "Patrols the islands and the water."

"From now 'til winter, it's just crazy for him out there," added Aunt Therese. "College kids, tourists. Come down here gettin' drunk, then gettin' themselves into all sorts a trouble. Not respectin' the water."

"You remember when Viktor had to find those young men from New York City?" asked Gerta, chuckling.

Her friend began to laugh. "You talkin' 'bout them three boys that stole Otis Payne's little eight-foot jon boat?"

"They steal this little boat and do not even know how to operate it," said Gerta to Layla, her round face turning pink as she laughed. "It is late at night, and they are very drunk. They think to go out to the ocean and catch a sailfish to take back to the city to show off to their friends."

"Thank the Lord they *didn't* know what they was doin'. Jon boats meant for cruisin' up and down the little creeks and byways for turtle and cats and such. Catfish," Aunt Therese said hurriedly, seeing the expression on

Layla's face. "They're sure not meant for catchin' a fish weighin' upward a hundred pounds and swimmin' nearly fifteen knots. If they *had* managed to get out in open water and by some miracle snag them a sailfish, all them, and Otis's boat, too, would still be at the bottom of the sea."

"My Viktor, he finds them late in the night. Stuck to their knees in the mud on the far side of Daws Island, drained almost dry by the mosquitoes, crying like babies," Gerta said, slapping the table.

The two old women laughed uproariously.

"Jesus Christ," said Layla.

"Well, Christ and Viktor Williams," said Aunt Therese, sucking her teeth. "But sweet heaven, if he don't spend half his time savin' idiots from themselves."

Layla grinned, her earlier mood lightening inside the laughter of the two old friends.

"Where's Aunt Jayne?" she asked. "I saw the truck out front from my window."

"Child, that ol' thing doesn't run two days out of five," sniffed Aunt Therese, helping herself to a biscuit. "A friend picked her up for her aerobics class over to the senior center."

"Her . . . really?" Layla had a vision of her plump aunt, jumping around, arms flailing with a roomful of elderly men and women, house music pumping through loudspeakers. "That's . . ." She bit back a laugh.

"Yessir," said Aunt Therese. "Twice a week, she struts outta here in that shiny leotard thing and that pink headband to get her exercise on."

"Therese, do not tell these stories of your sister," said Gerta, giggling.

"Well, am I lyin'?" She batted her eyes mischievously and took another bite of her biscuit. "Actually, I *am* lyin' . . . about the leotard. She got one, but only wore it once. Said it made her look like one a those balloon animals you see at the carnival."

Layla inhaled coffee into her lungs.

The old woman pointed a finger at her sputtering niece. "But she does wear that stupid headband."

Gerta rolled her eyes and waved a tiny hand at her friend to shush her. "So, you met Charlotte yesterday, yes?" she asked, tone light. "How did you find her?"

Layla stiffened, her mood deflating. She slid low in her chair, not answering, pulling at her tangled hair.

He walked to the water's edge and put the gun in his mouth.

"Charlotte was just Charlotte," said Aunt Therese into the silence. "Cranky, rude, talkin' all mysterious. You know . . . Charlotte." She tried to laugh. "Layla, baby? What is it?" Aunt Therese frowned, leaning close. "Layla?"

"Did anyone ever shoot themselves out on Scotia Island? Right around the time Mom would have left for college?"

Her aunt reared back, upsetting a coffee cup, the muscles in her jaw working. "Why you ask that for?" Her voice was choked.

Layla opened her mouth, closed it again, the two of them silent as coffee crept across the table. Gerta looked from her friend to Layla and back again, her face pinched in confusion. The sound of a chainsaw drifted through the open kitchen door.

Aunt Therese leaped to her feet. Grabbing a dish towel, she began frantically sopping at the spill.

"You know what?" she said. "I got some a that key lime pie left over from last Sunday. It'll be just the thing with this coffee."

"Therese . . . ?" began Gerta.

"I'm an old woman, Gerta," Aunt Therese snapped, interrupting her. "If I can't have pie for breakfast now just 'cause I want to, then life ain't worth livin'."

She bustled about the kitchen, clearing the biscuits and sausage from the table, her movements jerky, frenetic. Yanking the pie from the refrigerator, she slammed it onto the table, then stood breathing hard, clenching and unclenching her fists.

"Why you ask that for?" she asked again, eyes guarded. "About someone shootin' themselves out there?"

Before Layla could respond, she went on.

"There was a boy. Silas. Silas Brown. Related way, way back. Like everybody. Remember 'cause it was so terrible. Killin' yourself is a sin before God and ain't nobody ever in memory done such. Either before or after."

Tension oozed around them, seeming to slow time.

"I was already off island. Not long married." Aunt Therese stared through the open back door. "Came back for the funeral. Only a few days before Elinor left for school. Bad, bad time."

"Do they know what happened?" asked Layla, her voice barely above a whisper. "Why he . . . killed himself?"

"Didn't make no sense. Silas was a little bit of a scoundrel. Not a bad fella overall, but terrible full of himself, and way too handsy with the girls for his own good. His momma found him on the beach. He had . . ."

Aunt Therese closed her eyes, shuddering.

"Funny thing is. I don't hardly remember your momma or Charlotte at the funeral. I remember packing up her things a few days later. Remember her and Charlotte actin' funny. Standoffish. Never saw them like that with each other. Figured they just couldn't figure out their goodbye. Especially with everybody so upset over Silas and everything."

She stood, silent, lost in the memory.

"Folks started talkin' about dreams again. Terrible dreams. Didn't last long, but it got the old folks recollectin' 'bout the olden days. About the dreams from Grandaddy Flynn's time."

She turned to face Layla. "I still don't see . . ."

The two locked eyes, aunt and niece, and Layla watched as slowly, something like understanding began to form in Aunt Therese's eyes.

"Sweet Jesus," breathed the older woman.

17

GEMMA

Bekka was gone.

Bekka, her man, and her babies had simply vanished from Ainsli Green.

Gemma searched everywhere on Scotia. Everywhere in her dreams. Her friend was gone.

Day by day, it grew harder for Gemma to distinguish between what belonged to the waking world, and what belonged to dreams. She knew well that if the braid binding night to day twisted too tight—if she found herself lost—then she needed to look for clues: a horse on an island where none existed, birds that made no sound as they flew through the sky, a long-dead ancestor seen working the fields. And always there was the bracelet, the talisman gifted from the ancestors to lead the way back, the pale white shells, their heart shapes tinged in lavender.

But Gemma was seeing signs everywhere now: as she kneaded dough for the biscuits, as she hung the linens to air.

Voices in the shadows.

Hoofprints in the mud.

"Am I dreaming now? Am I dreaming? Am I dreaming?" She whispered this refrain all through the day, rubbing at the skin of her wrist to assure herself that the bracelet was not there, that she was awake, rubbing until she bled. Her lips moved constantly, mouthing the question over and over, oblivious to the fact that the few slaves still remaining on Scotia Island now drew back at her approach. But this time—this night—when she finally stumbled over Bekka, she knew it was a dream. Bekka's dream of Scotia.

"Bekka?"

Her friend stood framed in the door to the wash shed, her hair floating like dark silk, free around her face. She was grinning the gap-toothed smile that

Gemma had known from the time they were bitty girls tromping through the rice fields together.

"Bekka?" she said again.

Bekka stepped into the shed. "I gots to go, ooman. Freedom callin'."

"Don't." Gemma tried to move toward her, but her dress was heavy as iron, her feet stuck fast to the dirt floor. "Stay here. You be free by and by. When the buckra stop they fightin', you be free."

In the tiny space, Bekka's laugh sounded like glass chimes. "Don't want that kind of free. Want my babies to know they letters and they numbers. Want them to do more than muck in the mud for someone else's rice and pull fish out the sea for they supper."

"Ain't nothin' wrong with fish for supper," Gemma said. She tried to smile.

"Co'se not," said Bekka. She laughed again. "Love me some fish."

"Out there, that they war. Yankee, 'Federate, don't mean nothin' to us." Gemma was pleading. "Old man die and they forget about us out here on this tiny ol' place. That make us free."

Bekka shook her head, her expression suddenly sad. "Or they don't. We be sittin' here waitin'. End up trapped like crabs in a barrel. No place to hide. No place to run. Just a different kinda slave. Hear tell they's already places nigras be free. Negro teachers, doctors even." Bekka waved her arm behind her. "'Magine that? Negro doctors! Just like the buckras!"

"Don't go, Bekka," whispered Gemma. "Please, don't go."

Her friend came and wrapped her thin arms around Gemma's waist. She pressed her cheek against Gemma's breastbone, as if listening to her heartbeat.

They stood, holding on to each other in silence, the soapy humidity of the wash house settling onto their skin, until Bekka straightened and took a half step back. She reached up to Gemma's face, a small hand on either side, and pressed hard.

"You listen, ooman. This place, this island, it a boil in your spirit. And what you do with a boil, eh? You lets out the poison so's it can heal up proper. Come with me, Gemma. Leave this place be, so's your spirit can heal up. You stay here you be lost forever. You stay here, you die!"

Gemma looked past her friend. Through the open wash shed door she could see a patch of bright blue sky, a stand of pine trees.

I could do, she thought. Take my girls and leave this cussed place. And for a moment, she saw all those things she'd seen in the dreams of others—the dreams of her old mistress, the other buckras who came to Ainsli Green from off island: cities lit up with so many gaslights that night was like day, carriages drawn by *horses the color of midnight, Negro ladies wearing wide petticoats of stiff lace, just like the white ladies. She could see them now, those colored ladies, twirling in the shadows, just beyond the loblollies.*

But . . . she'd caught glimpses of other things in the dreams of those visiting buckras, too, back when the colonel still entertained other planters and business-men at Ainsli Green. She'd seen horrors in the nightmares of the black oystermen that plied the sound. There were other things out there beyond the water, things besides the magic lights and pretty dresses. There were monsters. Monsters that wore the faces of men.

Stay, she wanted to say again to Bekka. It ain't safe out there.

Scotia Island was almost hers. Time. She just needed a little more time. The next dream . . . or maybe the next one after that, and the colonel would sign the deed papers. She knew it. And here, on the island, her island, she could protect them all. Would protect them all, because she had the power to walk in dreams. But Bekka was already moving away, floating as if made of feathers toward the door, and the sunlight, and the freedom she thought waited for her across the water.

"Don't you go forgettin' 'bout me," Bekka called.

It was hard to see her. The white gown she wore blended into the glare of the sun. Gemma tried to keep her eyes on her friend, strained to memorize every line on Bekka's face, the slant of her eyes, the way her ears sat on her head, but the light overwhelmed her.

"Bekka," she cried out, covering her face. Slowly, the light faded, and when she dropped her hands, Bekka was gone and she was alone in a dark, empty place.

"Mama, come quick. Somethin' wrong wit' Marigold."

Gemma blinked. She was standing at the wash line, a damp sheet bunched in her arms, her middle daughter staring at her with frightened eyes. When had she started hanging the wash? She frowned at the wet bundle in her arms. She was hanging wash in the dead of night.

And Marigold?

Jessamine said something was wrong with Marigold? She tried to make sense of the words. In the days since Bekka had disappeared from the island, things seemed to come to Gemma through a fog. She rarely slept more than a few hours, and those hours were most often filled with shadow and threat. She'd tried pushing herself toward the colonel. She was out of time. The old fool was trying to die on her, but she couldn't focus, kept getting lost in gray nothingness.

"Mama, you hear me? I say Marigold sick."

Gemma inhaled sharply. "What you mean, Marigold sick? Saw her at breakfast. She alright then."

"No, Mama." Jessamine shook her head, frowning. "She wasn't. Been poorly for days. Remember? I been tellin' you. Now she can't get up. Burnin' up fever."

Gemma stared at her daughter. Just a few hours before, she'd pulled a sweet potato from the ash and shared it with Marigold. Jessamine and Lavender had been propped against the cabin wall, waiting their turn. Her girls, always such good girls, always minding so well.

No, that was wrong. She pinched herself hard in the armpit. She was remembering something from a long time ago. This morning . . .

She couldn't remember this morning. She squinted up at the sky and fingered the cross around her neck. What time of day was it now?

"Mama!" Jessamine's voice was sharp.

Gemma flung the sheet carelessly over the line and followed her daughter. The slave quarter was nearly deserted. There were fewer than two dozen slaves left on the island now, and those that remained were either too frail to leave or had abandoned Ainsli Green's schedule in favor of their own. A handful of sturdy cabins had sprung up on the other side of the island, away from the fields, in a shallow depression protected from the summer storms.

Inside the dark cabin, Marigold was a vague, shadowy lump against the far wall. Lavender looked up when her mother and sister walked in, her eyes huge in her slender face.

"She burnin' up," she said, echoing Jessamine's words. She dipped a rag in the bowl of water at her feet and dabbed at Marigold's face. Jessamine held back as her mother squatted next to Lavender and touched Marigold's cheek. Gemma hissed, resisting the instinct to yank her hand away. Touching her daughter's skin was like touching an open flame. Marigold was, indeed, on fire.

"Marigold?"

The only answer was a low moan. The girl shook so that her teeth rattled, and the sound was loud in the little hut. Her round cheeks had sunken in, the skin eerily shiny and clinging tight to the bones of her face.

Jessamine had said days. Could it be that her child had truly lain sick for so long? And yet, Marigold's drawn features and ragged breathing bore testimony to Jessamine's words. Gemma choked back a sob.

"Marigold," she said again. "You look at me, gal, when I talkin' to you."

Marigold struggled to open her eyes and Gemma forced herself to smile.

"You gon' get better. You hear me? You not so growed you gets to do whatever all you please in my house. I'm a fix you somethin' and you gon' be alright."

Marigold's eyes fluttered closed, but she managed a weak nod. Gemma pointed at Jessamine, who stood hovering in the doorway.

"Bring them coals inside a here. Make it hot as you can without burning us down. Lavender, you keep her wrapped tight and her head raised up. I be back directly."

She was at the cook house and back in minutes. She scooped hot water from the cook pot outside their hut and broke sticks of cinnamon into it, followed by willow bark and a spoonful of honey. Back inside the hut, she once again dropped down beside Marigold and rested the shivering girl's head on her lap. Marigold's skin was clammy, the sour smell of sickness oozing from her pores.

"Here now." She placed the steaming liquid to her daughter's lips. "You drink this."

Marigold took a small sip and began to cough.

"Unh-unh, li'l girl. We gon' take our time and you gon' get this down. Every drop. Got to kill off this sickness."

Time stretched wide then fell back in on itself, and in the stifling heat of the cabin, Gemma was only vaguely aware of the comings and goings of her other two daughters: Lavender freshening the water and bathing her sister's forehead and lips, Jessamine stoking the coals to force the fever. As her oldest daughter sweated and moaned, Gemma held on tight.

At some point, many hours later, as she felt herself begin to drift toward sleep, she felt the ripple of Marigold's fever dream and tried to seize hold. When they'd been sick as little girls, it's what she would do: slip into the currents of their uneasy dreams, soothing them with visions of the magical spirits that lived in the forest and bright angels that could spin sugared treats out of thin air. She fought off the demons that sickness brought with her sharpest knife and the mistress's iron fry pan.

For a moment, she had it. She was standing atop a tall hill. And there was her Marigold in a pretty dress, dove-gray satin with sky-blue stripes, just like the old mistress used to wear. Her daughter was standing in a boat that had grounded itself on a sandbar. She was only a short way off the beach, yet she seemed so very far away. And she was crying.

And then she was gone.

Gemma felt herself rolling downhill, rolling, rolling—no sound, no light—just rolling. She began to scream, terrified that it would be like this forever—her daughters, Ainsli Green, everything, lost—as she tumbled toward nothing in the darkness.

18

"So? What happened down there?"

Layla's back was turned to the room, but she could see her brother clearly reflected in the French doors of the balcony. A steady stream of headlights lit the parkway below, twinkling like stars in the dusk.

They hadn't yet spoken about her trip to Port Royal. Will had been waiting at the airport and she'd thrown herself in his arms, overcome by too many emotions to name. It wasn't until she'd stepped back from him that she noticed how drawn, how tired he looked, though it had barely been a week.

"Crazy trip?" he asked, surprised by the uncharacteristic display. "You okay?"

"Fine." Will shrugged. "Tired. Show's kickin' my butt."

They'd driven, mostly in silence, back to Will's condo, though Layla could sense the puzzled looks he shot her when he thought she wasn't looking, the questions he was anxious to ask.

Now, after dinner, he stood watching her, wineglass in hand.

"Layla?"

She turned just as Chuck came back into the living room.

"Baby's down," he said, sprawling on the couch. Will nodded, his eyes never leaving his sister.

"What happened?" he asked again.

"It was kind of like family curse meets Lifetime movie," she said. She tried to laugh, but it sounded false, even to her. Will raised an eyebrow as he sat on the couch next to Chuck.

She inhaled. The savory aroma of the evening's curry dinner still wafted in the air. Raking a hand through her hair, she let her eyes drift over the muted abstract painting mounted above the fireplace. She didn't want to talk about Port Royal. More specifically, she didn't want to talk about Scotia Island.

She closed her eyes, saw the man emerge from the woods and walk to the water's edge in the moonlight. Saw him raise his gun. Bile rose in her throat.

"Lay?"

Layla opened her eyes to find both men staring at her with concern.

She laughed again, the sound coming out as a hiccupping sob. Chuck, wide-eyed, made as if to rise from the couch, but she waved him off.

"Granny Bliss wasn't just a twin," she said. "She was a conjoined twin."

"Wait, what?" said Will, his eyes widening. "I never heard that before."

Yes, she could tell this story. This story was safe.

So she told them the story the Aunts had told her: about the trip across the water to the white doctor, about their great-grandfather taking Granny Bliss and Great-Aunt Mercy home to die, about the strange dreams of the naked woman and the ravens that had haunted the dreams of the people of Scotia Island.

She forced herself to keep her voice light, amused, as if to say she could hardly believe it herself. And, sitting in her brother's airy apartment, the smell of dinner all around them, she could almost convince herself it was all just a weird family anecdote. Amusing. Benign.

"They each had a scar, right here." She pointed to the center of her breastbone. "For the rest of their lives."

"Jesus Christ," said Chuck when she was done. "It all sounds so Southern Gothic."

"That is . . ." Will shook his head. "That is just wild, man!"

She smiled. "You know that scar on Mom's forehead? She got it trying to fly."

"What?" The men said the word in unison. They both leaned forward as she told them about her mother's leap from the roof, about her drinking in the woods with Buddha.

"Well, damn!" said her brother when she was done. "Flying? Drinking with Cousin Buddha? There can only be one logical explanation."

"And what's that?"

"Crazy Elinor was abducted by aliens in college and replaced with Type A Elinor."

The three burst into laughter, trying to muffle the sound so as not to wake the baby.

"And what about the mysterious cousin?" asked her brother.

"I met her," said Layla after a long moment.

"And . . . ?" asked Chuck.

"And nothing," murmured Layla, hunching her shoulders. "She basically . . . She fed us, then kicked us off the island."

"Kicked . . . ?" Will sat back on the couch, frowning. "What do you mean kicked you off the island. She can't kick you off the island. Half of it is yours."

"Well, not 'kicked off' exactly. But she was . . . not happy to make my acquaintance. Apparently, she and Mom had . . . issues."

Will chuckled and sipped his wine. "Well, you two have that in common at least."

"Yeah." She gave a hollow laugh. "We really bonded."

"Have you decided what you're going to do about the island?" asked Chuck.

She looked at her brother and brother-in-law and sighed. "I have no idea. And right now, I can't even think about it."

She suppressed a yawn.

"You can stay here tonight," offered her brother.

"No. I'm going to go on home. I just need to sleep in my own bed, I think." She smiled. "But I will take some of that curry with."

Chuck laid a hand on Will's shoulder. "You've got an early call in the morning. Why don't you go check on the baby then crash. I'll get her home."

In the car, Chuck turned to study her. "Did something happen, down there, Layla?"

"No, nothing." Layla stared through the windshield, not meeting her brother-in-law's eyes. "It was fine."

"Was it?"

She locked eyes with him. "It was fine!"

He held her gaze a long moment, clearly wanting to say more, then sighing, put the key in the ignition. But he didn't turn it. Instead, he sat staring at the steering wheel.

"Chuck?"

He looked up. "We're glad you're home, Layla."

His expression sent a jolt of alarm through her. "What is it? What's wrong?"

"It's just Will . . . He's not sleeping." His blue eyes were wide with worry. "He tosses and turns. Cries out in his sleep. He's exhausted and he looks terrible. I swear, I'm thinking about divorcing him."

He tried to laugh, but the sound stalled. "He says he's having these terrible nightmares but then says he can't remember anything about them. It seems . . ."

He sat for a long moment, gazing off into space. Finally, he shook himself and started the car. "Oh, honey, listen to me. I sound just like my bubbeh. Forget I said anything. I'm sure between Elinor's death and the shoot and everything, he's just a mess. Right? He'll be fine. Who doesn't have trouble sleeping every now and then?"

As they pulled from the parking garage and out into the street, Layla felt a chill. Will doesn't, she thought.

One night. Two. Then three. She wasn't sleeping either.

She hunched over her drawing table, a sketch of a pecan tree, the ruins of Ainsli Green behind it, spread out before her. It was well past midnight. She was wearing an oversized yellow caftan with black-winged pigs—the same thing she'd been wearing for the past two days.

She was supposed to be sketching knees, arthritic knees. She had a looming deadline. But it was the ruins of Ainsli Green that she drew again and again. Always with the silhouette of a man standing in the shadows. But the sketch never felt quite right. Something was always off. It was too light or too dark or just . . . off.

For the past three nights she'd awakened in the darkest hours, the flotsam and jetsam of dreams—or nightmares, she wasn't sure—playing in her head: a long, dark hallway cluttered with furniture, sketches—her sketches—fluttering like snow from a moonlit sky, her mother, standing in the dark, wearing a white blouse and white skirt.

Fragments.

Pieces of dreams that didn't fit together.

She'd wake, sharp-edged slivers of images in her brain, then get up to sketch Ainsli Green. She was taking her pills, but she couldn't decide if they were making things better, or worse.

"A Dreamwalker," she whispered. "I am a Dreamwalker."

Except, now that she finally knew what she was, what she could do, she couldn't sleep. Layla snorted.

Sleep.

She put her head down on the pile of sketches.

She just needed to sleep.

———

She heard the water before she saw it, the soft shush as the ripples kissed the sand. The moon was full, and it lit a silver pathway on the black water all the way to the Atlantic. A chorus of cicada song undulated from the woods behind her.

Scotia Island.

She stood staring out to sea, breathing in the cool, salt-heavy air.

"Wuffuh you come here?"

The voice came from behind her.

Layla flinched but did not turn around. "I don't know," she said quietly.

"You think you surprise me?"

"No," said Layla.

"Humph," said Charlotte, coming to stand beside her. "Your momma was a liar."

Her tone was almost pleasant. Layla said nothing.

"Powerful Dreamwalker, me. But dreams only reach so far," said Charlotte. "You know that?"

Layla made a noise and turned to find Charlotte watching her. She was at least two inches shorter than Layla, and she was dressed as if going to a party. Her pale blue head scarf perfectly matched the pale blue of her dress, the crystal buttons on the cuffs gleaming in the moonlight.

"No?" Charlotte cackled. "No. That's right. You don't know nuthin'. 'Cause your momma had secrets. So many secrets."

"So . . . ?" asked Layla.

"Your momma went away. I searched and searched. Found traces in Jayne's and Therese's dreams. But . . ." Charlotte sighed and turned back to stare at the water.

"You know Elinor invite me to her wedding? All swonguh. Portun. Play like she barely know me." She spit onto the sand. "But me one know her. Yes. Like she thowed way her old life and get new one easy."

She was silent for a long moment, the muscles working in her jaw.

"Then you got born. Could see her clear for a spell. Couldn't figure what you was though," she said finally. She touched the bracelet that glowed at Layla's wrist, identical to the one on her own. The two women studied each other, the gentle murmuring of the water the only sound.

"Are you walking my brother's dreams?" asked Layla.

Charlotte snorted.

"Dem come. Wantuh tek we island." She waved her arm, indicating all of Scotia. "First sweet mout' then dem say taxes. Dem say tourists. Conservation."

She spit again.

"Comeyahs. You."

The full moon had been replaced by a rising sun. One raven, then another landed on the beach and Layla backed away.

"Are you walking my brother?" she asked again.

"Oonah never tek this island," snapped Charlotte.

"I don't want it."

Charlotte reared back, her mouth open in surprise.

"I don't want it," Layla repeated. "I don't want this. I don't want any of this. Just leave us alone."

Charlotte crossed her arms, frowning. "Then wuffuh you comeyah?"

"I wanted . . ." Layla shook her head. "I didn't know about . . . this."

She swept out an arm, taking in the beach, the bluff, the sea. Taking in Charlotte. "My mother never . . ." She shook her head again. "I didn't know. I thought if I came, I could understand. Me. Her."

"Elinor?"

Layla nodded.

Charlotte laughed. "Ain't no understandin' waitin' here, girl."

She stared, eyes narrowed, and Layla thought she saw a flash of pity. Then without another word, Charlotte nodded and walked away. An unkindness of ravens wheeled overhead.

19

Layla hunched over her worktable, the sun streaming through the living room window falling on the sketch of the nose and sinuses. It had been nearly a month since her return from South Carolina, and she'd fallen into a sort of languorous routine.

The nights had become uneventful, the rare dreams benign. She talked to the Aunts every few days, worked on her sketches, cleaned up her apartment, went running. Twice, she'd met Will—who was sleeping better—at her mother's to continue boxing up things. She had even, almost, managed to convince herself that her mother and Charlotte had not caused a man's death.

The knock at the door startled her. Glancing at her watch, she was surprised to find that it was already late morning. She was wearing her flying pig caftan, her hair bunched on top of her head and held with a chip clip.

"Evan!"

Her brother stood beaming on the other side of the door, an overnight bag at his feet, an expensive-looking calfskin portfolio tucked under one arm.

"What are you doing here?" she cried, dragging him into the apartment.

"I have a meeting in Philly later tonight and arranged to have a long layover here to check in on you." He raised one eyebrow, appraising her. "You look . . ."

"Fabulous?" She yanked the clip from her hair and jammed it in a pocket with one hand, clearing papers from the couch with the other. "You want coffee? Did you see Will?"

"Yes, and no, not this time. Couldn't make it work. I can only stay for a hot minute," he said accepting a cup from her. "Talked to him this morning though."

Layla dropped into the chair across from him. She gripped her cup, barely able to contain her joy at seeing her older brother.

"So," said Evan, sipping his coffee. "That sounded like some trip you had down in Port Royal."

"It was . . ." Layla squinted, searching for the right word. "Informative."

"Will told me about Mom. Her jumping off the roof." He was laughing. "Oh my god!"

"That and the drinking and the driving." She shrugged, grinning. "I mean . . . right?"

"Oh." Evan put his cup down and pulled a file from the portfolio. "Remember before you headed down there, I said I had a guy?"

"Yes?" Layla answered slowly.

"Well, I had him do a little digging. He did a title search and looked into some of the deed restrictions. It's really fascinating."

"Evan," she said, a sense of unease rippling through her.

"He hasn't had time to do a full valuation of the property yet. We're working on getting a full survey done. Hopefully in the next week or so."

"Evan," she said more loudly, her alarm growing.

"Oh," he said. "Did you and, what's her name? Charlotte? Go over some of this already?"

Layla laughed out loud. "Uh, no! We didn't really have much conversation."

Her brother sat quietly for a long moment, studying her. "You know, sweetie. Whatever you decide about that island is fine. The decision is yours. It's an amazing piece of property. A piece of history that's been in our family more than a century and a half."

He ran a finger around the rim of his cup, absently staring off into space.

"Properties like that're getting bought up or simply seized all up and down the coast. Outsiders coming in and taking it."

Dem come. Wantuh tek we island.

"It just makes sense to have all the i's dotted and t's crossed, whatever you decide, right?"

She nodded, pushing away the growing nervousness. Yes, of course, that made perfect sense.

Layla thumbed slowly through the papers Evan had left. For hours she'd been sitting on the floor beneath the living room window, reading and rereading the title papers. There was her mother's maiden name: Elinor Louise Palmer, near the top of one page. On the bottom of another page was her own name, Layla Grace Hurley, and the date her mother had signed her share of Scotia Island over to her.

There was Granny Bliss's signature bequeathing her share to Elinor. Gracious bequeathing her share to her twins Bliss and Mercy. As the years led further into the past, the pages faded, copies of copies of copies, the signatures harder to read. But it was the last document that riveted her. It was a photocopy, the ink faded and barely legible. She held it up to the light.

> *January 1, 1862*
> *Colonel Rupert K. Everleigh of Charleston, S.C., and Scotia Island, S.C., transfers the 842 acres of Scotia Island, all buildings and the contents therein, to Gemma, a colored woman, and her descendants into perpetuity.*

Layla stared at this page for a long time, emotions raising goose bumps on her arms.

Gemma. A colored woman.

Her distant ancestor. A distant dreamwalking ancestor.

Year after year. Decade after decade, this island had belonged to her family. She felt a rush of pride, a sense of belonging to something big. Something important.

She closed her eyes and saw herself walking the sandy bluffs, sea birds wheeling overhead, watching the sky turn scarlet as the sun dropped below the horizon. She pushed the thought of Charlotte from her mind. Charlotte did not belong in this vision.

Evan was right. They needed to make sure all the i's were dotted and t's crossed.

Comeyah.

She heard Charlotte's voice in her head. Heard the snarl. And Layla squared her shoulders. Charlotte could call her whatever she liked. Layla belonged to Scotia.

20

GEMMA

She woke from a fitful sleep, bathed in sweat. Jessamine's fire had burned to charcoal, and the tiny cabin was an oven.

Gemma pushed herself up and bent over her daughter. Marigold's eyes were closed. She seemed to be sleeping, but her breathing came in short, rapid bursts accompanied by an alarming rattling sound from somewhere deep in her chest. Even in the darkness, Gemma could tell her daughter's color was wrong. She blotted the girl's face with a damp cloth, wetting her lips, brushing the matted hair from Marigold's clammy forehead.

"Wake up, child," she whispered. "You wake up right now, hear?"

The only response was a gurgling in Marigold's throat as her breathing caught, stopped, then restarted. Gemma ground her teeth and looked around. Lavender sat slumped near the door, her head on her chest, snoring lightly. Jessamine was nowhere to be seen. With a last glance at her sleeping daughters, Gemma stepped from the sweltering cabin.

It was just past middle night. A buttermilk-hued moon hung in the sky like a tiny fingernail, the sound of cicadas rising and falling like music, wrapping her in a vibrating cocoon of insect chatter. She inhaled deeply, and the air blowing in from the sea cooled her lungs.

Mine, she thought. All this here be mine.

As she walked toward the manor house, she kept an eye out for Jessamine. Her middle daughter had never liked the night. It was not like her to wander the dark.

At the threshold to the house, she hesitated, a chill spiraling down her spine.

In normal times she could be thrashed for this. For coming to the big house uninvited. For walking through the front door. But these were not normal times. Still, rubbing at the raw place on her wrist, she felt a shiver of dread as she grasped the door handle.

She pushed the door open and stepped into the foyer, wincing as the hinges squealed in protest. The house smelled stale, like dust and mildew. With no one to beat the carpets and sweep the floors, with no slaves left to latch the windows against the elements or to sop up the damp that was inevitable on an island, the house was beginning to disintegrate—slowly, steadily, from the outside in.

Ainsli Green felt deserted. But it was not. Somewhere deep in the house, a few slaves hung on, more out of habit than loyalty: Cora the cook; the groomsman, David; Aron. A few others. And her master. He was still up there, locked away in his room, still alive . . . just.

She lit a lamp and began to move through the silent house. It felt dangerous, and a bit thrilling, to roam the empty rooms at will. In the music room, the piano the mistress had loved so stood exposed in front of a half-open window, the view to the sea obscured by darkness, candle wax melted onto the polished maple wood. A crystal punch bowl lay shattered on the dining room floor near the fireplace, shards of glass twinkling like stars in the lamplight. A dozen delicate teacups were lined up on top of the lace tablecloth in the center of the table, as though in preparation for guests.

Gemma made her way into the colonel's study. In all her years, she'd rarely entered this room. It smelled of him: old paper, expensive cigars, and the clove cologne he always wore.

Setting the lamp down, she ran her hands over the wall of books beside the tall windows. All those black squiggles on white paper. How could there be so many words in the whole world? What did the buckras say to each other in all those books?

She knew how to make her own mark. Mistress Lucy had given her lessons along with the tarts.

Gemma: A half-moon with a tongue, three fingers one atop the other, two mountains and a pair of upside-down wings. Those marks were her name.

GEMMA.

She could make her name on paper, and soon she would put it on the paper that would make Scotia Island hers. It was the only thing the buckras respected, stronger than a promise, stronger than their own word, the one thing they would honor.

She picked up the lamp and walked back out into the hallway, closing the study door behind her out of habit. She found herself at the foot of the wide staircase that led upstairs. Hand on the railing, she hesitated. He was up there, alone, trying to die. Something moved in the shadows of the parlor, and she whirled, jerking the lamp high.

"Who be there?" she cried out. But there was no answer.

"Fool da," she muttered, her voice shaking. "House be nekkid."

Lamp held high, she backed away from the stairs until the back of her legs touched the hard, straight-backed bench reserved for guests, though there'd been no guests at Ainsli Green in a very long time. She sat.

"Not dreamin' now. Not yet."

The shadows twisted and sighed around her, and she gripped the lamp with both hands, closing her eyes against them.

"Not dreamin' yet."

"You want your mama."

Gemma started. The fire in her lamp had gone out, the oil burnt to nothing. Light leaked through the wide windows on either side of the front door. She set the empty lamp on the floor at her feet.

Rupert Everleigh stood halfway up the stairs in a burgundy dressing gown, tied at the waist with a gold belt. Beneath it, his gray wool trousers were neatly pressed but stained. And he was barefoot, his toenails long and yellowed.

"What that you say?" she asked.

The old man scratched his head and flakes of dry skin swirled in the light. "I said, you want your mama. You lookin' for Tuesday."

She stared, both fascinated and repulsed at the sight of bits of the colonel drifting delicately in the dawn light.

Rupert Everleigh gave his head another good scratch then limped down the stairs. He plopped onto the bottom step and crossed his legs, his bare feet bright in the dim light, squinting at her as he played with the tasseled end of his belt.

"'Cause I been lookin' and lookin'," he said. "Searched every which a way and just can't seem to find her."

"No," said Gemma quietly. "Ain't seen my mama."

Rupert Everleigh was watching her.

"Why you need my mama for?"

The old man glared at her. "I need her. You get her in here," he commanded. "You hear me? Right now."

And then he was behind her. They were at the beach, the island at their back, the sun rising like a fresh orange out of the deep, blue water.

She could smell him. His old buckra smell: tobacco and sweat and dirty hair.

"Don't you want to know?" he whispered. His tongue flicked her earlobe and she jerked.

"Gafa," she snarled. "Go way! You binnuh dead and not even know it!"

She turned and the sand shifted under her feet, throwing her off balance in the cold water. He was propped against a piece of driftwood on the rocky beach, watching her. She waded from the surf, her thin dress slowing her, weighing her down. She stumbled onto the sand and stopped, glaring at him.

"Don't you want to know?" he asked again.

"Know what, gafa?"

"She bewitched me. Tuesday. Wasn't natural. Knew that, but couldn't help myself. You know why it is you're so obsessed with Scotia Island? Why you can't leave with the other coloreds and go hunt for your false freedom?"

She clenched her hands at her sides and said nothing.

The old man began to laugh, a high-pitched, phlegmy sound that dissolved into a wheeze. He clutched his chest, slumping to the ground, panting for breath. She watched him through narrowed eyes.

"You infected. You got Ainsli Green and this whole cursed island in your blood. It's a disease. Ain't no cure. Once it gets inside, it eats you alive. Why you think I came out here to die with nothin' but niggers and rice around me?" He pointed a bony finger at her, his arm trembling with the effort. "You got the sickness."

The old man was watching her, his gaunt face blazing with the light of pure malice.

She felt herself growing cold, as if she was dying inch by inch, and when the ice reached her heart, she began to laugh. And then, her hands were around his throat, her nose against his face. She breathed in deep, smelled the fear and rage leaching off his skin, and she laughed again.

"You gon' sign that paper, Colonel. Know why?"

She loosened her grip just enough to lean back and look into his eyes. He blinked slowly but said nothing.

"'Cause you don't, I ain't gon' let you ever die. It be you and me for always and always on this island. Just you and me . . . Father!"

21

Layla turned onto Kalorama Road and let out a squeal of excitement. Finding parking near her brother's condo was always a challenge, and there, like a miracle, was someone pulling out at the end of the block.

She'd texted Chuck and Will the night before that she wanted to come to dinner. She'd sweetened the pot by offering to stop at the Florida Avenue Grill and pick up three orders of smothered porkchops. Chuck had responded yes almost as soon as she'd hit send. Will had still not responded, which was unusual, but she assumed he was a yes as well. He never could resist a soul food dinner, especially from the famed Florida Avenue Grill.

Layla'd been in a state of near euphoria since Evan had dropped off the documents about Scotia Island. She'd spent hours poring over them and nearly as much time doing Google searches on the Gullah islands and the history surrounding them. She was excited to share her findings with her brother and his husband. She had gone to South Carolina looking for answers about her mother and returned with more questions. Yet since returning home, she'd felt an inexorable pull back that seemed to grow stronger the more she found out about her mother's birthplace.

She threw the file-laden backpack over her shoulder and grabbed the plastic restaurant bags, the rich smell of fried pork and thick onion gravy making her mouth water. She was grinning as she trotted up the stone stairs to the condo and rang the bell.

Will opened the door and her grin collapsed. The last time she'd spoken with him, he'd said he was sleeping better, that the show was going great. He'd said he had some days off coming up and was going to get some rest, maybe meet her at their mom's and do a little more packing up.

But the man standing in the door looked anything but rested. The pallor from weeks before had returned. His eyes were bloodshot and he hadn't shaved in days. Layla saw a few gray hairs in the stubble.

"Will?"

He stared at her vaguely, then blinked. "Hey, Lay!"

"I . . ." She frowned. "I brought dinner. What's wrong with you?"

He shook his head, tried to laugh. "Nothing. Sorry, I didn't get back to you." He stepped aside, letting her into the house. "Totally lost track of time."

"You look like—"

"Let me take that." He took the bags, then rushed away, busying himself in the kitchen. Chuck, standing by the dining table, caught her eye and shook his head ever so slightly.

At dinner, Layla tried to engage her brother, but he was irritable, giving curt, one-word answers. Initially, Chuck tried to cover, gushing enthusiastically over the porkchops, the collard greens. But finally, even he gave up, and the three of them ate in awkward silence.

"You're the best. Feel free to bring dinner by anytime," said Chuck. He stood and bent to kiss the top of Layla's head. "I'm going to go get some work done."

He gave them both a look before disappearing down the hall toward his office. Will sighed and dropped his face in his hands. She sat, silently staring at him until he looked up.

"What?"

"Really, Will?" She raised an eyebrow and cocked her head. The expression he always gave her when he suspected she was being less than forthcoming. "You look like shit."

He laughed, and for a moment, the fatigue seemed to drop away. "Well, that's sweet."

"Seriously, dude." She leaned forward in her seat. "I just talked to you a few days ago. You said things had slowed at work. That you were getting rest. But . . ."

She waved her hand in front of his face, taking in the beard stubble, the bloodshot eyes.

"I was. Until a few days ago. And then . . ." He picked a napkin off the table and began to slowly tear it into pieces.

"Will?"

"When you have those dreams—" He stopped. She waited, watching as the napkin turned, bit by bit, into confetti.

"Remember how you used to always say your dreams were real?" he said finally. He laughed, the sound hollow in the brightly lit condo. "I've been having these dreams about Scotia Island, about Charlotte. I mean, I'm sure it's only because we were talking so much about it, but . . ."

He scratched at his beard, sighing. "But, these aren't like any dreams I've ever had in my life. Everything was so . . . I don't know . . . vivid. I mean, I could smell the water, Lay."

"What did you dream?" Layla asked quietly, wary.

He shrugged. "So, I'm out there on that island. And there's this little house. It's got all these windows on this porch. And there were these . . ." He frowned. "Jars? I guess? With flowers in all the windows."

Layla went still, a chill snaking through her before settling painfully in the pit of her stomach. She had never described Charlotte's house to her brother.

Will seemed not to notice. He stood, went to the bar, and poured himself two fingers of scotch. "Chase was there. He was just crawling around in the grass. But something was wrong. I couldn't get to him. And she was there, Charlotte, just watching from the trees."

He shook his head and downed the scotch in one gulp. "It just felt wrong," he said.

"Did she say anything?"

"Yeah." He gave a dry laugh. "She said, 'Tell your sister she's a liar.'"

Layla tried to breathe, but the chill in her gut had turned into a solid thing, forcing the air from her lungs.

"But Lay." Will looked up from his glass. His eyes were glazed with fear. She watched him swallow, and swallow again. "This morning when I woke up, there was sand in Chase's crib."

Layla stood in her darkened apartment, the muted swoosh of traffic leaking through the living room window. She dropped the never opened backpack on the couch and slid down beside it, her fists clenched to control the tremors. Will had had one of *those* dreams. It was a warning. She was sure of it. Charlotte was sending a message. But why?

She thought they'd had an understanding, a sort of truce. She wasn't a threat to Scotia Island, or to Charlotte. If anything, after everything she'd learned, it felt as if they should be allies in protecting the island.

She needed to talk to her. To Charlotte. If Charlotte had something to say to her, then she needed to say it directly to her. She sat in the dark for a long time, thinking, before finally making her way into the bedroom and pulling a small duffle bag from under the bed. She'd brought back a few of her mother's things from the Aunts'. Flicking on the bedside table, she opened the bag and pulled out a handful of pictures, including one of the few photos of Charlotte alone. In it, she was sitting on the beach, eyes closed, legs outstretched in the surf. Aside from the pictures, there was a small hair comb with shiny plastic jewels, the kind a small girl might like, and a bracelet of colorful, braided yarn.

She spread everything on the bed, then turned out the light and stretched out next to the items. She lay there for a moment, eyes closed, then had a sudden thought. Retrieving the backpack from the living room, she pulled the papers out and gently placed the one with her mother and Charlotte's name on it under her pillow before lying down again.

She needed to communicate with Charlotte, but as she lay there, she realized she'd never tried to reach into a specific person's dreams before. Her dreams had always appeared random, seeming to choose her.

The ridiculousness of lying on top of personal items of her mother's and cousin's suddenly struck her.

"Should just get a Ouija board," she muttered, laughing softly. "Or sacrifice a goat."

She felt water on her face and looked up. The sun was just rising. Dew clung to the tips of leaves, sparkling like crystals. Beneath her feet, she felt the pressure of uneven cobblestones. All around her, narrow, overgrown walkways wound drunkenly between grave markers, mausoleums, and ancient crypts.

She knew this place.

Père Lachaise.

The last vacation her whole family had taken together had been a week in Paris. While her father and brothers had taken boat rides up and down the Seine and haunted the arrondissements for the best macarons, Layla and her mother had wandered the city's famed cemeteries.

Something flashed in the trees and Layla moved toward it. She found her mother kneeling in front of a small headstone, wearing what her father called her cemetery sweater, the thick, white cable-knit turtleneck she always wore on her trips.

There were other people in the cemetery, but they were off in the distance, their whispered conversations reaching her as a faint murmur. Her mother was using a charcoal stick to do a tracing of the headstone. Layla moved close and sat in a nearby mound of grass to watch. She could see that it was the grave of a young girl, Yvette Abadie, 1899–1914. Her mother looked up and smiled, then went back to her tracing.

Layla leaned back into the grass and closed her eyes. She could feel the sun playing on her face as it filtered through the leaves.

"Layla?"

Layla sat up. Her mother was watching her, a smile playing at the corners of her mouth. She held the tracing out.

Layla reached for it, then froze. It was not a rendering of the tombstone, not the dates or the small daffodil in the center of the headstone. Rather, it was a sketch of their family, roughly drawn but easily recognizable: Layla's parents, her brothers, herself. And in the background, the vague outline of several other figures.

Her mother was watching her, no longer smiling. She forced the sketch into Layla's hand.

"Family," she said.

22

SUMMER

South Carolina in late July was even hotter than South Carolina in early June, the air viscous, gel-like. The soft greens of late spring had given way to brilliant emeralds and over-lush jades, and the clouds hovered at the top of the trees, blinding in their whiteness. The whole world felt jarringly Technicolor, surreal. The first time she'd come to South Carolina looking for answers. Now she was back, looking for Charlotte.

Charlotte.

She'd tried night after night to find Charlotte in the world of dreams. But either she was too inexperienced, or her cousin didn't want to be found. Charlotte's dreams had proved elusive. For the first time in her life, Layla craved the dreams, yet her nights had gone dreamless, quiet, and the irony was not lost on her.

If she could not reach Charlotte in the night, then she would have to come to her in the day.

"So, you came back."

Layla inhaled sharply, turning at the unexpected voice.

Viktor Williams stood smiling at her just inside the baggage claim door, his hands thrust deep in his pockets.

"Yep," she said. "I came back."

"Good," he said as he took one of her bags. His smile widened. "I hoped you would."

Layla raised an eyebrow, surprised. "Really? Why?"

He had already started across the narrow walkway toward the parking lot. At the question, he stopped, turning to look at her. "Why?"

She nodded. "Yeah, why?"

"Well," he said, cocking his head, brow wrinkling. "Because you seemed a mysterious sort. And I do love a mystery."

He grinned and resumed walking. "'Sides, Oma seemed right taken with you."

She smiled, shifting her backpack between her shoulders, and followed him across the parking lot.

"How'd you get trapped into picking me up?" she asked, once the truck was located and they'd settled in.

"Your tantes' truck finally gave over," he said, giving her a crooked smile. "So, I volunteered."

They drove the same circuitous route that Aunt Jayne had driven the last time. As they roared along the curving back roads of Port Royal, she rested her head against the seat and inhaled the warm, sweet-smelling air rushing through the truck's open windows.

The Aunts' old truck was parked in its usual place under the sugarberry tree, the sun glinting off the rust scabs. An old tractor sat sideways near the porch, as if someone had been mowing the patchy lawn and been interrupted. The Aunts were nowhere to be seen as Viktor pulled up close to the porch. Layla stared at the house, not moving.

"I know you haven't been gone all that long, but they're thrilled you came back," he said.

She nodded. "They're kind of wonderful."

"They are," he agreed. He seemed to hesitate. "So, can I ask you a personal question?"

She tensed, then brought her shoulders up slightly, an intimation of a shrug.

"Your mom and the tantes weren't close?"

She said nothing.

"You know why?"

She exhaled slowly through pursed lips, then shook her head. "Not really. No."

Viktor sighed. "That's kinda sad, isn't it? Family is everything."

Family.

She fixed him with a look. "Is it?"

He blinked, surprised.

Pushing open the door of the truck, she climbed out, dragging her bags behind her. "Thanks for the ride."

She turned and walked toward the house.

23

From the Aunts' wide porch, Layla watched the warm day leach away, the sky changing from an impossible shade of plum, deepening to navy at the edges. Beyond the trees, the low hum of the cicadas notched into a higher register. An ice-filled glass appeared on the porch step next to her. She turned to find Aunt Therese offering a bottle of Canadian Club and shook her head no.

"Suit yourself." Aunt Therese groaned as she settled herself on the porch next to her niece. She took a deep drink from her own glass and sighed. "But it's just the thing for nights like this."

Layla stared into the darkening yard. It was becoming hard to see anything except shadows moving against darker shadows. "It's not the nights I worry about, Aunt Therese. It's those horrible mornings after."

"Well, I guess that's right." Her aunt chuckled. "Those can be a bear. That's why you got to ease into drinkin'. Train."

"Train?" Layla smiled. "To get drunk?"

"Train to not get drunk," said Aunt Therese. "Drinkin' ain't no different from anything else. Like dancin' for example. Drinkin' right's all about rhythm and pace, buildin' up a tolerance. Not doin' too much all at . . . what?"

She stopped midsentence.

"Seriously?" Layla was staring at her, incredulous.

Her aunt took another slow sip from her drink and cocked her head. "Seriously."

Layla laughed.

They sat watching the sky darken, flickers of light tracing the path of fireflies.

"Aunt Therese," said Layla, breaking the silence. "You got that paperwork I sent? About the title?"

Her aunt nodded. "Gave me a funny feeling," she said, patting her chest softly. "Seeing Momma's name. Grandma Grace's. That old paper from when the land first got deeded to our family."

"Did Charlotte see it?"

"We had Damien, one of the neighbors, carry it out there. He got people out on Scotia still too. Goes out regular."

"And?"

Aunt Therese looked at her over the rim of her glass. "And nothin'," she said, after a long moment.

"But . . ."

"Time to go in," Aunt Therese said, abruptly rising and cutting her off. "Mosquitoes gonna eat us alive out here."

In the foyer, the sound of running water came to them from the upstairs bathroom, and Layla suddenly realized how exhausted she was. The trip, the worries about Will, the sense of urgency that she felt to talk to Charlotte, all pressed down on her like a weight. She turned to tell Aunt Therese good night and gasped.

In the hazy illumination of the overhead foyer light, her aunt was trembling, her lips pressed tightly together.

"Aunt Therese?" She took the bottle from the old woman and set it on the bottom step. "What is it? Do you want me to get Aunt Jayne?"

Aunt Therese shook her head. "No, baby. I'm fine. It's just the heat and the excitement of your comin' back to visit," she said. "And . . . and I guess I'm not as well trained as I used to be."

She nodded at the nearly empty bottle at the foot of the stairs and tried to laugh. The sound caught in her throat. "Why you back here, Layla?" she asked.

"I . . ."

Aunt Therese eased herself onto the step. "What do you see when you look at me? Look at us?"

Layla frowned. "I don't . . ."

"You know what you see? You see what all young people see. Two old ladies. Funny. Feisty. Not doin' too bad for our age, but two old ladies. You ever notice how nobody never calls a twentysomething feisty?"

"Aunt—"

Aunt Therese held up a hand to stop her. "Young people look at old people, at us, and the outside is all we are. All we ever were. Like we can't see. Can't hear. Like we ain't got good sense."

She laughed bitterly, stroking the whiskey bottle with one thumb. "So, pleased as I am that you're here, I'm a ask again. Why you back here, sugar?"

For a long moment, they locked eyes, old woman and young. Layla was the first to look away.

"Charlotte," she said, sliding onto the step next to her aunt.

"Hmmm?" Her aunt waited.

"I saw her. Back home. Dreamed her. Or she dreamed me." She shook her head. "I told her I didn't want to take Scotia from her. That I didn't want it. That I didn't want anything from her."

Aunt Therese squinted at her. "And she seemed okay with that?"

Layla nodded.

"She seemed to be," she said. "Then later, I found out Evan had had his people start the title and deed search. He had some people go out there to do surveys so . . ."

She stopped. Aunt Therese had jolted upright in alarm.

"Wait," she cried. "All them papers you been sendin' us? He had folks, actually goin' out there? To the island?"

Layla blinked. "Well, I guess so. Yeah?"

"White people? Outsiders?"

"I don't . . ."

"Damien said he thought he saw folks out there takin' pictures. Goin' around the island. And if he saw them, you can bet Charlotte saw them too."

"But . . ." Layla shook her head, alarmed by Aunt Therese's reaction, but not quite able to fathom the reason for her aunt's distress. "They were just there to get documentation. Proof that Scotia Island belongs to our family free and clear. That it has for over one hundred and fifty years."

"Do you think any of that matters?" snapped Aunt Therese. Layla drew back, stung by the vehemence in her tone. Upstairs, the water turned off.

"But, Aunt Therese," she persisted. "It's a good thing, right? If Charlotte wants to protect the island, now she has legal documentation, proof of—"

Aunt Therese snorted. "Because ain't no white mens ever tried to cheat a contract when it comes to colored folks."

She buried her face in her hands, then straightened, reaching for Layla's hand. "I know you thought you were doin' a good thing, baby. But I guarantee you, Charlotte isn't going to see it that way at all."

Layla was quiet for a long time.

"No," she said, finally. She thought of her brother's bloodshot eyes, the sand in her baby nephew's crib. "I don't think she does."

24

She'd tried to sleep. Tried, once again, to reach out to Charlotte in her dreams. Instead, she'd ended up lying awake most of the night replaying her conversation with Aunt Therese, her sense of dread mounting as the hours ticked by. She imagined Charlotte, out there on the island, watching from the shadows as strangers circled the in the waters, drones buzzing the treetops, taking pictures.

In the darkness, Layla squeezed her eyes tight. She needed to get back there, needed to explain. It was a misunderstanding. They, she and Charlotte, could work together to protect Scotia Island.

The thought made her smile a little. The idea that she could be a part of preserving something old and precious.

Her inheritance.

She imagined herself rehabbing one of the decrepit cabins at the Old Place, spending summers there painting, the cicadas the only sounds at night.

She'd go out to the island. Explain to Charlotte. Get her to understand. It would be okay. Everything would be fine.

She woke the next morning to the sound of mourning doves, the smell of food cooking. She lay still, eyes closed, the sun streaming through the window, warm on her face.

Just a misunderstanding.

Sitting up, she grabbed a towel and clean clothes, then shuffled to the bathroom for a quick shower.

After, she made her way downstairs to the kitchen, hesitating in the doorway. The table groaned with food—eggs, sausage, bacon, fried potatoes. Aunt Jayne stood thumbing through papers at the counter.

"Good morning." Layla twisted her still-damp hair into a messy bun on the top of her head the cranberry red of earlier in the summer now exchanged for a deep blue.

"Mornin', sugar," said Aunt Jayne, turning. "Set yourself down there and get some breakfast."

Layla sat and poured a cup of coffee. "Aunt Therese still asleep?"

Aunt Jayne flinched. "Therese's feelin' poorly this morning," she said with a tight smile. "I'm going to get that truck towed to the garage to get fixed this morning."

"I was kind of hoping to get out to Scotia today," said Layla.

"Not sure that's going to happen today, sugar," said Aunt Jayne, spearing a sausage. If she was surprised by Layla's statement, she showed no sign. "But if the truck takes too long to fix, I'll see about borrowin' you a ride down to the dock."

They ate in silence.

"Why?" asked Layla, finally.

Her aunt frowned. "Why what?"

"Why did you and Aunt Therese come to D.C.? Why did you give me all that stuff about Scotia Island?" She gripped her cup hard, the warmth seeping into her hands. "I'd gone my whole life without knowing. You had to know how Charlotte would react. Or at least have some idea. Her history with my mom. Why even start all this"—she waved her hand in the air—"drama?"

Aunt Jayne's eyes were cold, despite the smile. "Did you think we didn't know about Scotia before them papers you sent? Didn't know how valuable it is? Our ancestors' blood and sweat and tears soaked into that ground. Charlotte got no children. What you think happens when she goes if no one lays claim? You don't think those comeyahs show up like maggots? Build tennis courts over top the graves of our people. Try to erase us?"

"So, you needed me?" said Layla.

"Family always needs family, sugar," said Aunt Jayne. "For one thing or 'nother."

Layla gave a derisive laugh. Her aunt shook her head slowly.

"Wasn't no lie we came to say our goodbyes to Elinor. Wasn't no lie we want to try and mend what got broke in this family," she said. "But the big truth is, you needed to know about that island. You needed to know about your gift."

Layla shook her head. "And what if I don't want any part of . . . any of it?"

Aunt Jayne laughed bitterly. "Oh, honey! Ain't never been no point in *what ifs*." She leaned close. "And now that you do know," she said softly.

"Can you say for true, you want no part of it? The island? Your history? Your gift?"

Layla pushed to her feet. "I'm going to go for a walk. I just need to . . ."

"Baby . . ."

"It's fine. I just need to clear my head."

"I'll just wrap you up a plate for later."

Layla turned and fled from the kitchen.

The area surrounding the Aunts' house was shot through with narrow paths and winding roads. She went down one, only to find that it ended at an old house much like the Aunts'. Backtracking, she chose another path, wider than the first and covered in gravel. Eventually it led her to a two-lane asphalt road that ran in an uninterrupted straight line, climbing gradually until it disappeared over a low hill in the distance. Twisted gray oaks and shoulder-high chartreuse grasses rose on either side of the road. The high-pitched whine of insects drifted from the vegetation. The only human sound came from the occasional jet that tore through the periwinkle sky, high overhead.

She felt like the only person left in the world, and the feeling was not an unpleasant one.

She'd spoken with Will just before drifting off to sleep the night before. He'd sounded exhausted, and more than a little confused as to why she was back in South Carolina. All she'd said was that she had to take care of some business involving Scotia Island, which was true.

"Hey!"

She spun, momentarily losing her footing on the road's sandy shoulder. Viktor was out of the truck in an instant.

"Hey," he said again, coming to her side. "Sorry! Wasn't tryin' to sneak up on you."

"No, no, I'm fine," she said, waving him away. "Just not paying attention." She laughed self-consciously. "Good thing you weren't a mugger or something."

He grinned. "Lucky for you, not a lot of muggers hang out on these back roads."

He thrust his hands into his pockets and leaned against the hood of the truck. "Speakin' of which, where in the world you tryin' to get to out here in the middle of the Lord's armpit?"

"Nowhere."

"Well, that'd be about right then, 'cause this road leads to nowhere for a good long while."

"Really?" She laughed and touched her hair, realized it was still scrunched in a clip from her shower. She pulled the clip free, shaking out her hair and letting it fall to her neck. It was still early but the day was already hot.

"And what a coincidence! It just happens I'm goin' nowhere myself. Wanna ride?"

She hesitated, then climbed into the truck.

"Know the Tantes showed you off all over the Royal last time," he said, starting the engine. "You get a chance to see much of Beaufort?"

"I didn't see any of Beaufort." She shrugged. "I saw Port Royal and the island and that was about it."

He shot her a look from the corner of his eye. "I heard. How'd that go?"

"Probably about how you heard." She stared at the road through the windshield, feeling the rise and fall of the truck in the pit of her stomach as it rolled through the countryside.

"You see any ghosts out there?" he asked.

"Ghosts?"

Viktor nodded. "Scotia Island's s'posed to be filthy with 'em. Supposed to be the reason it's cursed. Nobody around these parts wants anything to do with the place. Only folks go out there is folks from there or them that's still got people out there . . . or folks from out of town."

"Like me."

He grinned, his eyes still on the road. "Yep, like you. The odd developer from up north comes down from time to time wantin' to put condos or some such out there. But so far, that hasn't worked out so well."

Layla thought of the newspaper article: THE MYSTERY OF AINSLI GREEN. "Only scary thing I saw out there was my cousin, Charlotte," she said.

"And?" He shot her a look.

"And she was scary enough."

"And yet here you are, back again," he said, chuckling.

"Yep," she said, keeping her eyes fixed on the passing countryside. "Here I am again."

"Well," said Viktor. "Crazy relations are common as ticks down here. I mean, are you even really from the South if you ain't got at least one drunk uncle and a half dozen peculiar cousins?"

Layla shot him a look and laughed.

The drive from Port Royal to Beaufort took only a few minutes through picturesque countryside. For nearly two hours they drove through the streets of Beaufort, past Easter candy–colored houses and old churches with pointed spires, Viktor maneuvering his truck beneath towers of ancient live oaks dripping with moss, and down palmetto-lined brick roads. He was a good guide, full of anecdotes about the places they passed. It was fun to pretend that she was simply a tourist visiting a charming, antebellum town, that this was a date.

"Used to use the tombstones in there for operating tables during the Civil War," he said, as they passed St. Helena's Episcopal Church.

"Robert Smalls, the slave turned congressman, is buried yonder," he said, pointing toward the Tabernacle Baptist Church. "Not far from the founder of Beaufort Town."

He seemed to know something about every massive old house they passed, to have a story about each graveyard. They'd finally stopped for lunch at a tiny place near the water.

"This whole town looks like a movie set," she said.

They were sitting outside the café, overlooking the water, a wide, green umbrella shielding them from the sun. A handful of boats, their sails bright against the sky, plied back and forth on the silver water as gulls swooped overhead. Viktor nodded.

"It should. So many movies get done down here that some of these old houses are bigger movie stars than Marilyn Monroe. This place got the best frogmore stew around," he said, scanning the menu.

Layla frowned. "I, uh . . ."

Viktor threw back his head and laughed. "No frogs. I promise. And it's delicious."

It had turned out to be not so much a stew as a spicy buffet, jumbled together and dumped on newspaper right onto their table: shrimp and sausage and potatoes and corn, all meant to be eaten with their fingers. And it *was* delicious.

Layla felt a satisfying grogginess overtake her as they sat in overstuffed silence watching the boats out on the water.

"It's a wonder you know."

Viktor's voice seemed to come from far away. She turned her head to look at him. He was slouched in his chair, studying the water, one finger tracing the rim of his ice tea glass. She blinked, her eyelids heavy from the heat and the food.

"It's this place." He turned to look at her. "Anything can happen. There's magic here."

"You're a cop." She smiled slightly. "You believe in magic?"

He shrugged. "Magic? Energy? A force? Doesn't matter what you call it. There's something here. Something out on our islands. Sometimes it's incredibly beautiful. Sometimes . . . not."

He grinned.

"Beaufort's haunted, you know. Just like Scotia. Can't turn around without runnin' into one spirit or 'nother. Out that a way . . ." He pointed out over the water. In the distance, she could see a line of traffic moving slowly across a bridge. "People come from all over to see the Land's End Light."

"Land's End Light?"

"At night, out where the land ends, folks see strange lights. I seen 'em myself. Some say it's the ghost of a decapitated Confederate soldier searchin' for his head by lamplight. Others say it's the spirit of three slaves who got hung out there for runnin' away."

The hair on the back of her neck stood on end and she shivered.

"Don't you ever feel it?" Viktor focused on the bright water. "Things that defy explainin'?"

Layla stared across the glittering water. And said nothing,

25

"Truck's gone," said Viktor as they pulled into the yard and parked in front of the house. "Tante Jayne must a got that tow."

Except for a rectangular patch of yellowing grass, the space beneath the sugarberry tree was empty. Aunt Therese was sitting in the shade on the porch swing. She seemed to be sleeping.

Viktor turned off the engine and studied the old woman through the windshield. He gave a pained grunt. "She drinkin' again?"

Layla twisted in her seat to look at him. "Again?" she asked, surprised.

"It was a real bad time after Uncle Joe died. For all of us." He watched the old woman on the porch. "But she seemed to get right again. After a while. To get her feet back up under herself. But since your momma died . . ."

He shot her an apologetic look, his voice trailing off.

"How long ago did he . . . did Uncle Joe die?"

"Six, seven years ago," he answered. "My junior year of college."

Layla followed his gaze through the windshield. Had her mother reached out? Come down for the funeral? Layla frowned. Trying to remember. Until recently, she hadn't even known there'd been an Uncle Joe. She had a vision of her mother sitting at her desk at work, filling out a condolence card, sending a tasteful flower arrangement. As if her brother-in-law had been just another client. She felt queasy.

Viktor was still watching Aunt Therese through the windshield. "Oma's worried about her. *I'm* worried about her."

Layla thought uncomfortably of the previous night. Of the nearly empty bottle of whiskey on the bottom step. The smell of liquor wafting off her aunt.

He sighed. "We should get her in the house. Can't be good for her sittin' out in this heat."

They got out of the truck and headed for the porch. As Layla's foot touched the first step, Aunt Therese opened her eyes.

"Hey there," she said, smiling. "Where'd you find my boy?" She appeared stone cold sober, but even from several feet away, Layla could smell the alcohol seeping from her pores.

"I found *her*, Tante," said Viktor. "Wanderin' out there on the back roads. Decided to give her the grand tour of Beaufort."

"Well, isn't that nice. And what'd you think of ol' Lettuce City?"

Before Layla could answer, Viktor stepped around her. "Tante, I am just parched. I would kill for some sweet tea."

"Well, ain't no need for killin'," laughed the old woman. "You just got to follow me into the kitchen." Viktor offered his arm. She took it and pulled herself to her feet with only a hint of unsteadiness.

The house was cooler than the front porch. Late afternoon sun streamed through the windows, bathing everything in a golden glow. Aunt Therese pulled a glass pitcher of tea from the refrigerator. Her hands shook as she poured it into the glasses, but she waved away Viktor's offer to help.

"Jayne finally got them to tow that piece of junk outta here," she said, sitting down between Layla and Viktor. "Truck isn't worth spit, but she is unnaturally attached to it." She frowned. "You babies hungry? Let me fix you somethin'." She stood.

Layla and Viktor shook their heads.

"We're stuffed. Viktor introduced me to frogmore stew on our grand tour. Apparently, it has everything in it except frogs," Layla said.

"Frogs are an underappreciated delicacy," said Aunt Therese, sitting back down.

Layla's face twisted and Viktor and Aunt Therese laughed. Layla felt herself relaxing in the warm kitchen as she recounted for her aunt some of the places Viktor had taken her, his stories about Beaufort. When he stood to go, she glanced at the clock over the sink and was surprised that nearly an hour had gone by. Outside, the sun had drifted closer to the horizon.

"I gotta run. I told Oma I'd pick up a couple of things for her over to Port Royal." A shadow crossed his face as he looked at the old woman. "You alright, Tante?"

"Course I'm alright." The woman squinted up at him. "Right as rain. Why you askin'?"

"You just look . . . tired, that's all." He bent and kissed the top of her head. He hesitated for a heartbeat, then touched Layla's shoulder. "See y'all later."

He was gone before Layla could thank him for showing her around.

She turned to find Aunt Therese staring at a space somewhere beyond the table. All the sparkling energy of the past hour seemed to have left with Viktor.

"Aunt Therese?" said Layla, uneasy.

The old woman blinked vaguely at her niece. "The boy's right," she said with a wan smile. "I am a little tired. I'm a go lie down for a bit. No tellin' what time Jayne might be comin' back. You get hungry, you help yourself, hear? There's plenty."

She stood and headed down the hall toward the stairs.

Layla sat at the table a while longer, then began to wander aimlessly through the house. It wasn't a big house, and nothing appeared to have changed from the month before. In fact, nothing seemed to have changed in decades. In the dining room, a large crystal punch bowl sat in the center of the lace-covered table. A computer the size of a toaster oven sat on a scuffed table beneath the window in the sitting room across from the front hall stairs.

It took her several long seconds of fiddling to figure out how to turn it on. The monitor glowed green and the cursor flashed in the bottom left-hand corner, but nothing else. After a few minutes, she finally gave up trying to get it to boot up and returned to the kitchen.

She poured herself another glass of tea and fished out an ice cube. Closing her eyes, she held it against her throat, shivering at the delicious bite of cold on her neck. With Aunt Therese upstairs sleeping and Aunt Jayne still not home, it was eerily quiet. Dropping the ice back into the glass, she walked out into the front yard, thinking about what Viktor had said about her aunt's drinking. About Uncle Joe.

Layla would have been in high school, would have remembered her mother mentioning a death in the family, remembered her coming down to South Carolina for a funeral. But there was no such memory, and she couldn't shake the image of her mother sending an impersonal condolence to Aunt Therese, the thought that even then, when her sister needed her the most, her mother had not returned, even briefly, to her family.

Layla shivered and stared up at the blue bottles twisting lazily in the tree branches, sparkling as they caught the late afternoon sun.

Every time she thought she had a clearer sense of her mother, that maybe this was a person she could have liked, could have been friends with, another detail emerged blurring that image, suggesting otherwise. Was her mother a fun and adventurous person ready for anything? Or was she cold and distant, calculating? Maybe she just shed personalities and facades like a pair of designer heels.

You know about snakes girl? They shed they skin over and over. Moving along through life.

A prickle of tears stung her eyes, catching her by surprise. She swiped roughly at her face, then with a last glance at the bottle tree, turned and headed back to the relative coolness of the house.

She was standing in a park. The misting rain felt wonderful on her face. There were bottles in nearly every tree, visible as vague spots of color in the gray haze.

Closing her eyes, she inhaled, feeling something like contentment. This place felt safe and peaceful, but she'd learned long ago to be on guard. Dreams needed to declare themselves and even then . . .

There was a path, the stones cool and slick with moss beneath her feet. She followed it, her eyes drawn again and again to the flashes of blue in the branches overhead.

"Layla?"

Her mother stood several yards ahead, just to the side of the path. Once again, she wore a wedding dress, but this one Layla recognized. Heavy satin, simple, a chapel train. It was elegant, the way her mother always presented to the public. This was the wedding dress from the photograph that hung in the front hallway, the wedding dress that nestled in piles of vanilla tissue paper in the attic, wait-ing for her *wedding day.*

Her mother stood, hands clasped in front of her, head cocked. Layla knew that look, had endured it her whole life. Appraisal. Examination. The scrutiny to ensure that the outfit was right, the hair in place, the conversation appropriate. She waited. Expecting to feel the familiar flicker of anger, prepared to defend herself against . . . whatever it was that wasn't quite right this time. But, to her astonishment, she felt only a hazy sense of bemusement. And tiredness. Even in the dream she was so very tired of it all. She smiled sadly.

"Why?" she asked, quietly.

Her mother frowned, seeming confused. "Why, what?"

"Why?" Layla laughed, the sound loud, harsh in the fog. "Let's see. Why did

you leave here and act like this . . . like your family never existed? Why did you let me think there was something wrong with me all this time?"

Her voice was rising. She inhaled, blew a hard breath out slowly through her nose. Her hands shook and she pushed them deep into the pockets of her jeans.

Her mother smoothed the front of her gown again and again, not meeting her eyes. "Do you remember the stories I told you when you were little?"

"What?" Layla blinked. "What are you talking about?"

"The one about the queen who swam in the ocean of dreams. Remember?"

Her mother stepped toward her, hand outreached as if to touch her face, but Layla recoiled, batted the hand away.

"No," she cried. "You don't get to do that. You were cold and cruel to the people who should have mattered the most. You were cold and cruel to me!"

"I just wanted you to be normal," said her mother, her voice pleading. "I just wanted to be normal."

"And I wanted you to love me."

Layla felt it the instant Charlotte appeared. A shift in energy. An electrical current traveling along her skin. Unpleasant. Persistent. A burning where the shells of her bracelet circled her wrist.

"Love?" Charlotte's voice was hard. "Can't love. Never loved. Only herself. Always herself."

Charlotte had entered her dream, hijacked it, but she only had eyes for Elinor.

"Can't keep her word," Charlotte went on. "Thinks fancy outside changes ugly inside."

"Just stop it," snapped Layla's mother. "You always wanted too much. Always. Too much."

Charlotte charged, teeth bared.

"Charlotte!"

Layla moved to intercept her, her instinct, in spite of everything, to protect her mother. The older woman whirled, eyes wild.

"And you," she hissed. "Suckled on the same poison as you momma. Liar! Liar!"

For a moment, Layla stood, unmoving in the face of the woman's rage. "That's not . . . ," she managed at last. "That's not what . . ."

She was at the beach, no longer in control of her own dream, ankle deep in water, Charlotte watching from several yards away. There was something *wrong with the water. Thick, sticky, it sucked at her legs, threatening to pull her down. Layla felt a tremor of fear.*

"What is wrong with you?" she yelled at the old woman. "Stop it! I didn't lie to you. I was trying to help. Leave me and my family alone."

"Liar," spit her cousin, not moving. "Oonah all liars."

Layla fought against the water that was not water, struggling to step onto the beach. She lost her balance and fell to her knees, feeling the gooey substance suck at her thighs, drag at her arms.

"Charlotte," she screamed.

The old woman watched her for a moment longer, then turned and walked away.

Layla thrashed, fighting to free herself, her shoulders beginning to burn, her breath growing short with the effort. This can't happen like this, she thought, panic beginning to build. It can't. It never happens like this. And then she was under. She inhaled, felt her lungs lock, felt herself engulfed by terror.

"God Almighty!"

Someone was pulling on her, trying to roll her over. She couldn't see. She couldn't breathe. She lashed out, kicking her feet, trying to break free.

"It's alright! You gonna be fine! Come on, now. Breathe for me, girl!"

She was forced onto her side, and she vomited hot, brackish water. Coughing violently, she tried to sit up.

"Whoa, now. Not just yet."

She opened her eyes. Two men she'd never seen before—a chubby, white man and a chubbier black one—stood over her, framed in a blinding light. Holding her arms on either side, they helped her up. She found herself sitting on the bank of a narrow stream, surrounded by tall, sharp-edged grass. The light was coming from a lantern suspended on a pole several feet away.

"What the sam hell you doin' out here?" asked the white man.

"I . . . ," began Layla. She stopped, confused. She didn't know where "out here" was.

The black man leaned forward, offering her a handkerchief. In the blistering light it seemed to glow.

"My name's Lewis," he said. "And that there is Arlo." He pointed over his shoulder at his companion. "We was giggin' flatfish out yonder and saw you go in. Arlo fished you out. Took some doin'."

Layla ran a hand through her hair. There was mud everywhere. Thick and smooth, it clung to her jeans, her shirt, her hair, the now familiar smell of sulfur clogging her nose, stinging her eyes. She clutched the handkerchief and blinked, confused.

She'd come into the house and finished her tea. Texted Will. She'd gone upstairs to lie down until Aunt Jayne came home. And then . . .

"What was you doin'?" Arlo asked again. He was staring bug-eyed at her. He seemed to be considering whether to throw her back where they'd found her. "Look up and you facedown flailin' away in the mud like you tryin' to swim to China straight through the creek bottom."

"Arlo!" hissed Lewis. He shot his friend a warning look before turning back to Layla. "Who your people?" he asked her.

She gave him Aunt Therese's and Aunt Jayne's names. Her voice was hoarse. There was a bad taste in her mouth. "I'm staying with my aunts."

She started to shake, and the clattering of her teeth could be heard over the cicadas.

"Our truck's parked back yonder," said Lewis. He pointed into the darkness. "We gon' get you home. Can you get up?"

She nodded and looked over his shoulder. He sensed her hesitation and smiled.

"It's alright. I knows Miss Jayne and Miss Therese from church." He paused. "You must be Elinor's girl. I didn't know her so well, but I was real sorry to hear 'bout her passin'."

He pulled a cell phone from the front pocket of his overalls and held it out to her. "You best call your folks and let 'em know you alright. They liable to be out their minds right about now. You wanderin' around in the middle of the night."

Arlo appeared at her side with a blanket. He draped it around her shoulders. It smelled like gasoline. Layla took the phone from Lewis and stared at it, trying to remember the Aunts' number. But all she could see was the thick green water closing over her head, sucking her down.

"It's alright, honey." Lewis gently took the phone from her hand and punched in the number. "I got it. Miss Jayne? How you? It's me, Lewis Banks. Me and Arlo down here on Little Frog Creek. Got your girl here with us."

By the time they pulled up in front of the house the sun was shimmering at the edge of the horizon, the sky blushing the pink and orange of dawn. Every light in the house was on. Layla sat slumped, unmoving in the back of the truck until Arlo opened the door. The two men walked her to the porch, standing close, but not touching her. The Aunts waited silently side by side on the porch, watching her come.

She stopped at the foot of the steps and stared at the peeling paint, unable to meet their eyes. "Aunt Jayne . . ."

"Shhh." She wasn't sure who said it, but suddenly they were both there, their thick arms wrapped around her, closing her in, sheltering her. She sagged against them and began to cry.

26

She hadn't showered, hadn't changed her clothes. She lay curled in the center of the bed, still wrapped in the gasoline-smelling blanket, trying to make herself as small as possible. She'd taken a pill and now she was drifting in a sedative haze, where time meant nothing, where everything meant nothing. Her last coherent thought, before the pill kicked in, had been the image of Charlotte, her teeth bared, eyes blazing with rage. It seemed unlikely that any explanation she had to offer would resonate with the old woman. But then, even that thought had slipped away into a gray, cottony nether place where there were no fears, no worries, no thoughts at all.

Aunt Jayne had come up to check on her—minutes ago? An hour? Once, sometime later when she opened her eyes, she thought she saw Gerta, Viktor's grandmother, sitting there on the foot of the bed, her pink face floating in the sunlight streaming through the window.

"This secret," she said. "It is very beautiful, a gift from God."

Then Layla had drifted back to sleep.

When she opened her eyes again, she was alone, and she was sure she had imagined the tiny German woman talking to her from the end of the bed. Groaning, she sat up. Her mud-caked clothes were stiff and streaked with gray-green slime. Her hair and skin reeked of pluff mud. She felt unstrung, every breath an effort. She considered lying down again, but before she could give in to the urge, Aunt Jayne appeared in the doorway.

"Telephone." She held the phone out. "It's Will. He says he's been trying to reach you."

Layla took the phone from her aunt, her other hand going instinctively to the pocket where she kept her cell. It was empty.

"Hello?"

"Where the hell have you been?" Will's voice shook with emotion. "I've been burning up your phone for the last twelve hours. What is going on? What funeral are you talking about?"

"Funeral? What?" She shook her head, confused.

"That's what I'm asking," said Will, his voice rising. "You sent me like seventeen texts. And didn't none of them make any sense after 'How are you?' Talking about blue bottles and flowers and funerals and queens. What the hell is going on down there, Lay?"

Again, Layla instinctively reached for the missing phone. She remembered sending a single text. And then, nothing.

"I lost my phone." She forced a laugh. "And I have no idea about those other texts. That's . . . crazy."

"Well, someone has a warped sense of humor," said Will, his tone softening.

She realized he thought someone else had sent the texts. "Hmm" was all she said. "Well, how *are* you?" she asked, desperate to change the subject.

There was a silence that stretched long across the phone line. "Fine. Mostly. Still not sleeping well. Still having those crazy dreams."

His voice was strained. He sounded as used up as she felt.

"Lay, I just wanted to . . . I wanted to apologize."

She frowned, confused. "For what?"

"For all those times I made fun of you when you'd get up in the morning and try to tell us about your dreams. For blowing you off." His voice cracked. "I mean, night after night of this . . . I can't even imagine what it must have been like for you. Having these dreams that feel so . . . so real. And . . . well, I'm sorry for being such a dick."

Her breath caught in her throat. She didn't trust herself to speak. "Well, you're still a dick," she said, finally.

"Nice," her brother said, chuckling softly. "Anyway . . . sorry." After a moment he asked, "How long're you going to be down there?"

"Will," she said, slowly. "I think maybe Charlotte might have something to do with the dreams you've been having. Maybe."

"Crazy Cousin Charlotte?"

"Yes." She tensed, her heart beating hard, waiting for the familiar snark, the dismissive laugh.

"How?" asked Will quietly, instead.

She blinked, surprise bringing tears to her eyes. She hesitated, unsure of where to even start. Despite her brother's apology, she wasn't sure how much to say or how much he would believe. "She seems to be able to get inside people's heads," she said after a long moment. "To make them dream things."

"Like some kind of hypnosis?"

Layla bit back a laugh. No, she thought, not even a little bit like hypnosis. "I guess."

"But how could she be doing that from all the way down there?"

"I'm not sure. But it seems strongest when she's upset or angry."

"Upset?" Will's voice was rising again. "What the hell does she have to be upset about? We don't even know her."

"She thinks we're trying to cheat her out of Scotia Island." She explained about the survey Evan had commissioned, the title search, giving the CliffsNotes version of dreamwalking.

"Shit," her brother swore softly.

"Yeah." Layla sighed. "Shit."

"Well, can you make her stop?" There was an edge of desperation in his voice.

"I don't know." Layla closed her eyes. "But I'm going to try."

Long after they'd said their goodbyes, Layla sat cradling the phone in her hand. A part of her—not a small part—felt, if not exactly gleeful, vindicated. *See?* she wanted to scream into the phone. *See? How does it feel? How does it feel to have your dreams, your nightmares, follow you into the daylight?*

She knew it was cruel and mean-spirited. Will was struggling.

And yet . . .

From some deep well of willpower, she'd finally summoned the energy to drag herself to the shower. It had taken long minutes and persistence to rid herself of all traces of the thick mud that clung to her like the slime her niece Ashley was so fond of. By the time she'd finished and changed, she felt drained.

The house was eerily quiet as she rummaged through the kitchen cabinets. She needed coffee, strong and hot and sweet. Sitting at the kitchen table, head bowed over her cup, the steam from the coffee curling the hair around her face, she wondered distractedly where the Aunts had got off to.

She glanced up and grunted in surprise, inhaling coffee into her lungs that triggered a fit of coughing. Viktor was standing in the doorway in his uniform, his eyes hidden behind mirrored sunglasses.

"Jesus Christ," she sputtered, once she could speak.

"Mornin'." Viktor slid into the chair across from her.

Layla blinked then looked away, concentrating on the oversweet liquid in her cup. She was certain that by now, he'd heard all about the incident from the night before. As had probably everyone else within a fifty-mile radius. I'd be really embarrassed if I had the energy, she thought. Grimacing, she took a big gulp of coffee.

"You scared the livin' daylights outta everybody last night," he said, long after the silence had grown awkward. He carefully placed his glasses on the table between them. She could see herself reflected in the lenses, the image distorted. "Nobody even knew you were out the house."

"Including me," she said dryly. She took another sip of coffee, feeling the undissolved granules of sugar cling to her tongue.

"If those two ol' boys hadn't a been out there giggin' flatfish, you coulda died," he went on, his expression neutral. "What the devil were you thinkin'?"

"Thinking?" She blew out a slow breath, struggling to keep the bitterness out of her voice. "I wasn't thinking. I was . . . asleep."

Blinking in surprise, he sat back in his chair. "Sleepwalkin'?"

She thought of all the times she'd found herself in a neighbor's yard late at night. Of the unexplained scratches and bruises, the soiled nightgown. Of how often she'd woken in the morning, her bed littered with leaves or rocks, one time an expensive, sealed cigar.

"Yes" was all she said, finally, nodding. "I . . . sleepwalk sometimes."

"Hunh," he said. He ran a thumb over the edge of his glasses. "When I was a kid, there was this boy. Used to have night terrors, his daddy called them. Would find him time to time, wanderin' the road out by his house. Didn't matter how hard they tried to lock that boy in. Once he even showed up on our back step in the dead of night. Didn't remember a doggone thing the next day."

He grinned. "But don't ever remember anybody ever findin' him butt deep in creek mud though. That's kinda crazy."

Layla's face flamed hot. She pressed her lips into a hard line and dragged her fingers through her still-damp hair.

"Interestin'. It's interestin'," he added quickly, seeing the look on her face. "Does that happen often?"

"Often enough." She leaped up from the table and began to bustle around the kitchen, wiping counters, opening the refrigerator door, closing it again. "Do you want coffee? Something to eat?"

"I'll take a coffee," he said. "Black."

She poured him a cup, then freshened her own, before sitting back at the table, aware he was scrutinizing her.

"It's always happened. Ever since I can remember," she said, answering the question he hadn't yet asked.

"And wasn't no treatment for it? No medicine."

"My parents tried everything. I don't think there was a pediatrician or sleep doctor on the Eastern Seaboard we didn't see." She laughed mirthlessly. "Hypnosis, acupuncture, warm baths, soft music, pills."

She sighed, remembering. "There was even a period when they were supposed to come into my room and wake me up every hour or so. Trying to break up my sleep pattern or something."

She stared at her fists, clenched tightly on the table. "That lasted about a week."

"That must a been awful."

"It wasn't great." Layla shrugged not meeting his eyes. "Where are the Aunts?" she asked, changing the subject.

"They went to the market downtown with Oma. They thought they'd just let you relax here today after . . . after all the excitement last night."

She crossed her arms and locked eyes with him across the table. "And you're here to babysit." It wasn't a question.

"I wouldn't put it exactly like that," he said, squirming slightly in the hard kitchen chair.

"No?" She smiled grimly.

He flushed and fiddled with his sunglasses, spinning them round and round on the table, the silence growing increasingly uncomfortable.

"So, today . . . ?" he asked at last.

She sighed. "Today, I guess, I'll just try to figure out how to get on the internet."

He laughed. "Well, good luck with that. I think the tantes think the internet is some sort of magic. And out here, I s'pose it might as well be. Kinda comes and goes whenever."

"Great. I lost my phone. I can't get Wi-Fi. And I have some emails for work I need to send."

"I could drive you into Beaufort," he said. "You could get a new phone and the library's real close if you need to get online."

"Is that part of your babysitting duties?"

He rolled his eyes.

Magic. Medicine.

Medicine. Magic.

Layla had been silent as they drove the short distance to Beaufort. The words Viktor had spoken in the kitchen had sparked something, the germ of an idea. The phone store was only a short distance from the library, and Viktor offered to drop her off then pick her up when she texted.

And now, she'd been sitting in the downtown Beaufort Library for an hour and a half, scouring the internet and reference texts and scientific journals.

Activation hypothesis.

REM sleep disorder.

Gamma aminobutyric acid and glycine deficiency.

Piled high around her were books on dreaming and brain imaging, sleep disorders and neurotransmitters. There were articles on skeletal muscle disengagement and the association of disordered sleep and Parkinson's disease. She'd hoped her background in medical illustration might help her understand at least some of what she was reading.

It hadn't.

Layla peered at her notes. They were as indecipherable as the books towering over her. And nothing she read seemed to relate to what she had. What Charlotte had.

She dropped her head onto her arms and gave a snort of laughter. The medicine idea had been a bust, and she doubted any books she found on magic would yield better results.

She stood, stretching as she raked a hand through her hair. Slinging her purse over her shoulder, she headed for the front door, leaving the mountain of books behind. Nothing had changed what she already knew about dreamwalking, which she was forced to admit was barely anything.

She dreaded the thought of going out to Scotia Island to face Charlotte directly, but there seemed to be no alternative.

Layla stepped into the afternoon sun and was immediately hit by a blast of wet coastal heat. She stood, unmoving in the doorway, taking small sips of breath, letting herself adjust to the hot air, before making her way toward a shaded area at the top of the staircase leading down to the street.

Magic and medicine. She muttered the words, worrying them like a sore tooth.

Last night proved, if nothing else, that she couldn't just walk into Charlotte's dream and take her on. She was only just beginning to understand what this thing was she could do. In the past, she'd been a passive bystander, dreams seeming to choose *her*. Random.

But Charlotte.

There was nothing random about the way Charlotte entered dreams. She had had years to use it, to practice. And she was wielding it as a weapon.

Layla felt a quiver of fear. What if Charlotte didn't believe her, or didn't care, that the men she'd seen, the papers Layla had sent for her to look at were all a way to protect them? To protect Scotia Island? She shook her head, breathing hard.

"Hey you!" Viktor was walking up the stairs carrying two drinks. He held one out toward her and she took it, sighing with pleasure as her hand closed around the icy cup. He sat down beside her in the patchy shade. "Hot enough to melt the scales off a snake, isn't it?"

She raised an eyebrow. Despite the sweltering heat, he looked as crisp and freshly pressed as he had in the Aunts' kitchen hours before. She pushed a lock of sweaty hair out of her face.

"You get your emails answered?" he asked.

"My emails?"

He cocked his head. "You said you had emails to check on."

"Oh, right. Yeah. Got everything done. Thanks." She held up her new phone. "Phone's all charged and already texted the Aunts. Told them you were on the job. Keeping me in your sight at all times."

Viktor groaned softly. "Stop already. They were worried and I knew it was going to be a light day at work."

"Fine," she said, relenting. "Thanks for the drink."

His phone beeped and he glanced at it. "Do you mind if we make a quick stop on the way back? I need to drop off Oma's prescriptions." He grinned. "And of course, she wants to see for herself that you're all in one piece."

This time it was Layla's turn to groan.

Gerta Williams lived in a senior community at the end of a long row of identical apartments. Layla followed Viktor into his grandmother's. Like the woman herself, the space was bright and compact. Light spilled through the skylights in the living room and through the open patio door.

"Oma?" called Viktor.

"Oh my god," gasped Layla. The stark white walls were covered in vivid, modern art, the canvases imaginatively arranged. On the mantel, over the gas fireplace, was a small piece by Dale Chihuly, one of her favorite artists. The twisting swirls of orange and gold glass reflected the sunlight that streamed into the room, casting bright rainbows onto the ceiling.

"You like these?"

Reluctantly, she turned her attention away from the artwork and toward the German woman.

"They're beautiful," she breathed. "These pieces are fantastic!"

Gerta smiled and plucked at the frilly apron tied around her middle. "You see me and expect paintings of kittens, yes? Lace doilies everywhere."

"You got your kitten and lace doily moments, Oma," Viktor said grinning.

"You hush, now." Gerta pinched his cheek, then clasped Layla by the wrist. "Come, *kleines*. We have coffee on the patio."

A small lawn separated the brick patio from a narrow strip of parking lot but it, and the neighbor next door, were nearly obscured by a thick planting of roses and tree peonies. Containers edging the patio were bursting with angel's trumpet and begonias.

Gerta saw Layla looking and sighed. "I miss my garden. I had so many beautiful flowers. One gets old and there are so many things that away." She flicked her wrist as if tossing something aside.

Viktor squeezed his grandmother's hand and Gerta rewarded him with a smile before pouring coffee from a silver urn into delicate china cups. She handed one to Layla.

"*Leibling,* leave us women to speak in private, please," she said to her grandson.

Viktor looked startled. He glanced at Layla as if for an explanation, but she was as taken aback as he was. She sat motionless, her cup halfway to her mouth.

"Well," he said finally. "I guess I could go take a look at that cabinet door I been meanin' to fix."

He hesitated, but Gerta merely smiled more brightly and sipped her coffee. He grunted softly and disappeared into the house.

"Do you believe in evil?" asked Gerta, once they were alone.

"I . . ." Layla laughed nervously. Caught off guard by the question, she was unsure how to answer. "I guess."

"Therese has been my friend for many years and for all this time she doesn't trust to tell this thing about your family." Gerta gave her a tiny smile. "Until now."

She studied Layla over the rim of her cup for a long moment. "It is not necessary for one to *be* evil to do evil things," she went on. "A caged animal is not evil, but will do whatever it takes to survive. Attack. Kill. Use all that is at hand. Not good. Not bad. Survival. Yes?"

Gerta turned her head to stare past the rosebushes, some old sorrow playing across her smooth face, her cup balanced in her palm, seemingly forgotten. Behind her the large yellow blooms of the angel's trumpet bobbed on the breeze.

Layla gripped her cup and said nothing.

The old woman shook herself and reached to touch Layla's wrists. "I do not understand it so much, this thing, I think. In the waking world there are things to keep Charlotte in check: laws, her . . . isolation out there on that island. But in the night, she roams free. She fights to protect what she believes is hers. What *is* hers. She is angry. Frightened, *nein*? Caged."

The hair on the back of Layla's neck prickled.

"All done, Oma," said Viktor, walking out onto the patio.

"So," said Gerta, straightening in her seat. "You have a boyfriend?"

"*Oma!*"

His grandmother ignored him. "Because this one, he needs a nice girl. That last one, *ach*!" She rolled her eyes, her face twisting in disgust.

"Are you kiddin' me, Oma?" cried Viktor, his face red. Layla pretended to inspect the pattern on her china cup, biting her lip to hold back a laugh, the tension of just moments earlier dissipated.

"Because I am old, I lose many things," said Gerta. She grinned and patted Layla's wrist. "But because I am old, I say whatever I think."

"Unbelievable," muttered Viktor.

Gerta yawned. "*Entschuldige*. Pardon me. We will see each other again soon, yes?"

The old woman stood and laid a hand on Layla's shoulder. "Do not forget, *Schatz*. An animal has nothing to lose when backed into a corner."

She kissed the top of Layla's head and walked into the house.

"Okay, what was that all about?" asked Viktor as they climbed into his truck.

"What?"

He shot her a look. "All that talk about animals and bein' cornered and all."

Layla shrugged. "It was nothing."

Victor raised an eyebrow. "Well, alrighty then."

She felt him watching her but forced herself to look straight ahead, until finally, he gave a small shake of his head and fired up the engine.

27

GEMMA

The sun thrust a golden spear of light across the water, its tip not quite reaching the shore where she sat. Far out on the horizon, dark shapes appeared, then disappeared.

Dolphins. There were dolphins, swimming out there, where the water became deep.

Must be like flyin', only in the water, she thought. Salt 'gainst your skin. Goin' fast. Goin' anywhere the water goes. Anywhere in the whole, wide world.

Gemma closed her eyes. Pain shimmered bright in the pit of her stomach, as if her morning yam had contained ground glass.

Jessamine was gone. Vanished like a haint in daylight. She'd looked and looked. Calling her girl's name until her throat bled. Gemma could no longer sense her child's soul. The thread that bound Jessamine's life to hers had been somehow, cruelly severed.

And Marigold? Marigold was dead.

Was that right?

It didn't feel right.

It felt like a dream, a bitter-tasting, demon-driven dream.

She needed to get up, needed to go look for signs. The signs would help her find her way.

Dream world or waking world?

The signs would tell her for sure.

But she was afraid. Afraid that if she moved, the glass that was making its way through her gut might grind her insides to a bloody mess. Gemma rolled her eyes to the side and thought she heard her eyeballs crackle inside their sockets. She swallowed hard. If her insides were filled with glass, then this was a dream.

Except . . .

. . . except she could hear the night creatures in the trees beginning to stir and, just beyond her feet, the water whispering against the smooth beach stones, exactly the way it should.

Signs.

There had to be a sign somewhere, something to guide her out of this nightmare and back into the world, because this had to be a nightmare, a horrible, unending nightmare. She kneaded her wrist, obsessively working that place with her thumb where the shell bracelet should sit if this was a dream. But there was only a bloody scab from the constant rubbing and rubbing and rubbing.

And there was a vague pressure beneath her fingernails. A hazy memory of howling like an animal, of clawing wildly at the soft earth that covered her child's grave. She raised her hands to her face. Her nails were broken and bleeding, reddish-brown dirt caked beneath them, the knuckles scraped and raw. Dropping her hands back into her lap, she fixed her gaze once again on the sea, searching the horizon for signs of the dolphins.

Dolphins, she thought, just like birds. Flying. Free. Happy. She bet they were happy.

"Mama?"

The hand on her shoulder was warm through the fabric of her shift, solid, and Gemma recoiled. That hand felt real. At least as real as anything else around her. And yet . . .

"Mama, you got to get up now."

Inside her head she was screaming: Let me be! She pressed her lips tight, forcing the words to stay inside her mouth.

The pressure on her shoulder increased to the point of pain. Why wouldn't the girl just go on now? Why wouldn't they all go on and just leave her to her misery?

"Get up from there," said Lavender gently. "It 'bout to come dark. You been sittin' and sittin'. Time to come in now."

Gemma moved her eyes. This time there was no mistaking it. Her eyeballs crackled when they moved. She laughed, high-pitched, hysterical. Maybe while she'd been screaming for Marigold to come back to her, she'd broken her eyes. Maybe she would go blind. She would be glad for it, then she'd never have to see another bad thing in her life. She moved her eyes up, then down, she rolled them sideways as far as they would go. She laughed harder, rocking back and forth, pounding her battered hands on her thighs. Tears poured down her face as she laughed and laughed.

Then, Lavender was in front of her, shaking her hard. Gemma's head snapped back and she bit her tongue, tasting blood.

"Stop that! You stop that right now and get up from there! You come on with me."

Her mother stopped rolling her eyes. The laughter slid into a moan before dying out. "Where?"

"Home."

Gemma shook her head side to side. "I ain't done."

"Done what, Mama?" Lavender's narrow face was pinched, her eyes glittering with fear . . . and something else. Anger. "Whatchu doin' out here?"

When her mother didn't answer, Lavender wrapped one thin arm around her, dragging her to her feet. Holding tight, she forced Gemma to walk, refusing to release her until they were back at their hut.

The quarter was unnaturally quiet. A single cook fire burned at the far end of the row. Scotia Island had become a land of ghosts.

"I's dead?" Gemma asked, standing, unmoving in front of their open door.

"No," whispered Lavender. "You's alive."

"But Marigold, she dead? Jessamine gone?"

Lavender hunched her shoulders, then bent to stoke the ashes of their fire, not answering. Sparks leaped into the air, swirling in the darkness like fiery, orange butterflies.

"You got to eat," she said, once the fire had sprung to life. "They's crawfish and grits."

Gemma didn't move. "You wrong. I's dead. Least good as."

Lavender stood. She stepped to her mother and pinched the flesh above Gemma's elbow, hard. "Feel that? You feel that, Mama? Then you not dead."

Gemma shook her head and moaned.

"What you want, Mama? Ainsli Green? You still wantin' Ainsli Green?"

"Ainsli Green a pile of stones and dead fields," snapped Gemma, showing the first glimmer of life. "Ain't nothin' here no more."

Lavender's sharp intake of breath was loud in the empty quarter. "Nothin'?" she said sharply. She leaned close. Until Gemma could feel her warm breath on her face. "I's here. You don't see me here? Right here? I ain't nothin'."

Gemma turned her head to look at her. The crinkly sound in her eyes was still there but her insides felt the tiniest bit less jagged than they had down at the shore. She stared at her daughter in the firelight.

"Yeah, baby, you still here," she murmured. "You not nothin'."

She blinked, then gazed over her daughter's shoulder, in the direction of the manor house. She barely recognized her island. With no one to work the pumps and gates, the rice fields had either dried up completely, or the weeds had choked them to death. Even if there had been the slaves to weed and harvest the rice, the Union ships had formed a blockade, separating the islands from their markets on the mainland. If there even still were markets. Silt had settled in the supply ponds, turning the water the color of weak coffee. And day by day, the forest edged ever closer to the big house, reclaiming its own.

Gemma spooned grits into her mouth and, under Lavender's unrelenting glare, forced herself to swallow. "Gon' put my head down for a bit," she said, crushing a crawfish between her fingers and sucking out the sweet meat.

Lavender glanced at the sky. The turquoise sky flamed scarlet and peach, the air cooling fast. She nodded, her smile not quite reaching her eyes. "Go on and rest, Mama. I'll clean up."

Gemma folded herself onto the pallet and stared up at the timbered ceiling. She didn't understand how it was that the deed papers remained unsigned. It was coming on late fall and still the master fought her. From some deep reserve of will, as if it were the one thing that kept him clinging to life. This nightly battle in his dreams.

Word came across the water. The Union men made promises. Land. Freedom. Broke that promise. Made new ones.

She didn't know those Yankees. Didn't know their boss man Lincoln. She did know *this* place. Knew Rupert Everleigh. And she knew that a buckra's promise without paper was just wind on your face. There. Then not. She needed his mark on that paper. Needed it to protect her family.

At the thought of her family, she moaned, pressing her sore tongue against the roof of her mouth. Marigold. Jessamine. Lavender. She closed her eyes and rubbed and rubbed at her wrist.

The house glowed, as if the mansion were a giant lantern. Music drifted from the open windows out into the darkness to meet her as she approached. Rupert

Everleigh's house no longer perched at the crest of the hill; instead, it appeared to rest in a field of black feathers that grew from the ground like stalks of corn, reaching nearly to her shoulders. She walked, arms stretched wide, the feathers caressing her skin as she passed. Every so often she stopped to pluck one free, and by the time she reached the house, her arms were filled. In the light spilling from the open windows and doors, she saw that the feathers were streaked with blood, the quills glittering like bits of crystal.

Heart pounding, Gemma threw them down, the quills ringing sharply against the wooden porch floor. Uneasy, she stepped across the doorsill and into the house. There were people dressed in fancy party clothes lining the main hall, which seemed to stretch forever. When her eyes finally adjusted to the light, she cried out in delight. There was Tuesday, her mother. And her son, Leo, who'd drowned just days after his twelfth birthday. Behind him stood Marigold, her hands resting protectively on her brother's shoulders, an expression of contentment on her face.

Gemma laughed and clapped her hands. Lavender was wrong. She was dead and this was heaven. Even the old mistress, the colonel's mother, the woman who'd snuck her sweets and taught her her letters, was there. It struck her odd that the white woman should be in the colored heaven, but maybe the rules of the dead were different.

Her mother, her son, the old mistress smiled and waved at her, and Gemma opened her arms wide, wanting to embrace them all, but as she stepped toward them, the floor seemed to buckle. There was the slightest hitch in the music and she hesitated, before trying again. This time the floor lurched hard, throwing her off balance. She tumbled to her knees. The hall went black, the music clanging to a discordant stop.

Gemma scrabbled to the wall, the grits and crawfish from her supper boiling up into her mouth. Vomit splattered the wall, the hem of her shift.

A faint light appeared in the distance, and she groped her way toward it, but no matter how long she walked, the light hung there, just out of reach. She felt a pressure inside her head, a folding sensation, as if her skull might collapse on itself. She clutched at her wrist, squeezing hard, the shells biting into her skin. She felt a prickling down the middle of her back, faint at first, but it grew, then grew some more, until it felt like fire against her skin. Gemma cried out in pain. In fear. This was not her dream.

And then she was back out on the front porch of the main house, her family gone, her shift damp and rank with vomit.

No.

Wake up.

This is wrong.

The warning was a roar in her head. And she wanted to listen. She was so tired, she ached.

Not yet, she thought, *not quite yet.* Her hands shook as she stepped into the big house for the second time, the main hall empty this time. They shook as she climbed the front staircase. The window was open in the colonel's room, the cool November breeze not quite freshening the sour-sweet smell of decay that hung in the air.

"Never thought it would come to this."

She inhaled sharply. The voice seemed to come from the very air.

The old man was buried among the bed linens, his pale face blending into the rumpled sheets. She edged close to the bed and perched herself stiffly in the nearby chair, watching in silence as he fought to untangle himself from the bedclothes.

"Sumbitch," he swore. He flailed, a sheen of sweat breaking out on his gaunt face. He managed, finally, to free his legs and sit up, wheezing as he clutched at the bedposts.

He was dressed in a dark morning suit, his white, high-collared shirt crisp beneath an emerald-green waistcoat. As he struggled to stay upright on the bed, a ream of documents tumbled to the floor, and Gemma saw that the bed held many more. She bent to pick up the paper closest to her feet.

"You leave that be," snapped Rupert Everleigh.

She glared at him and continued to study the paper before glancing back up at him.

Rupert Everleigh's sparse, white hair had become full, the color of wet sand, the color it had been in his youth. His long face was still thin but now sported a healthy glow. The morning suit that just moments before had nearly swallowed him up, fit snugly on his straight, muscular frame. The colonel was, once again, the young man that had, in the not so distant past, owned one of the most prosperous cotton and rice plantations in the Sea Islands. He was smiling.

"I could fight you, you know," he said. "I got one good scrap left in me, I bet."

She shook her head. "'Tain't no use, Colonel. You ain't got the time, nor me neither."

Her master sighed. "Probably right." He pointed toward the bedroom door. She turned to see his daughter, Nell, standing there, still holding the body of her son. Gemma wondered if they had died together like this, the mother holding the child. She wondered if Nell would hold her son like that for all eternity.

"Nell's gone hasn't she."

"'Pears so, suh."

His seemed to crumple then, his face, his body all sharp angles, telegraphing his pain. "Then there's nothing for it, I s'pose."

He stroked the papers surrounding him in the bed absently, blinking rapidly in a futile effort to hold back tears as he gazed at his daughter.

And then the papers began to change. First the one Gemma held, then those scattered on the bed, on the floor. The ink seemed to run, then shift, the words changing on the page as they watched. The colonel's mouth gaped open.

"Damnation," he swore, leaping to his feet. He swatted the documents away from him.

Their eyes met, slave and master, and in that instant, just for an instant, they were bound together in mutual confusion.

Gemma stared at the paper in her hand. As she watched, Rupert Everleigh's signature began to appear on the bottom of the page, slow, labored, as if her master was straining to get each letter just so. So intent was she on the document she held, that at first, she failed to register that he had gone still as stone, his breathing fast and ragged.

Looking up, she followed his gaze. She went rigid, the document that was still birthing her master's signature falling from her hand.

Lavender stood in the doorway. But it was a Lavender that Gemma had never seen. Still small in stature, she was in that moment barely recognizable as the quiet child Gemma had raised to womanhood. She stood straight as a rod, her eyes flashing fire, her mouth set in a hard line. In one hand she held an old-fashioned quill pen, its long black feather dark against her pale cotton shift, ink dripping from the nib, staining her fingers, the wooden floor.

"You not . . . you can't be here," Gemma managed to say. "A Dreamwalker walkin' with a Dreamwalker. You can't . . ."

Lavender looked at her and smiled, and that smile froze something inside Gemma, terrified her. She took a step back, closer to Rupert Everleigh than she ever wanted to be. She did not know this woman who stood before her, this stranger who wore the face and form of her daughter. This woman who felt like fire and storm.

"Mama," said Lavender, that hard, dangerous smile reflecting in her eyes. "I can be wherever I need to be. I's a Dreamwalker."

28

"You hungry, sugar?" Aunt Therese placed a ham on the kitchen counter and began to pick nervously at the brown sugar glaze. Aunt Jayne appeared to be trying to pound a ball of dough to death at the kitchen table. Neither looked directly at her.

"A little," said Layla.

Aunt Therese nodded and turned to get a plate, seemingly relieved to have something to do.

The Aunts had been in the kitchen, pretending to not be waiting for Viktor to drop her off. Layla gave them an edited version of her trip to the library and her visit with Gerta, and then an uncomfortable silence had descended over them. Neither aunt appeared willing to bring up the incident from the night before.

"I see the truck's fixed," Layla said, trying to fill the awkward void.

Aunt Jayne grunted. "It's runnin' for now," she said, not looking up. "Don't know 'bout fixed."

Aunt Therese set a plate of ham and black-eyed peas on the table. Layla caught the scent of whiskey on her breath as she leaned close.

"When do you think we could go out to the island?" Layla asked. She poked at the thick slice of meat on her plate.

Aunt Jayne slammed a fist into the mound of dough, rattling the table, startling the other two women.

"Ain't nobody need to be goin' out to that island," she said quietly, not looking up.

"What?"

"Ain't nothin' for you out there." Aunt Jayne pointed a dough-encased finger. "Just heartache."

"What are you talking about?" Layla stared slack-jawed at the two sisters. Aunt Jayne returned her look, her round features tight. Aunt Therese gripped the back of a chair and stared at the floor. "I need to talk to Charlotte!"

"And last night you ended up near asphyxiated in mud out in the Little Frog!" Aunt Jayne snapped. She wiped her hands and slid into a chair across from her niece, arms crossed tight across her chest. "Don't seem like Charlotte's in a particularly talkative frame of mind. So we're thinkin' the best thing for it might be to get on up outta here before . . ."

"Before what?"

"Before she gets like she was before," murmured Aunt Therese.

"Before?" Layla looked from one woman to the other. "What happened before?"

The air thrummed, a long, wordless conversation taking place between the sisters, each of them seemingly suspended in that moment before everything is irrevocably changed.

"When your momma left, Charlotte, folks hereabout, went through a bit of a bad time," said Aunt Therese.

Layla said nothing. The Aunts had not mentioned this before.

"Your momma did come back home," her aunt went on. "A few times."

"She . . . what?" Layla shook her head. "But I thought . . ."

"She came down with Andrew. Your daddy," said Aunt Jayne. Her fists were balled on the table beside her plate, the veins bulging in her hands. "She wanted us . . . wanted Charlotte to meet him. Not sure what she was thinkin'. To show us she done good? To make amends for forsaking her kin? Anyway . . ."

She opened her hand, spread her fingers wide on the table. "Andrew," she said, a faint smile playing at the edge of her lips. "Everybody loved them some Andrew Hurley. Almost enough to make up for Elinor playin' at city girl and stayin' gone."

"Especially Charlotte," said Aunt Therese softly.

The nascent smile vanished. "Yeah, especially Charlotte," agreed her sister.

"What happened?" asked Layla, unconsciously speaking in a near whisper.

"They got married. Your momma and daddy," said Aunt Therese.

Layla frowned, confused. "So?"

"So, Charlotte went and lost her goddamn mind," snapped Aunt Jayne. Her sister flinched.

Layla stared.

"She went to that wedding. Didn't nobody think that was a good idea.

Charlotte on a good day could be . . . unpredictable. Barely said nothin' to nobody. Got all dressed up—"

"She looked nice," interrupted Aunt Therese.

Aunt Jayne shot her a withering look. "She got all dressed up then stood in a corner like some doggone potted plant all evening, giving everyone, us, your daddy, Elinor, the evil eye. When your momma tried to get her to dance, to come sit with the bridesmaids and have some cake, Charlotte liked to knocked her down gettin' outta there."

Layla tugged at her hair, frowning, remembering Charlotte's version of the wedding.

"She did say something to your daddy before she hightailed it out of there," said Aunt Therese.

"What?"

The Aunts shrugged in unison.

"Nobody knows," said Aunt Therese. "But after the wedding things got . . . bad."

The sisters were silent for a long moment.

"We went out there. Out to Scotia. After," said Aunt Therese. "To check up on her. Make sure she was doin' alright."

She shook her head.

"She wasn't. Found her out there huddled in the bed. House closed up. Hot and foul smellin'. Don't think she'd bathed in days. Wouldn't say a word."

"Auntie Mercy was doin' poorly by that time," said Aunt Jayne. "Didn't really want to call Charlotte's sisters. They'd been lookin' for any excuse to get her off that island since forever. So, we brought her back here with us."

"Then things got worse," said Aunt Therese.

The Aunts exchanged a look.

"The nights were just awful. She would be thrashin' around. We had to get special locks for the windows and the doors 'cause she'd wander off. She took to yellin' out names and . . ." Aunt Therese flinched.

"Names?" asked Layla.

"Just names," answered Aunt Therese. "She'd call out names in the dead of night and then later we'd hear about how the person whose name she called hadn't shown up for work. Or they took sick. Or got themselves arrested for fightin' or something. There was this cousin, he . . ."

"They found his dog wanderin' the streets. House burnt to the ground," said Aunt Jayne. She clenched and unclenched her hands. "Never did find him."

Layla sat rigid, her mouth dry, a frisson of fear settling in the pit of her stomach.

"And we could feel it," Aunt Therese went on, her voice low. "It was her. We knew it was her. Could just see it. Like little flashes in the back of our eyeballs. Charlotte mad mad. But still, she wouldn't say nothin'. Just sat there, day by day, all fire and poison."

"Doctor said she was depressed," said Aunt Jayne, her tone scornful. "She's depressed? For what? How he know she's depressed if she just sittin' there like a tree stump? He gave her pills. Don't know why doctors always think there's a pill for everything. But we gave 'em to her anyway. Wasn't nothin' else workin', was it?"

"Did they work?" Layla asked the question, though she wasn't sure she wanted to hear the answer.

"At first," said Aunt Therese. "And then . . . that plane crashed."

Layla's head whipped up. "Plane?"

"Been on those pills about a week. Had been sleepin' quiet. Her, and us too. Finally. Actually, talkin' a fair little bit. Askin' about maybe going back out island after the holidays."

"Then it started up again," said Aunt Jayne. "Her yellin' out in the night. One name. Wasn't nobody we knew. But she just kept at it. Three nights, four. And we had a bad, bad feeling. We surely did."

She made a choking sound. "On Christmas Eve, a pilot over to the Marine base got up from bed, got into his jet plane, and flew that thing smack into the ground."

"Oh. My. God," whispered Layla. She tasted vomit in the back of her throat; an image of the man on the beach, shotgun in hand, flashed in her mind.

"Saw his picture, his name on the news the next morning," murmured Aunt Therese. "The name Charlotte had been yellin' out in the night."

"We had no choice. Had her locked up in that sanitorium," said Aunt Jayne. "Over in Savannah."

"They put her on even more pills," added her sister softly. "Couldn't barely talk. Let alone dream. When they let her go, we stayed out there with her. Fixin' her food. Lookin' out for her. Stayed on Scotia nearly half a year. Doin' for her."

"And she forgave you? For . . . locking her up."

"What choice did we have?" snapped Aunt Jayne. "And she did . . . nothing," she said, her voice softening. "Just retreated to her little piece of the world. Scotia. Everything fine, long as she's left to herself. Mostly."

She shook her head.

"We made a mistake," Aunt Jayne went on. "We thought you needed to know what you are, where you come from. To know your family. I thought Elinor was a fool." Her shoulders sagged. She seemed to deflate, and somehow this surrender was more terrifying than her rage. "But maybe Elinor wasn't the one that was the fool."

"Last night won't happen again." Layla raked her fingers through her hair, not sure this was true, even as she said the words.

"She's in my head every night," Aunt Therese spoke softly. Her hands quivered with the effort of holding on to the chair. "Those echoes. All those years out there on that island. She was like an ember, just smolderin' away. Then Elinor died. And you came, and it was like pure oxygen to her. That ember just . . . exploded." She looked up and locked eyes with her niece. "And I think it's going to be bad again."

Layla felt a chill. She thought of the young pilot, the jet screeching toward the earth and exploding in a ball of fire.

"You should go," interrupted Aunt Jayne. "May not make a bit of difference, but still. You got to. For you. For us. For everybody."

Layla fought the urge to hurl the plate of ham and black-eyed peas across the room. "If she's going to do that again, that thing where she turns people's dreams around, if you think all those terrible things might start happening again, then that's even more reason to try and stop her!"

"How?" snapped Aunt Jayne. "Stop her how?"

"I don't know!" She dug her nails into the table and struggled to keep her voice even. "But do you think running away is going to help?"

The two sisters were silent.

"Do you want me to leave?" she asked.

"Oh, sweetheart! We don't *want* you to leave." Aunt Therese reached for her hand. "We want you to be safe."

"And if I leave, will I be safe? Will you?"

Again, the sisters said nothing.

"Okay, then," Layla said, pushing to her feet. "Since it doesn't seem to matter where I am, I might as well go out to Scotia Island then."

She turned and left the kitchen.

Upstairs in the room beneath the eaves, she threw herself across the bed and screamed into the pillow. She had no idea how things could have gone so completely wrong. She'd been unhappy before—unhappy and maybe a little bit crazy, but now she was unhappy and crazy and under attack.

Eyes still closed, she frowned. Despite her bravado in the kitchen, the idea of confronting Charlotte again made her physically ill. Charlotte was powerful. And she had hurt people. Made them hurt themselves. Did that make her a murderer? She jerked upright. Gerta had asked if she believed in evil and the question had seemed so peculiar, so random.

"A caged animal has nothing to lose."

Gerta's words sounded in her head. But was that true?

Layla dug in her bag for her phone and texted Will: U ok?

His only response was two thumbs-up. Irritated, she punched in his number, then deleted it.

Her notes from the library were scattered all over the floor, and she picked them up, flipping through them. Was there anything there at all that might help her reach Charlotte?

Too wound up to sleep, she crept down the stairs. The kitchen was empty, and she stepped out onto the front porch. She could hear the soft tinkle of the bottles in the tree above her, invisible in the darkness. She stood staring at the stars, the same stars her mother had once stared at. Was Charlotte out there now staring at this same sky? Or was she already asleep, walking in someone's dream, causing pain? Finally, fatigue and the unrelenting mosquitoes drove her back inside and up to her room.

She was standing in a gray space. It was warm and empty. But for all that, it was not featureless. The air around her seemed to vibrate, to pulse, and there was the murmuring of voices, the sound of a crowd before the concert begins.

She'd heard this before. So many times before, but for the first time in her life she knew what it was she was hearing. It was the whispers of other dreamers, and she realized with a start that she could choose. She glanced down at the shell bracelet glowing on her wrist and laughed out loud. Closing her eyes, she took a deep breath in through her nose, arms held away from her body, listening, feeling. When she opened her eyes, she was in a huge auditorium.

She was alone, but the auditorium was decorated as if for some kind of ceremony. Red, white, and blue bunting hung from the ceiling, the doors, the window frames. Outside, planes roared overhead, and she could hear the sing-song cadence of men counting off a quick march.

Marine base. I'm on a Marine base.

Even without looking outside, she knew it was a Marine base.

Hearing laughter, she climbed the gleaming bleachers to peer through one of the high windows that lined the big hall. Out on the patchy grass, standing in the sun, was a woman about her age, her red dress catching the sunlight like a flower. Aunt Therese.

She was walking Aunt Therese's dream.

There was a broad-shouldered man in uniform with her. Handsome. Skin the color of burnt ginger. They were holding hands in the bright afternoon sun, and they only had eyes for each other.

Joseph.

The Marine's name came to her. Aunt Therese's late husband. Layla's Uncle Joe. Layla could feel their happiness, their love, and tears threatened again. They were so young. She turned to climb back down the bleachers so she could go outside to them, but the auditorium was gone.

The grayness had returned, as had the discordant throbbing, the buzz of voices. Other dreamers dreaming. She hesitated.

She could still feel it, that connection, tethering her to her Aunt Therese and Uncle Joe, feel the thrum of happiness her aunt was feeling but there was something else happening out there in the gray, something urgent.

Reluctantly, she turned away, turned toward the gray, the other dreams. There was an odd sensation in her head, and then she was in a room not much bigger than a closet, the walls lined with books and magazines, rising as high as she could see. Somehow, she knew there was a treasure buried in those books, and she had to find it. She began hauling books from the wall, but there were always more. She pulled faster, and faster still, until the pile of books reached her waist and she could barely move. She needed to get out, but she couldn't leave until she found . . . something. She had to find the thing. Whatever the thing was. She had to.

"I got egg salad."

Layla inhaled sharply, startled. There was a girl, just visible on the other side of a short wall of books.

"What?"

The girl held a sandwich out toward her, impossibly large and bright yel-

low with yolk. The girl was young, nine or ten, plump and shiny faced, her long cornrows pulled back into a ponytail. It was a girl Layla hadn't spoken to since she'd left her sprawled beneath the playground swings in the third grade— Angela Morris, her grade school nemesis.

"Egg salad," said Angela again. "Wanna trade?"

"I don't have anything to trade."

"Then what's that?" Angela pointed to the bracelet on her wrist.

Layla looked down at the bracelet encircling her wrist. "No." She shook her head, crossing her arms to hide it. "You can't have this."

The girl shrugged and pushed her sandwich into her backpack. "I got something to show you. Wanna see?"

Layla hesitated. She hadn't found her treasure, but she didn't want to stay in this room of books anymore. "Okay."

Angela grinned and then they were walking down a hallway, Layla trailing behind. They pushed through the large door at the end of the hall, and then Angela was gone. The sensation, that feeling of a folding inside her head, was quicker this time, the gray just a flash, warm, velvety, like stepping through a curtain.

Layla was on a stage and there, huddled in a small circle of light, was her brother.

"Will?"

At the sound of her voice, he jerked, but he didn't seem to fully register her. She ran to him and threw her arms around his neck. His skin was clammy and cool. And he was trembling.

"Layla?" His voice was that of an old man's.

"Will, what is it?" He seemed terrified.

"Lay, I don't want to be here."

Frowning, she grabbed his hands. "Dude, it's a dream." She squeezed his fingers hard. "Wake up, okay. Just wake up."

"I can't." He shook his head. "I've tried and tried. All the doors are locked." He pointed. "And he won't let me out."

She turned. They were in a small theater and from the front row, a man sat smiling up at them. She swore under her breath.

Oliver. The man Will had been in love with before Chuck. A man that had broken his heart.

"Shit," she muttered. Trapped forever with the person you had once loved with all your heart, a person that had treated that love like garbage. "Charlotte, you sick twist."

She was sure Charlotte had planted this terrible thought in her brother's head. "What?"

"Ignore him," she said, turning back to Will. "Just come on."

She dragged him to the back of the theater and pushed against the door; it was locked. She tried another door, then another, but it was no use. It was just as Will had said. The doors were all locked. They weren't getting out that way. Behind them, at the front of the theater, Oliver began to clap.

She gave him the finger, fighting the urge to charge down the aisle and punch her brother's ex-lover in the mouth. Beside her, Will slumped in a seat and covered his face with his hands. She needed to get him out. Needed to get him to wake up.

A thought flashed through her mind, bright as a flare. Something from the jumble of journal articles and textbooks. One of the few things she'd read in the library that she'd understood. About logic and dreams not being able to coexist, about the inability to hold on to concrete details in a dream.

What if . . . ?

She squatted down next to her brother.

"Will," she whispered. "What's your phone number?"

He raised his head to look at her. "What?"

"Your phone number. What is it?"

Maybe if she could just get him to . . reboot, if she could get the reasoning part of his brain fully turned on . . .

Will was staring at her.

"Listen to me," she said. "I need you to tell me your phone number, your cell phone number."

He'd changed it less than six weeks before. He would have to reach to remember. He screwed up his face with the effort.

"I don't . . ."

"Yes, you do! Say it!" She willed her voice to stay calm, willed herself to ignore the applause behind them. "Tell me your cell phone number and then you can go home. You can go home and see Chase and Chuck."

"Chase? Chuck?" The confusion appeared to clear for a moment, and he looked at her fully for the first time. Behind them the applause had stopped. "I can't . . ."

"You can. Think, Will. Think really hard."

He gripped the seat in front of him, his eyes locked on hers. "Two, zero . . ." He dug his fingers into the velvet fabric.

"See? You can do this."

"Two, zero, two." He was sweating. *"Five, seven . . ."*

Suddenly, it was much brighter. Around them, the seats began to fade, growing fainter with each number.

"One, four . . ."

They were alone now, just the two of them, in a great, white space.

"Come on, Will!" She felt strong, confident. They were almost there.

"Eight . . ." And then she couldn't hear him, could barely see him.

"Will?"

Layla jerked awake. She lay staring at the low ceiling. Sunlight twisted and shimmered across the ceiling and wall, the light splintered into countless rainbow shards by the panes of glass in the octagonal window. She felt focused, light, a glimmer of hope burgeoning in her chest.

For the first time since she was a small girl, this thing she had, this thing she could do, didn't feel like a bad thing. Didn't feel like a thing she needed to fix. It had never happened like that before. She had never chosen.

Unconsciously, she stroked her wrist. And she had done a thing. She had guided Will out of his own dream. She was not as strong, not as skilled as Charlotte. But maybe she had stumbled onto something. Her own secret weapon. A way to defend herself. And her family.

Science and magic.

Layla glanced at her phone and jerked upright. It was early, but there was a text from Chuck: Call me.

She punched in the number.

"What's wrong?" she demanded with no preamble when her brother-in-law answered.

"Good morning," said Chuck, laughing.

The knot that had been forming in her chest loosened. "Morning," she said. "Sorry. What's up?"

"Will just wanted me to check in and see how you're doing. He said you texted last night."

"Yep." She thought of the uncharacteristic emoji. "Is everything okay?"

There was silence.

"Chuck?"

"Okay, so a day or so ago I would have said no," he said, finally. "But this morning he woke up at the crack of dawn. And he was humming."

Layla blinked. "Humming?"

"I haven't seen him in this good a mood in the morning since . . . Well, I've never seen him in this good a mood. And the crazy thing is he was yelling out in his sleep half the night. Thrashing around. I just knew he was going to wake exhausted like he has for the past week or so."

Layla grinned, relief flooding through her. "Well, that's a good thing, right?"

"For him," said Chuck, laughing. "I don't know how many more nights I can take with your brother yelling out his phone number in the middle of the night."

29

She maneuvered the Aunts' ancient truck through the narrow, curving streets of downtown Port Royal. Layla'd been restless all morning; the news of her brother, the night's dream, and the Aunts' revelations from the night before clanged relentlessly in her head. She'd paced the rooms of the house like a caged animal, and when she'd wondered aloud about maybe taking the truck for a drive, just to get out of the house, Aunt Jayne had all but thrown the keys at her.

By late morning she found herself here. Both sides of the street were lined with old homes, small antique shops, bookstores, and quaint boutiques. Layla pulled into a parking space beneath a massive old oak, the Spanish moss dangling from the branches gently brushing the truck's roof.

She climbed from the truck and began to stroll the thickly shaded sidewalk, taking in the art galleries and bed-and-breakfasts. One quirky shop sold lighthouses, clocks, and figurines carved from driftwood that had been collected from the beaches of the Carolinas. At a small bookstore, she bought a coffee table book about the flora and fauna of the tidal marshes of the Sea Islands for Chuck.

There was a small cottage next to the bookstore that had taken on a new life as a café. Layla stopped and bought an iced coffee and, as an afterthought, three slices of caramel cake. Taking her drink, she sat at one of the tables tucked in the garden at the side of the café. It was cool under the trees, the air thick with the scent of magnolia and rose. She sipped her coffee and studied the sky. Sitting in the cool greenness of the garden, she felt a sense of calm she hadn't felt since her mother's death.

Her phone pinged, and she glanced down to see a warning that a major storm was churning its way north up the Atlantic, but there, in the sweet-smelling garden, it was hard to feel alarmed by the reports of the vicious winds and surging waves said to be working their way toward them. The sky was a cloudless, crystalline blue, and a brisk breeze freshened the summer air as people bustled about the little town.

She picked at her cake. Despite everything the Aunts had told her, she knew with absolute certainty that she had no choice about confronting Charlotte. She could go back to Baltimore but there was no guarantee of protection there. There was no guarantee of protection against Charlotte anywhere.

She stuck a finger in the caramel icing and popped it in her mouth, sucking absently as she gazed out at the street. Charlotte would keep coming after her, after her family as long as she saw Layla as a threat. As long as she felt she had nothing to lose.

Nothing to lose.

Layla kept coming back to that thought again and again. What did Charlotte have to lose?

And then there was the island itself. Increasingly, she found herself drawn to it. The beauty and the stillness. Her family's long history there. It felt like a place to belong.

A hard gust of wind knocked over her nearly empty coffee cup, and from blocks away came the sound of church bells striking the time. Three o'clock. She shot another look at the sky. It seemed to be growing darker. Feeling a flicker of nervousness, she picked up her packages and headed for the truck.

They were outside when she drove up: Aunt Therese on the porch swing shelling peas, Aunt Jayne on her hands and knees pulling weeds away from the foundation near the steps.

Aunt Therese looked up. Layla mounted the porch steps. "You have a good outing?"

"I did." She watched the Aunts work for a minute.

"They say it's supposed to storm." Layla held up her phone and once again glanced uneasily at the sky. It was definitely growing darker and the wind was picking up.

"Oh, sugar, it's gonna storm alright. Don't need no phone to tell me that," said Aunt Therese, laughing. "Old Arthur keeps me plenty updated."

"I brought you guys something from town." Layla held up the white bakery box.

"You brought us some Sweet Dell's? Well, holy hallelujah," exclaimed Aunt Therese. "I haven't been in there since they redid the gardens."

"Little Rodelle's place," said Aunt Jayne. She stood with a groan. Pulling off her gloves, she stepped onto the porch and squinted into the bakery box. The frosting of the caramel cake gleamed like gold against the white cardboard. "Rodelle's cakes ain't never been as good as her momma's."

"Well, whose is?" said Aunt Therese. She took a bite of the cake, making sure to get every drop of the caramel icing off the plastic fork. "But it is still some mighty fine cake."

Aunt Jayne reached for a piece and her sister rapped her knuckles with the fork. "Unh-unh, Jayne. You know you not 'sposed to have cake with your sugar."

"Really, Therese?" Aunt Jayne put her hands on her hips and glared. "So, you eatin' all that up like you ain't never had a slice a cake in your life, is just you lookin' out for me, then?"

"Yes, ma'am!"

"Mm-hmm."

Layla grinned, feeling a sudden flood of warmth toward the Aunts. No matter how things worked out, she was glad they had come back into her life.

She suddenly threw her arms around the two old women, the shopping bags swinging awkwardly on her wrist.

"Oh," cried Aunt Jayne, patting her stiffly on the back.

Layla released them. "I need to put this stuff away."

Aunt Jayne cleared her throat. "Well, I'm a put supper on in a bit."

Layla nodded. As she walked into the house, she could hear Aunt Jayne yelling for her sister to stop eating all that cake.

Layla bit into her piece of fried chicken. There was corn on the cob and beans fresh from the garden, and of course buttermilk biscuits. She was still getting used to the fact that no matter how stifling hot it was outside, supper was always something incredibly heavy, something amazingly delicious.

"You all aren't worried about the storm?" she asked. Outside the sky had turned the color of a bruise, purple with streaks of green. Intermittent flashes of lightning lit the kitchen.

The Aunts shrugged in unison.

"No point in worryin'," said Aunt Jayne. "You just put up anything that might fly off, close the shutters, and wait for it to blow over."

"What about evacuating or something?"

Her aunt snorted. "Girl, evacuate to where? This house done stood up to storms nearly a hundred years. Ain't nothin' gonna bring this old place down. We're as safe here as anywhere. Time to time, yard gets flooded out yonder, but usually worse that happens is we lose a few shingles and some tree branches."

"Florence was pretty bad," said Aunt Therese. "And Dorian wasn't no picnic either."

"Yeah. It does seem like the big ones gettin' bigger evey year," agreed her sister. "But still we've stood it alright and fared better than a lot of folks."

"It's going to be fine, child," said Aunt Therese. She helped herself to another drumstick.

"But . . ." Layla hesitated, thinking. "What about the islands? What happens to the people out on the islands? On Scotia?"

"Da wata da bring we, an de wata gwine tek we bak," Aunt Jayne murmured.

"What?" asked Layla frowning.

Her aunt shook her head. "Sometimes," she said, speaking slowly. "Crazy and mean as she is, there are those few times I am righteous glad she's out there. Protecting Scotia. Protecting the home place. Making sure those comeyahs stay away."

Layla blinked.

"They come and they come. All those folks from outside. From up North," explained Aunt Therese. "They come and they build their fancy condominiums and their seawalls to protect their pretty boats. Plowin' up the grass and fields for golf courses and tennis courts. Hikin' over the ancestors' graves and rippin' out the oyster beds and the marshes. Then the storms come. Nothin' to hold back the water and then that water takes those islands. Bit by bit."

She gazed through the back door.

"Charlotte out there. She defends Scotia and Scotia defends her and the people still there. Makes those comeyahs go away. Makes them afraid. They come to Scotia and Charlotte scares them off."

"But they don't stay scared off," added her sister, quietly. "Money always gonna be stronger than fear."

They were silent for a moment, each lost in her own thoughts. Their sorrow and anger hung in the air.

"But that's what the surveyors and the title search was for," Layla said quietly. "They can't take it away from us if we don't want them to. If we have clear and definitive ownership."

Aunt Jayne gave a harsh laugh and gazed at her with something like pity. "Oh, sweetheart. Even if that were true, you can't be naïve enough to think these white folks don't bend and twist the law 'til it screams. Charlotte doesn't want your help. She doesn't want anything at all from you."

"It's not a matter of what Charlotte wants, Aunt Jayne. Scotia Island is as much mine as it is hers," said Layla.

"Layla," began Aunt Therese.

"No, Aunt Therese. It feels right to me. This place. Whatever I said before, I *am* grateful to you both for Scotia, for my history." And not for the first time that day, Layla felt tears well. "It's our legacy. Our family's. And I want to help protect it."

She stood. "I want to work with Charlotte. I have to work with Charlotte." She was quiet for a moment. "But if she won't work with me. If she won't listen . . ." Layla clenched and unclenched her fists. "Well, I'm not afraid of Charlotte."

A gust of wind blew something against the back door, and they all jumped. Aunt Jayne locked eyes with Layla.

"Well," she said, her voice like steel. "You should be, child."

30

It had finally started raining, hard, sending water sheeting through the window and onto the floor. Layla pulled the window tight and sopped up the water with a T-shirt. Outside, the Aunts' truck was already nearly covered in leaves and broken twigs.

Layla was agitated and uneasy, and despite the thick darkness, it was too early to sleep, though she doubted she could have anyway. She tried downloading a movie to her phone, but each time it would drop out after only a minute or two, a victim of the Aunts' magical internet.

Finally giving up, she stretched out on the bed and stared at the ceiling. The supper conversation played in a continuous loop in her head. She was not the enemy, but Charlotte had apparently decided she was no different than the developers who periodically came sniffing around, anxious to build marinas on the beach.

Despite her brave talk in the kitchen, she *was* afraid. Terrified.

Somehow, she had to convince this distant cousin that they were allies, that they were stronger together, and that she, Layla, had as much right to Scotia Island as she did.

The storm was ratcheting up. Outside the wind pummeled the house, tree limbs lashing at the siding. She wondered what Charlotte was doing this very moment, alone in her tiny house out on the island.

Probably plotting my demise, she thought darkly. She gave a dry snort.

She woke from a fitful sleep with a start. She lay for a moment, listening to the rain pound the low roof overhead. It was still coming down hard but the wind had died back, rendering the sound more soothing than terrifying.

She fumbled for her phone to check the time, and as her fingers closed around it, she stopped. Frowning, she sat up.

Smoke?

Was that smoke?

She stood and sniffed at the air. She was sure of it.

Smoke! There was smoke!

Clutching her phone, she yanked open the bedroom door and froze. Smoke was drifting up the staircase, shimmering faintly in the glow of the hall night-light.

"Oh my god!" she cried.

She took an instinctive step back.

Aunt Therese! Aunt Jayne!

Layla frantically tried punching in 911 as she raced down the stairs, her heart pounding in her throat.

The smoke was thicker on the landing. She banged on the nearest door. "Aunt Therese! Aunt Jayne! Fire! Get out! There's a fire!"

The door opened and Aunt Therese stood, weaving unsteadily in the threshold. "What?"

Layla yanked her aunt into the hallway, ignoring the woody, sweet smell of whiskey on her breath. "We have to go!"

Fighting panic, she thrust her aunt toward the stairs and whirled toward Aunt Jayne's door. It was unlocked—and empty. She whirled to follow Aunt Therese.

"Where's Aunt Jayne?" The air grew darker, thicker, as they raced down the stairs. Her throat burned, every other breath a cough. She could hear the fire now, a faint crackle, the air hot on her face. "Aunt Therese, where's Aunt Jayne?"

Their address. The 911 operator was asking for their address but Layla's mind had gone blank. Her only thought, to get out. Get the Aunts out. She yelled her aunts' names at the operator.

"Just hurry," she screamed.

At the foot of the stairs Aunt Therese came to an abrupt stop. "Sweet Jesus!" she cried.

The door to the kitchen was wreathed in flame. Smoke raced along the ceiling, billowing into the hallway toward them like a deadly river. The curtains on the back door, the wallpaper glowed a vivid orange. And in the center of the inferno, unmoving, stood Aunt Jayne. Aunt Therese yanked free of Layla's hold and was halfway down the hall before Layla had time to comprehend what she was seeing.

"No!" She lunged at the old woman, catching hold of the back of her nightgown. "No, Aunt Therese!"

Her aunt outweighed her by nearly eighty pounds, and panic made her strong.

"No! You can't get to her that way." Layla struggled to stop her, screaming to make herself heard over the roaring blaze. In the narrow hall, the heat had grown unbearable. In desperation, she rammed her body into her aunt, using the momentum to drive the older woman back. Aunt Therese stumbled backward, toward the door.

"Jayne!" screamed Aunt Therese, still fighting to get to her sister. "Jayne."

"No!" Layla pushed frantically using her shoulder as a plow, eyes stinging, her head pounding from lack of oxygen. "No, Aunt Therese! Get out! I'll get her!"

They tumbled out onto the front porch.

"Jayne," moaned Aunt Therese.

Hunched over her knees, Layla coughed violently, each wheezing breath a knife blade down her throat. "I'll get her," she managed to say. "Stay here."

In the distance, sirens punctuated the sound of rain and fire.

Straightening, Layla staggered toward the back of the house. It was still raining hard and her feet skidded on the rain-soaked grass. Smoke was beginning to pour from every window on the first floor.

"Aunt Jayne!"

Three feet inside the screen door, Aunt Jayne stood, still motionless, holding what looked like a newspaper in one hand. Wind and rain blew through the open door, pushing the fire away from her, but it was only a matter of seconds before the entire kitchen was engulfed. The air felt superheated, singeing Layla's face, blistering the skin on her forehead.

She grasped the handle on the screen door and screamed, the metal red-hot. Whipping off her shirt, she wrapped it around her hand then flung herself into the burning kitchen, trying to ignore the flames, trying to ignore the horrifying heat.

"Aunt Jayne!"

She grabbed her aunt. The old woman's eyes were closed, her sweat-drenched face blank. As if she was asleep. Layla grabbed the front of her shirt and pulled. Aunt Jayne took two steps and stopped. Something exploded in the inferno behind them and Layla screamed, her voice drowned out by the fire's own. Her mind was a swirling black hole of panic. Her only thought was to get away from the terrible heat and the choking smoke. They had to get out or they were both going to die.

Still holding on to her aunt, she pulled, backpedaling hard, dragging her toward the door. They were nearly out, her aunt right at the threshold, when Layla lost her footing on the wet porch boards. She went down hard, bringing Aunt Jayne with her, her aunt landing half in and half out of the house. There was another small explosion and Layla scrambled to her hands and knees.

Gasping for breath, her eyes swollen from the smoke, she crawled to her aunt and grasped her beneath her arms, struggling to pull her away from the house, but Aunt Jayne was dead weight and Layla fought for traction on the rain-soaked grass. She watched in horror as the hem of Aunt Jayne's housecoat began to smoke. Suddenly, like a ghost, Viktor materialized from the haze. He yanked her to her feet.

"Go," he yelled. "I'll get her. Go!"

Layla staggered blindly toward the trees, the rain cooling her face, her lungs, the skin on her bare shoulders. She'd lost sight of Viktor in the smoke, but moments later, he reappeared, Aunt Jayne over one shoulder, the hem of her housecoat in flames. By the time she reached them, he'd extinguished the fire in the wet grass. She fell to her knees beside him, reaching for Aunt Jayne.

"You alright?" he asked.

She nodded, not trusting herself to speak. The yard was filling with firefighters, and Viktor pulled her up and out of the way as paramedics rushed to Aunt Jayne's aid.

"How?" Gripped by a spasm of coughing, it was all she could say.

"Police scanner. Heard the address and . . ." He shook his head.

They watched in silence from the shelter of the tree line as the paramedics loaded Aunt Jayne into the ambulance and Aunt Therese climbed in behind her. Viktor reached for her hand and she grabbed hold.

"Was she . . . ?" he said at last, his voice strangled. "Was Tante Jayne asleep?"

She looked up at him, and she could see the reflection of the fire in his eyes. She gave the tiniest nod and began to cry.

31

Gerta hurried down the hospital corridor toward Layla and Viktor, her round face flushed with distress. When she reached them, she flung her arms around them both, and the three of them clung to each other in a tight, awkward embrace. The top of Gerta's head barely reached Layla's collarbone, but Layla leaned into the contact as best she could.

"Therese called," cried Gerta, stepping back to look up at them. "I barely know what she is saying!"

"There was a fire. Aunt Jayne was caught in the house."

"*Mein Gott!*" murmured Gerta. "She is hurt?"

"Her gown caught fire," answered Viktor. "She has some burns on her legs. But she's going to be okay."

Gerta was shaking her head. "I do not understand. It was the stove? Something with the storm? What?"

"We don't know yet, Oma," said Viktor. "The fire seemed to start in the kitchen. That's all we know right now. And Tante Jayne . . ."

He shot a look at Layla, who flinched.

"Tante Jayne was a little bit . . . confused," he finished.

"Confused?" The old woman looked from her grandson to Layla, then back again. "What does this mean, confused?"

Neither of them answered.

"*Ach,*" huffed Gerta impatiently. She stared at them hard for a long moment. She seemed about to say something more then changed her mind.

"Therese is with her?" she asked instead.

"She's in there," answered Viktor. "Tante Jayne's sleeping."

Gerta pulled a set of keys from her handbag and held them out. "Layla and Therese will stay with me until things are settled." She looked Layla up and down. "You saw the doctor?"

Layla shook her head. The paramedics had examined her at the house. She had second-degree burns on her hand and first-degree burns on her face. And every breath felt as if a hairbrush were being forced down her lungs. But she'd refused transport to the hospital. What she wanted now more than anything in the world was a shower and some sleep.

"Sleep then," said Gerta, as if reading her mind. "A hot shower. Things will be better then." Gerta chuckled. "Or perhaps not worse."

She dropped the keys into her grandson's hands, then hurried past them into Aunt Jayne's room, leaving Viktor and Layla alone in the hallway.

"You really should let someone take a look at you. You inhaled a lot of smoke," he said.

She held up a hand to stop him. She'd let the EMTs put a bandage and some ointment on her face and hands at the house, had even sat for a few minutes in the back of the ambulance breathing in oxygen, but now, she just wanted to go. Her hands were shaking. She balled them tight against her chest, swallowing hard.

"I'm fine," she said, her voice hoarse. "I'm just going to go check on the Aunts real quick before we go."

He opened his mouth as if to say something else, then seemed to think better of it. He nodded and leaned against the wall to wait.

Aunt Therese was sitting in a chair next to her sister's bed, a thin hospital blanket wrapped around her shoulders. Gerta was beside her, one small hand resting on her friend's shoulder. She looked up when Layla walked in, but Aunt Therese hardly seemed to notice.

Layla glanced at Aunt Jayne. She lay still and silent in the hospital bed, her heavily bandaged legs visible beneath the covers. She looked fragile, insubstantial.

"They got her sedated," said Aunt Therese to no one in particular.

Layla squatted beside her. "Aunt Therese, I'm going to Miss Gerta's now. Why don't you come? You need to rest. Aunt Jayne is sleeping and Gerta'll stay with her."

She looked up at her aunt's friend, who nodded.

Aunt Therese's eyes never left the motionless form on the bed.

Layla sighed. "Alright, then. I'll be back later, okay?"

She leaned to give her aunt an awkward hug, and Aunt Therese grabbed her wrist, holding her hard enough that she could feel the bones grind against each other.

"Baby, you stay. Or go," said Aunt Therese, her voice raw. "Whatever you think best. You do what you need to do. You are family." Her eyes locked onto her niece's. "Always family."

Layla inhaled. "Aunt Therese, I know that. It's okay. It's going to be . . ." Her aunt's grip tightened on her wrist and she hissed in pain.

"No!" The word ricocheted around the small room. "It's not! Not okay at all."

Gerta was watching them, her expression puzzled.

"Me and Jayne, we thought . . ." Aunt Therese's voice broke. "But we made a mess of things. We surely did. Scotia. Shoulda just gone on and let it alone, but we thought . . ."

She choked out a half sob, before taking a deep breath. She tried to smile. "No, no, no! You're right, child. Everything's going to be just fine."

She held on to her niece another moment, emotions playing across her brown face, then let go with a sigh.

Layla looked at her mother's older sisters. They barely resembled the bright, brassy women that had appeared at her mother's funeral just months before. They looked tired and beaten. They looked old.

"It is going to be okay, Aunt Therese. I promise you," said Layla.

Her aunt smiled, but it was a promise they both knew she might not be able to keep.

"You gon' be able to sleep if you drink this?"

Layla took the cup of coffee he offered without looking up and nodded. Her clothes were damp and reeked of smoke. Her face felt tight and swollen, and the burn on her hand throbbed in time with her heartbeat. Viktor found an old bottle of pain medications in the back of Gerta's medicine cabinet.

"Don't believe Oma would mind," he said, handing her the bottle. "Considering the circumstances."

Layla gulped down two, not bothering to read the bottle.

A hummingbird flitted back and forth over the angel's trumpet on the patio, and the wet grass sparkled in the morning sun. But Layla wasn't seeing the bright summer morning on the other side of the glass. She was seeing fire: yellow and orange—the color of Gerta's Chihuly—climbing the kitchen walls, devouring everything in its path. She was seeing Aunt Jayne on her back, eyes closed, seemingly deep in a calm sleep as her housecoat smoldered around her ankles.

"How you holdin' up?"

She blinked. Viktor was watching her from the other side of the small dining table. She shrugged. Even that smallest of movements exhausted her. Everything exhausted her: moving, thinking, breathing.

"Tante Jayne was sleepin'." It was not a question.

She gave a small nod.

"Was she sleepwalking, you think? Like when you went into the creek the other night?"

Layla stared into her cup. The heat was uncomfortable through the bandage, and she shifted it in her hands. She could feel the faintest blurring at the edges of her pain, a slight wobble behind her eyes. She closed her eyes and sighed.

"Layla!"

She blinked and looked up. He was staring at her, his brow creased with concern, and she realized that he had been talking to her.

"I'm sorry. What?"

"I said, Do you think maybe Tante Jayne might have accidently caused that fire."

She suppressed a yawn. She was so tired. "Charlotte caused the fire."

Viktor gave a surprised laugh, his eyes widening in surprise. "What? Charlotte? Your cousin out on the island Charlotte?"

She gazed at him, unblinking. He laughed again, then frowned.

"What the devil are you talkin' about?" he said when she said nothing. "What are you saying?"

Layla sipped her coffee, wincing as the steam washed across the angry skin of her face. "Maybe she was trying to scare us. Maybe more. I don't know. I just know she's pissed and she caused that fire."

He sat back in the chair, mouth open, gaping at her, his expression flitting between amusement, disbelief, and worry. The faint blisters on his cheeks looked like a new sunburn. He ran a hand over his face and studied her through red-rimmed eyes. He looked as tired as she felt.

"Okay," he said, finally, with a forced chuckle. "I'll play along. How exactly did Cousin Charlotte, who I'll bet hasn't stepped foot off that island in like, I don't know . . . a million years, cause that fire?"

Layla's jaw tightened at the tone. She knew that expression, had seen it more times than she could count on the faces of neighbors and teachers and psychologists through the years. Had seen it on the faces of her own family. He was humoring her, nothing more.

"When you were a little boy, your grandmother used to tell you stories about demons that could come down chimneys and through keyholes," she said, her voice cold, flat. She heard his sharp intake of breath. "They would sit on a dreamer's chest and make them dream terrible dreams. It terrified you."

She'd seen a bit of this in one of Gerta's dreams the first time she'd visited; had watched Viktor at five, maybe six years old, sitting at her knee, eyes round, terrified. He was looking at her the same way now, his golden skin suddenly pale.

"Oma . . . Oma told you about that?" He stared at her, his mouth open in surprise.

"Alptraum." Layla's eyes were locked on his. "They're called alptraum. You believe they're real. And I think you know your grandmother didn't tell me about that. Would never have told me that."

He was up from the table. His eyes had gone dark, hard, and she could see the muscles working in his jaw. "Just what the hell are you playin' at here?"

She gripped her cup, her eyes never leaving his face. "I need to tell you something."

32

She lay sprawled across the bed in Gerta's guestroom, eyes closed. Images flickered across her closed eyelids: thick, green water tugging at her ankles, Aunt Jayne standing in the kitchen, fire racing up the walls. Aunt Jayne lying in the grass, eyes closed, asleep despite the chaos, despite the burns.

She was sure she'd never be able to fall asleep, but when she opened her eyes again, the light filtering through the crisp, white curtains had changed to golds and ambers.

She sat up with a groan. Her face hurt. Her hand hurt. The muscles in her back and sides hurt. She tugged at her hair which still emitted the acrid stench of smoke in spite of her long shower.

A plastic shopping bag hung from the post at the foot of the bed. Layla peered inside and let out a strangled laugh. Inside were two T-shirts, a pair of jeans, and a set of underwear. The thought of Viktor agonizing over a selection of bras and panties for her both amused her and made her want to sink through the floor. She pulled on one of the T-shirts and the pair of jeans. The T-shirt was a size too big and the jeans barely made it past her full hips. They were, she realized with a pang, the only clothes she now had in South Carolina.

Viktor was still sitting in the same place he'd been when she'd gone to lie down hours earlier. She could see his reflection in the glass patio door. He looked pale and shell-shocked.

"Thank you," she said, pointing at the clothes. He gave a barely perceptible nod. She sat down at the table and waited.

She'd told him everything: about her family, about what Charlotte could do—about what *she* could do. His response had been disbelieving silence. He sat staring at her now, his expression grim.

"All that stuff you were sayin' before. That dream stuff. That stuff about Charlotte and the island and your momma and all the rest. That's all the God's honest truth?" he said, finally.

She nodded.

He was silent for a long time.

"I was nine when my folks split up," he said at last. "My brother, Felix, and me came down here from Boston to live with Oma and Opa. They raised us. Them, and for all intents and purposes, Tantes Therese and Jayne too."

He locked eyes with her, and his expression was hard and angry. "Except for my brother, those three old ladies, Oma and your aunts, are the only real family I got on this earth. This dreamwalkin' thing you're talkin' about, I don't understand half of it, and I'm not sure how much to believe, but if Charlotte had anything at all to do with hurtin' them, then I think it's time we took a little trip on out to Scotia and have us a come to Jesus meetin' with her."

Layla simply nodded once again.

Viktor's boat was newer than the Aunts' and much more powerful. She felt the engine's vibration through her body, and as they flew across the water, the wind whipped her breath away. Unlike when she'd ventured out to Scotia Island with the Aunts, this time there were no stories of mysterious twin babies or naked women. No talk of black birds filling the sky. There was only the sound of the water splashing against the boat's hull and the rhythmic drone of the engine.

"You talked to your brother last night?" Viktor raised his voice to be heard over the boat noise.

"The night before," she said.

She leaned forward to peer through the windscreen. Everything was shrouded in a tattered gray mist. She could only see a few feet past the bow, but Viktor had assured her the fog would burn off by the time they reached the island. Twisting a strand of hair around her finger, she sat back and closed her eyes.

She'd conferenced with both Will and Evan. Her brothers had been horrified when they'd heard about the fire, about Aunt Jayne. It had taken long minutes to calm them down, to be heard over their frantic cross talk, their insistence that she come home. Right now.

"I can't," she said. "I need to get the Aunts settled in."

"Well, then I'll come down there," said Will.

"What for?"

"I could . . . I don't know. Something."

Layla laughed, softly. "There's nothing you can do for the Aunts. Not right now. Maybe in a few weeks. I'm fine."

She'd had to assure them again and again that she hadn't been hurt. That she would come home as soon as she could.

"Chuck's going to go put money in your account later today," Will had said, finally relenting.

"I don't—"

"Do you have clothes?" he interrupted. "A place to stay? Do you? Yeah, I didn't think so," he went on before she could answer. "Then you're going to need money. And please go to a real store, not one of those back-alley resale places you're always shopping in. You look homeless ninety-five percent of the time."

"Not homeless," Evan interjected. "Artsy."

"Oh, my god, you guys," she groaned, shaking her head, though they couldn't see it. "Shut up, already."

True to his word, Chuck had wired her five hundred dollars, Evan another thousand. She'd spent yesterday settling into a small bed-and-breakfast in Port Royal to give Aunt Therese and Gerta their space and buying some essentials in town for herself and the Aunts.

Before she'd ended the call with her brothers, she'd said, "I love you dudes." There'd been a moment of surprised silence before Evan muttered, "We love you too." Will had simply said, "Yeah, whatever, man."

Curled up in the boat seat, she snorted at the memory.

She opened her eyes. Just as Viktor had said, the fog was lifting. Spread out before them was the crystal blue water of the sound, and there, far out on the horizon, loomed the gray hulk of Scotia Island.

33

For the second time in as many months Layla stood on the long wooden dock at the edge of Scotia Island. The sea birds screeching overhead and the sound of the water lapping against the side of the boat was all that broke the silence.

"When was the last time you were out here?" she asked.

"When we were young, we would come out with the Tantes for the reunions and the fall oyster fest. Some weekends. Not so much now. Don't think I've been out to the island in a year? Probably longer."

"Really?" she said, surprised.

Viktor shrugged. "No real reason to."

He took off his sunglasses and studied the sandy trail that led to the top of the bluff. "Believe it or not I've only met your cousin a handful of times, but I've heard the stories. Everybody's heard the stories . . ." He cut himself off and put his sunglasses back on, the muscles of his jaw working.

"We should go," said Layla, turning away.

"Yep."

They stopped at the crest of the hill, and once again Layla was struck by how both empty and complete Scotia Island was. A world out of the world, as if nothing beyond the horizon existed, or mattered. Despite everything, regardless of her reason for returning, it still felt right. Just standing there, she could feel a calmness take hold, her heart rate slowing, beating in time with the waves washing up on the beach.

They made their way along the narrow, sandy trail that snaked through the brush. For a quarter of an hour they walked in silence. Though they were healing, the morning's heat made the blisters on her face burn; sweat plastered her T-shirt to her back.

"This the right way?" Viktor asked behind her.

"Yes," she said, breathing hard. She stopped in the patchy shade of a buckthorn shrub. "I think."

The truth was, she wasn't sure. She'd only been to Charlotte's the one time and that had been with the Aunts. Viktor handed her a bottled water from the pack slung across his shoulder, and she pressed it to her face, sighing with relief before gulping half of it down.

"I'm pretty sure it's just up there." She pointed to a vaguely familiar-looking hedge several yards ahead.

When the little clapboard cabin appeared just beyond a sparse stand of loblollies, Layla gave a whoop of joy. It looked exactly the same as the last time Layla had seen it. There were flowers in jars glimpsed through the windows, and a forlorn-looking nightgown fluttering on the clothesline. Layla wondered if it was the same one as before. And there, beyond the house, the sun glinted off the bottle-filled trees. Layla could feel her heart pulsing in her throat; every movement, every sound sent her senses firing. She took another swig from the water bottle, futilely trying to moisten a mouth that had suddenly gone dry.

Pushing his sunglasses up on his head, Viktor studied the shadows around the house, his eyes darting back and forth, seeming to take in everything at once.

"So?" he said, his voice low.

"So," she said, taking a deep breath. "I guess it's time for that meeting."

She walked from the cover of the trees, chin up, back straight, telegraphing a confidence she didn't feel. She banged hard on Charlotte's door.

No answer.

She turned the doorknob and found that as before, the door was unlocked. Heart pounding, she walked through the sleeping porch and into the kitchen.

The massive kitchen table was filled, edge to edge, with baskets of fruit: blueberries, blackberries, elderberries, the strange round fruit she recognized as muscadine grapes. A pot of water simmered on the woodstove, flooding the room with sweet, fruit-scented steam.

The last time she'd been here, they'd never left the kitchen. A hurried exploration showed that aside from a small bedroom and bathroom and a compact storage area off the porch, there was little else to the house.

Layla swore under her breath and forced herself to breathe slowly, to focus. Charlotte had to be nearby. She stepped back outside where Viktor stood waiting.

"She's not in there. But she can't be far. The stove's on."

"Should we go look for her?"

Layla shook her head. "No, even when she's not here, she's here," she said, echoing Aunt Therese's words. "She'll be back soon."

They were sitting quietly, side by side against the wall behind the table, when Charlotte walked in minutes later. She shuffled past them to check the pot on the stove before turning to the baskets of fruit on the table. It took her a moment to register the man and woman on the other side. She froze, blinking wildly in the steamy room. Layla glanced at Viktor. His arms were crossed, his hands loosely clenched on the tabletop. She stood and the old woman hissed, teeth bared.

"*Wuffuh* you in my house?" she hissed. "Go'way!"

Layla moved warily around the table. She opened her mouth then closed it, trying to remember her plan to explain to Charlotte about the surveyors, the title searches, to offer her help against the developers that would try to cheat them out of Scotia Island and steal their family's legacy.

But now, face-to-face with her cousin, the words stuck in her throat. All she could see was her brother's haggard face, the fear in his eyes as he told her of finding sand in his son's sheets. She saw the flames crawling up the walls of the Aunts' kitchen. Aunt Jayne asleep in the rain, senseless to her burns, the destruction of her house.

The woman standing in front of her had done terrible things. Layla clenched the fabric of her shorts, forcing herself to keep her hands at her side.

"Charlotte," she managed, her voice thick with emotion. "We need to talk."

"You not gon' be vexin' me with no talk," cried Charlotte, pointing her walking stick. "You goin' to get away. All *dis'yuh*, it b'long to me one! I says you not here, you not here!"

Layla felt the fury ignite, deep in the pit of her stomach, felt it catch hold and roar up into her chest, scorching her lungs, searing away her breath. She took a step toward the woman, who narrowed her eyes but did not back down.

"It was you, wasn't it?" said Layla. "You made that fire happen."

Charlotte's eyes flicked past her to the door, as if measuring her chance of escape.

"I know it was you. You walked in Aunt Jayne's dream. You made her start that fire." Layla raised her hands as if to strike the woman, saw Charlotte flinch. "You are a sick, twisted, old woman."

Charlotte reared back, quivering with rage. "Oonah not come me house and talk'um dat langwidge to me. Go'way!"

"I'm not going anywhere! You are going to listen to me."

"Liar!" Charlotte snarled, the sound low and dangerous. "You comeyah! You tongue is poison. Every word. You got nothin' to say to me."

"I never lied to you."

"Liar!" Charlotte screamed, spit flying, peppering Layla's face. "I see them mens taking pictures, measure this, measure that. I see them boats goin' round and round Scotia."

"Charlotte—"

"Get out!"

"No," yelled Layla. "I will not! You almost killed Aunt Jayne." She slammed a fist down on the edge of the sink and was gratified to see a flicker of fear in Charlotte's eyes.

The old woman was breathing hard, the sound ragged and uneven.

"What do you want, Charlotte? You think I betrayed you? I didn't. You think my mother betrayed you? I don't know. Maybe she did somehow, but that was a long time ago."

"What time got to do with a damn thing, girl?" Charlotte was suddenly calm. A sly look flashed across her face. "You think you know Elinor?"

Beneath the suddenly cool voice, Layla sensed danger. It penetrated her anger, sending an alarm through her gut.

"*I* knew Elinor. Your momma left here. New face. New mouth." Charlotte was speaking English now, the words slow and precise, so that there was no mistaking their meaning. "Pretty clothes. Proper lady. Shook the Gullah off like it was just dirt on her shoes."

She flicked her hand in the air.

"Wasn't no thing gon' stop Elinor to make her pretty life. And oh, she was strong. Walked the dream of anyone who could get her there. Walk. Walk. So strong. Could find a dream that wasn't yet hardly a dream. Twist it around."

Her eyes glittered with malice, and something else. Something that looked like pain. Layla tried to swallow the bile that had worked its way up her throat, tried to back away. But she stood fixed in the damp kitchen, rooted in place.

"Know why she got off this island fast fast? She broke that boy. Walked his dream night after night 'til he walked out there in that water and shot hisself."

Layla's head snapped up and she gasped as if struck, remembering the dream. The boy who'd walked from the woods with the gun.

"He . . . he raped her," whispered Layla. "He . . ."

"Rape?" Charlotte's eyes widened in genuine surprise. "That what you thought you saw? And I know you saw. Yes, you did. Wasn't no rape. Your momma open her legs for him, like she open 'em for half the boys on Scotia." She laughed, the sound like rusted metal. "Only difference was, that boy, Silas? His seed took root, but then, he didn't want no more of Elinor. He want another gal. Oh, but she wouldn't have that, would she?"

"Stop it."

"Silas wouldn't give her as much as a howdy do. Act like she was some poor relation he ain't never shared a meal with. Let alone a bed. He done already got everything he wanted. Elinor begged me. Begged me to help her get rid of that thing growin' inside her. Make everything like it was before. And then it was time for justice."

"Stop it," Layla said again.

"So, she walked him, over and over and over. Until she broke him."

"You're the liar," hissed Layla.

Charlotte shook her head. "I a lot a things, but I ain't never been no liar."

Layla took a step back, vaguely aware that Viktor had come to stand behind her. Every fiber of her body screamed at her to leave. Leave now!

"Secrets, so many secrets." That sharp-edged smile again. "She runs. Far, far. And then she meet your daddy."

Layla was shaking her head. No. She had to stop her. Whatever Charlotte was about to say, she had to stop her. But all she could do was hold up one trembling hand. Viktor was saying something to her, but the only words she registered were Charlotte's.

"She saw your daddy, and she was going to have him. But even with her new pretty ways, she had to be sure. 'Cause what a man like that want with some backwoods Gullah girl." Charlotte grinned. Layla struggled to breathe in the steam-filled kitchen. Sweat ran fast between her breasts.

"I mean, your daddy was a fine man for certain," Charlotte went on. "Ooh, but she walked that man's dreams until—"

"Shut up!" screamed Layla. She lunged and felt herself caught from behind. "Just shut up!"

"Don't," whispered Viktor in her ear. "Let's just go."

"Fuck you! You're a liar and a fucking psychopath," screamed Layla. "I know what you did. You think I'm going to let you hurt my family? Is that what you think?"

Charlotte made as if to follow, but Viktor held up a hand. "Enough," he said.

"You know what my reward was for keepin' all her secrets? That one, and all the others?" screamed Charlotte at the frenzied girl as she was being dragged toward the door. "Gettin' locked up in the nuthouse. Locked me up like I was the crazy person. She got the pretty life. And I got locked away."

Viktor dragged the thrashing Layla from the house, Charlotte's words following them. And then she was outside. She jerked free of Viktor's grip and staggered a few feet before doubling over and vomiting into the sparse, sandy grass. Finally, she stood, shaking hard. Whirling to face the house, she screamed and screamed. Until her head felt as if it might explode; until her voice gave out. And then she dropped to the ground, head on her knees, gasping for breath.

Viktor touched her shoulder and she jerked away.

Slowly, her breathing slowed and the tremors that racked her body stilled. She sat back and held her face to the sky. It was overcast but the warm breeze calmed her. When she opened her eyes, Viktor was sitting about ten feet away, quietly watching her. She'd almost forgotten he was there.

"Well," said Viktor finally. "I think that went well."

Layla gave a sharp bark of laughter. Staring at the ground, she took a quivery breath and swiped at her face. Neither spoke for a long moment.

"It's not true," Layla murmured, not meeting his eye. "What Charlotte said, it's not true!"

Her head snapped up at Viktor's silence. He returned her look, his expression carefully neutral.

"Layla, I didn't know your mother," he said cautiously. "And I barely know your cousin."

"You think—"

"I don't think anything," he said, interrupting her. "I know that there are three sides to every story and that part of what she said was to get inside your head."

She looked from him to the small house, then back again. Except for a faint plume of white smoke drifting from the brick chimney, there was no sign of life.

"She basically said my mom was a murderer and a whore, and that my parents' whole life together was some kind of endless dream fuck!"

"I heard."

She waited for him to say more, to offer up reasons why none of what Charlotte had said could possibly be the truth. Instead, he sat silently, pulling at the spiky grass. She felt her anger smoldering in her chest.

"Let's just go," she said, leaping to her feet. She pushed her way through the hedge and onto the sandy trail that led back down to the pier, not turning to see if he was following.

34

Layla stumbled down the path, oblivious to the biting insects, the sting of the tall, sharp grass against her bare arms. For as long as she could remember, she'd wanted to feel like she had a place where she belonged. And for a few weeks, she'd felt like this might be her place, that these were her people. When she'd stood in the Old Place, she'd felt a connection, like an umbilical cord, stretching from her mother to Granny Bliss to Gracious and beyond, linking her to this land, to this thing only they could do.

She tripped, caught herself before going to her knees, Charlotte's words thundering in her head.

"What a man like that want with some backwoods Gullah girl?"

Memories of her parents spooled out before her in the afternoon sun. Her dad and her mom dancing in the backyard. The way her mom looked at Daddy when he was working on one of his projects. The story of how they'd met at a street fair in Adams Morgan.

Layla moaned as something broke inside her. It wasn't a lie. Her parents' life together couldn't have all been a lie.

As she walked, the anger slowly began to die, like a fire going dark. And she realized she felt nothing, just a hazy numbness. There was sadness, but she felt detached from it, as if observing it from some great distance.

And it was okay, this vague not feeling. She'd felt some version of this her whole life, her feelings fluttering outside of herself. This was familiar, safe.

She reached the crest of the hill and glanced back. Viktor was far behind on the trail, moving slow. From where she stood, the sky slowly blended into the sea, far out on the horizon. It was an odd shade of blue, and she could see a hazy demarcation of hues. She took a deep breath, taking in every detail, the birds wheeling high above, the scent of the thick woods behind her, the feel of the air against her skin. And she let the tears fall. She cried for what she was. She cried for what she wasn't. This beautiful, mysterious place that had never, would never belong to her.

She would go home and deed it to the Aunts, she decided. She was fairly certain she could do that, though the thought of it caused a deep ache in her chest. She could almost hear Evan's howl of protest; she had no ready explanation for him, but this had to be over.

"Wasn't no rape. Your momma open her legs for him, like she open 'em for half the boys on Scotia."

Layla ground her teeth as she turned to look in the direction of Charlotte's cottage. No, this had to be over.

Viktor finally caught up to her and they walked in silence back down to the boat.

On the pier, he jumped into the boat, holding up his hand to stop her when she made to follow him. She watched, frowning as he put on a pair of headphones and turned on the radio and the boat's radar. He squinted up at the sky, slowly shaking his head from side to side, then pulled off the headphones.

"What is it?" she asked.

"Another storm blowing in," he said, peering at the radar's screen. "Looks to be a bad one too. Was just s'posed to be a quick shower but . . ." He shrugged.

Layla glanced at the sky. The faint demarcation of earlier had settled into distinct lines, the ash color closest to them turning to slate then indigo where it met the sea on the horizon. She looked back at Viktor to find him unloading rucksacks from the boat onto the pier.

"It happens," he said, catching her eye. "Weather out here can turn on a dime and that's a bad sign."

He pointed at the quickly changing sky above them.

"A sign of what?" Apprehension cut through the chaos that had been cluttering her thoughts, thoughts of her mother, the island, Charlotte.

"A sign that we won't be goin' back out on open water anytime soon today." He jumped from the boat, throwing another large canvas rucksack onto the pier. "Radar showin' a fair amount of ugly weather chargin' in off open water."

"You don't think we could make it back to Port Royal before the storm?" she asked, hopefully. "It's not that far."

He continued to check the latches on the boat's forward hold as he looked up at her. "'Magine you're itchin' to get off Scotia, but that's how folks get killed out here. Overestimating their skill, and underestimating Mother Nature."

"Storms," she muttered. "Shit."

Viktor gave her a sympathetic smile. "'Tis the season."

She sensed the tension under his light words.

"Should find us some shelter," he said, straightening. He picked up the larger of the two sacks, shifted it to sit flush against his back. In the few minutes they'd been standing there, the temperature had dropped. The air tasted metallic on her tongue.

"We should head to the Old Place," he said, picking up the larger of the two sacks sitting at their feet. "It's not too far."

She nodded and picked up the remaining rucksack. He turned and started back the way they'd come.

"Ain't the Ritz," he said over his shoulder. "But at least we'll be out of the wet."

She sighed and followed him back up the sandy trail, focusing on moving forward and staying upright. Hiking uphill was much harder with a pack on her back. Sand from the shoreline swirled in the air, stinging her face, her arms.

"What is all this?" she panted, motioning to the packs.

"Gettin' caught out in the open sort a comes with the job, so you got to pretty much be prepared for anything."

As they headed into the woods toward the Old Place, she kept a watchful eye on the darkening sky. She couldn't decide which was worse: being trapped on an island with a huge storm blowing in or being trapped on an island with Charlotte.

They were nearing the trail leading to the Old Place when, without preamble, the sky split in two. There was a flash of lightning, then the rain began to pour with terrifying ferocity. Within minutes, the trail was a slippery mess, booby-trapped with hidden rocks and twisting vines. They moved as quickly as they could, half trotting, half sliding. As they crested the slope overlooking the Old Place, Layla pointed to her mother's old house, and they made a dash toward it.

There was a rusted padlock on the door, but the door itself was barely connected to the frame by bent hinges, giving easily when Viktor leaned his weight against it.

"Sorry," he murmured, though it wasn't clear where his apology was directed.

Forcing their way through the packed sleeping porch, they found themselves standing in the kitchen, a thick layer of cobwebs covering every surface. A trio of saplings had forced their way through the wooden floorboards in one corner, and pale gray mushrooms sprouted from the rotted wood of the windowsill. The storm had turned the afternoon to twilight, the little house held hostage by deep shadows.

"Here."

Layla jumped. She turned to find Viktor holding out a small lantern, not much bigger than a car remote. She switched it on, and the bright LED light forced the darkness to the edges of the room.

Viktor flicked on a second lantern and placed it on the metal counter.

"Well, isn't this cozy?" said Viktor, grinning.

Layla batted a strand of cobwebs away from her face and shrugged off her dripping rucksack, coughing as dust swirled up from the floor, irritating her still-raw lungs. She glanced out the door. The rain had formed a solid, impenetrable wall of water. A clap of thunder seemed to explode directly overhead, and she gave a startled yelp. She turned to find Viktor calmly going through the contents of one of the rucksacks, seemingly oblivious to the storm raging around them.

"I'll be back," she said.

"Be careful," said Viktor. She saluted and was rewarded with a grin.

Though bigger than Charlotte's, this house, too, was small. The sleeping porch they'd come through had been nearly impassable, packed almost to the ceiling with discarded tools, building materials, and bits and pieces of machinery. Off the kitchen, she discovered a sitting room, a bookcase taking up one wall; an armless rocking chair and a wide love seat, the stuffing bursting through the faded velvet upholstery, were pushed against each other on the other.

She pulled a book from the bookcase. The pages were faded and swollen with moisture, the cover slick with mold. Wincing, she placed the book back, wiping her hand on her wet jeans. Next to the love seat was a door. Layla pulled on it, the doorknob squeaking in protest, but it had swelled in its frame and was stuck fast.

"Guess what I found."

She stopped fiddling with the door and turned. Viktor stood in the doorway, a glass jar filled with clear liquid held high above his head, clearly pleased with his find.

"What is that?"

"Moonshine, girl! Found it in one of the cupboards. This here is one hundred percent pure white lightning." He grinned. "Have a seat and let me introduce you to one of the South's finest traditions."

She perched on the edge of the love seat. "You are not seriously going to drink that, are you?"

"Sure. Why not?" He twisted the top off the jar and inhaled deeply, nodding in approval.

"Why not?" She gaped in disbelief. "Uh . . . because that stuff is probably at least fifty years old. It can't possibly still be any good and you could . . . I don't know . . . die."

Viktor threw back his head, laughing as a gust of wind rattled the house. "Little girl, allow me to explain the realities of white lightnin'," he said, exaggerating his Southern drawl. "Can't nothin' live in moonshine. Can't nothin' spoil moonshine. Only three things guaranteed to survive the end times: cockroaches, Twinkies, and moonshine liquor."

She snorted, watching as he took a small swig. He made a face before letting loose a low-pitched growl.

"Ooh. Wee," he gasped, shaking his head from side to side like a wet dog.

He held the jar toward her. "Your turn."

"Yeah. No, I am not doing that!"

"Come on," he urged. "Where's your sense of adventure?"

"Ha! Seriously?" She raised an eyebrow. "I am sitting in an abandoned house, on an island, in the middle of a storm. I just had the absolute funnest visit of my entire life with a woman who could kill me in my sleep, and you're questioning my sense of adventure?"

She jumped as something crashed outside the house. "You know what? What the hell?"

She took a sip, felt her tongue and throat ignite. Coughing violently, she tried to swear, but that only seemed to stoke the fire in her mouth.

"Good, right?" Viktor was grinning.

Through teary eyes, she glared at him, then gave him the finger. Scooching back on the love seat, she took in small breaths, trying to quell the inferno in her gut. The moonshine was like liquid fire, at least at first, by the third sip, not so much. The coil of angry tension that had been nesting at the bottom of her gut since she'd been dragged from Charlotte's house began to unwind.

"Hold up there, champ!" Viktor took the jar from her. "This ain't a drink for beginners."

"Aunt Therese said you have to train yourself to drink right." She laughed, remembering.

"Yeah," he said. His smile faded slightly. "I bet she did."

She immediately regretted her words, remembering his concern about Aunt Therese's drinking. He was watching her now, questions in his eyes.

"Well, you talked to her," he said, finally.

Layla snorted and rolled her eyes. "Yep."

"So, what now?"

Layla shrugged. "Not a clue." She took another sip from the jar. The sound of water dripping through the ceiling echoed from the kitchen.

"You know," he said, after a long moment. "Does it really matter how your momma and daddy started lovin' each other? I mean, it was the day to day that kept them together, that *kept* him lovin' her, right?"

Something seized inside Layla and she winced. She clamped her eyes closed and shook her head. The movement caused the room to momentarily tilt. She didn't want to think about her parents. She didn't want to think about anything.

"You hungry?" asked Viktor, changing the subject.

Layla opened her eyes. "You have food too?"

He laughed. "Wouldn't be much of an emergency kit if it didn't include somethin' to eat."

He disappeared into the kitchen and quickly returned with a package of nuts and several oranges. They sat side by side, eating in silence as the storm seemed to settle directly overhead.

"I'm sorry," said Viktor.

Layla hunched her shoulders but said nothing as he went to check the weather radio.

"Might as well rest up. We're going to be here awhile," he said, returning with a hoodie, which she gratefully took. She peeled off her rainsoaked top and replaced it with the dry one as he looked away.

He slid to the floor and closed his eyes, his head resting on one of the rucksacks. Layla sat for a moment, eyes closed, her back against the love seat, smelling dust and decay, but she was too restless to sleep. Standing, she picked up one of the lanterns and began to wander the small house, her feet squishing inside her wet shoes.

At the closed door beside the bookcase, she stopped. Holding the tiny lantern in her teeth, she began working the doorknob, the edges of the door. She was excited when she felt it give slightly, and after a few more minutes, it creaked open. Holding her lantern high, she peered in.

Behind the door was a large closet, and like the porch, it too was filled with the detritus of the previous occupants. There were boxes of empty glass jars similar to the one they'd drunk the moonshine from, fishing gear, more books, piles of crumbling papers. On a low shelf was a stack of neatly folded but faded and rotting linens. Layla pulled down the remnants of a large bedspread and saw what appeared to be a bible tucked beneath.

She carried the bible and the bedspread to the love seat and propped the lantern against her thigh. Balancing the bible on her knees, she carefully opened it, the leather spine creaking. There was the sharp scent of molded paper, and despite the dim light, she could easily make out the names on the crumbling page marked "Family Record." She traced her finger backward up the list of names. There was her mother. And her mother's mother. And her grandmother's mother.

Elinor.

Bliss.

Gracious.

Lavender.

The men and women the Aunts had spoken of, all real on the pages of this decaying bible. Some of them echoed the names she'd already heard; many others formed wide branches, filling out the leaves of her family tree.

Different handwriting. Different inks. Filling up two full pages.

The words blurred, the result of her tears and the moonshine. A few feet away, Viktor was snoring softly. Layla curled herself tightly on the love seat, the bedspread across her legs, the bible tucked against her stomach, and closed her eyes.

She was standing at the door of the old house. The rain had stopped but a thick fog obscured everything. The air felt heavy, fecund.

"Layla? Baby girl?"

She stiffened, then slowly turned. Her father stepped from the shroud of the fog and into the light cast by the tiny lantern.

"Daddy?"

He stood there, sawdust on his pants, wearing the ratty green sweater her mother hated. He was holding a cigar, and the smoke from it curled up into the shadows.

"Hey there, baby girl."

She flung herself into his arms, burying her face in his broad chest, smelling the warmth of him, the Old Spice cologne he always wore, crying softly.

"You're smoking again," she said, sniffling into his sweater.

He laughed and his whole body shook. "Yeah, never really quit. Your mother just thought I did." He hugged her tighter. "So that'll be our little secret, okay? You know how she gets when she disapproves of something."

She smiled and held on, gripping his sweater in her fists, feeling the coarse fibers between her fingers.

"Mom's dead, Daddy," she murmured.

He reared back, his eyes wide with surprise. "She is?"

She nodded.

"Oh, baby girl. I'm so sorry." He pulled her close again, his breath warm against her ear.

She squeezed her eyes closed. She just wanted to stand there, breathing in his scent, feeling the scratch of his beard stubble against the side of her face, feeling his heart beating in his chest.

"Daddy?"

"Hmmm?"

"Something bad's going to happen."

He squeezed her tighter.

"Can you make it go away?"

"It's going to be okay, baby girl."

"Is it?" She wanted to believe him.

"Layla!" The voice came from behind her, and she jerked around.

Her mother stood a few feet away, arms crossed, watching them. "You've been pulling on your hair again, haven't you? It's no wonder it always looks a hot mess."

"Leave the girl alone, Nor," said her father.

"Stand up straight, honey," said her mother, ignoring him. "You have such beautiful bone structure, but you're always slouching."

Her mother reached to flick Layla's hair back from her face and straighten her collar, and Layla recoiled from the touch. Saw her mother wince.

Her mother had done something terrible. She frowned trying to remember what. She stared at her mother for a long moment, feeling anger and grief, then anger again.

Confused.

And then, she hugged her, surprising them both.

Her mother stiffened. "Oh for . . ."

For just a second, her mother returned the embrace, before pulling away. She grabbed Layla's face and stared into her eyes. "You are my beautiful, precious daughter and I loved you the best I knew how."

She turned to her husband. "We have to go, Andrew." She eyed the cigar. "And get rid of that thing."

A noise came from inside the house, catching their attention. As the three of them stood just outside the door, listening, the sound came again, louder. Layla dashed toward the house.

"Viktor?"

She ran into the parlor and skidded to a stop, letting out a scream. Viktor still lay sleeping on the floor, and there, crouched in the center of his chest, was an animal. No, not an animal. Something else. The size of a raccoon, it had long claws and an almost human face. It was wearing a black fedora. As she stumbled into the room, it turned its head and bared sharp, canine teeth, hissing.

"Get away," she cried. "Get!"

The creature hissed again, arching its back as if to leap at her. She backpedaled. She needed a weapon, but there was nothing in the parlor but old books and the tattered bedcover. She whirled toward the porch, registering with a sharp pang that her parents were gone. Grabbing the first heavy thing she could find, a rusted hubcap, she raced back toward the parlor. The creature was gone. But so was Viktor.

35

Layla jerked awake, flinging herself upright on the narrow love seat. The lantern, the rucksack, the jar of moonshine, nearly empty now, were there on the floor. Viktor was not.

She leaped up, racing to the kitchen then back again, calling his name. Knowing he wouldn't answer. She yanked open the front door and peered out. The storm had retreated, but it was now deep night and there was only blackness and swirling fog on the other side of the door.

"Viktor?"

The light from the lantern she held hit the curtain of fog before bouncing back to her. Swallowing hard, she stepped warily into the darkness, the lantern held high in front of her. A quick search of the Old Place revealed her as the only occupant. Trembling, she gripped the lantern tight, unsure what to do next. Viktor knew the woods, this island, he knew how to survive. She tried to convince herself that he was fine.

But it was dark and he hadn't taken his light. And he wouldn't have just taken off in the middle of the night. An image of the creature in the fedora snarling atop Viktor's chest flashed in her mind. He was in trouble and she needed to find him.

Slowly, carefully, she picked her way back toward the pier, struggling to stay on the narrow trail in the dark, jumping at every sound. The boat sat wedged against the pier, bobbing gently in the now calm water. Viktor was not there.

Layla whimpered softly, feeling herself balanced dangerously on the sharp edge of panic. Something thrashed in the woods and she gave a yip of fear.

"Fuck!"

She closed her eyes, opened them, breathing hard.

"Fuck, fuck, and fuck," she muttered.

She turned and headed back up the trail. She had no idea where she was going. She just knew she had to keep looking. She'd been walking only a few minutes when she heard something. A cry.

"Viktor?"

She held the tiny lantern high and peered into the darkness. Teeth clenched, she stepped from the trail, pushing aside the thickly growing bushes, mud sucking at her shoes. She'd only gone a few yards when she thought she saw something move in the shadows. She crept closer.

There!

The fog was lifting, and under the clearing, moonlit sky, she could plainly see Viktor just ahead at the edge of the trees. She moved toward him, crying out as she sank shin deep in thick, muddy water, falling forward. The lantern flew from her hand, landing a few feet away, and she held herself still, trying to slow her panicked breathing.

Slowly, she worked her way toward Viktor. What had appeared to be solid ground was in fact the edge of a marsh. Thick mud grabbed at her feet, her legs, threatening to pull her down. She thought of that night on Little Frog Creek and for a moment she froze. It took her several seconds to realize that the sound she was hearing was her own terrified sobs.

"Come on, Layla," she whispered.

Struggling to keep her footing, she forced herself to move, finally reaching his side. She grabbed hold of his arm.

"Viktor?"

He stood staring, unseeing. He did not resist as she dragged him, inch by painful inch, out of the marsh. Retracing her steps, it took them more than a quarter of an hour to work their way back to the Old Place. She was covered in insect bites and trembling with exhaustion, her shoes given up to the glue-like mud somewhere back on the trail as she settled Viktor back on the parlor floor. Securing the door as best she could, she curled beside him and cried herself into a deep, dreamless sleep.

"Layla!"

Someone was shaking her, hard.

"Layla! Layla, wake up."

She swatted at the hands, tried to roll away. "What?" she cried. "What is it?"

She pushed herself to sitting and opened her eyes to find Viktor standing over her. Eyes wild and bloodshot, his clothes torn and muddied, he was barely recognizable as the man who'd brought her to the island just the day before.

"What the hell happened?" he asked. "What is going on?"

She scratched at her blistered feet, not answering.

"Layla!" he yelled.

Her head snapped up and she saw, reflected in his eyes, the same panic she'd felt as she searched for him.

"You were sleepwalking," she said, quietly.

"I don't sleepwalk." His voice was brittle.

She said nothing.

"I was dreaming," said Viktor, finally. "The alptraum came to steal my dream. I could feel his teeth on my throat."

He raised a hand to his neck.

"I . . . ran. I was running in the woods and . . ." He shook his head. "And then I was lost."

He was looking past her, his eyes unfocused. "There was someone there, but I couldn't see them in the dark. I just knew they were there. Somehow, they helped me find this lake. I was trying to figure a way across. Trying to find a way home."

"I found you in the middle of the night. Standing in the middle of a marsh," said Layla.

They locked eyes in the brightening parlor.

"Charlotte?" he asked.

She gave a barely perceptible nod. Viktor looked down, his face twisting, and when he looked back up, his pale-colored eyes were hard as stones.

"We need to get the hell off this island," he said.

36

Nine days.

It had been nine days since their disastrous trip to Scotia Island. Nine days since Layla had confronted Charlotte. Nine days since Charlotte had walked Viktor's dream and abandoned him in the marsh.

Viktor was avoiding her. She'd texted him a handful of times, but there'd been no response. She understood. She could only imagine how angry, how terrified, how confused he was. But still—it stung.

She'd run into him a few days after it happened. She'd gone to Gerta's condo to check on Aunt Therese. He was leaving and saw her coming up the walkway. Even from a dozen feet away, she'd heard the sharp intake of breath, seen his eyes dart in alarm, before he regained his composure and fixed a neutral smile on his face.

"Layla," he said.

"Morning." Her attempt at a smile was only slightly more successful than his.

He nodded, put on his sunglasses. "Oma and Tante Therese are having coffee. Tante Jayne's all settled in with her family in Savannah for now?"

"She is."

"Glad to hear it," he said. He made as if to step around her. "Okay, then. You take care now."

"I'm staying in Port Royal."

Viktor stopped. His head swiveled slowly in her direction, his eyes hidden behind the reflective lenses.

"Oh?" he said, warily. "For how long?"

"Indefinitely. There's some things I need to finish. With Charlotte."

He flinched. There was a long pause and then that careful, noncommittal smile reappeared. "Well, good luck with that."

"Viktor."

Layla reached out a hand to touch his arm and sensed him shrink away. She pulled her hand back.

"Viktor," she tried again. "I am so sorry."

"It's all good, Layla." He stood a moment longer, his eyes still hidden behind the glasses, then nodded. "See ya."

Layla was at the door to Gerta's condo when she heard him call her name. She turned. He was standing next to his car, the door open.

"Be careful, ya hear?" he called, and then he drove away.

Now, days later, she sat staring through the window of her bed-and-breakfast, her dinner growing cold on the fancy antique side table. On the boat ride back from the island, she'd realized with a certainty she felt in the deepest part of herself that Charlotte would never leave her alone, would never leave her family alone. Not if she stayed away. Not if she deeded her share of the island to the Aunts.

And so, she had decided to stay. Until she could figure a way to end things with Charlotte.

On the other side of the glass, she could see the flicker of fireflies.

She'd tried that first night and the night after that and the night after that to find Charlotte in her dreams. She'd stumbled on dreamers, so many dreamers, but not Charlotte, never Charlotte. She wasn't sure how or when it would happen, she just knew she was not leaving, could not leave, until it did.

She glanced at the two pills on the table next to her congealing grits and shrimp. Picking them up, she stared at the tiny blue ovals in the palm of her hand. She couldn't remember the last time she'd taken one. Her world had flipped inside out. Before, she would have done anything to avoid the dreams. Now, she needed them.

Her magic pills.

Tonight, she needed a different kind of magic. She needed to sleep. She needed to dream. She placed the pills on her tongue and washed them down with sweet red wine. No, she was not leaving until she finished things with Charlotte.

The sun was shining bright through the ruins of Ainsli Green, the tumbled remains of the old chimneys shimmering against the morning air. The air was cool, fresh, the smell of the ocean swirling around her. It was early, and everything—the grass, the leaves on the trees—still sparkled with the night's dew. Layla glanced at her wrist, saw the white of the shell bracelet glowing there.

Scotia Island.

She closed her eyes and tried to imagine her cousin. The slight, sinewy frame, the dark, angry eyes. The sweet smell of the hedge that surrounded her house. Layla concentrated hard, trying to fix every detail in her mind.

She could hear the murmuring. Dreamers, there were so many dreamers out there. She could feel the pull of them, like the gentle tug of an outgoing tide, but she forced herself to focus. She needed to stay here. In this dream.

The tiny, smudged windows of the sleeping porch, flower-filled jars on every sill. The huge kitchen table that dominated the tiny kitchen. The lonely nightgown fluttering on the clothesline.

Layla felt something shift around her, the tiniest vibration in the air against her skin. She focused, her eyes still closed. There was the slightest ache in her head. Not pain, not quite. All around her, the dreamers whispered.

The smell of the berries Charlotte had collected. The feel of the steam against her face.

And then she heard it. The clink of glass against glass. And she was there, standing in the shadow of the trees abutting Charlotte's house, the wind playing a discordant melody with the bottles strung among the branches. She was there, in Charlotte's dream.

Charlotte was standing in the sunny yard, feet bare. Young, laughing, her face turned to the sky. Her hair was loose and wild around her brown face, a crown of flowers riding low on her forehead. And there was Layla's mother, barefoot as well, screaming with delight as she chased a small, spiky-haired dog round and round the tree.

Watching the scene, Layla hesitated, disarmed by the innocence, by the pure joy she was watching.

But these women, her cousin and her mother, had caused so much pain, had hurt so many people. Had caused people to die. And Charlotte was still hurting people. Layla took a deep breath and stepped from the cover of the trees.

Her mother saw her first. She stopped, the ball she was about to toss to the dog held in midair. Charlotte turned, her eyes widening first in surprise, then narrowing in rage.

"Oh," she said.

Layla stood, feet wide, tense, waiting. "Hello," she said when Charlotte said nothing else.

She forced herself to walk closer toward her cousin, who seemed to age with each step Layla took. Forced herself to smile. "I'm here now," she said. "With you."

She saw something flicker in the other woman's eyes.

"You think this somethin'? You bein' here?" Charlotte said, finally. Her voice was as dead as her eyes. "That ain't nothin'! That just a l'il party trick."

"Yeah, I do," answered Layla. "Think it means something."

She glanced over Charlotte's shoulder. Her mother was gone. The house and the bottle trees were gone. Instead, they were standing in a field of high grass surrounded by debris: a broken porch swing, a rowboat covered in moss; a tattered bedsheet hung from a tree, fluttering like a ghost in the breeze, a pile of moldering books and papers.

"You think I don't hurt you 'cause you blood?" snarled Charlotte.

"Blood?" Layla laughed bitterly. "What do you care about blood? Blood? Family? That means nothing to you."

Layla was surprised to see a flicker of pain in her cousin's eyes.

"You don't know me, girl," said Charlotte. "I'm the only one hold true to family. And you gon' leave!"

"No. I'm walking in your dream. You're not walking in mine and I'm not leaving. Not yet."

The two Dreamwalkers circled each other warily in the trash-strewn field.

"You gon' pay for this!"

Layla bit back the angry retort. "Then do it. Wake up now. And then tomorrow night or the night after make me pay."

She forced herself to smile though she felt her gut twisting in fear. She had no idea what Charlotte could do. Could she wake herself and throw Layla out? Could she twist this dream and trap Layla somehow? Could she hurt her?

She leaned close to the woman who was slowly growing older.

"There's things even you can't do in dreams. You're just an old, bitter woman."

Nothing to lose.

Gerta's words echoed in Layla's head and she frowned, thinking hard.

"They all think you're crazy, don't they?" she said, her voice low. "A crazy, old woman living all by herself out here on the island. Trying to scare people off, and when that doesn't work, messing with their minds."

Charlotte was watching her, her eyes slits of rage in her round face.

"They locked you up, didn't they," said Layla. "Filled you with so many drugs you couldn't even talk, let alone dream." She gave a harsh laugh, her voice dripping with venom. "You think you're safe out here? You think that can't happen again? You think we can't lock you away somewhere and just lose the key? Someplace far away where you will never see Scotia Island ever again?"

She didn't see the walking stick until the very last minute, barely managed to get her arm up to protect her face. The blow sent a tsunami of pain roaring through her forearm and into her shoulder. She screamed, staggered back, looked up in time to see Charlotte winding up for another blow.

"No," screamed Layla. She pushed the old woman, who skidded on the wet grass before going down, the tip of the walking stick delivering a glancing but painful strike to Layla's thigh.

"Shit!" Layla snatched the stick from the fallen woman. She held the stick over Charlotte's face, quaking with white-hot rage, tears of pain streaming down her face. She swung, barely missing the old woman's face, relishing the look of terror there.

She swung again, then threw the stick into the high grass. "I know what you're afraid of," she said, her voice hoarse with fury.

And then they were inside a building, the floors carpeted, the smell of antiseptic permeating everything. The concrete walls painted an industrial green. A hospital. They were in a hospital.

A fat white woman ran screaming past them, hospital gown flapping wide to show her naked buttocks beneath, feces smeared across the backs of her thighs. Charlotte cried out and cowered against the peeling wall.

There was the murmuring again, and for a moment Layla was distracted, catching the hint of Jean Naté drifting in the air. Somewhere, out in the world, the Aunts were dreaming, but Layla forced herself to push that aside.

"I ain't feared of you!" Charlotte whispered, but her eyes, wild, darting, gave lie to her words.

"You should be," hissed Layla. "If not here, then out there. I am a Dreamwalker. Maybe not as good as you, but good and getting better. If you keep coming after me, keep coming after mine, I will have you locked away in some concrete loony bin, drugged out of your skull for the rest of your life."

She flicked her hand at the hall around them.

"You ain't nothin'," murmured Charlotte, her voice barely audible.

"I am your blood." Layla was tired and her arm was sending agonizing jolts of pain through her whole body. "And I know what you did. What my mother did. You did terrible things. You hurt people. You're still hurting people. You are cruel and you are broken. And you don't deserve this gift."

Charlotte opened her mouth to protest.

"Don't! I know what you did. I know what you are." Enraged, Layla could barely get the words out. "I am your blood. But I am nothing like you."

She felt it then, a rumbling. The world around them seemed to glitch. And as Layla watched, the walls, the ceiling began to crumble, disintegrate, tiny bits breaking away before fading into nothing.

Charlotte had flattened herself against what was left of one wall. "She promised," she said.

"What?" Layla frowned, confused unsure of what was happening around them. "Who? Who promised you what?"

"To love me," said Charlotte. "Your momma promised to love me."

And then they were on the beach. The air shimmered, the wind stirring up miniature golden sand tornadoes at their feet.

Charlotte stood a few feet away. She was old again. She stared at Layla, her skin a sickly gray.

"She promised," she said again. "We was bound, your momma and me. I did for her, gave for her. Held her secrets close."

Her breathing became ragged, and she faltered, swaying for a moment on the uneven sand. "You are my blood. You are her blood," she said, her speech slurring. "You are . . ."

Her knees buckled, and she crumpled in slow motion onto the beach.

From somewhere far away came the sound of a bell ringing.

37

LAVENDER
1862

Out near the horizon, where the silver water turned to navy, she could see them. Dolphins: making their way through the deepest part of the sound as they threaded a path toward the Atlantic.

Standing thigh deep in the water, Lavender thrust up an arm and waved. She laughed. She knew it was ridiculous, but she still felt that somehow they sensed she was there. The thought made her happy. She stood watching and waving until it was too dark to see, before wading back to the gravelly shore.

It was pitch dark in the woods, and she had no lantern as she made her way back to her cabin, but her step was sure. She knew this island as well as she knew her own face. Her feet had never walked on any other land.

The woman and old man sat side by side at the cabin door, exactly as she'd left them before going to wave to the dolphins. She nodded to them then went to stoke the fire under the pot that held their supper.

"Bird's roostin' on the shore," she said. "And look, Momma." She pointed. "Moon's got a caul. Gon' storm by mornin'."

Lavender expected no response from her mother, and she got none. Her mother hadn't spoken a single word since that night. The night she had followed her mother into the colonel's dream.

They'd stared at her, her mother and the colonel, her mother's expression so shocked that Lavender had almost laughed.

What are you doin' here, her mother had asked. And Lavender had answered, *What I had to do, Momma. What you couldn't.*

And she had.

For weeks she'd practiced the colonel's mean, spiky signature, stealing papers from the study that no one ever entered anymore. Slowly, pains-takingly copying each line, each swirl until even *she* could not tell the difference.

And in those weeks, she'd humored her mother, had let Gemma believe that she still needed her voice, her hand to guide her in the world of dreams. But in truth, she didn't need her, hadn't needed her for a very long time.

She had been the quiet one. They'd all thought that. And she had let them. But quiet was not the same as harmless. Not at all.

She could feel it—power—flowing through her veins like warm mo-lasses, filling her up. Unbeknownst to her mother, she'd reached as far as the mainland. She'd walked the Yankee buckras. She'd even found the old colonel's nephew and spent more than one night unlocking the doors in his mind where all the dark things, the bad things, were hidden. She smiled. He would never be a threat to them. Not ever.

"I did what you couldn't," she said, letting the dark quill drop to the floor, the ink leaving a petal-shaped stain on the wood.

Her mother had been failing. Lavender had watched as Gemma wan-dered closer and closer to that fragile edge that separated awake and asleep. Had watched as her mother stumbled across and then back again like a drunkard. And then they lost Marigold. And Jessamine disappeared. And Lavender had to act. Her mother was used up, her mind breaking into tiny pieces.

They'd stared at her that night. Her mother confused, the old colonel horrified that yet another of his niggers had found a way into his dreams, this one holding a signed deed to all of Scotia Island.

"Get out," he'd screamed.

But Lavender only laughed. "It be okay now, Colonel. You stay here. You see you little girl. You boy. Eat you fine food. Watch the darkies in the field."

She spoke gently, humming a lullaby from his long-ago childhood, soothing him. And as she spoke, his face relaxed, his eyes focusing on something far, far away. She was going to leave him in that gray dreaming place. Where he would be happy and they would be safe.

Gemma cried out behind her, and Lavender turned. Gemma was shak-ing her head no.

"It's alright, Momma." Lavender squatted in front of her and gripped her fingers. "He gon' live, Momma. And we gon' have Scotia Island for always."

She squeezed her mother's fingers tight, warding off further protest. "He's gon' live," she said again. "Oonah jus' let go, hear?"

And this time Gemma seemed to register the threat running beneath the words. Lavender stood and kissed her mother on the forehead.

"See you in the mornin'."

But in the morning, Rupert Everleigh had been sprawled at the foot of the bed, wearing his fancy dress coat. Lavender first thought he'd finally decided to die, and that would have suited her fine. But when she leaned close, she could smell his sour breath, could just detect the faint rise and fall of his chest beneath the starched nightshirt.

Her mother had been there, too. Still perched at the edge of the chair, eyes open but unseeing. Lavender called to her, shook her until her teeth clacked together like clamshells. She'd pinched her cheeks hard enough to leave bruises, but Gemma had sat in that chair, hearing nothing, seeing nothing, and Lavender realized that her mother had finally lost her way back to the waking world.

She moved them then—the old man and her mother—to the slave quarter. It seemed the thing to do. Except for two of the other cabins, they were alone there. She knew from her nightly wanders that the war still raged. That the Southern buckras were being pushed back. But here on Scotia Island, at Ainsli Green, the war was already over.

The few black people left had scattered themselves across the island. They fished, harvested rice for themselves and their families, built cabins of their own design. They made plans to raise their children in peace, and answered only to the weather and the rising and setting of the sun, belonging only to themselves.

Lavender spooned stew into a bowl and went to sit between her mother and her ex-master.

"It 'bout time to clean you whiska," she said, using a clamshell to place stew between Rupert Everleigh's lips. He smacked loudly and she smiled.

She took turns feeding her mother and then the old white man, talking to them as she did. She told them about the cabins being built on the leeward side of the island, about the headstones that young Aron was helping some of the men carve for the old slave cemetery, about the fire that had nearly leveled Ainsli Green's cook house during the summer. They never talked back, her mother and the old man, but she was rarely lonely. Simon, the rice driver's brother, had taken to coming over most evenings. He was

Ainsli Green's master carpenter, and it was he who'd had the idea to make the grave markers. He had also carved her a fancy box of heart pine. She'd put the deed paper inside and hid it in the cemetery.

And then there were the nights. Most nights, she put the master to bed on Jessamine's old pallet, before tucking her mother in on Marigold's. Every few nights, she visited her mother in her dreams, curling against Gemma's back, feeling her warmth, holding her tight. And in the darkest part of night, she would let herself slide into that shadowy place where her mother now lived, neither awake, nor asleep.

Sometimes she found Bekka, out there on the mainland. Her baby was walking now, and her man was helping to make the railroad. Freedom sat heavily on Bekka. She missed the sharp bite of the island's salt air, the transparent blue of the sky. Sometimes Tuesday, the grandmother she'd never known in the waking world, sat beside her and her mother, humming as she braided baskets of sweetgrass.

Gemma seemed not to know her daughter was there. She drifted untroubled among her memories—old and older still—traveling the bright rooms of her dreams. But it gave Lavender comfort to walk by her mother's side, to watch over her, to see what she saw, even if her mother never saw her. Wandering forever in her dreams, her mother seemed to be at peace at last. As strong as she was, Lavender wasn't strong enough to bring her back to the waking world with her. Or maybe it was that her mother simply didn't want to come.

Many nights, Lavender tried to find her sister. She missed Jessamine. On those dark nights, she searched and searched, reaching into the world for Jessamine's dreams, but they were never there. She hoped it was because her sister was just too far away to reach. She hoped she was happy too.

The old master dreamed, but Lavender rarely walked there. His dreams held no interest for her. She had taken what she needed from them.

She wiped her mother's face and went to sit by the fire. The storm was moving in fast from the sea. She could smell it. She hoped Simon would come soon. She closed her eyes and smiled. Tonight, she would walk by her mother's side in her dreams, and she would whisper the words she whispered every night.

"It ours, Momma. We did it. Ainsli Green is ours."

38

FALL

Standing on the beach, paintbrush in hand, she shook out her arm. The cast had been off nearly a month, but her arm still ached, a constant, dull thrum of pain radiating to her fingertips. She closed her eyes, waiting for the images in her head to begin to take shape on the canvas in front of her. Laughter and snatches of conversation floated across the sand, registering as pleasant background noise. She adjusted the plaid beret her father had given her all those years before. She and Will had finally finished the long, slow process of cleaning out their mother's house and she'd found the beret in a box, tucked in a far corner of the attic. It squeezed her forehead like a vise grip, and it still emitted the faint smell of mothballs, but she liked the sensation of having it on her head, liked the idea that her father had bought it for her all those years before.

"Nice hat."

She looked up. Will was grinning as he walked toward her. Behind him, down the beach, Chuck was running back and forth in the surf, Chase tucked under his arm like a football. Viktor stood at the edge of the grass line taking pictures. When he saw her looking, he pointed the camera in her direction. She waved.

"I like your boyfriend," said Will, coming to stand beside her.

"Not my boyfriend."

"Well, he should be. He's cute."

Layla rolled her eyes. There still existed a palpable tension between her and Viktor, but between the Aunts and Gerta, it had been nearly impossible for them to avoid each other. They subsisted now in a sort of uneasy, slow-moving friendship.

"And if you two ever do decide to get married," he persisted, grabbing her hand, "I play golf with one of the best event planners in D.C."

"Oh my god. Shut up." She snatched her hand away, punching him in the arm. Grinning, he dropped to sit in the sand at her feet. Layla swished her paintbrush in a jar of water, then plopped down beside him. They watched the gulls spinning and turning in an elegant dance over the water.

He sighed.

"It really is beautiful here," he said.

She nodded. "Yep."

"I like it, Lay, the idea of turning Scotia Island into an artists' colony. It's a brilliant way to protect the island. But you do know it's going to be a ton of work, right?"

She shrugged. "Gotta work somewhere."

"Lay?"

She turned to look at him. He scooped sand with his hands, letting it run through his fingers as he studied her face. "What happened down here? Really?"

It had been three months since the fire, three months since the final confrontation with Charlotte. She'd been back home only a handful of times—to help him close up their mother's house and to pack up her life and move to South Carolina.

She smiled. "I told you what happened."

He held her gaze. "But did you, though?"

Her smile faded, but she didn't look away. "I came down to clear up some stuff with Charlotte that got stirred up after Evan started all that legal research," she said, keeping her voice neutral. "Then there was a fire and Charlotte had a stroke."

At every mention of Charlotte, her brother flinched.

"But what about the dreams?" He asked the question so softly, she almost didn't hear.

Layla frowned, peering intently into his face. "You're not having . . . bad dreams again, are you?"

He shook his head, not meeting her gaze. They sat together in silence, each lost in their own thoughts, Will pushing the sand into piles.

"You're not going to tell me, are you?" he asked, finally.

She watched the piles collapse slowly back into themselves and said nothing.

"And what about her?"

Layla followed his gaze to where an old woman sat motionless in a wheelchair, gazing out at the water.

Layla stared at the unmoving figure for a long moment then looked at her brother. "She's family," she said slowly. "And family takes care of family."

Viktor strode up just as Will opened his mouth to say something.

"Y'all ready to head up for some lunch?" he asked.

Will closed his mouth and stood. "You want us to carry her up?" He jerked his head in the direction of the wheelchair.

Layla pretended not to notice the dark shadow that crossed Viktor's face. From the moment she'd insisted Charlotte be brought back to the island after her stroke, Viktor had made no secret of his feelings.

"No, go on up," she said. "We're just going to sit out here a bit longer."

Viktor eyed her warily. "Layla?"

She met his eyes and smiled. "It'll be fine. Really."

She waited until he disappeared at the top of the dune with her brother, then padded over to her cousin.

"Hello, Charlotte."

The old woman sat silently in her chair, staring unseeing at the silver-blue water. Since that night she'd not spoken a single word. The doctors were calling it a stroke. But Layla knew it wasn't only the stroke that kept Charlotte silent, withdrawn. She was drifting in that place of half dreams and memories. A place where she seemed happier than she'd ever been in the waking world.

She and the Aunts had brought her back to the island, convinced her sisters in Savannah that this was where Charlotte would have chosen to be, that they would care for her as long as necessary.

But it was Layla who spent most nights out on Scotia Island, alone with Charlotte, in Charlotte's tiny house. Out on the island, where the nights were indescribably dark and the sky glimmered with a million stars.

On those nights, Layla curled in the chair next to Charlotte's bed, slipping into the gray place with her.

And there, wandering beside her cousin, Layla watched her mother and Charlotte playing in the waves, watched them as they lay in the grass counting stars. And in that place where Charlotte had chosen to stay, Layla had met her great-grandmother Gracious, her great-grandfather Finn. Had watched Grandaddy Finn dig a pit and roast a pig, had listened to her grandmother and mother and cousin singing and gossiping late into the night as they shucked oysters. And she understood why Charlotte didn't want to leave.

Layla stared down at her cousin. Family looked after family, but the truth was far more complicated. In those dreams, her mother sat at the knee of Granny Bliss and learned the way of the Dreamwalker, as did Charlotte. And Layla, hovering at the edges in the shadows, listened, and learned too.

Something had happened to *her* that night too. The gift had changed yet again. Day and night, there was a buzzing on her skin, like a faint electrical current. And the dreams—the dreams were magnificent. She could walk wherever she wanted, in whoever she wanted. With just a whisper in a dreamer's ear, she could bend desire, reshape thoughts. And with Charlotte near, she was stronger still, hopscotching dreams through the night, plucking memories and fears and hopes, experiencing adventures through others, acquiring amazing amounts of knowledge. She reveled in this new feeling of power.

"Not settling. Not even a little," she murmured. "And guess what, Mom? Still no dental insurance." Layla laughed out loud.

A flicker of movement caught her eye and she looked down. Charlotte had shifted in her wheelchair. For a fraction of a second, she seemed to be watching her, her eyes glittering with awareness.

Layla met her eye and touched the older woman's arm, feeling the sharp quiver of power brighten beneath her hand.

"This is ours, Charlotte," she whispered. "Forever ours."

Layla waved her arm, taking in Scotia Island and everything beyond it. "Anything we want is ours. We are the last Dreamwalkers."

Acknowledgments

The writing of a novel is a collaborative effort. The writer may put the words onto the blank page, but the very fortunate writer has a team of wonderful people that bend and shape, buff and shine those words until they are the best they can be.

I have been a very fortunate writer, and I will be forever grateful to Joanna Volpe, my amazing agent, and the entire team at New Leaf Literary. Your ongoing support and confidence in my words and my stories mean more than you know.

I owe a huge debt of gratitude to Lindsey Hall, my brilliant editor at Forge. Her frequent *whys* pushed me to look deeper into the heart of the story and find its clearest truth.

I want to give a special thanks to Tamara Butler, Ph.D., the director of the College of Charleston's Avery Research Center for African American History and Culture, who took time from her busy schedule to discuss some of the nuances and historical perspectives of the Gullah Geechee experience. I also would like to thank author and editor Savannah Frierson, who was kind enough to read an early copy of *The Last Dreamwalker* and offer her insights into South Carolina Lowcountry life.

I am also thankful to the staff at my day job, Angie Hinojosa, Kylee Ladd, Vickie Vargas, and Rob Conner, who, on way too many mornings, cheerfully tolerated a sleep-deprived, under-caffeinated, cranky human during the long writing and editing process.

And finally, as always, I am so very thankful to my many friends old and new, and to my family, Kenneth, Jonathan, and Logan, for their love and support. Love always.